Dark Moon Seasons

I0645860

Valerie Griswold-Ford

WWW.DRAGONMOONPRESS.COM

Dragon Moon

Dark Moon Season

Copyright © 2009 Valerie Griswold-Ford

ISBN 10 1-896944-89-2 Print Edition
ISBN 13 978-1-896944-89-0

Dragon Moon Press is an Imprint of Hades Publications Inc.
P.O. Box 1714, Calgary, Alberta, T2P 2L7, Canada

Dragon Moon Press and Hades Publications, Inc. acknowledges the ongoing support of the Canada Council for the Arts and the Alberta Foundation for the Arts for our publishing programme.

The Alberta Foundation for the Arts
COMMITTED TO THE DEVELOPMENT OF CULTURE AND THE ARTS

Alberta COMMUNITY DEVELOPMENT

Canada Council for the Arts   Conseil des Arts du Canada

Printed and bound in Canada or the United States
www.dragonmoonpress.com
www.v-gford.com

Dark Moon Seasons

Valerie Griswold-Ford

Dedication:

For Florence and Doris
I'm only sorry I didn't finish it in time.
We miss you.

Acknowledgments:

Thank you to my wonderful editor Tina and my publisher Gwen,
for putting up with me when this novel took on a life of its own.
Thank you to Donna, Kathy, Beth, Barbara, Rob, Mike, Erik,
Shade, Domy, Lai, Beard and everyone else who read parts of
this book and critted it for me. And thank you to all my fans, who
have waited so patiently for this sequel.

Prologue

"Aftershocks"

"Now what do we do?"

The question spun through Justin Greystone's head, chased by several others that snapped and clamored for his attention. Chief among them was wondering who had unleashed the massive magical surge that had blown the roof off of Gene-Tech's secure building? It had felt familiar, but then again, with the number of powerful Mages he'd been associating with lately, he really couldn't go by "familiar."

Thunder rolled overhead, echoing the grumblings of the residual earthquakes as the building shifted again and a veritable snowfall of concrete chips cascaded around them. Justin stumbled, nearly knocking Rick Jackson off his feet.

"We can't stay here, Justin," Rick said, his face pale beneath the grime. "What do we do?"

"We have to find the office," he said, swinging around and peering through the destruction. The emergency lights threw a hellish orange glare over the carnage, and Justin tried not to focus on the stretchers with their still passengers on the other side of the spell chamber.

"What office?" Rick asked.

"Alex Masterson's office. We need to get the files from the experiment." Justin stumbled again as the floor moved.

"We need to get out of here," Rick repeated. "This place is about to collapse in on itself. Not to mention the fact that the cops will be here any minute."

"I can stabilize it if we need, at least for a few moments," Justin said, hoping he wasn't lying. "But we have to find those files. We need to find out what he did."

Despite Rick's worries, Justin knew it would be at least twenty minutes before the police responded to the explosion — Gene-Tech was set far back from any roads, the better not to be bothered by anyone official. The building crashing down on them, on the other hand, was a distinct possibility, and they'd left both Nikki and Alenya unconscious in the spell chamber.

Nikki. His thoughts turned dark again as they moved through the creaking twilight. *What am I going to do with her now?*

Her pale, serious face, dark blue eyes shadowed with magic and old pain, swam before him briefly and his heart ached. She was so young, so unready... Justin cut those thoughts off ruthlessly. *We were all too young,* he reminded himself. *We dealt with it. So will she. We'll just have to help her, if she'll let us.*

"Jus, over here."

Rick had ranged in front of him, the AK-47 he'd taken off a dead guard earlier in the night held low and confident. Now he stood in front of a locked door.

"You're sure?" Justin said, running a hand over the door. Rick nodded, and Justin backed up. "Then let's do this."

The AK-47 chattered as Rick blew away the lock and then kicked the remains of the door into the office. They stepped through the doorway, and Justin wondered briefly why there were no magical protections.

"Because he was that damn secure?" Rick said.

"Not Alex Masterson," Justin replied, looking slowly around the opulent office. A mahogany desk dominated the room, in front of a whiteboard covered with notes. Two file cabinets sat across from it, and a large table was pushed up against the wall opposite the door. Justin took a step towards the cabinets, then paused and walked over to the desk instead.

The rich mahogany wood glowed under the light coating of dust from the ceiling, and as soon as his fingers touched it, Justin knew he'd hit gold. Protection spells flared to life, vibrating with barely-contained Power, and he swore. This was going to take far too long...

"Are you certain they're in there?" Rick said, reading the scowl on his face accurately.

"They have to be. Where else would he hide them?" Justin reached into his pocket and pulled out a small Swiss Army knife. He mumbled a few words under his breath and then popped open the larger blade. "Do you have any gum?"

"What?"

Justin glanced up at the shocked expression on Rick's face and chuckled. "I'm serious. Do you have any chewing gum?"

"Why?"

"So I can short-circuit these spells for a while and open the desk."

Rick gave him another dubious look but dug into his pockets. "Sorry, MacGyver, I'm all out."

"Damn." Justin looked around the room. "Hell. It's a small magic." He whispered under his breath and a small stick of chewing gum appeared in his hand. He unwrapped it and popped it into his mouth, chewing enough to soften it and then spat the sticky lump onto the dusty desktop. A few more whispered words, and he drew the blade through the middle of the gum, cutting it in half. Sparks raced over the surface of the desk for a second, and then died. "Just a little sympathetic magic. I hope this works."

"You hope?"

"Yep." Justin closed the blade, pocketed the knife and reached for the top drawer tentatively. No sparks flared, and he breathed a sigh of relief. "Come on. I don't know how long I can keep this hole open."

They grabbed every piece of paper they could find in the desk, then checked the filing cabinets, which proved to be empty. Justin risked a little more magic, even as the floor swayed beneath them, and shoved all the papers into a small pocket of space that he saved for emergencies. Then they booked it back to the spell chamber, hoping they could get out in time.

"What is causing this?" Rick shouted as an ominous rumbling began somewhere beneath their feet.

"Magic... whatever Nikki did was so strong that it literally weakened the walls," Justin shouted back. *That, and Shanna. . . no, don't think about that now.* "We have to get out of here!"

As they burst into the spell chamber, the ceiling behind them crashed to the ground. "I'd say our grace period is up," Rick said, scooping up a prone body from the floor. "I. . shit!"

"What?" Justin looked up to see Rick shift the body to one side.

"Nikki's bleeding, badly." Rick shook his head. "We need to leave, now."

"Agreed." Justin pulled Alenya's limp body into his arms. "Get over here."

"You're going to do more magic?" Rick shuddered but stepped closer.

"You got a better idea?"

Unfortunately, while the spirit was willing, Justin had been running on fumes for a while. He managed to get all four of them out of the crater that the secure building was forming, but only to the lip, and then he stumbled, rain hitting him like accusations. Outside of the dubious safety of the building, the storm howled, and they were all immediately soaked.

"Sit," Rick commanded, dropping Nikki next to him. "I'll get us out of here."

"How?" Justin asked, shifting Alenya's dead weight across his lap.

"Plan B." Rick jerked his chin towards the parking garage. "Luckily for you, I know how to hotwire a car."

Justin stared at him, and then laughed. "You're brilliant."

"I try."

It only took Rick a few minutes to return with a suitable vehicle — an older Jeep that rumbled a tenor counterpoint to the thunder above and below it as they loaded their two unconscious burdens into the back. Justin spent those minutes marveling at the sheer destruction that one single Horseman could wreak. *No, not just a single Horseman,* he corrected himself silently. There had been another, and he knew that signature very well...

What are you up to now, sister mine? Why now?

He hadn't formulated an answer by the time Rick pulled into Vashti's driveway. The Earth Lord's farmhouse was hunkered down against the storm, and the woman who had trained him met them at the door. "Bring them," she said, turning and leading them through the corridors to the massive kitchen that crouched at the center of the building. The warmth from the fireplace crept slowly into Justin's bones as he laid Alenya gently onto the large table, and then he turned to Vashti.

"Why did she start the Cleansing?" he asked, rain streaming down his face like forgotten tears and ignoring Rick's gasp of horror. "What happened?"

"She's your sister," Vashti replied, raising one dark eyebrow at him. "Why ask me?"

"Because you and your fellow Councilors are involved in this up to your eyebrows," Justin said, trying not to sound accusatory and knowing he was failing miserably. "And quite frankly, I'm tired of being jerked around. What is Shanna doing that is so important no one can know about it, and how does Nikki fit into it?"

"Why don't you ask her?" Vashti told him, going to the large stove and removing the whistling kettle from it. "It's not as if she tells us everything either. And before you explode at me, young man, let me remind you that the StarChild does what she wants, whether or not her Council approves. And she did not blow up the Gene-Tech facility, as far as I could tell. That was the lovely young woman on the table behind you. So why don't you tell me what happened tonight where you were, and worry about things you cannot control when we have time?"

Justin bit down hard on the retort that hovered behind his lips, trying not to lose his temper, and Rick jumped in. "Nikki's hurt," he said, from the head of the table where he'd laid her. "Badly. I think he hit her heart."

Vashti turned quickly. "Why didn't you say so?" she demanded, hurrying to his side, her hands busy on Nikki's still body as soon as she reached the table. "Get Morgan, Justin."

Justin turned and ran, the habits of years deeply ingrained. He finally found the other Earth Lord in his study and blurted out, "Vashti needs you — hurry!"

When they got back to the kitchen, Justin hung back, shocked at the amount of blood coming from between Vashti's fingers. "Holy shit, what did he do?"

"Heart and lungs," Vashti said curtly, and jerked her head at her brother. "I need your help."

Both Rick and Justin moved away, not wanting to be underfoot. "Is that why she did it?" Rick whispered, his eyes glued to the body on the table. "Is that why she killed them all?"

"I don't know," Justin whispered back. "I really don't know." But he did. *That's why Shanna had to start the Cleansing,* he realized, ice crawling through him again. *She had to call that Spirit up, or Nikki would have died.*

Instead of a dead Horseman, we've got. . . He blocked the images from his mind.

Nikki's body jerked, and Rick moved forward instinctively, but Justin grabbed him, glad for the distraction. "Let them save her," he said, holding his friend back. "They can do it. I promise."

Time slowed to a crawl; the howl of the wind outside an eerie, keening counterpoint to the deep, liquid sounds of breath moving through the ruins of Nikki's chest. Morgan and Vashti cast in well-oiled unison, Power rising and falling through the flickering firelight, sweat-stained faces gleaming as they fought to repair the damage caused by Alex's knife. Eventually they both stepped away and washed their hands, then Morgan picked Nikki up and took her out another door. Rick watched him go, questions rising, but Justin caught his attention and shook his head.

"She needs rest now," Vashti said, dropping heavily into a chair near the fire, her normally chocolate face ashy with exhaustion. "I don't know how she survived, but..."

"She killed them all," Justin told her, and her face paled even more. "All of them?"

Justin nodded. "Which explains the Summoning. Shanna couldn't let her die."

"Balance forgive us all," Vashti said. "What else happened?"

Justin leaned back in his chair, suddenly realizing how tired he was. "We lost Andreas," he admitted. "He escaped with Alex and the other Blood Mage."

"And one of the breeders," Rick added from where he was leaning against the fireplace. "I saw him roll one of the gurneys through that Gate just before things went to hell."

"So we've got two Blood Mages, a rogue Shadow Lord and an innocent girl with a babe in her belly that's been exposed to bastardized versions of the Summoning Spells on the loose, and you have no idea where. Is that what you're telling me?" Vashti looked from one exhausted young man to the other. "Do you have any good news?"

"No one saw us," Justin said. "Well, they did, but they're all dead. Isn't that good?"

"It'll have to be." Vashti sighed and looked up at the ceiling. "I just wonder how long it will take us to pick up the pieces this time."

Justin wondered the same thing.

"What do we tell Nikki?" Rick asked, breaking the silence. "She'll want to know what happened."

"You lie," Vashti said, and when they both started to object, her voice cut across their words like a sword. "You lie until your tongues turn blue and fall out if you have to, but you lie. Do you really think she'll be able to handle what she's done? Until you hear further from me, you lie."

"You can't keep her in the dark forever," Justin warned. "The news. . ."

"The government won't let information leak for a while, especially with Shanna casting tonight," Vashti said. "I warn you, Justin. If you don't obey the Council in this, not even your sister will be able to protect you."

"Is that a threat?" Justin asked quietly.

The kitchen, his home away from home for so long, grew cold and dark as he waited for her answer. "No," she said. "A warning only." Her dark eyes avoided his. "For all our safety, Justin, do not fight this. Please."

He didn't answer.

Chapter One

"The World in Tatters"

"Holy shit."

Chief Petty Officer Derek Reynolds, US Navy First Class currently on assignment to the Pentagon, thought that sentence summed up the situation rather nicely, even if it did sound odd coming from the refined mouth of his superior officer. As he looked out over the remains of the GeneTech Research Facility, part of him marveled at the sheer power needed to wreak such havoc on this level. The rest quailed: he'd seen bomb sites that had more architecture still standing.

Originally, three buildings had formed a triangular complex, with one building backed into a manmade hill. The two buildings in front were still standing, although he wasn't sure for how long: their facades were cracked and dented, and pieces of them scattered across what had been a well-trimmed lawn. The sign that once read "Gene-Tech Research Facility" in stiff letters was now so much slag, destroyed by whatever had roared from the depths of what Derek assumed had been the secure wing.

That building had vanished entirely: in its place was a smoking crater, filled with a sea of rubble that shifted and moved beneath the feet of the emergency personnel as they dug, looking for survivors. The rain poured down from darkly scowling clouds and the lightning bolts slammed into the sodden ground, making the rescue even more treacherous. The thunder grumbling overhead was echoed by snaps and crashes from below as the remains of the building continued to settle into its grave. Emergency workers of every stripe swarmed over it like flies on a corpse, looking for the smallest flicker of life.

"Shit, what a mess," Derek's commanding officer continued, looking not at the rescue operation but the swirling storm above her. Even with his gloves on and his Senses muted, Derek could see the tendrils of Earth Magic huddling close to Lt. Amy Elder, Earth Mage First Class, as if seeking shelter from the behemoth above. "I hate storms."

"And storms hate Mages," Derek replied, his mouth twitching as he tried not to smile at her. *Telling your CO she looks like a drowned rat is not conducive to your career,* he reminded himself. *Even if it's true.* "So you're even."

Amy shot him a dark glance, then looked at the young officer who had guided them in past the security checkpoints. "What hospital are you quarantining the survivors at?"

If there are any survivors. Maybe from the other buildings...

"What survivors?" Officer Petrolus said. "We've been at this for almost four hours, and all we've pulled out are bodies."

Derek and Amy both sighed, and he continued, "Not that there might not be survivors buried deeper in the rubble, of course, and that's what we're all hoping for, but the crews haven't found anyone yet..."

"How many bodies?" Derek asked, and Petrolus pointed to a corner of the activity, where a large tent had been hastily erected. The two naval officers walked carefully across the slick ground, the policeman trailing behind them. Taking a hold of the edge of the canvas with one gloved hand, Derek looked at Amy, then flipped the doorway open.

"God in Heaven," he said, looking at the rows of body bags. "How many people were in there?"

"According to the logbooks we found in the other buildings, the entire complex was on lock-down," Petrolus said, looking down at his shoes as if he couldn't face them. "There was some sort of super-secret government project going on in the secure wing, and if Masterson's security precautions are indicative of his state of mind, he was really paranoid about this one."

"What did the other guards say about it?" Amy asked, as Derek looked back in at the rows of bodies.

Petrolus hesitated, then said, "Maybe I'd better just show you."

Sweet Mary, Mother of God, what happened here? Derek thought a few minutes later, standing in the lobby of the main building, staring in shock at the woman behind the desk. She had grey, teased hair and too much eye makeup, but the kind lines on her face reminded him of his grandmother. A pink turtleneck snuggled underneath a bright patchwork sweater, and he was absolutely convinced that she'd be wearing sensible shoes and slacks as well. Her head was slightly bent forward, balanced on her hand as if she were concentrating on the book open on the desk in front of her.

She was stone dead.

"Are they all like this?" Amy asked Petrolus, her voice echoing in the stillness.

"All of them," he said. "Dead, with not a mark on them. As if someone had stolen the very life from them. Even the lab animals are dead." His radio blatted static, startling them all, and he lifted it hastily to his ear. "Yeah? Okay, I'm coming." Then he looked at them hesitantly.

"Go," Amy said. "We can find our own way around."

He bolted, a frightened rabbit escaping the circling shadows of vultures and hawks. The door thudded hollowly behind him, reminding Derek of the closing of a mausoleum.

"There had to be over four hundred people employed by this facility," she said softly. "Four hundred genetic scientists and Mages, working on all sorts of cutting edge projects. Including, apparently, a secret government project."

"And they all died in one fell swoop," Derek said, running one gloved hand along the edge of the granite desk and shivering as Power hummed through the silk. "On All Hallow's Eve."

"Just as the StarChild sealed off a very large portion of Vermont and Quebec," Amy finished, folding her arms across her chest. "There's no way this isn't connected."

"We don't know that." Derek raised his head. "I haven't found any traces of her magic."

"You also haven't taken your gloves off," Amy pointed out. "And Shanna Greystone knows how to cover her tracks better than most — you know that."

Derek had to admit she was right. "You're supposing that she knew of this place."

"And you're supposing she didn't." Amy turned and looked back at the dead receptionist. "Who else do you know with this kind of Power?"

He didn't have an answer for that. Doubt and death hung heavy on the air, magnified by the storm that howled overhead, and he found himself loath to do the job he'd been sent to do. Once the gloves came off, he would be open to the images and memories lying in wait for him.

"How long have you been in the field, Derek?"

The question caught him by surprise. "Fifteen years, ma'am," he replied, wondering if she was worried about how he'd handle this, considering it was their first assignment together.

"Have you ever seen anything like this before?" Amy asked, further surprising him.

"No, ma'am," he admitted.

"Damn."

He was about to answer when the door slammed open and Petrolus skidded into the room. "Lieutenant! We've found a survivor!"

Amy and Derek ran out the door after him, the melted, crushed ground crunching like shattered glass under their feet. They reached the edge of the crater just behind several EMTs who slithered down into the remains of a large chamber, dragging a stretcher behind them. "Who?" Amy demanded, grabbing Petrolus by the arm. "Who did you find? Masterson?"

"Not unless he's had a sex change," Petrolus said. "This one's a woman."

A badly-damaged woman, Derek saw as they lifted her gently onto the stretcher. Short blond hair clung stubbornly to her lacerated skull, slicked with blood and darkened with dust, and her lab coat was in tatters. He slid carefully into the dim cavern.

"Wait," he said, stripping off one dull brown glove. "Don't move her yet."

"Hurry up," the EMT said. "She's lost a lot of blood."

"I'll be quick," Derek said, placing his bare hand on her cheek. "But we need to know what happened here."

Pain! Blood! Terror! A barrage of images slammed into his mind, one after the other, in rapid succession like a machine gun of emotion. Woven into the stream were two images, each terrifying in their own way: a simple rag doll, lying in the midst of a destructive rainbow that burned away shadows, and a young woman with dark hair and dark blue eyes who turned towards him, the flesh melting off her face, leaving a skull that burned with dark energy. A ghostly hand came out of the darkness, skin hanging in shreds from its delicate bones, reaching for him as he fell. The image shattered as he stumbled back, breaking his contact with the woman's skin.

"What did you see?" Amy was suddenly next to him, holding him up as the EMTs wheeled the comatose woman out of the darkness. "What happened to her?"

"God help us," Derek whispered, and she paled. "What the hell was Masterson doing here with these people?"

"Are you going to be okay?" one of the other EMTs asked, looking sharply at him, and he shook himself, reminded of his job.

"Yes, go on." Derek blinked, looking around as the man hurried off after his companions. With his ungloved hand, he reached out for the wall, wondering what he would find. Now that he'd invoked his talents, he could hear the background Magic whispering, muttering, moving like a thousand ghosts in the rear of his mind, each jostling the others to make him listen, and he shuddered. What had happened here?

"Are you certain this is a good idea, Derek?" Amy asked.

"Good idea or not, it's something I have to do, ma'am," he replied, and laid his hand against the crumbling concrete. A familiar sullen chill sank through his palm and Derek frowned, then peeled away part of the wall. "Look at this, ma'am."

"Amy," she corrected him, leaning over and looking at what he'd exposed. "I keep looking for my mother when people say that, and out here, no one will care. Just call me Amy and we'll be fine. What is it?"

"Iron," Derek said and she shuddered. "Why would he build a secure wing for working magic in that had iron interlaced in the walls? Iron short-circuits spells."

"Not all of them," Amy said, touching the rebar he'd uncovered with a fingertip. "But it would make it damn hard to cast anything of substance in here, especially Earth Magic. Iron grounds spells — in fact, the way it's buried in here — it's almost like he was trying to guard against Earth Magic. But that's ridiculous. Earth Magic is the magic of genetics — why keep it out if you're doing genetic magic?"

"Because you're paranoid?" Derek asked, running his ungloved hand on the bar and raising an eyebrow. "The spells are gone now, but if I'm reading these traces right, he had some sort of shielding spells on these."

"Shielding against what?" Amy asked.

"Earth Magic, definitely," he replied. "And...what the hell is this?"

The trace shimmered along his nerves, an odd, tangled note of Power that didn't resemble anything he'd ever sensed before, cutting cleanly through the remains of the shielding spells. Derek concentrated, trying to tease out more of the trace, but it defied his attempts to untwine its signature, so he committed it to memory and raised his hand.

"What?" Amy asked, and he shook his head as he pulled his glove back on.

"I don't know. But this just got a whole lot weirder."

The ground shook again, and concrete powder fell around them, a white mist in the rain. "Let's get out of here," Amy said, reaching up and pulling herself out of the hole. "I want to go back to those other buildings."

"Yeah," Derek said slowly. "Let's go."

As they crawled out of the remains of the building, the back of his neck prickled, and he paused, looking back into the semi-darkness. *What secrets did Alex Masterson have hidden here?* he thought, wondering if he really did see a shadow moving along the remains of a hallway. *And what will it cost us to uncover them?*

As he watched the Sensitive follow the Earth Mage up out of the crater, Lucifer pondered his options. *She* would not appreciate any interference in her plans, but for the moment, everything of consequence was gone from this place anyways, so he saw no reason to interfere in the mortals' investigation. Let them look. They would find nothing to tie *her* to anything. Although the Sensitive would bear watching — he was powerful, and could be a problem.

From his vantage point within the World Walls, Lucifer could see the storm energy swirling around the remains of Gene-Tech, hungry fingers of raw Power muddying the magical traces of what had happened Halloween Eve. By tomorrow, the events that had occurred in the spell chamber that lay in ruins would be lost to all but the most Sensitive, and his Lady would be safe from discovery. He stalked the wreckage, adding his own trail to the maelstrom, further obscuring who had been there and what they had done.

The taint of the Balance sat in his mouth, a residue like arsenic that weighted down his limbs, threatening to drag him down into the morass. How had the Balance managed to take the girl back? They had been so careful with the spells, and yet the child had channeled a Horseman. But how?

Lucifer.

Her voice, soft and deadly, stroked across his mind. *Yes, my Lady?*

Come home, my Lucifer. We have a guest.

He smiled, a dark, predatory smile. He enjoyed her guests. They always screamed so nicely.

Chapter Two

"Dreams Within Dreams"

I'm dreaming. I have to be.

Sylvia Richards looked around the hall, wondering whether to be bemused or scared out of her wits. Gone was the damp hole in her side caused by her erstwhile second's knife, as was the dark spell chamber: in its place, ivory pillars spiraled up to a cathedral ceiling, draped in multihued mist that softened the cold stone. Deep plush rugs muffled the footsteps of the various beings that wandered in and out of the audience hall, and she found a small bit of amusement at the entire scene.

So my mind retreats to a King Arthur fantasy when I die, huh? I guess there are worse things. As long as Merlin and Morgan le Fay don't decide to beat me up, I'm probably okay.

Sylvia decided a bit of wandering was the smart thing to do — if she was going to be trapped here for any bit of time, she figured knowing the lay of the land was a good thing. As she took a step forward, a flash of silver caught her eye.

So you couldn't even kill me correctly, huh, Ashcroft? Some Blood Mage you are. She regarded the slim silver soul cord wrapped around her ankle with a dispassionate eye, wondering how far it would stretch, and if it would be worth it to break it now, even though that would kill her body, wherever it lay. *If I could. Maybe one of these folks would oblige me. Then I wouldn't have to face whatever's waiting for me if I manage to recover.*

As if I could be that lucky.

She pushed a stray blonde hair from in front of her face and looked around, trying to figure out where the doors to this endless hall were. Not that it really mattered, in the end: even if she found a door, she wasn't sure she'd be able to pass through it.

The silver cord proved to be less of a hindrance than she'd thought; in fact, she soon forgot it as she prowled among the columns, not sure what she was looking for but knowing she couldn't stay still. The denizens of the mist left her alone, for the most part, although several bared teeth at her in a silent warning to stay away.

Mist, Sylvia thought, reaching for a sliver and feeling the cold. *Could I be in a Chaos realm? How did I get through the Walls?*

Could someone have summoned me? Oh goddess, Alex, what were we really playing with?

Eventually, Sylvia reached the front of the seemingly endless hall; at least, she assumed it was the front, considering it was dominated by a large marble throne. The throne was gorgeous, but it was the woman seated upon it who took her breath away. Sylvia drew back behind one of the columns to study her further.

Her long, pale hair flowed down over one shoulder, a waterfall of silk and shimmer that blended in with the mist that clung to her like a second skin. Rainbows glimmered in her pastel eyes; her pallid lips were currently pursed as she listened to some sort of strange spirit Sylvia couldn't identify. This, clearly, was the ruler of this little pocket dimension, but for the life of her, Sylvia had no idea who she was.

And then, as if she'd felt a gaze on her, the woman turned, and Sylvia was trapped by those odd eyes. She shrank back against the pillar as the Lord (she had to be, with the presence she radiated) rose from her throne and came down onto the floor.

"Well, well, well, what do we have here, my children?" The Lord's voice flowed over Sylvia, full of languid interest and sharp scorn. "I do believe we've got a mortal skulking among us. You know what that means."

Laughter and shouts arose from the spirits that clustered around the Lord, and Sylvia went cold. *This sounds bad...*

The pale eyes were cold. "Run, little mortal. Hope you can keep ahead of my children. They haven't had a new toy in a while."

Sylvia didn't need to be told twice. Hoping for death was one thing: to face it, in the form of the mob of Chaos creatures behind her was something else entirely, and she realized that she wasn't quite ready to give up yet. She bolted into the mist, hoping to lose herself in the fog, wondering if there were any Shadows she could use to protect herself, reaching out as she ran, hoping to feel the familiar magic sing in her blood, but there was no darkness that welcomed her. Nothing but the endless mist, the shifting rainbow of illusion and fog, and the shouts of the crowd behind her.

I can't let them catch me. The thought pounded in her head. *I have to get out of here. Even though I'm sure it's just a dream, that I'm not in a Chaos realm, I can't let them catch me. You can die in dreams.*

Of course, I'm dying anyways, but I'd rather not hasten the journey any.

Knowing where she was would have made it easier, and she didn't even have the time to stop and Gate to somewhere more familiar. She fumbled in her pockets as she ran, hoping to find something useful but they were empty. *I need a mirror or something. Something I can break. Anything...*

Something shattered in front of her and she flinched back. Glass shards lay on the ground, as if by magic; Sylvia didn't even stop to think. She grabbed the nearest shard and slashed her palm open, then turned and faced the mob.

Power surged around her, fueled by the blood pouring from the open wound in her hand and her own desperation. It wasn't much of a shield, but it kept the most vicious of the spirits back.

"What, a little mortal mage is keeping you at bay? Shame on all of you."

The Lord pushed her way through the crowd to the edge of Sylvia's shield. "Honestly," she continued, her silky voice sharp-edged with scorn. "It's not as if..." And then she stopped as she looked at Sylvia.

"Leave us," the Lord commanded, and her troops, snapping and snarling in disappointment, began to melt into the fog. "Leave us, all of you."

Sylvia didn't falter, even when the room emptied and only the Lord looked back at her. "Silly child, why didn't you show yourself fully?" the Lord said, her odd eyes unreadable. "I would have never sent them to chase you had I seen who you were."

"Who I am?" Sylvia laughed harshly. "What are you talking about? I'm a dying Shadow Mage, trapped in her own mind. What's so special about that?"

"Oh no, child." The Lord shook her head, a strange smile playing about her pallid lips. "You are so much more than that." She moved through Sylvia's barrier as if it were smoke, and Sylvia shuddered at the Power surrounding her. "Look at me."

Her rainbow-slick eyes captured Sylvia's gaze, drawing her into a spider web of Power and promises, and within the shimmer lay the barest hint of her heart's desire.

"I can protect you, Chosen," the Lord whispered. "I can keep you safe from those who would hurt you, would use you. Let me help you."

Let me help you. The words echoed deep within Sylvia's mind, digging deeply for something that she knew she couldn't let the strange Lord have, no matter what she promised.

"Why should I trust you?" Sylvia tore her eyes from the Lord's hypnotic gaze and backed up. "You tried to kill me too."

"Mortals who stray into this realm are fair game, Chosen." The Lord shrugged elegantly. "Which is why you should accept my offer — I can protect you. Here, in my home, you will be safe."

Sylvia somehow doubted the Lord's idea of "safe" was the same as her own. *But what choice do I have? And it will give me time to figure out what the hell is going on. I swear, Ashcroft, if I ever find you, I'm going to eviscerate you for this.* "You can protect me?"

"Oh yes, Chosen. You'll be very, very safe." The Lord smiled at her. "Come with me."

"No!"

Nikki Jeffries sat bolt upright, fire burning in her chest and the image of the pale woman with the rainbow eyes shimmering in her mind. Snow slashed against the window above her head; the room was unfamiliar, and she panicked. *What is going on?*

She threw off the covers and hissed as pain pulsed along her breastbone, but gamely swung her legs over the side of the bed. One thought fluttered in her head: that she had to get out of there. Had to run. Had to flee.

"Where do you think you're going?"

The deep voice startled her even more than the cold floor beneath her bare feet. Nikki jumped; her hand came up and she pulled at the Shadows around her, weaving a protective shield.

Then she saw who was standing in the doorway and felt very foolish.

Morgan came into the room and set the tray in his hands down on the nightstand by the bed. "You know, it's warmer in the bed," he rumbled, amusement rippling through his voice. "I'll even turn on the lights so you don't have to eat in the dark."

Nikki dismissed the Shadows and climbed reluctantly back into bed. It was warmer, and now that the panic had subsided a bit, she noticed how exhausted she felt. "Where am I?" she asked, as the Earth Lord turned on the lights and the room sprang into view. "What happened?"

Morgan turned back to the nightstand and retrieved the tray, then set it across her knees. "You're at the farm," he told her. "Safe, for the moment, because no one knows you're here."

"Safe from who?" The steam from the bowl tickled her nose with the fragrance of garlic, onion and basil; she picked up her spoon and dug into the homemade tomato soup, suddenly realizing how hungry she was.

"Who do you think?" Morgan moved around the room, straightening things, and Nikki suddenly realized how little she knew about what had happened.

"Alex got away, didn't he?" Anger rose within her when he nodded, and her jaw clenched. "That son-of-a-bitch. I'll..."

"You'll finish your dinner and then sleep," Morgan interrupted, frowning at her when she scowled at him. "You need to heal."

Her free hand went automatically to her chest, and Nikki flashed back to the spell chamber at Gene-Tech, and the cold steel of Alex's knife as it sank into her breastbone, crushing her heart beneath its weight... "He stabbed me in the heart," she said softly, and Morgan nodded. "Then how am I still here?"

"How do you kill Death?" Morgan asked her, and Nikki shuddered as her own words came back to haunt her. "Your Horseman kept you alive. It's not time for you to go." He gestured at the tray. "Finish your dinner, or Vashti will wonder."

She finished the soup, but pushed the sandwich aside. "I'm not that hungry."

Morgan reached out to take the tray and Nikki put her hand on his. "Morgan, what will Alex do now?"

The Earth Lord paused, and she could feel the sadness in him. "He will try again, child. They always do."

"So what do I do?"

"You heal now." Morgan smiled at her, a smile tinged with both sadness and hope. "And then you defeat him. That's what you do."

Once the door closed behind him, Nikki laid back down on the soft pillows and listened to the snow shushing against the glass above her head. *That's what I do,* she thought sleepily. *But what about that pale woman? What does she do?*

And why was I dreaming about Sylvia?

She fell asleep before her mind supplied an answer.

Chapter Three

"Going Nowhere"

"How's the view?"

Alex Masterson didn't even bother to turn from the dirty window. "It sucks," he snapped, his temper worn thin by four days of constantly being on the run. "It's disgusting here, and this damn storm is screwing with everything I try to cast. How the hell am I supposed to work under these conditions?"

"It's better than a cell," Tony Ashcroft pointed out, and Alex heard him shut the door. "And that storm is also screwing with the police's tracking spells. We might actually get a chance to breathe for a bit." Paper rustled on the table in the corner. "I brought subs."

"Did you also bring an idea of where to go from here?" Alex retorted, finally turning away from the dreary vista outside the window. Charleston was supposed to be a lovely Southern city, but the roach motel that Tony had found for them squatted in the midst of a gloomy industrial park, crowded with factories that belched black smoke. "I'm serious, Tony. We need a secure spot to finish those spells, or in five months we're going to have a monster on our hands."

"I know that, Alex." Tony pulled a chair up to the table he'd put the subs on and cracked open a can of soda. "But we have to let the heat die down at least a bit before we try and hook back up with Andreas. He's got the breeder safe, and she's stable for the moment. We have a bit of breathing room."

"That bit of breathing room gets shorter every day we waste," Alex replied. Unease gnawed at him, a sinking sensation that time was slipping away, that he had to get somewhere and finish things before they found him. "Did you manage to get the copies of the spells?"

Tony shook his head and picked up a piece of his sandwich. "Someone got there before me."

"What?" Alex clenched his fists to stop from beating the man. *I need him, at least for the moment, because I can't go outside without running the risk of being recognized,* he reminded himself silently, holding on to his temper with effort. *It's the storm — the storm is riling you up. Calm down and approach this rationally, Alex. Think. You can do it.*

Tony was watching him, chewing slowly, and Alex didn't like the calculating look in the Blood Mage's eyes. Probing for weakness, as always — it was a trait he'd encouraged before. Now, having it turned on himself, he felt almost trapped.

It was not a sensation Alex was familiar with. Nor one he enjoyed.

"They took everything?" Alex said, after taking a deep breath. "Even from the desk?"

"Yes." Tony swallowed and then set the sandwich down. "But it shouldn't matter. Doesn't Andreas have another copy?"

Alex cursed at himself for not thinking about that. "He should. That bastard has shit hidden away everywhere." His belly ached; not from hunger, but from the hastily-bandaged stab wound Nikki had gifted him with the night of the explosion.

Nikki. His eyes narrowed as he thought of her: the experiment's miracle child, the proof that the spells worked. Too bad she had a spirit to match her benighted mother's. He could have used her on their side.

But they worked. She's proof. So once we get back to a place we can finish, we can breed as many soldiers as I can sell. And once those contracts are fulfilled, then I can retire and watch the chaos.

Tony cleared his throat, pulling Alex from his thoughts. "What?" he asked irritably.

"I said, I think we should really consider hopping around the

US for a bit, muddy our trail, before we settle in." Tony held up his hand. "Let me finish before you blow a gasket. We've got a number of people on our tails, and most of them would rather smear the two of us across a large portion of the country. The good news is that they're tracking us, not the breeder. So let's give them something to follow, and let Andreas keep her hidden."

Alex had to admit it was a good plan, even as he chafed at the delay. "How long?"

"If we could, I'd say for at least a month. But that's not feasible right now." Tony took another bite of his sub. "Unless Andreas can put the breeder into a stasis spell?"

"Sure he can. It's not going to stop that baby growing, though." Alex started to pace, running his hand through his dark hair. "Not without serious issues, that is. And the last thing we need is a superhuman idiot savant."

Tony grunted. "It was worth a shot."

Alex continued to pace. "We need to have this settled within the next month — the spells can wait that long. But we need a place to cast on this side of the Walls. I'm not about to go casting in a Shadow or Dawn Lord's backyard and risk them showing up to claim my prize."

"What about the Earth Lords?" Tony asked.

"What about them?" Alex retorted. "Those passive fools haven't got the balls to step in and do anything to stop us. Don't let Andreas fool you, Tony. I'm far less worried about them and their damn Council than I am about our clock running out."

"And the StarChild?"

"What about her?" Alex snapped. "She's busy in Vermont. And since we're not in Vermont, I doubt she's worried about us."

Tony didn't answer, and Alex turned to look at him.

"What?" he demanded.

"Nothing," Tony said, and shook his head. "You're the boss."

"And don't you forget it." Alex turned back to the window and scowled at the rain beating on the glass. "Let's find somewhere sunny next."

"I'll do my best."

"Let's find somewhere sunny next."

Alex's words rang in Nikki's ears as she sat at Vashti's kitchen table watching the fog rise up from the new snow as the sun set. The dream had played over and over in her mind all day — Alex and Tony bickering in some ratty motel room, with pouring rain a steady backdrop to their quarrel. She'd finally given up on sleep and come downstairs to find Vashti cooking something in a deep pot. To her surprise, the Earth Lord hadn't sent her back to bed, but had instead told her to take a seat and then pulled out a frying pan.

"You look troubled, child," Vashti said, cracking eggs into the pan.

"Bad dreams," Nikki said, pushing her dark hair back from her face. "They seem to come a lot lately." The image of Alex rose in her mind again, and she took some solace in the fact that he'd looked distinctly the worse for wear.

Unfortunately, she couldn't tell if the dream was real or something her mind had created to remind her of the fact that she'd let him get away.

I should have stabbed him a few more times, she thought, taking out her aggressions on the plate of eggs and hash browns Vashti had just put in front of her. *In the head.*

"Are you going to eat those or destroy them?"

Nikki's head snapped up as Justin slid into the seat next to her, his hazel eyes alight with mischief. "I mean, seriously," he continued, filching a slice of bacon from her plate. "What did those poor eggs ever do to you?"

She scowled at him. "What do you want?"

"Touchy today, aren't we?"

Nikki threw her folk down, admitting defeat against her breakfast. "I feel useless here," she complained. "I can't do anything! And it's not like I'm broken! I'm fine!"

"You were stabbed in the heart, Nikki," Justin said, shifting from humor to seriousness. "Alex collapsed your lung. Rick and I thought you'd bleed to death on this table. Pardon us if we want to baby you a little."

Nikki lowered her eyes, trying to hide the rebellion she knew he could see anyways, and wanting to scream at the same time.

"I'm fine," she said finally, when she could control her tone. "And babying me won't find Alex."

"No, it won't," Justin agreed, and she looked up, surprised. "Which is why I'm here to spring you."

"Really?"

"Really." He laughed at her expression. "Go grab whatever you have."

She went flying up the stairs, grabbed the few articles of clothing that someone (probably Justin, although she hadn't even really thought about it) had brought over from the Inn and then looked around, wondering what to put them into.

"Will this work?" Vashti's voice came from the doorway; Nikki looked up to see the dark Earth Lord holding out a small backpack.

"Thank you." The words suddenly seemed inadequate and Nikki flushed. "I mean..."

"Don't worry, child." Vashti smiled at her, her dark eyes soft, the grandmother Nikki had never had. "We're here if you need us. Just be careful when you leave here. We've protected you so far, but beyond the boundaries of this farm, you're on your own. There are those who will be looking for you."

"Alex." Nikki nodded.

"Not just Alex," Vashti cautioned. "You were not quiet at Gene-Tech and there are more dangerous things in this world than one megalomaniac. He isn't the only one who'd like to study you."

Nikki froze, chilled by the implications of Vashti's words.

"Just keep a low profile," the Earth Lord continued. "And remind Justin to do the same. Let the storms keep your signatures clouded. Don't give anyone official the opportunity to come after you." And with that last bit of advice, she hugged Nikki briefly and then left the room.

Her words rang in Nikki's ears. Nikki packed the backpack mechanically, suddenly aware of what she'd done on Halloween. *So much for being anonymous,* she thought, slinging the bag over her shoulder. *Maybe going after Alex hadn't been such a good idea.*

Then again, I really didn't have much choice. Hell, this is a lovely mess, isn't it?

Justin had brought his car: a little dark green BMW that somehow screamed corporate clone at her, something completely at odds from what she knew of him. Nikki slid into the leather interior and raised her eyebrow at him. "Nice car."

Justin grinned. "It was my sister's — she upgraded but didn't want to get rid of this one, so she gave it to me."

"Your sister can afford a BMW?"

"My sister's a magical consultant," Justin explained, backing carefully out of the farm's driveway. "It pays well."

Nikki filed that piece of information away for later — she had a feeling that it might be something she was good at. "Good to know. Maybe I'll look into that."

They passed the ride in companionable silence. Justin was lost in his thoughts, and Nikki could only see Rick's face in the thinning fog. Grey clouds hung over the road, and she could taste snow again on the wind. When they pulled into the driveway at the Inn, Nikki's heart clenched.

"Are you okay?" Justin asked, parking the car.

"Yeah." Nikki looked over at him, even managed a smile. "Let's go."

Chapter Four

"Shards"

"I need answers, people, and soon. The President is not amused by all this."

Derek leaned back in his chair, letting the harsh, tense voice of his boss wash over him. Rear Admiral Ismael Hayden hadn't gotten to the position he now enjoyed at the Pentagon by losing his cool, but even Derek had to admit that the twin situations in New Hampshire and Vermont would stress anyone out. Especially given the increasing pressure Ottawa was no doubt bringing to bear on Washington, given the fact that part of Quebec was now sealed off by the StarChild's barrier. *Luckily, we're not responsible for that,* he thought, savoring the warmth of the coffee cup he cradled in chilled hands. *This is bad enough without having to cope with an international incident on top of it.*

The rain had turned to snow and still fell outside the trailer he and Amy had commandeered as their own, adding to the odd stillness of the scene. It was almost a funeral atmosphere — not inappropriate, but odd. *At least the cold is keeping the bodies from decaying,* his mind whispered cynically. *So we can save some money there. Washington should be happy with that. No wasted money, not us.*

"We're still pulling bodies out," Amy replied, drawing Derek back to the conversation at hand.

"Still?" Another voice interrupted her; Derek frowned, trying to place the speaker, which became easier as the man continued to talk. "How many people did Masterson kill there?" *Oh yeah, that must be Paul. Can't mistake that accent. Canadian Magical Police, if I remember correctly. I'll have to ask Amy about him afterwards; I think she mentioned having met him before.*

"We don't know," Amy said, frustration evident in her voice. He looked up to see her tugging on the end of one of her short dark curls as she rolled her eyes. "The secure building must have had more than one project housed there — you don't build a facility that big for one experiment. But we can't find records on anything else being run in there. We haven't found whoever came in and blew the rest of the building up the night after the first explosion either. They used some sort of magical bomb, but the residuals don't match any traces we have on file. So..."

"And how did they get in to blow it up in the first place?" Ismael asked sharply. "Why didn't the local police have officers watching? And where were the two of you?"

"We'd gone to the hospital with the only survivor," Amy said. "I thought with all of the activity, the site would be safe. Unfortunately, all we had were mundane officers. We're dealing with Mages here, and the local police force doesn't have that much in the way of magical infrastructure. Anyone who was big in the local FBI network was scrambled up to Vermont the same night. So we're a little short on the magic side."

"Can't you enlist some of the locals?" Ismael asked her.

"We have." Amy dropped the curl she'd been tugging and buried her forehead in her hands. "There's not a lot up here that's willing to work with us, especially since we don't know who to trust. The saboteurs Gated in, knocked out the guards, dropped their bombs and Gated out again. That tells me two things: they knew the area, and they had at least one powerful Mage on their side."

"Could it be Masterson himself?" Ismael asked, and Amy shrugged.

"Could be. Could be the StarChild, although I'm being told that there is no way she'd do that," and Amy shot Derek a look that spoke volumes about what she thought of that. "It could be someone completely new, which scares the shit out of me."

"The StarChild has not left Vermont." Derek sat up as he realized who was speaking. Baird McClannahan, it had to be. No one else sounded quite like Baird. *Shit, they must be really concerned to drag him out of Washington.* "I can guarantee you that."

"How?" Ismael demanded.

A low chuckle flowed over the conference line. "Because my partner has been in her constant company for the last two weeks."

Amy and Derek exchanged astonished looks. "Jonathan's *inside* the barrier?" Amy blurted out. "But he's been..."

"Reassigned," Baird said smoothly. "Temporarily."

What, now the StarChild has her own agent? Derek's eyes widened. *Or is this just more evidence that things in Washington are a lot more convoluted than I thought?*

Don't think, came Amy's mental advice. *Worry about our situation, and let Baird worry about his partner.*

Sound advice, but Derek continued to ponder the significance of that particular situation for a while, only half-listening to the conversation that swirled around him. He was abruptly brought back by Amy poking him in the arm.

"Hmm?" he said, blinking.

"Are we boring you, Chief?" Ismael's voice, flat and full of menace, crackled over the phone line and Derek straightened.

"No, sir. Sorry, sir." *Shit.*

"Then would you mind answering the question, Chief?"

Derek squirmed, looking over at Amy. *Help.*

He asked about what you've found in the ruins so far, she sent, a sympathetic smile on her face.

"Well, honestly, sir, we've found a lot, but we don't know of what." Derek clenched his fingers around his coffee cup again, knowing what that statement would bring. "Unfortunately, between two explosions and the Storm above us, the site is a magical mess. Not to mention the Chaos magic that blew through."

"Chaos magic?" Paul interrupted again, a note of panic in his voice. "What do you mean, Chaos magic?"

"Just what I said, sir." Derek said, "Something big and Chaotic ran like a bull through a china shop right through the middle of the site, and ruined most of my traces. I have four Sensitives working with me — two clairaudients, a clairvoyant and another psychometrist, but it's slow going. We've got to untangle everything before we can even hope to start committing anything to the evidence file."

"How long?" Ismael asked, and Derek shrugged again, even though he knew the admiral couldn't see him.

"As long as it takes, sir," he said. "We're working 14-hour days right now, trying to figure it out."

"Don't burn out," Ismael warned. "We don't have anyone to spare to help you."

"Yes, sir."

"Now, what did the Healers report?" Ismael asked. "What about the autopsies that have already been done?"

"Preliminaries on the bodies from the two intact buildings suggest that everyone died of the same thing," Amy said, and Derek breathed a sigh of relief that he was done. "Heart failure."

"Traces on the bodies?"

"Bollixed, like everything else," Amy said. "The only thing they're certain of is that the Power signatures are not fully human."

"Lord magic?" Ismael groaned. "Good god, just what we need."

"They aren't sure what they've found is Lord magic, sir," Amy said. "They just know it's not fully human."

"What the hell was Masterson doing?" Ismael exploded. "Baird, tell me you have some good news for me?"

As the talk turned from the New Hampshire site to the Vermont site, Derek leaned back in his chair, his mind going over that particular tidbit. The Healers on site were absolutely confounded, and he didn't blame them. *If it's not Lord magic, and it's not human, and it's not the StarChild, then what is it? Little green men? That's pretty much all we're missing at this point.*

The conversation wrapped up soon after that, and Amy hung up the phone. "What's on your plate today, Derek?"

"More of the same." He drained his coffee cup and then got up to refill it. "I'm heading back down into the hole. I think we're getting closer to the office section. I hope, anyways." Turning back to her, he offered the coffee pot. "More?"

"Derek, why don't you believe the Chaos magic came from the

Storm?" Amy asked, holding her cup out.

"Because there's too much of it." Derek filled her cup and then put the coffee pot back while he tried to sort his thoughts out. "If this is leakage, then this Storm is a lot bigger than any of the Earth Mages are telling us."

"This is a huge Storm," she said.

"Not that huge. If it was, then why aren't we finding this kind of leakage elsewhere?" Derek leaned against the cabinet the coffeepot was set on. "No one else is reporting these levels of Chaos magic — not even up at the Barrier. Baird and Paul didn't mention anything about high levels of Chaos magic. So how can it be the Storm?"

Amy sipped her coffee, wrinkling her forehead. "This place makes my head hurt," she complained. "I wish we could find those records."

"Me too," Derek said. "Do you think that's why the second explosion happened?"

"To cover the theft? Most likely." Amy stood up and stretched, then pulled her coat on. "Come on, time for us to get to work."

They separated once they got outside: Amy went off to the temporary morgue, to help catalog the dead and record the Healers' finds, while Derek went back to the crater that had once been the secure wing.

What continued to amaze Derek was how much of the building Masterson had constructed into the hill that backed the complex. They were still discovering tunnels and rooms, deeper than the explosions had managed to penetrate, as they cleared the debris.

Now if only we could find the remains of his office, Derek thought sourly, climbing down into the building. The police officer at the bottom of the ladder nodded to him, and Derek set off through the tunnel, stripping off his gloves as he did.

The feel of Chaos enveloped him, slick and jagged at the same time, a cacophony of sensations that skittered along his nerves as he strode through the semi-lit hall. The orange emergency lights cast odd shadows in front of him as he moved deeper into the labyrinth, playing tricks with his mind.

Somewhere in this morass is the truth of what really happened,

Derek mused, stopping to look into the remains of what they thought was a break room. *It may take us a while, but we'll figure it out.*

"Chief?"

One of the clairaudients flagged him down as he moved through the corridors. "Yes, Jessie?" Derek said, coming over to her. She was older than he'd originally thought, and one of the most thorough clairaudients he'd worked with. If someone was going to find something, it was going to be her.

"Listen to this." She laid her hand on his arm and then put her other hand on the desk she was sitting at. There was a moment of fuzziness, and then Derek heard what she'd found.

"We have to have four viable infants to fulfill the contracts," one male voice said.

"I realize that, Alex," another male voice snapped. "But your precious lead researcher is starting to lose her nerve. Why you insist on keeping her around..."

"Just do your job, Tony," the first voice replied icily. "And if she gets too squeamish, kill her."

"Very good, Jessie," Derek breathed, breaking the contact. "Get it on tape for me."

"Of course."

———

What did you find, Sensitive?

Lucifer narrowed his eyes as he watched the Sensitive pat the woman on her arm, smile and head off. Once he was sure the man had gone out of the area, he stepped out from the Walls and touched her, searching ruthlessly for what she'd found and shared.

Bah, just Alex, he thought, dropping her arm and shoving her backwards in disgust. *Stupid woman.*

He strode back through the Walls angrily, wishing he knew why he was so concerned about the Sensitive. *It's obvious that they haven't found anything. Why am I still here?*

But something still nagged at him, a small, niggling fear that something here still connected Madness to the experiment.

Something that would bring the Sensitive and the Council to their doorstep, and if the Council came against them, Lucifer would be powerless to protect her.

The Council must not know. That thought pounded in his mind. *The Council must not get involved.*

Even if I have to kill every mortal connected with them.

CHAPTER FIVE

"A GLIMPSE OF THE PAST"

Nikki rolled over and eyed the grey skies distastefully. *It's only November, and I'm already done with snow,* she thought, fighting the temptation to roll back over, pull the comforter over her head and go back to sleep. *Honestly, will it never end?*

But spending the last week in bed had made her heartily sick of sleeping. Now that she was back at the Inn, Nikki was starting to make her own plans to find Alex and finish what she'd started on Halloween. "I just need to know where he went," she said out loud, thumping her fist on the bed in frustration.

"Are you still complaining?" Sarah Connors came into the room, carrying a breakfast tray. Rick followed his cousin in, carrying a small package that he tossed to Nikki. "Now what's wrong?"

"The same thing that's been wrong for the past six months," Nikki said, struggling to sit up and not dump the package on the floor. "Alex Masterson is still alive. What's this?"

"You tell us," Rick said, perching on the end of her bed and stealing a piece of bacon off the tray Sarah set in front of Nikki. "It's addressed to you."

"You mean I'm actually allowed to open my own mail?" The statement came out a little harsher than she meant and Nikki flushed. "I'm sorry, Sarah, that was rude."

"But understandable." Sarah smiled at her, radiating patience like a saint, and Nikki felt even smaller. "I'll be back for the tray later."

"So open it already!" Rick urged, stealing another piece of bacon as Sarah left. "Who's sending you stuff from London?"

"London?" Nikki turned the padded enveloped over. "I don't know anyone in London." She pried open the taped-down edge and pulled out a pair of cardboard inserts, taped together. A folded letter fell out onto the covers, and she set aside the cardboard to pick it up.

"Dear Ms. Jeffries," she read out loud. "As per our instructions, here is the key to your new home. Enjoy." She looked at Rick. "I now have a house. But from who? Who knows me? And who would know I was here now?"

"I can think of a few people, but not why," Rick said, craning his neck and leaning over to look at the letter. "Anything else in the package?"

Nikki handed it to him and picked up the cardboard inserts. "Just this."

The key that was taped to the inside of the cardboard was large and copper. Nikki pulled it from the cardboard and ran her fingers over it: even now, after who knows how many years in the hands of the London bank, it still held the whisper of Teraisa's Power, the darkness of the Shadows that had consumed her murmuring to her daughter. "My mother sent this." *Which explains how they knew to send it.* "But why now? And how did she tell them to send it to me?"

"Does it matter?" Rick said, drawing her attention back from the key. "Let's see where Mill's Pond is." When she stared at him blankly, he waved another piece of paper at her. "This fell out of your packet as well. It's got an address on it in Mill's Pond, New Hampshire, which I've never heard of."

"Look online," Nikki said, pointing at her laptop and attacking her breakfast while he was getting directions. Then she got out of bed, grabbed a pair of jeans, a tee-shirt and underwear and went into the bathroom to get changed from her pajamas.

She paused while dressing to look at the slim scar on her chest, the only reminder of Alex's attempt to make sure she didn't interfere in any of his new plans. Vashti and Morgan had done a great job, closing a wound that should have taken months to heal. *A wound that should have killed me,* Nikki corrected herself silently, staring at the slender white line meandering down the edge of her left breast, barely visible against her pale winter skin. She ran her finger down it, feeling the scar catch against her fingertip just a bit. One physical reminder.

"Nikki? You ready?"

Rick's voice jarred her out of her thoughts. "Yeah, hang on." She slipped on her clothes and then ran a brush through her hair and deemed herself decent. "Let's go."

Mill's Pond, it turned out, was only about an hour north from Sarah's. Nikki let Rick drive while she navigated with the map he'd printed out. The key she'd been sent was in her jacket pocket, and she wondered what they'd find when they got there.

Oh, stop it, she finally told herself irritably. *It's a house. Nothing else.*

Yes, but it's your mother's house, her mind whispered back. *Who knows what she's left you there. And what if it's only in the Shadow Lands? What will you do with Rick?*

That was something she hadn't considered. "Hey, Rick, do you still have that talisman Justin gave you?" Nikki asked out loud, and grinned when he fished it out of his pocket. "Oh, good."

"It lives in there now," Rick said, giving her a grin. "Between you and Justin, I never know where I'll end up, so I figured rather be safe than sorry."

"You were a boy scout, weren't you?"

"Guilty as charged," he admitted.

"Were you any good?" she teased, settling back against the seat.

He shook his dark blonde head. "Nah. I quit early on."

"You actually quit?" Nikki asked, mock-astonished. "I don't believe it."

The rest of the ride passed quickly as they bantered back and forth. Nikki was surprised at how quickly they fell back into a comfortable zone; it was hard to believe that six short months ago, she'd been back in Connecticut, planning her life after college. Somehow, she hadn't really expected to be trying to stop a megalomaniacal madman from destroying the world.

How far out of whack my life has gone, she mused, as Rick slipped a CD into the player and the familiar sounds of Christmas carols washed over her. *I can't believe it's only two months until Christmas. When will I find time to shop?*

Then she laughed silently at herself. *We need to save the world, and I'm worried about Christmas shopping. Priorities, Jeffries, priorities.*

"What road are we taking again?" Rick asked, interrupting her thoughts.

"Um, Silver Lane," she said, consulting the map. "Should be a right."

"Gotcha." He executed the turn smoothly despite the snowy roads. "How much longer?"

"According to the map, it should be right over the hill," Nikki said, sitting up a bit. "In fact, it should be right in front of us."

They topped the hill, and Rick stepped on the brakes, stopping the car. They both stared in silence at the house that presented itself to them at the end of the road.

"Dearest goddess," Nikki breathed, awed. "Do you feel that?"

Darkness. Pure elemental darkness hung over everything, from the neatly shingled roof to the dark green hemlocks in the front yard. Nikki had only seen one house like this in her life: Alenya's, the Shadow Lord who had raised Justin and taken Nikki in to train her after her powers first awakened. Alenya's large palladium mansion, set deep in the Shadow Lands, had been obviously the house of a Shadow Lord — her presence could be felt in every stone and flower that surrounded it. Teraisa, however, had been a mortal Shadow Mage before Alex's experiments had turned her into something more, and her home was on Earth, not within the Shadow Lands. The amount of cold Power that permeated the dwelling spoke of just how much a part of the Shadows she had truly become.

And if this is what happened to my mother, what did the experiments do to Caran Masterson? And to Alex himself? Goddess, this is just the Earth side of it — do I even dare to go into the Shadow Lands there?

"Do you really want to go in there?" Rick whispered, obviously shaken.

His senses must be in overdrive, Nikki thought absently. Out loud, she said, "I do. You can stay out here if you want, though. I won't mind."

It took him a few minutes, but Rick shook his head. "No, I can't let it get to me like that." He drove slowly down the hill; the Shadows parted before them like black lace curtains drawn back by inquisitive old ladies. The house glowered down at them as they pulled closer; even though she was now the owner, Nikki felt like an intruder. The mother she had never known had watched her grow up from here; as the front door loomed in front of them, dread grew in her stomach, a lead weight.

The driveway stopped at the set of small stone steps that mounted up to the massive front door. Nikki slid out of the Cherokee, her legs unsteady, and approached the door. The large key snicked the lock open and the door swung open noiselessly.

"If Lurch comes out and greets us, I'm running."

Nikki jumped and gave a little shriek as Rick spoke from right behind her; the atmosphere of the place had made her forget she hadn't come alone, and his voice shattered the solitude like glass. He raised his eyebrows at her.

"Jumpy much?"

She rolled her eyes at him and sternly told her heartbeat to slow down. *It's just a house,* she said silently. *No matter who lived here before. It's just a house.*

Too bad I don't believe that.

The door creaked a bit at the last minute as she pushed it open wider, and every horror movie Nikki had ever seen rushed through her head in a mad dash of blood and gore, shading her vision red for a moment. *It's just a house...*

"So, are we going to go in, or are we going to decide this is a really bad idea and get the hell out of here?" Rick asked her quietly.

"Since when have we backed down from something just because it was a really bad idea?" she joked weakly. Just the sound of their voices seemed to raise the gloom a bit. Nikki wondered how long it had been since the walls of the house had heard anything other than whispers.

Gathering her courage, Nikki pulled the key from the lock, dropped it back into her jacket pocket and stepped in. Small pale blue magelights sprang to life as her boot heels cracked on the marble floors, gunshots of sound that echoed through the house as she ventured further into the foyer. There was something in the house, something that watched her, judging, contemplating, and she had the uncomfortable feeling she knew who it was.

It was creepy. It was also par for the course for her life lately.

"Do you know where we're going and what we're looking for?" Rick asked as he followed her in. She shook her head, then paused as a thought hit her.

"She wanted me to come here now, specifically," Nikki said, looking around the foyer. "Which means I'll bet she left me something important, and if she's anything like I think she is, she'll have hidden it. Let's see if we can find her workroom." She looked around. The foyer had a long hallway that ran off in either direction, and there was a staircase leading up to the second floor in the center of it. "You go that way, I'll go this way. Let's check this floor before we go upstairs. I really feel like I need to find her workroom."

"Sounds good," Rick said, and headed off. She watched him go for a moment, surprised at how quickly he agreed, and then shook herself and went down her own hall, peeking in each room curiously.

She found a kitchen that was remarkably homey, and a small dining room, as well as an old linen closet full of dusty cloth, but no workroom. A glance in Rick's direction found him shaking his head; he'd obviously struck out as well. They met back at the stairs.

"Well, you are the proud owner of three sitting rooms," he reported. "And one very scary closet that I think once held either brooms or your mother's equivalent of Farnsworth."

Nikki giggled at the thought of Alenya's dour butler. "Well, the kitchen isn't that scary. And the dining room isn't too bad either. The linen closet is another story."

"I hope you know a good cleaning service, Nikki, because there is no way Sarah's coming out here to help you fix it up. Not unless you get rid of the Shadows." Rick's smile was pure mischief, and it coaxed an answering smile out of her.

Then she looked up the stairs. "Well, I guess we go up."

The second floor appeared to be all bedrooms — Nikki figured she could have most of her friends from college over and still have room left over. But still no workroom.

"Did you find anything?" Rick called from down the hall. She was about to answer when she opened the final door and stopped, stunned.

Nikki had only met her birth mother once — when Teraisa had led her and Rick into Gene-Tech on Halloween to rescue Alenya and stop Alex. Even so, the flavor of the former Shadow Mage's magic had imprinted itself on her psyche, a unique signature that still held a faint taste of the Mage she had once been. And that signature was all over this small room.

Teraisa's bedroom was light and airy, a decided contrast to the gloom of the rest of the house. It was painted a pale lavender, a color that was echoed in the darker trim and the bedspread. It was as if the Shadows had never been allowed to desecrate this room, but that wasn't what had caught her breath.

The mantle over the fireplace on the opposite wall was crowded with pictures. Pictures of Nikki from birth onwards. Teraisa may not have raised her, but she had apparently kept a very close eye on her daughter as she grew up.

Or maybe not, Nikki thought, moving towards the pictures. She picked one up: it was a winter scene, with her on a sled. Her adopted father Marc had been pulling her along; the girl in the photo was only about six or so. Plump pink cheeks glowed from the cold of the winter afternoon; her snowsuit was brushed with white, mute evidence of how many times she'd fallen off the sled that afternoon. Smiling at the memories it brought back, Nikki replaced the photo, noticing that they stopped when she was approximately thirteen. *I wonder why? Was it too hard to sneak into the house?*

"Maybe at that point you were getting too subconsciously sensitive to the Shadows." Rick's voice came from behind her, once again answering her unspoken thoughts.

"You know, six months ago, that would have freaked the crap out of me," she said, turning to look at him.

"Six months ago, you wouldn't have been here at all," he replied. Nikki sighed, unable to refute that.

"Six months ago, I was a normal human being."

He didn't answer. She looked away, not wanting to continue the conversation, and the doorway tucked in the corner of the room caught her eye. Not really thinking it would be more than a closet, Nikki went over and opened it. The narrow iron staircase that wound upstairs surprised her.

"Well, that's one way to keep your workroom private," Rick said, coming up behind her. "I doubt she let anyone in here."

Nikki drew in a deep breath. "Well, let's go see what's upstairs."

"Are you ready?"

Am I?

They climbed the stairs in silence, the iron cold under their hands. The room opened up before them, taking up most of the third floor of the house. Despite the fact that Teraisa (as far as they knew) hadn't been back to the house in at least a week, a fire still burned merrily in the fireplace, and there was not a speck of dust. "Do you think she's been back?" Nikki murmured, looking around at the heavy mahogany furniture.

"Dunno." Rick's amber eyes went a little unfocused, a sign she recognized as his stretching his Talent out to "read" the Power signatures in the room. *Yet another indication of how much I've changed, that this doesn't bother me at all,* she mused privately, not wanting to disturb him. "I don't think so."

"Well, let's see what we can find here," Nikki said, looking around the room. "Where do you want to start?"

They ended up splitting up: Rick started over by the window, where a small desk and filing cabinet stood. Nikki, on the other hand, closed her eyes and opened her mind to the Shadows around her, trusting her mother's blood to guide her to anything that Teraisa might have wanted her to find.

Behind her closed eyelids, she watched dark purple and black Shadows rise, wrapping their icy fingers around her, whispering seductively. Despite the fact that her grounding was in the Earth sphere, thanks to the magics that created her, it was the Shadows that made her feel truly alive. The Shadows in the workroom caressed her, welcoming her into their world and, when she asked if there was something she needed to find here, they answered in the affirmative.

She stretched her hands out in front of her as the Shadows pulled her gently through the room. The sound of Rick shuffling papers and opening drawers faded as the faintest sounds of what she realized was a beating heart began to fill her ears. It grew, never stopping, a steady "thump-thump" that vibrated through Nikki, giving her the sensation of walking through a giant womb.

Her fingertips encountered stone; Nikki opened her eyes to see the tip of a gargoyle's large, hooked nose. Deeply set gemstone eyes, flickering with reflected firelight and Shadows, regarded her intently as he squatted on the mantel above the fireplace.

"Hey Rick, look at this."

Rick looked up from Teraisa's desk. "He's an ugly little fellow, isn't he?"

"I don't know," Nikki said, continuing to inspect the small creature. "I think he's kind of cute." She ran her fingertip down the length of the nose to the side of his face. "I wonder where...ow!"

The gargoyle suddenly turned and sliced open her finger with one wicked claw, drawing blood. As Nikki yanked her hand back, a single drop of blood fell into the gargoyle's outstretched hand, a glowing red jewel that the creature regarded intently. The blood sank slowly into the stone, and the creature's onyx eyes began to glow a deep, dark sapphire blue. Almost the color Teraisa's eyes had been the last time Nikki had seen her.

"Trust no one," the gargoyle croaked, and to her surprise, it stepped to the left of its perch, revealing a dark hole in the wall. Nikki peered in but she couldn't penetrate the gloom.

She cupped her right hand and concentrated on filling the hollow of her palm with light. As steeped as the house was in Shadow, it was hard for her to summon the magelight; Nikki had to grit her teeth and reach far down into the ground for enough Earth energy to ignite it. *One of these days, I need to figure out how to actually do things while I'm immersed in Shadows,* she thought absently as pale green light began to spill from between her fingers. *This is getting old.*

"You're not planning on sticking your hand in there, are you?" Rick had walked over while she was creating the magelight and now stood looking over her shoulder, watching her with interest.

"Not without seeing what's in there first," Nikki said, opening her fingers carefully and letting the magelight float out into the small hole. "I can't imagine my mother would leave something of value in here for just anyone to find." She jerked her head at the gargoyle, which had hunkered back down in his new spot and was still watching them intently. "After all, I've bled enough today."

The green light crept forward, illuminating what appeared to be a small box set far back in the hole. Nikki exchanged a look with Rick, who shrugged.

"Any ideas on what it is?" he asked.

"Well, let's find out." Nikki spread her hands and Shadows flowed from her fingertips. The effort of keeping both the Shadows and the magelight under control made sweat bead on her forehead, but she clenched her teeth and reminded herself that she was a Horseman. A mythical being that could depopulate cities, if the legends were true. *I can certainly handle doing two spells at once, dammit! One little gargoyle is not going to stop me from getting that box!*

Her Shadows wiggled forward, ebony snakes intent on retrieving the prize bathed in the green glow of the magelight, and hooked themselves around the edges of the box. A chill crept down Nikki's spine on soft kitten paws as the box slid forward. *This is too easy,* she thought, as her Shadows inched the box towards her hands and the magelight flickered out. *Way too easy.*

But nothing exploded; the gargoyle stayed motionless as the box came out of the hole and settled gently into her hands. It was an elaborately carved black box, made of a cool substance Nikki couldn't identify.

"So open it," Rick urged, and she tilted it, looking for a latch. The box hummed slightly as she turned it over and the gargoyle laughed, a sound like rocks falling into a pool of water.

"Trust no one," it repeated, and launched itself off the mantel at Nikki, who nearly lost her grip on the box as she tried to duck out of the way and fell. The edge of one wing sliced her cheek open as the creature flew by; it cackled and zipped down the iron staircase.

"Wonderful," Nikki said, climbing back to her feet and swiping at her bleeding cheek with one hand. "Now I've got a bloodthirsty gargoyle loose in my house, and a box I can't open."

"Maybe you can hire an exterminator for the gargoyle," Rick joked, and she chuckled. "As for the other..." His voice trailed off as she touched the box with her bloody hand and then gasped.

Images flashed through her head: a dark Shadow, leaning over her childhood bed as she slept, cutting a lock of the younger Nikki's hair, and then a mad succession of faces, old, young, and in between; then a rose garden, lush and warm, the scent of the flowers a heady perfume that invaded her nostrils. The barrage was so immediate and stopped so suddenly that she swayed on her feet, and Rick had to grab her before she fell over again.

"You okay?" he asked, putting her back on her feet.

"Yeah, I think so." Nikki blinked, trying to get her bearings again. "It was...I don't know." The box in her hand gave an audible click, and the lid tilted open. "Blood," she said softly. "She tied it to my...oh, weird."

"What?" Rick leaned over her shoulder to get a closer look at the boxes contents.

Lying inside were locks of hair, all different colors and lengths, tied with slender colored ribbons. Nikki went over to the table slowly and then lifted them out and laid them down, one by one, until she reached the last, which she hesitated over.

"Whose are they?" Rick asked.

"I'd imagine they belong to everyone involved in the original Soldier project," Nikki said, stroking the lock that she knew had come from her. "All the donors, and the children. Maybe even some of the researchers involved."

"But why?" he said, frowning. "Are you sure?"

"Pretty sure," she replied, and turned the box around so he could see the lock she hadn't touched yet.

It lay nestled on a black velvet pillow, threaded through a platinum ring that had a perfect diamond heart surmounting it. A shining length of shimmering gold, dulled only by the blood encrusting it.

"Who...?" Rick asked, reaching for it.

"I don't know," Nikki replied, pulling the box away. "But I know that this one," and she picked it up, "is mine. And if mine was in here, it only makes sense that these others belong to the others in the experiment." She quickly repacked the other locks, suddenly chilled. "Let's get out of here."

Chapter Six

"Lifelines"

Justin stretched, popping his shoulders and arching his back as he got slowly to his feet. "We need to take a break," he told his foster mother, who gave him a mutinous glare. "I'm serious. We've been scrying all day — you can't continue at this pace. You need to rest."

"Kith doesn't have time for me to rest," Alenya snapped, getting up and swaying slightly. "We don't know how long he'll survive in that Cube."

Wincing in guilt at the mention of the Shadow Lord who had helped raise him, Justin nevertheless shook his head. "You can barely stand, Alenya," he said bluntly, knowing she wasn't going to like hearing what he had to say. "You're not going to help Kith by killing yourself looking for him."

"He's right," a new voice said from the doorway, and they both jumped. Cassandra stood there, her white robes luminous in the semi-twilight of the hallway. "You need to take a break, Alenya."

"I'm fine, Mother," Alenya said and then swayed again before settling back into her chair. "I don't need anything more than something to eat."

"And a good night's sleep," Justin chimed in firmly.

"Definitely," Cassandra concurred, coming into the study and gesturing at the magelights, which brightened. "You look like hell."

"Thank you for that," Alenya said, baring white canines at her mother. "Perhaps if your lover was trapped in a Shadow Cube by the misbegotten son-of-a-bitch who incidentally sired you, you'd look less than perfect as well."

"It's entirely possible," Cassandra said, unruffled by her daughter's vitriol. "Then again, considering that the misbegotten son-of-a-bitch was my lover at one point and is also missing, maybe you should realize that not everything is working out perfectly for everyone else either right now, and listen to us."

Justin blinked, trying to follow the logic in that sentence. *Either I'm more tired than I thought, or Cassandra's being even more obtuse than usual,* he decided, when it failed to scan a third time. *Or both.*

"Justin, you need to go home as well," Cassandra continued, and despite himself, he raised an eyebrow at her.

"And since when is this not my home?" he asked her. "Am I no longer welcome here?"

She didn't even have the grace to flush. "You know what I mean. Go back to the Inn and rest for a while. I'm sure Nikki and Rick would like to see you."

And if that's not a dismissal... "I'm sure they would," Justin replied evenly. "However, I promised Alenya I'd help her."

"And you have," Cassandra said. "And now I need to talk to her. Without you here."

That stung. A lot. "Why?" he asked.

Cassandra turned to look at him, her face bland. "Because you're still a mortal Mage, Justin, no matter who your sister is, and this doesn't concern you. I have Lord business to discuss with my daughter. Now leave us, please." When he gaped at her, she frowned. "I won't ask politely again."

"Behave, Mother," Alenya said. When Cassandra turned back to her, Alenya continued, "This is still my house. Don't go telling my foster son that he's not welcome here."

"No, I'll leave," Justin said bitterly, walking towards the door. "Trust me, Lord business means Council business. And I've had enough of the Council to last me a lifetime."

He didn't slam the study door behind him, but he did shut it precisely. *Damn Council,* he thought mutinously as he strode down the corridor to the Gate Alenya kept active in the secondary workroom. *Always so damn secretive. They'll get us all killed before they'll unbend enough to tell us there's something wrong.*

The Gate swirled slowly in the semi-darkness of the room as he opened the door, and it only took Justin a moment to calibrate it to the Gate in Sarah's pantry. The chill of the Shadow Lands left him as he stepped into the pantry, and the enticing smell of hot coffee perked him up a bit. That, and the sounds of Nikki and Rick talking.

"Is that coffee?" Justin asked as he came into the kitchen. "Please tell me I'm not dreaming."

"Nope," Nikki said, getting up and pouring him a cup. "There's plenty." She handed him the cup and then squinted at him. "Although I think you need sleep more than coffee," she said. "When did you last go to bed?"

"Last night," Justin said, sipping the coffee gratefully. "But I was up spellcasting all day."

"No luck finding Kith yet?" Rick asked, as Nikki went to the refrigerator and started pulling things out and piling them on a plate.

"Nothing," Justin said in disgust. "Alex and Andreas are keeping their heads down. Of course, I can't really blame them, considering that not only us, but the Council and probably the US government are all after them as well." Nikki set a plate of leftover chicken, couscous and asparagus in front of him and he smiled up at her. "Thanks."

"No problem." She sat back down at the table and picked up her own steaming mug. "Let me know if you want more."

Justin picked up his fork. "So what have you two been up to?"

To his surprise, they looked at each other and hesitated before Nikki said, "We went to my mother's house today."

"It's still standing?" Justin said, blinking. "I would have thought Alex would have razed it to the ground when she vanished."

"I would have loved to see him try," Nikki said wryly, and he gave her a puzzled look. "Trust me. It wouldn't have worked."

"If you say so." Justin shrugged. "Find anything interesting?"

"My mother left me something." Nikki pointed to the thin scratch on her cheek. "What do you know about gargoyles?"

"She left you a gargoyle?" Justin said, nearly choking on the couscous as he tried to laugh and eat at the same time. "Wow, special."

Rick got up and pounded him on the back while Nikki glared at him. "Not exactly. The gargoyle was hiding this. Once he scratched me, he left, but I don't know that he's not still in the house somewhere."

The intricately carved black box was gorgeous, but it was what coursed through him when Justin picked it up that sobered him instantly. "Holy shit," he breathed, feeling the chill from the box tiptoe through him. "Where the hell did she get this?"

"What?" Nikki asked, raising one dark eyebrow at him.

"This is a Shadow Box," Justin said slowly, turning it over and looking at the various carvings. "Very rare — and the Shadow Lord that made it was very talented. These don't leave their creators usually. What's in it?"

"Hair," Nikki told him. "Locks of hair. Can you tell who made it?"

"That's what I'm looking for," Justin said. The carvings were intricate, and it took him several minutes to give up. "If there's a name on here, I can't find it." He set the box back down on the table. "Which begs the question, of course, of where Teraisa got it. Like I said, these don't usually leave their creator's hands. How did she get one?"

"A gift, maybe?" Rick said, and Nikki and Justin exchanged long glances.

"Maybe," Nikki said, picking the box back up. "And maybe the owner just didn't need it anymore." She looked up at Justin. "So, have you been tossed out or did you just decide you needed a warm bed to sleep in tonight?"

Justin grimaced. "Cassandra came by to talk Council business with Alenya, so I was instructed to find myself somewhere else to be."

"Council business?" Nikki asked, and he grunted. "What is this Council, anyways? You never really did explain what they do."

"They're a bunch of stuffed shirts who have nothing better to do than run people's lives," Justin said sourly. "Not that I have any strong opinions or anything." She gave him a disbelieving look and he sighed. "Okay, the Council of Nine is the ruling body of the Elemental Lords. Technically, they're an advisory body to the

StarChild, but they pretty much run the Lands, as much as anyone can. Trying to get a bunch of Elemental Lords to do anything together is a lot like herding cats, and almost as frustrating. They'll listen to the StarChild, and pay lip service to the Council, but really, Lords are an independent bunch, and most of the time they do what they want."

"But what *is* the Council?" Nikki insisted. "Who's on it?"

"Nine Lords," Justin said. "Three each of Earth, Shadow and Sun, if you read the older books."

"Sun?" Nikki said, and he nodded.

"The legend is that the Dawn Lords are descended from the union of Sun and Magic, just as the Shadow Lords came from Magic and Shadow, and the Earth Lords from the Earth and Magic," Justin said. "It's pretty, and probably false, but hey, who knows. Anyways, the Council is always nine members, and it takes at least one of each to cast the Summoning Spells. Supposedly. And the StarChild, of course, but maybe that's just window dressing too."

Nikki sat back chewing over that while Justin finished his dinner and Rick refilled his coffee cup. "So what's the plan for the next few days?" Justin asked, getting up and putting his dishes in the sink.

"I've got a book to write," Rick said regretfully. "Which is where I'm headed now. I'll see you guys later."

As he left, Justin turned to Nikki. "Plans?" he prodded, when she didn't answer.

She shrugged. "I dunno. I need to find Alex. I just don't know how."

"You still have all those files, right?" When she nodded, Justin spread his hands. "Let's start working through them tomorrow."

Nikki looked at him for a moment, then nodded again. "Yeah, I guess."

"You guess?" Justin sat down opposite her again. "What's up, Nikki?"

"Do you think they're really dead?"

The question startled him. "Who?"

"My mother. And the ghost of the Dawn Lord." Nikki's eyes darkened. "Which means Lords can really die. Do you think my mother is dead now?"

Justin drew in a deep breath. "Yes, Lords really can die," he said finally. "But in this case, I don't know, Nikki. We know the Dawn Lord was dead. But your mother — I don't know if someone that consumed in Shadows could even be considered alive." She winced, and he laid a hand on her arm. "I'm sorry. I'm tired, and my mouth is running away with me. Let's talk again tomorrow — I might be able to come up with something more productive then. Okay?"

But as he followed her upstairs to the room Sarah had told him he could use at any time, Justin wondered what else he might end up doing. Cassandra had been ominous, more so than usual, and ordering him out was not her normal mode of operations. *Something big is going on,* he decided, opening the door to his room. *And it's going to drag us all down if we're not careful. And personally, I'd rather not end up like that Dawn Lord.*

Now what do I do?

The rose garden was flush with new growth, fragrant blooms nodding their heavy heads in the warm breeze. Trimaris del Sole sat at a small stone table, a glass of wine forgotten in front of her, and pondered her options. Unfortunately, there were a lot fewer of them than she would have liked.

I could go to the Council, she thought, one finger tracing the pattern inset in the tabletop, the stone warm under her touch. *Admit I was the Dawn Lord involved in the insanity this time, and take my punishment. That would be the smart path.*

"Yeah, if you've got a death wish."

She looked up as her sister's voice broke the sleepy silence. Kymara del Sole stood by the gate, her hands on the latch, an arch look on her face. "My only wish is to be done with all of this," Trimaris replied, watching her enter the garden and drop into the other chair. "Or to go back twenty-three years and stop you and Andreas from even starting."

"Good luck." Kymara ran one finger around the edge of the wineglass in front of her. "He's a stubborn bastard, my Andreas." The love in her voice still touched her sister.

"He got you killed, you know, Ky." Trimaris reached out and removed the wineglass from her ghostly sister's grasp. "I don't see why you still love him."

"Because it's not all his fault," Kymara said, the light in her eyes dimming for a moment. "But that's not the reason I'm here."

"Oh? To what do I owe the pleasure of this visit?" Trimaris gave in and took a drink of the wine; the sweet, slightly sticky liquid slunk down her throat, leaving a faintly metallic aftertaste. The taste of the blood that now lay partly on her hands.

Kymara's next words turned the metallic to dust.

"The StarChild has started the Cleansing."

Trimaris nearly choked on the wine. "What? How did she know?"

"She's the StarChild, Tri." Kymara shrugged. "I'm not sure it's just this, though."

"What?" Trimaris' head spun. "What else could have possibly spurred her to do that?"

"Whatever she's sealed up in Vermont with," Kymara replied. "You do watch the news, don't you? I know you've devoured everything you could find about the explosions."

"That's because I was responsible in large part for those explosions," Trimaris said, clenching her hand around the stem of the wineglass. "I can't help it."

"What are you talking about?" Kymara gave her a sharp look.

"Nothing," Trimaris said, looking away. "What do you want here?"

Her sister looked at her for a moment longer before continuing, "I know she started the Cleansing, because dead or not, I'm still a member of the Council. I need to know why."

"So what, you think I should just invite her here to tea and ask, 'So, Shanna, why start the Cleansing now?'" Trimaris threw her head back and laughed. "We were screwing around with the Summoning Spells, Kymara! Andreas and I were casting them that very afternoon! I'm just surprised she didn't come and take care of us right then!"

A shocked silence descended on the sunlit garden. When Kymara did speak, it was in hushed tones. "You started casting the spells that day? Where?"

"Right here." Trimaris pointed to a corner of the garden, where she could still feel the taint of Shadow lying across the grass. "He figured it was safer this way."

"And you didn't stop him why?"

Trimaris couldn't stop her skin from crawling. "Because he threatened me with the same fate you met if I didn't help him. And I still don't have any reason to believe he wouldn't have done it."

When she looked back, her younger sister was staring at her, her blue eyes troubled. "I can't blame you for that. So what did you do, Tri? Cast through a Gate?"

"Not quite." It had been an amazing bit of spellcasting, and even now, Trimaris could appreciate the artistry of Andreas' skills. "He translocated part of the spell chamber from the secure wing to here."

Kymara's jaw dropped. "But, but, you can't do that!"

"I can't, no. But Andreas could, and did. How he did it, I don't know." Regret etched pain on her tongue as she closed her eyes. "I figured it was safest not asking."

She heard the chair rub against the ground as Kymara got up, and opened her eyes again to watch the ghostly Dawn Lord pace, her brow furrowed in thought. "She must have really sunk her claws into him," she heard Kymara mutter. "That's the only explanation."

"What are you talking about, Ky?" Trimaris asked her finally. "What are you so worried about?"

"You really have shut off your brain, haven't you?" Kymara said, swinging around to look at her. "Think, Trimaris! What keeps Earth separate from the Dawn Lands, you twit?"

"The World Walls," Trimaris said. "So?"

Kymara shook her head. "How do you think he broke those Walls?" When her sister continued to stare at her, Kymara threw her hands up in exasperation. "He was using Chaos Magic, Trimaris! Her magic!"

Trimaris paled. "Madness?"

"Who else?" Kymara resumed pacing, stalking around the garden, her robes brushing back the roses that reached out to her.

"Who do you think put him up to this in the first place?"

"But, but, how did he run into her? And why would he join her?" Trimaris' head was spinning. "Andreas is ambitious, but even he knows that Madness would as soon kill him as give him anything. What happened?"

"I don't know," Kymara admitted, stopping to finger a pale pink rose. "I didn't realize how much she was involved until after I'd died. It's easier to see the contamination in him that way."

"Lovely." Trimaris drank the rest of her wine, hoping for an answer in the dregs, but finding none. "So explain to me again why going to the Council wouldn't be the smartest thing?"

"How do you know he wasn't the only Council Lord involved?" Kymara said, still caressing the rose. "We have no idea how deeply Madness' corruption has spread through these lands. And I can't get close enough to the Council to find out."

"Why not?"

"Because when I died, I surrendered to the Balance," Kymara said. "If Madness has corrupted more than Andreas, they'll sense me, and I don't know how many I can fight by myself." She dropped the rose and shook her head. "I have to talk to the others. We may need to push up our schedule."

"Others?"

Kymara smiled. "Of course. Madness is obviously gathering her forces, Tri. Would you expect the Balance to do less?"

Trimaris shook her head. "So when do you go back to being the spoiled kid sister I actually remember?"

"She's dead," Kymara said. "Get used to it. And don't go to the Council. I'll be in touch." She vanished, leaving her sister sitting in the now empty garden, watching rose petals fall to the green grass and shrivel into dust.

Chapter Seven

"A View Beyond"

Sylvia leaned back in the wing chair, feeling the velvet brocade give slightly beneath her blue-jeaned legs and watched an illusionary sun set against the mountains, wondering what she'd see when the sun rose again. The Lord who owned the estate she was staying at was prone to changing everything at a moment's notice; she'd already experienced going to bed in a mountain castle and waking up to an ocean vista outside her window. Even the length of the days and nights seemed arbitrary, as did the number of suns and moons in the sky. *Which means I'm somewhere in the World Between the Walls, but I'll be damned if I can figure out where.*

Even the magic worked differently. She'd already tried to summon both Shadows and Earth spirits to her in the privacy of her rooms, but although she could get a Circle cast, nothing answered. But she could feel Power moving through the halls, so Sylvia knew it wasn't a dead zone. It just didn't add up.

So now what? she mused, watching the sun shade to a blood red as it balanced precariously over the jagged cliffs. A mug of tea oozed fragrant steam on the table beside her, but Sylvia ignored it for the moment. *I can't just sit around and wait for someone to waltz in and rescue me. I'm not a damn princess in a fairy tale, after all.*

And it was extremely clear to her that she wouldn't be allowed to leave on her own. The Lord she'd encountered so far had been very pleasant to her, but Sylvia had noticed the guards that followed discretely behind her and the fact that the same servant never came in twice to her rooms. That, combined with the fact that the halls seemed to empty when she left her rooms, gave her the distinct impression the Lord was isolating her. But why?

The sun continued to dance on the edge of the cliffs, slipping into a dark bed as twilight shadows crept over her balcony and into her room, dragging her thoughts into a deepening gloom. Sylvia looked down at her legs stretched out before her; her ankles crossed neatly, the silver thread around the right one gleaming in the growing darkness. *I've already survived a madman. I can't just sit and let another madman run what's left of my life.*

Especially since I don't know how much longer I have.

Her tea was still lukewarm when she finally reached for it, and the essence of tea leaves and dried fruit died on her tongue as she drank, still thinking about her course of action. *I need to find the library,* Sylvia decided, putting the mug back down on the table. *Even odd Lords like these have a library, and while I doubt they'll let me poke around in their workroom, the library shouldn't be off-limits.*

And if it is, I'll figure something else out.

She stood and stretched, enjoying the feel of jeans and tee-shirts. The first morning, Sylvia had woken up to find a closet full of ball gowns and medieval clothes, but those had vanished in the night and more familiar clothing had appeared. Even a lab jacket, which had made her smile.

"Useful," she murmured, slipping the jacket on and filling the pockets with a pen and paper. "Definitely useful now."

Sticking her head out the door, Sylvia noticed the hallway was lit with gaslights this time. Movement flickered at one end of the hall, but whatever it was ducked around the corner when she looked. Probably another guard; she shrugged mentally and slipped out, intent on prowling all night if she needed to.

She started ducking her head into every doorway that wasn't locked: most seemed to be bedrooms, and she wondered why there were so many empty rooms. A few opened into dining rooms or sitting rooms, but no library.

"Are you looking for someone?"

Sylvia jumped at the question. She spun around and shrank back; a male Lord stood looking at her, an amused grin playing on his sensuous lips. "I'm sorry, Chosen One," he continued. "Did I startle you?"

"A bit," she said, not relaxing at all and feeling the door handle press into the small of her back.

"Can I help you find something?" he asked, coming closer.

"I'm looking for the library," she admitted. The look in his dark eyes made her feel like she'd been caught stealing cookies from a cookie jar. "Is there one I can use?"

"Bored?"

"A little," Sylvia said, seizing on the excuse. "I'm not used to having nothing to do with myself."

His grin grew, and a dangerous light began to glow around him. "I can help with that, Chosen," he purred. "Let me show you exactly what Madness' realm can grant you."

Madness? Is that the Lord's name? "Just the library," she said, shrinking back even farther. "I want to do some reading."

He pouted a bit at that, but then cocked his head as if listening to another voice Sylvia couldn't hear. Then he backed up and offered her his arm. "Let me escort you to the library."

Sylvia took his arm warily, but he was true to his word and took her through the labyrinth of hallways to the library of her dreams. On the way, he introduced himself as Lucifer; when she asked if he was the Lord in charge of the realm, he shook his head and told her he was "just stopping over for a while, like most in this Land." He also gave her some hints on how to navigate Madness' house. Once he opened the heavy oak doors with a flourish, Sylvia forgot all about why she was there or any questions she may have had for the tall Lord. She stepped inside the room hesitantly, unable to believe her good luck.

Aisles upon aisles of bookcases marched into the distance, a cornucopia of knowledge that touched something deep inside her. "Is there a catalog?" she asked, her voice unsteady as she took in the vast array of books.

"Over here."

Joy of joys, it was a computer. Sylvia quickly pulled up a search window and didn't even notice when Lucifer left. The first word she typed in gave her a list, not only of books, but where to find them. She printed the list off and started hunting.

She dropped a large pile of books off in her room, and then set out once more. The twilight still hadn't deepened into true night, despite the fact that the sun had fallen behind the mountains hours ago, and there were two moons, one crescent and one full, hanging in a deeply purple sky. The gaslights flickered as she strode purposefully to what Lucifer had told her was the back door.

The door was small, unobtrusive and she nearly missed it as she was hurrying down the hall.   It wasn't locked, as he'd said, and with a delicious feeling of freedom, Sylvia slipped out into the moonlight. The scent of night-blooming flowers hit her nostrils, and she took a deep, greedy breath. *So this is what freedom smells like.* A maze of boxwoods stretched out into the distance, draped with flowering vines, and Sylvia decided to explore. Movement flickered behind her and she sighed, realizing she still had her bodyguard with her. *I hope you enjoy the walk,* she thought, grinning to herself as she skipped down the stairs into the maze. *Let's see if you can keep up.*

Walking into the maze was like walking into a florist's shop: the scent of roses, moonflowers, night-blooming cereus and others she had no name for enveloped her. She let the fragrances wrap around her as she wandered through the hedges, running her fingers along the vines.   It felt so good to be out of the house that she simply wandered, enjoying the sounds of the night around her. Her guard kept a respectful distance behind her, and Sylvia almost forgot that there were others in the area until she heard Lucifer's voice rumble out of the shadows.

"She suspects nothing."

Sylvia slowed to a crawl, certain the "she" referred to was herself. "Are you sure?" came a familiar female voice, the one he'd called Madness.

"Positive." Lucifer sounded far too pleased with himself. "She nearly wet herself when I showed her the library."

"You brought her to the library?" Sylvia's eyebrows raised at the tone in her voice. "Is that wise, Lucifer?"

"What can she do, my love? There's no way for her to get back to her body without one of us bringing her back. That keeps the Dying under our control. We have the Living as well — all we need to find is the Dead, and we can start the casting."

"But what about the StarChild?" Madness asked, and Sylvia could hear the fretfulness in the Lord's voice. "I have waited too long for this, Lucifer! I am not willing to wait another four millennia to make my bid."

"If we control the Three, what can the StarChild do?" he replied. "You've already crippled her by interfering with her Horsemen. All we need to do is find the Dead and make sure the final spells are cast on the child."

Even walking slowly, Sylvia lost the conversation as she moved down the row. She'd heard enough to pique her curiosity, and suddenly the maze lost its charm. She hurried to the next exit and back to her room, wondering what else she'd find in this odd realm, the door slamming behind her in her haste.

Bang!

Nikki jerked awake, her eyes wide and her heart pounding. Sleet hissed against her window, but other than that, the room was silent, and she laid back against her pillows, breathing fast but trying to calm down. *It's just a dream,* she said to herself, watching the shadows move on the walls. Lightning flashed outside and she heard another crack of thunder and realized what had woken her.

"Christ, it's just a thunderstorm," she said out loud, and then laughed. "Way to go, Jeffries. Some Horseman you are, scared of a thunderstorm."

The mention of the Horsemen brought back the dream, and she sobered. *Who are Madness and Lucifer? And why would I be dreaming of Sylvia again?*

This is so weird. I wish there was someone I could talk to about that.

But she couldn't think of anyone, and eventually she fell asleep again.

CHAPTER EIGHT

"SLICE OF TRUTH"

He saw her first, and slowed to savor the scene. The small café they'd agreed to meet at was quiet, set back from the street in a grove of sugar maples that were just beginning to turn. Her dark head was bent over whatever she was reading, and a nearly-empty iced glass radiated faint mist as it warmed in the sultry early autumn air. Wisps of dark hair escaped her braid and curled around her pale face, giving her a vulnerability he wasn't expecting. It was still hard for him to remember that the unborn child he'd lost all those years ago had actually grown up. *Odd,* he mused, leaning against a blue Volkswagen Beetle that was snuggled up to the curb. *Odd to think that one actually survived.*

I wonder if they all did?

"You can stop staring at me at any time," she said, raising her head and pinning him in place with serious dark blue eyes. Her mother's eyes: she had the same unforgiving expression Teraisa had often used on him, and he wondered if it was genetic.

"I was surveying the end result of a successful experiment," he replied, giving her a small half-smile and standing up. "Do you mind if I join you?"

Suspicion flared in her eyes. "Will you go away if I say no, Alex?"

"No," Alex admitted, closing the distance between them and pulling out a chair that he folded himself into. "We need to talk, Nikki."

Nikki tilted her head at him, as if measuring him for a casket.

"About what? How I'm going to kill you as soon as I find you?"

"Now that's inhospitable," he chided her. "Honestly, it's thanks to me that you're alive."

"What?" Nikki threw back her head and laughed. "Sweet Goddess, Alex, how egotistical can you get? It's thanks to you that I'm a freak of nature!"

"Special. I prefer special."

"Special, huh?" The gleam in her eyes both pleased and worried him. "Yeah, I guess you could use that word. It doesn't change anything, you know. I'm still going to kill you."

"Why?" he asked her, leaning back and stretching his legs out.

"Because it's my job now, Alex," Nikki told him. "You screwed around with spells you shouldn't have had any access to. And in doing so, you created your own destiny. Dammit, Alex, you're a Shadow Mage — you had to know you were punching holes in the Balance!"

Alex shook his head. "Not exactly. Andreas never told me what spells we were using. He ran everything — I just supplied the resources necessary."

"And all the weird shit that was happening around you didn't clue you in?" Nikki asked, narrowing her eyes at him. "I don't believe it. You're not that stupid."

"We were on the cutting edge of genetic manipulation," Alex reminded her. "Twenty-three years ago, the elemental Lords had only come out of the woodwork ten years earlier — no one was doing what we were!"

"You're right," Nikki said. "Everyone else was protecting the Balance. You were blowing the hell out of it."

"We were experimenting," he insisted. "I had no idea how deep Andreas would pull us in."

"It was still your duty as a Shadow Mage to cultivate the Balance, Alex." Nikki shook her head. "Blaming it all on Andreas does not absolve you." Then she gave him a keen look. "I wonder if I can kill you now — do you think it would stick?"

"No." They both looked up at the waiter who had just appeared to take their orders. "This meeting was arranged so you could get to know each other better. That's why they chose to make it a dream and make it here — we're neutral ground. No killing. Would you like to order now?"

"Damn," Nikki said, but there was very little rancor in her voice. "Oh well, I guess I'll just have to enjoy hunting you down in the real world then, Alex." She picked up the menu and handed it to him. "I'll have the portabella panini with the sweet potato fries, please. And another iced tea, no sugar."

Alex stared at her, a little bemused at how businesslike she was. *It's as if she doesn't even hate me,* he thought. *It's really just a job for her.*

"Sir?" The waiter's voice prodded him out of his bemusement. "Would you like something?"

"Rum and coke," Alex said, and looked down at the menu. "And, ah, the steak sandwich. Regular fries."

"Don't you dare die of a heart attack before I find you, Masterson," Nikki said, and he looked up to see a small smile playing about her lips. "I'll be very disappointed if that happens."

"Don't worry," he said, handing the waiter the menu. "I'm more likely to die from the belly wound you've already given me, which means you'll have your revenge in the end."

"You really think this is about revenge?" Nikki shook her head. "How egotistical can you get?" She leaned forward and laid her hand on his where it sat on the table, and the anger was gone from her eyes, chased by clear purpose. "It's nothing personal, Alex. You disrupted the Balance, and I'm an agent of the Balance. In order to restore the Balance, you have to die. That's all."

"So it wouldn't matter the situation?" he asked.

"Not really," she said. "Like I said, it's nothing personal. I'm not Frankenstein's monster, out to kill her creator because you made me a monster. I'll take full responsibility for being a monster, if I am. You, however, need to pay for what you did to the world in general, and to the people you ran roughshod over in particular, and there's no circumstances that I can see right now that absolves you or Andreas. You had plenty of warning that what you were doing was wrong. You had several of your researchers tell you that, and you either killed them or experimented on them. I've read the files."

"You either killed or experimented on them." Her words echoed

in his mind, and to his shock, a wave of guilt accompanied them, and a face rose from that wave. Cameron Hillerman. His one-time best friend, the Mage he betrayed in the worst possible way. Alex closed his eyes and winced, then wondered why the shot hit him so hard.

"Alex?" There was slight concern in her voice, and he opened his eyes to see her frowning at him.

"You're right," he said, the unfamiliar taste of guilt thickening his tongue. "You're absolutely right."

Shock raced across her face, a fast horse that left utter confusion in its wake. "What did you say?"

"I said, you're right." Alex sighed, wondering what the hell was wrong with him. "Maybe I need someone I can't kill or intimidate to help me out in that respect. Point me in the right direction."

Nikki continued to stare at him, and he could see her trying to process that revelation. When the waiter came up with their drinks, she pointed at Alex. "This is a joke, a construction of my imagination, right? It's not really Alex Masterson who just admitted he was wrong."

"No, it's really him," the waiter assured her, flashing white teeth in a grin. "Don't worry — he's been having these thoughts for a while, whether or not he's admitted them to himself. He just never had anyone he could talk to that he could admit that to. Look at his face — he's as surprised as you are. That's part of why this dream was set up — you two have more in common than you thought. Your sandwiches will be up soon."

"No way," Nikki said, as the waiter went back into the café. "We are nothing alike."

"Are you sure?" Alex said, picking up his drink and taking a careful sip. Dark rum exploded in his mouth, a smooth counterpoint to the acid bite of the coke, giving him a chance to study her. "I think he may be right."

"You're insane." Nikki pointed at him. "I am so not like you. You need a freaking moral compass to even come close to me."

"Are you volunteering for the job?" he asked, and she scowled at him.

"Not hardly."

"Why not?" Alex said, surprising himself by enjoying the banter. *I haven't had this much fun talking to someone since before we started the first experiment,* he thought. *She has so much of Cameron in her — I could almost imagine she was his daughter, not Teraisa's. Until I look at her, of course. Then her lineage is perfectly clear.*

"Because I'm going to kill you, you idiot, and saving your soul beforehand is just...wrong."

"Even if it needs saving?" Alex said softly, and Nikki hesitated, then shook her head and stood, shoving her chair back.

"Don't you dare appeal to my better side, Alex. I don't have one when you're concerned." She stalked off down the street, disappearing into the bright sunshine.

"Well, that went better than we hoped." Alex looked up at the waiter who had reappeared with a tray in his hands.

"It did?" Alex accepted the plate the waiter handed him.

"Sure. The place is still standing."

Alex couldn't disagree with that. The steak sandwich melted in his mouth; even though he knew it was a dream, the sensations were so real that he decided to stop questioning it and just enjoy it. Now that Nikki was gone, though, he wondered just who "they" were. *Pretty powerful, to pull both of us into a dream,* Alex mused. *I wonder if the Council could do it?*

His mind whispered a name in suggestion, but he shook his head. *I doubt the StarChild wants to do more than plug the holes in the World Walls with my guts,* he told himself, picking up a crisp French fry. *And the tone of this... meeting, if they want to call it that, didn't go along with that.*

"Mind if I join you?"

This voice was masculine, and very familiar. Alex looked up at the amused face of Cameron Hillerman and shrugged. "When have I ever minded your company, Cam?" he asked, and the ghost (or dream? Did it make a difference?) chuckled.

"Oh, I can think of a few times, Alex," he said, dropping into Nikki's abandoned chair. When the waiter came out, he ordered a rum and coke as well, then looked over at Alex. "You're looking tired."

"Being on the run is tough," Alex admitted. "I'm finding I'm not fond of it."

"You always were fond of your creature comforts," Cameron said, grinning. "You're in a world of shit now, old man."

"Tell me something I don't know."

Cameron's face went serious. "You need to be very careful with Nikki, Alex. Everything is not as it seems."

"See above comment." Alex snorted at the grimace on Cameron's face. "Seriously, Cameron, when has anything been as it seems on this project?" Then he smiled, staring off in the direction Nikki had stormed off in. "But damn, she's so perfect, Cam. She's everything we hoped for and more."

"She's Death, Alex. Literally."

"I know."

"She's going to kill you."

"I know."

"And this doesn't bother you?" Cameron said. "Hello, earth to Alex!" Then, as Alex continued to stare off into the distance, he sat back, shaking his head. "Good lord, you're not stuck on her, are you? Need I remind you that not only are you almost forty years older than she is, but she wants to tie your guts into garters?"

"No, she just wants me dead," Alex said, finally coming back to himself. "It's strictly business, and I can admire that. I can also work around it."

"She's right. You're completely self-absorbed." Cameron took a large swallow of his drink. "You really think you can change her mind?"

"I think I can give her some more options than she's currently considering," Alex corrected him, pointing with a French fry. "After all, I'm a businessman too, and if I can convince her that killing me won't help repair the World Walls and the Balance, I might even get her to let me help her fix things."

"Fix things," Cameron repeated, disbelief weighing down his voice. "Now you want to fix things?"

"I've always wanted to fix things," Alex said, popping the fry he'd been gesturing with into his mouth and looking off in the distance again. "I knew there were problems with the original experiments. There always are. But looking at her — I know we can work through them, create the hybrids we wanted. It's just going to take a little tweaking." He paused. "Just what you always wanted to hear me say, eh, Cam? Admitting that there were problems."

"Are you really sure you want to do that, Alex? You may not like the results you get."

Now that's an odd comment for Cameron to make. Alex looked back to see an almost alien expression peering out of his old friend's eyes as Cameron stared at him, a look that chilled him to the bone and made him realize that whatever was sitting across from him was not his best friend. No matter what he looked like. *Tread carefully, Alex,* his mind warned him, and he looked around for the waiter.

"Do you gentlemen need something?" As if his thoughts had summoned him, the waiter appeared next to the table, helpfully bland and yet somehow reassuring.

"Just the check, I think," Alex said. "I'm done here."

"Problems, Alex?" Cameron said, a whisper of menace threading through his familiar voice, and a frisson of something akin to fear walked down Alex's spine.

"Not yet," Alex said, wiping his mouth on the napkin. "But I don't like sharing my table with strangers."

"And what makes you think I'm a stranger?"

Alex smiled, and the expression carried none of its earlier warmth. "Cameron Hillerman died because he wanted to fix things. He would never sit here and try to talk me out of making things right. So I don't know who the hell you are, but I'm done talking to you."

Cameron's mouth twisted in anger, and then the image shattered, thousands of fragments of light and sound that blew over Alex, cutting into him like brilliant shards of glass and fury and then vanishing.

"Interesting," the waiter said, brushing debris off himself. "I wondered how long he'd stay before you figured it out. Dessert?"

Alex stared at him.

"Alex?"

The voice was wrong. As Alex continued to look at the waiter, the café started to waver. "Damn," the waiter said, shaking his head. "I can't keep you here any longer. You'll have to have dessert later." And the man reached out and pushed Alex backwards. "Don't forget us, okay?"

"Alex?"

Alex went tumbling backwards through a dark, cold tunnel, the warm café and sunlight retreating into the distance, with that irritated voice calling his name. As he rushed towards some sort of ground, wondering what would be waiting for him, the aches he'd left behind swarmed over him and he groaned. *Can't I go back to the dream? I felt so much better there!*

"Alex!"

"All right, shut up," Alex said, finally opening his eyes and squinting at Tony. Luckily, the final fall into the bed hadn't been too bad. "What?"

"Do not do that again." Tony's normally swarthy face was ashen, and Alex blinked at him. "I came in and you were barely breathing!"

"Really?" Alex blinked again. "Shit."

"Yeah, you could say that." Angry color bloomed in Tony's face, chasing the grey tinge away. "If you die on me, Masterson, so help me God, I'll find you and kill you again."

"God's not going to help you," Alex said, sitting up and wincing as the wound in his belly throbbed. "He hates you."

"The feeling's mutual," Tony retorted. "What the hell were you doing?"

"What?"

"What were you doing?" Tony repeated. "Look outside!"

Alex glanced out the window. Rain slashed against the window, a hissing overlaying the heavy rumble of thunder. "So it's a thunderstorm."

"It was clear an hour ago," Tony said. "And then this blew up out of nowhere. What kind of shit are you playing with, Alex? What were you looking for?"

Salvation? No, too strong. Maybe just answers. Alex closed his eyes for a moment. "I was looking back in my memories," he said finally. "Trying to see if Andreas had told me anything that might help us finish this."

"And?"

"Nothing," Alex said, hoping Tony would read his reticence as disappointment. "Any luck in finding us a permanent base?"

"A bit," Tony said, and the tone in his voice made Alex open his eyes and stare at him. "I think I have a place. I've just got to make sure it's close enough to where we stashed Andreas so I can drive over there and get them afterwards. That's what I was coming to tell you when I came in and found you trying to die."

They should have covered that better, Alex thought, but out loud all he said was, "Go tell Andreas to get ready to move, then. I want us settled as soon as possible."

"And what are you going to do?" Tony asked.

"Sleep," Alex replied, sliding back down and closing his eyes. "Just sleep." Before Tony left, he added, "Ask Andreas about the spells. I want to make sure we have access to them."

"Why?"

Andreas turned around and looked at Tony. The Shadow Lord stood in the midst of a sunlit garden, a pair of shears in one hand and a single blood-red rose in the other, looking almost mundane in soft pants and a short-sleeved tunic. In fact, if one ignored the long dark hair and the bandages around his eyes, he could be any older retiree in his garden, passing time on a warm winter day by babying his plants.

"Because someone broke in after the explosion and trashed the office, and took every damn piece of paper they could lay their hands on," Tony said, irritation apparent in his voice. Andreas silently congratulated whoever it had been; they had been sharper than the two he'd thrown his lot in with.

"Why did they beat you to it?" he asked, moving to another bush and selecting a large bloom. To his MageSight, the roses glowed with life and health, a welcome balm to his battered soul. Standing here in this garden, Andreas could understand why Kymara had loved her garden so.

One day, my love, we will have a garden together again, he thought sadly, snipping the rose. *I promise you. If we can incarnate a Horseman, there's no reason we can't incarnate a Dawn Lord. Provided, of course, that we survive the next few months, which is looking less and less likely.*

"Because they weren't on the run with three cripples," Tony snarled, bringing Andreas' attention back to the present. "And I got back there as soon as I could."

"But not soon enough," Andreas said, and Tony snorted. "Luckily for you and my wayward son, I have another set of the spells."

"Good. Where?"

"Safe," Andreas said, and smiled as he heard Tony growl. "Be patient, Tony. They are in a safe place, and no one will find them until I retrieve them."

"I could..."

"No, you couldn't," Andreas said, turning back around to the furious Blood Mage. "I'll retrieve them once the Lands quiet down."

"Alex thinks we don't have time."

"Alex should stop thinking," Andreas said, moving to the table he'd set out in the corner of the garden. "It gets us all in trouble."

"Well, at least we agree on something," Tony said, following him to the table. "But we need to start soon."

"The child is stable," Andreas said, setting the roses into a vase he had waiting. "We have at least another month before we need to start the secondary spells. Tell Alex to concentrate on finding us a safe place to retreat to, since the instant anyone tries to do any magic around here, the locals will swarm us." He paused. "You did remember that, did you not, Tony? I trust you did not Gate into the nearby area."

"I'm not that stupid," Tony growled. "I drove in from Houston."

"Good." Andreas sat down, admiring the roses and enjoying the feel of the sunshine on his skin. "Then I believe we are done. Come and collect us when you have a permanent place for us."

He could imagine the look of absolute fury on Tony's face at the blatant dismissal, and the sound of the Blood Mage stomping out of the small bungalow he'd taken over on the outskirts of this sleepy retirement town. It would have been a perfect place to finish the experiments, if not for one thing.

Trust Tony to find the only empty house in a retirement

community of Mages, Andreas thought, amused by the irony of it all.

"At least it has a garden."

"I should have known I couldn't hide from you," he said, as he felt her familiar presence brush up against him. Kymara stepped into the sunlight, glowing softly.

"I'm not the only one you can't hide from, my love," she told him, stroking his cheek. "The Balance is stirring. The Horsemen ride, and the StarChild has started the Cleansing."

"At least I can die in the sun," Andreas said.

"You don't have to die."

He laughed, a bitter sound that jumped the garden walls and echoed across the desert. "Of course I do," he said. "That's what the Cleansing is all about. Do you think either side will let me survive what I've done?"

"You can still make it right," Kymara said, kneeling in front of him and taking his hands in hers. "Bring the girl and come with me now, back to my garden. I can protect the two of you. I can help you. Please, Andreas, trust me and come with me."

He wanted to. Andreas could feel her warmth running over his skin like the heat from a second sun, but deep within his soul, an icy snake of hate and anger uncoiled, burying the warmth with despair, and he pulled his hands away. "Nothing can make it right now, and no one can protect me," he said harshly, getting up and hurrying inside. "No one."

Chapter Nine

"Storm Chased"

"What the hell is my subconscious trying to tell me?"

Nikki lay in bed, staring up at the dark ceiling, the scene from her most recent dream running through her head. *First Sylvia, then Alex,* she thought, clenching the covers in her hands as she tried to make sense of the strange dreams. *Why are they living in my head?*

The niggling thought that someone else was sending her the dreams whispered at the back of her head, but Nikki firmly shut the whisper out of her mind. "No one is messing in my head," she said out loud. "I'm not that paranoid yet."

Her chest ached as she lay there, and she rubbed her breastbone. "I am going to kill you, Alex," she said, as if to reassure herself. "And it really isn't personal anymore. It's just a fact. I'm going to kill you."

But what if he is sorry? That insidious voice was back. *What if he wants to make things right, like he said?*

"That was a construct of my imagination," Nikki said, giving up and getting out of bed. Sleet sheeted the window with ice and she scowled at it as she turned on the light. "And it still doesn't matter. He broke the Balance. He has to die." The Horseman within her agreed, but that other voice wouldn't go away.

There has to be a way to save him, it insisted. *We don't have to kill everyone who crosses us.*

"I cannot believe I'm arguing with myself about the fate of a criminal mastermind!" Nikki shouted, grabbing a towel and stalking into her bathroom. "I really must be going insane."

A hot shower improved her mood a bit, and her mind suggested an alternative to sitting around and reading more files from Gene-Tech. She came out of the bathroom rubbing a towel through her hair, the brisk strokes massaging her skull and waking her up even further. She tossed the towel on the bed and pulled on a tee-shirt and yoga pants, then crossed to her desk where an assortment of things she'd taken from her mother's house awaited her.

Running her fingers over the carvings on the top of the obsidian box caused a shiver to run down her spine again, and Nikki again wondered how her mother had come to possess the box. *Talk about secrets. Will I ever find out everything about her?*

Do I want to know everything about her?

She dismissed that line of thought and removed her fingertips from the top of the box. "Not yet," she said out loud. "There's another way, and it's probably safer."

Picking up a black bowl that she'd also brought back from her mother's house, Nikki went back into the bathroom and filled it with water. Then she went back into her room and set the bowl down in the middle of her floor before kneeling in front of it.

Kneeling there, Nikki closed her eyes and mentally probed the rest of the Inn. Justin was nowhere in the area, which was probably a good thing, considering he'd been reminding her to keep a low profile. *This is very low,* she thought. *All I'm doing is looking. Not loud at all.*

Rick was writing in his room, and deep in thought; he didn't even acknowledge her mental touch as she passed him by. Sarah was cooking down in the kitchen, and there were a few guests puttering around, but none of them were even marginally magically inclined, as far as she could tell. Also good.

Nikki opened her eyes and leaned over the bowl of water, watching the light dance on the black, glossy surface. "Time to use some of this Power I've been given," she said, and spread her hands out.

Dark-green Shadows rose up from the floor around her as she

called them, Earth Magic and Shadow Magic combined in a form that wasn't supposed to exist in one person. *You know, I bet I could call Light spirits too,* she thought idly, then pulled her thoughts back to what she was working on, coaxing the Shadows into the bowl where they spun clouds of darkness into the water. The bowl began to glow darkly and Nikki smiled in satisfaction.

"Now to bind it," she whispered, reaching up and peeling the scab from the slash the gargoyle had left on her cheek. Pain flashed as the skin let go, and Nikki watched two small drops of blood splash down into the water, adding to the small storm brewing in the scrying bowl, a pale echo of the weather she could still hear swirling high above the Inn.

"Show me my siblings," she whispered to the Power reaching for the blood, thin fingers of green-tinged darkness snaking lines through the diffusing crimson. "Show me how to find them, and where."

Miniature lightning flashed in the bowl, arcing across the surface of the water. When the lightning cleared, a blur of images jostled each other within the liquid, a visual static, as if the bowl were trying to "tune in" a specific signal. Nikki leaned over even farther, barely feeling the drain on her Power as the images slowed, gradually coalescing into a single picture: a painting of sugar maples at the height of their color, their trunks bleeding into pencil lines, the center of the illustration blank except for the sketched-in suggestion of figures. The painting leaned up against a wall, a bottle of wine tipped over in front of it, remnants of a pinot noir or cabernet staining the plush cream carpet beneath it. But no person. Nikki studied the image, memorizing it, wondering what it meant. *It must be a clue, but why show me only hints? Why not show me what I asked?*

Maybe I'm just doing it wrong.

"What does this mean?" she asked out loud, not really expecting an answer. "What about the others? Do I have to find the picture to find them?"

More visual static. Nikki watched the images slow again, settling on a large white building: a hospital or clinic, with an ornate cross superimposed over the picture. It pulsed once, twice, as if trying to impress upon her the importance of the scene, and then faded from view.

Nikki sat back on her heels, trying to make sense of the enigmatic images. Her gaze slid to the box still sitting on her desk, as if drawn there. *What if I add the hair to the water somehow?* She thought about that, wrinkling her nose. *There must be some way...*

Her door slammed open, distracting her. The water in the bowl sloshed as she skittered backwards from Justin's thunderous face as he stomped into the room.

"Just what the hell do you think you're doing?"

His hostile question startled her at first and she gaped at him for a moment. Then her own temper flared. "I'm doing what I need to do!" she snapped back at him, rising to her feet. Shadows from the bowl rose with her, feeding off the anger radiating from her, but she was suddenly too furious to notice. "Vashti told me I needed to find the other children! And Alex is still out there with a breeder, remember? Sitting on my ass isn't going to do anything, and no one else..."

Justin crossed the room in a single stride and cut off her tirade mid-syllable by grabbing her by the shoulders and shaking her hard. "You need to stop, dammit! Look outside and see what you're messing with!" And he yanked her around to face the large bay window that lit her room by day.

Nikki gasped at what she saw, anger drowning for the moment under shock and fear. The sleet that had been shushing softly against the glass was gone, replaced by a howling maelstrom that slashed icy claws against the side of the building, fighting to get inside.

"Do you feel that?" His harsh voice grated against her ear, barely recognizable as he held her against him, forcing her to see what was going on outside. "This Storm is so hungry, and you're right here, a tasty, foolish little Mage burgeoning with Power, barely shielded, not even casting within a Circle, because you're that much better than the rest of us. Ripe for the picking."

"Stop it," Nikki whispered.

"That's what I was trying to do, until you started flinging Shadows and Earth Magic around as if it were confetti, disrupting everything anyone in the area was trying to do, and all but lighting a damn beacon for anyone who might be looking for you! Not to mention riling up the Storm again! So tell your Shadows to get lost and start following fucking orders for once!"

She flinched back from the callous words and released her grip on the Shadows in the room, but a tiny thread of resentment poked through her panic. As the Shadows dissipated and the wind screamed, Nikki wondered how she was supposed to have known this would happen. She could hear fury, hunger and a strange pained glee ripple through the wind's howl, thousands of voices bellowing for her and she shrank back against Justin. "How could I have known?" she asked, despising the whining note in her voice. "Why didn't you tell me?"

"I've been a little busy!" Justin roared, spinning her back around to face him again. "And we told you not to attract attention!"

Nikki yanked her shoulders out of his hands, feeling her anger grow again as she stepped back. "I didn't think a simple scrying spell would attract any attention!" she shouted at him. "Maybe if you had taken the time to explain a few things before just vanishing on me, I would have realized that! But no, you just waltz in and out and expect me to twiddle my thumbs until you deign to notice me, until you've got something for me to do..."

"I've been helping to try and calm this damn Storm!" Justin interrupted her. "I'm sorry if that didn't fit into your schedule, but that's life. We thought we could trust you not to stir things up, but apparently not!"

"Maybe if you'd told me what you were doing, I wouldn't have fucked it up!" Nikki shrieked back, her fists clenching at her sides.

The Inn shook as a wicked bolt of lightning slammed down outside somewhere nearby, and thunder cascaded around them. Nikki had never experienced the convergence of a thunderstorm and a winter snow/sleet storm, and a small part of her was fascinated by what was going on outside her window.

Unfortunately, it was a very small part, as most of her was consumed by the irrational desire to strangle Justin on the spot, and then pound any information he might have been holding back from her out of his lifeless body. Her Horseman surged forward, approving of this plan, and not even the Inn falling down around her was going to distract her.

"All right, both of you, knock it off!" Rick suddenly ran into the room and thrust himself between the two of them, cutting her off from her intended target. Nikki glared at him, and he glared right back at her. "Tamp it down, Nikki, before you two kill all of us!"

She ignored him — he wasn't the one she wanted. Nikki bared her teeth and hissed at Justin over Rick's shoulder. "Supercilious, self-righteous bastard!"

"Stubborn, selfish bitch!" Justin snapped back at her. "No, spoiled brat would be closer, because the gods know you aren't acting anything like a responsible adult!"

"And what would a responsible adult look like?" Nikki snarled at him. "You?"

"At least I know what I'm doing!"

"And I would, if someone had bothered to explain anything to me! But you don't! You expect me to just magically know! Pull the knowledge out of the ether! And then you freak out when I try!"

Another bolt of lightning crashed down outside; the windows shook in their frames and Nikki stumbled as the aftershocks of the impact rippled through the Inn.

Even that didn't stop her from trying to kill Justin. Her view had shrunk to his hateful expression and the knowledge that she could and should kill him, that he deserved to die. And the glow in his eyes told her that at the moment he felt the same way about her.

"Nikki, Justin, *stop!*"

Rick's command went unnoticed. All Nikki's frustration boiled over and his voice was lost amid the raging of the Storm above and the emotions swirling in her head. She stretched her hands out, reaching hungrily for Justin with Power-laden fingers, red hazing her eyes and not even caring anymore who went down with him...

And then her vision exploded into a brilliant starburst of white light and pain. Nikki went over backwards, her fury doubled by the exquisite agony exploding from her jaw. Her head connected with something hard and everything went dark.

The world, when it came back to her, was pain. Most of it was centered on a tender spot on the back of her head, but her jaw ached and her teeth felt as if she'd been chewing concrete. Nikki attempted to open her eyes: bright light stabbed her corneas and she groaned, squeezing her lids shut again.

A cool compress slid onto her forehead, a welcome relief from the pain.

"Jesus, Rick, what did you hit her with?" Sarah's concerned voice echoed a little in her head. Nikki wanted to tell her she'd be fine, really, but the only thing that escaped her lips was another groan.

"My fist," Rick said, and Nikki flinched at the temper simmering beneath his even tone. "I figured you wouldn't want me using the furniture."

"No, that would have been overkill," Sarah agreed. "Here, talk to her. I'm going to check on Justin."

Nikki heard the door open and footsteps retreating. "Nikki, can you hear me?" Rick asked.

She settled for waving one hand weakly. Moving anything else seemed out of the question at the moment, and her mouth still didn't want to work properly. *Why did Rick hit me? And what happened to Justin?* She remembered him coming in, but then her memory descended into a haze of rage that she shrank back from exploring.

"Justin's fine," Rick said, and she felt his angry, slightly defensive presence move closer to her. "But you two were about to destroy the Inn with your little games. Do you realize what you were doing?"

Nikki couldn't answer that, so she poked at the haze for a bit, and images rose from the depths of the red. A blanket of shame covered her as she realized what had happened: she'd lost complete control of her Horseman, done the one thing the Council had been concerned about and nearly caused the deaths of innocents. *Bloody Hell,* she thought. *What kind of monster am I turning into? The kind that I accused Alex of making?*

"It wasn't just you." Rick put his hand on hers and squeezed it gently, his anger subsiding a bit. "Justin lost it too."

Yes, but Justin's not facing a possible death sentence from the Council, she reminded him, and felt him squeeze her hand again.

"I...I need to sit up," she finally managed to say, and his strong hands helped steady her as she sat up. Nikki realized she was on her bed as she felt the blankets shift beneath her. She put one hand on the cold compress on her forehead and forced her eyes open.

The dim lights cast shadows on Rick's face, giving him a skeletal cast that made her shiver for a moment. Lightning flickered occasionally outside, and thunder still rumbled, but not the bone-crushing rumbles that had shaken the Inn before. Nikki could still feel the Storm swirling above her, but the sensations were muted, as if behind glass.

"Sarah invoked the protections on the Inn," Rick said, and Nikki blinked at him. He chuckled. "You know, when Justin found out, he looked exactly the same way."

"Sarah's a Mage?"

"Not exactly," Justin said from the doorway, and Nikki looked over to see how bad he looked. Bad, and the icepack he was holding to the back of his head didn't look to be helping him any. Rick had gone for her jaw, but he'd punched Justin square in the eye from the looks of it. "The spells were laid on the house long ago, and she knew how to trigger them. More like a witch than a Mage, if anything, but not really a witch either." His gaze shifted from her to Rick. "Nice right hook."

"Thank you." Rick stared back at Justin, a clear challenge implicit in what he left unsaid. Nikki felt the tension rise between the two of them as they stared at one another for a long moment, then Justin shook his head minutely and Rick relaxed. Then Justin looked back at Nikki and his jaw tightened a bit.

"Now, without either of us losing our temper, would you mind telling just what you were doing that you decided you needed to use Storm energy to fuel? And why, in the name of anything that's holy, did you do it without casting a Circle first?"

Nikki took a deep breath and reminded herself and her Horseman that Justin was not the enemy. Then she said, "I was scrying. And I didn't cast a Circle because I don't know how."

Justin and Rick both stared at her.

"You're kidding," Justin said finally. "No one ever taught you to cast a Circle?"

She shook her head very slowly, trying not to aggravate her headache. "I'm not even sure what goes into it."

"But, but...oh hell." Justin looked disgusted. "No, of course they wouldn't. Alenya's got a permanent Circle in her workroom, and you haven't really cast anywhere else. Shit." He took a deep breath. "And what were you using as a focus?"

Nikki indicated the scratch on her cheek, and his eyes got even wider.

"You used *blood*?" When she nodded, Justin groaned and slumped against the doorframe. "Sweet Jesus, no wonder you were attracting all that attention! Nikki..."

Her jaw clenched. He must have seen the expression because he stopped. Then he said, "It's not your fault. You're right, we shouldn't have left you hanging. But I don't have time to train you, and damn, Alenya apparently left some large holes in your education, which makes sense, because she's not used to casting here on Earth. Be ready to leave early tomorrow."

"Why?" Nikki asked, frowning.

"Because we're going to take care of this once and for all."

That sounded ominous. "We're going to the Council?"

"No. We're going to Rothman House."

Chapter Ten

"Bits and Pieces"

"It's like trying to describe an elephant when all I have is a tail and part of one foot. I have no idea what I'm holding onto!"

Derek shook his head angrily and continued, "And really, all we have is pieces. Whoever trashed the scene knew what they were doing — the Chaos energy that got mixed into the building was enough to totally fuck up any sort of coherent signatures any of my Sensitives can read. Hell, all we find are random snippets of conversation and unrelated images! I can't find my elephant if I don't know what I'm looking for!"

"Calm down, Chief." The steel in Amy's voice cut across his ranting, and the use of his title reminded him that for all the casualness of their relationship, she was still his superior officer. He swallowed hard, trying to bring his emotions back under control and got up to start pacing around the small trailer.

"I'm sorry. This is just the worst crime scene I've ever had to deal with," he said after a few moments of thick silence.

"I know." Amy took a deep breath and then picked up her coffee cup. "I'm remembering why I hate dealing with civilians — it's always so damn messy."

Derek grunted agreement and looked back over at the box on his desk with distaste. "I have an entire building to sift through, with four very talented Sensitives, not to mention myself. And all we have to show for approximately ten days worth of work is a few fragmented images, a signature that might be a chimera for all I know, and a knife with Alex Masterson's blood on it."

"And a rag doll with no face," Amy reminded him. "Don't forget that."

"And a rag doll with no face," Derek agreed. "A rag doll with traces of magic on it, but who the hell uses a worry doll to base a spell in?"

"Well, would you confiscate it if you found it on someone?" Amy replied, and he conceded the point with an angry shake of his head. "We're dealing with very inventive people here. I have to give them that."

"And that's what scares me." Derek gave up on pacing and slumped back down in his chair. "Inventive people with access to Lord-level Power. Or, God help us, Lords themselves."

Amy didn't answer; when Derek looked over at her, she was frowning at her computer screen, obviously deep in something. *Probably more autopsy reports,* he thought, and sighed. *At least she's working. You should be doing the same.*

He reached into the box and pulled out the plastic evidence bag that held the switchblade they'd found in the rubble-filled main spell chamber. Two sets of bloodstains etched rust-colored marks on the slender blade: one set was Alex Masterson's, and the other was an unknown female. Derek slid the knife out and scowled at it as it lay on the desktop.

"I wish I could have found you before that Chaos Mage destroyed everything," he muttered under his breath. "Damn fool. What were you doing associating with Chaos Mages anyways, Masterson? And where the hell did you hide all your damn files?"

"Hmm?" Amy looked up, eyes unfocused. "What did you say?"

"Nothing," Derek said, stripping his gloves off. "I'm just muttering. This damn Storm is going to drive me insane."

"I can up the shields again on here," Amy offered, and he shook his head.

"No, I'll be fine." He took several deep breaths, slowing his heart and trying to quiet his mind. "Sorry. Didn't mean to disturb you."

"That's fine." Derek heard the soft click of her keyboard start again as she went back to her work.

The knife sat there, and he stared at it, wondering what he hoped to find. The Sensitive who had pulled it from the ruins had caught just a whiff of Alex's signature on it and had rushed it to the lab: the DNA test had confirmed that he'd been stabbed with it, as had a female unknown. So now it sat in Derek's lap to see what else he could pull off it.

Staring at it gets nothing done, he told himself irritably, and laid a bare hand on the blade, closing his eyes to concentrate better.

There was a flash behind his eyelids, and a rustling in his ears. Derek strained to hear the voices that murmured just out of reach, trying to figure out who was speaking out of the past to him as the office and the clicking of Amy's keyboard faded from his perceptions.

"Sorry, love, nothing personal," a male voice rumbled in his ear. Derek could hear the crash of thunder and the sharp retort of gunfire somewhere in the distance, and the floor shifted underneath him as if an earthquake was involved somehow, but no images.

"I doubt it, *love,*" a female voice snarled; Derek blinked as he realized how young she sounded. *Far younger than Dr. Richards,* he thought, straining to hear more. There was a wet tearing sound and a male gasp, and Derek realized he was hearing flesh ripped apart. "But tell me, Alex, how do you kill Death?"

That question chilled Derek to the bone. *Please, please tell me I didn't just hear what I thought I did,* he prayed, as the rumbling grew louder. The floor continued to pitch beneath his feet, and Derek began to wonder if this was a memory or really happening to him.

"Amy?" he called out, but the name was swept away by a mad, chill wind that spun him around, leaving him dazed. "Someone?"

Light pierced the darkness around him, and Derek peered out, hoping for something familiar. When he saw the young woman he had seen before, holding her hand out to him, he shrank back, suddenly terrified.

"Tell me, how do you kill Death?" she said, the pale flesh on her face melting away, revealing the skull he'd seen before. Her outstretched hand dripped skin in long strips as she reached for him, and her dark blue eyes, floating in her eye sockets, held him trapped.

There was no malice in her gaze, though. *She's not looking for me,* Derek realized, as fear iced his heart. *Is she? What's going on?* Magic shimmered in the air around her, a signature that he couldn't read and yet recognized...

He reached out to her, hoping to understand the Power swirling around her. She took his hand, and as the frigid bones touched his flesh, Derek realized where the fear he felt was coming from.

Her. She was the source of the fear, giving lie to the calm bravado radiating from her eyes. She pulled him close, and he tasted the sweet, cloying scent of her breath as she said, "It's nothing personal."

Light exploded around them and Derek was thrown backwards, slamming back into his body. Thunder roared above him, and the roof of the trailer sounded as if rocks were being thrown down upon it. The lights flickered, and his breath steamed in the cold air.

"What the hell is going on?" he asked, shaken. The knife blade vibrated under his palm as he spoke and he jerked his hand back as if the metal were suddenly alive.

"The Storm's hunting!" Amy shouted. "I don't know what, but something got its attention, and it's on the move!"

Derek started to answer, and then light exploded again. For a moment, he thought the trailer they used as an office had been hit by lightning; then he realized that the sparkles of light were still dancing in front of his eyes and he couldn't hear anything, not even the thunder...

Look closely, a voice whispered. Derek shivered as it passed through him, a mix of life and death that thrilled his senses and deadened his fears. *Follow the web. See where the spider sits, waiting for prey. Too bad the prey is larger than the hunter who hunts it.*

What? Derek watched the scene unroll in front of him, fascinated. A map of the United States lay before him, fully covered with a massive web of Power, so intricate that he couldn't follow individual threads. Crouched near him was a bloated spider, multiple eyes awhirl with Chaos, her massive abdomen swollen and distended, bathed in Shadows and Light, Earth and Blood.

She waits to release her children, the voice whispered, and Derek shivered again. *She feels secure in her domain, guarded by her mate, helped by traitors. All is in her web, and she rules her web completely.*

Then how can we stop her? Derek asked. *How can we fight that?*

There are champions. Brilliant flames leapt up from points on the web: thousands of them, varying in intensity from the merest flicker to five great pillars of fire that roared in the vast silence of the web. *She will not find the world as easy to conquer as she thinks.*

So we have to find the champions? Derek asked, as the spider began to stir, stalking along the web in a deadly dance that her size belied.

You won't be able to miss them. He swore he could hear amusement as the voice faded. *Just don't get in their way.*

"Champions?" Amy said later, as they drove back to the motel. The Storm had eased up a bit, but sleet still poured down, making the driving treacherous. Still, Amy kept looking over at him, her eyes incredulous. "You're kidding, right?"

The car skidded a little and she swore; Derek swallowed, fighting the urge to check his seatbelt again. "I wish," he said. "And I'm sure at least one of the signatures was the girl we're following."

"Could she be your spider?" Amy asked.

He'd considered that, and shook his head now. "I don't think so, although I could be wrong. The spider is old — I got a feeling that this has been in the planning for a long time. The girl I saw — she's young."

"Young. Great." Amy turned the car into the parking lot of the hotel and Derek breathed a sigh of relief.

"Young, and inexperienced," he said, as the car slid into a spot. Amy shut the engine off and then turned to look at him again.

"So you're telling me that we've got a kid with the magical equivalent of a nuclear bomb out there, and we're supposed to stay out of her way?" When he nodded, she shook her head. "You get to tell the Admiral that one."

What is going on? Lucifer stalked through the halls of the castle, his lean body vibrating with Power that he barely recognized. *Where is the Horseman getting this strength?*

The Storm that raged on Earth had its roots here, in the World Between the Walls, and it lashed the walls of Lucifer's home, a hurricane of fury and fear that drowned every other noise with its howling. The halls were nearly empty of Spirits, which didn't bode well for what he would find when he entered his Lady's bower.

Her subjects knew to hide when she was in this type of mood. If the Storm outside was any indication, Madness was in a truly foul temper.

Ice and snow hit his face as he opened the door to her private rooms: every window was wide-open, the wind tearing at the curtains that clung to their frames with frozen fingertips. Lucifer peered through the whirling flakes, searching for Madness.

"Lucifer!"

His eyes widened as she pounced on him out of the maelstrom, her rainbow eyes delighted.

"Do you feel this?" she cried, grabbing his hands and spinning him into the room. "Do you feel her?"

"I do," he said, trying to stop her, but she merely broke away, dancing through the snow that coated the fine rugs on her floors, her bare feet weaving intricate runes and her filmy dress clinging to her body, soaked from the sleet and rain. Lightning echoed in her laughter.

"Look, and tell me she is not my child!"

Lucifer gaped at her. "This...pleases you?"

Madness spun in a circle, a pale dervish of joy. "Can you not feel it? Only a child of Chaos could revel in this, and even as she fights it, she revels in the destruction." She stopped, the glow in her eyes drawing him to her. "We can use this, my love. She hears the call of Power and soon, she'll crave this. And that, I can use. Soon, she will be mine." Thunder crashed above, and Lucifer heard steel in her voice. "And once I have stolen her heart, the Balance will stand no chance at all."

CHAPTER ELEVEN

"BACK TO SCHOOL"

"So why Edgar?" Nikki asked Justin as she pulled the Jeep into the deserted parking lot. Despite the ongoing Storm and the chain across the entrance to the long driveway, the road had been absolutely, spotlessly clear; a fact that would have creeped her out had she not known who waited for them at the house.

Rothman House was still on the National Registry as a perfectly restored example of a late Georgian manor, but the house had been closed to the public since the death of its caretaker under mysterious circumstances last summer. It glowered down from atop its hill, backed by a stormy sky that still spit snow pellets down on them. The chill in the air reminded her of the first time she'd seen the house: when Francesca Childers, the art historian turned caretaker, had still been alive, sitting next to her and spinning tales that Nikki hadn't been able to believe.

At least the chill is just weather this time, she thought somberly. *And if I keep telling myself that, I might even be able to walk back in without help.*

"Because I don't have time to walk you through the basics, Nikki," Justin said, breaking into her thoughts. "And you need to learn...Gods, I don't even know what holes you might have in your education." He held up a hand as she bristled. "Not your fault. Alenya's not used to teaching rank amateurs — she probably forgot that you didn't have the same advantages her last pupils did."

"Her last pupils?" Nikki said, her anger fading under the brunt of her curiosity. "You and your sister?"

Justin nodded. "Shanna was nine when we went to live with her, and her Powers had already started to manifest. And since both our parents were Mages, we had already learned the basics."

"What happened to your parents, Justin?" Nikki asked the question that had been nagging at her since she'd first gone to Alenya's vast house in the Shadow Lands and learned of his past. "Why didn't you grow up here on Earth, instead of in the Shadows?"

He didn't answer at first; she waited, feeling the atmosphere in the Jeep grow heavy with sorrow. "Because great Power can bring out the worst in people," he said finally, turning and looking at her, hazel eyes dark with pain. "Something I'm sure you'll learn before long."

I think I already did. "I did this, didn't I?" Nikki said, and when he raised his eyebrows at her, she waved her hands at the weather outside. "The Storm. All these disturbances. I've seen the news, Justin — there's been a spike in crime since Halloween. Not only that, but the number of coma patients has increased, and most of them seem to be Mages or magically-inclined." When his jaw dropped, she shrugged. "I was a reporter. I know how to find things out."

For a split second, something that might have been naked fear ran across Justin's face; then he gave her a half-grin and she wondered if she'd imagined it.

"Not all of it, but you didn't help things," he admitted. "This had to be one of the worst Halloweens in centuries, and between you and my sister...well, let's just say there are a lot of things that need to be dealt with."

"Vermont," Nikki said, and Justin nodded.

"Right. While you and Alex were busy trying to magically disembowel each other, Shanna sealed off a large portion of Vermont and part of Quebec. I'm sure she had a good reason for it, but since she's not communicating with any of us, I can't tell you why. What I can tell you is that the Power she was using, combined with the forces we were trying to stop at Gene-Tech, ripped a big hole in the World Walls. It let in a few things we'd rather not have here on Earth."

"So there are what, Shadow demons or something?" Nikki asked, opening her door.

"I wish." Justin climbed out of the Jeep, shaking his head. "Shadow demons at least could exist here without upsetting the Balance that much, and we could send them back without having to rip more holes in the Walls."

She looked over at him. "What are you telling me?"

"There's a world between the World Walls, Nikki," Justin said, leading the way up to the front door. "Did Alenya mention anything about Chaos Magic to you?" When she shook her head, he sighed. "I'll add it to the list."

"So the Storm is fueled by Chaos Magic?" Nikki guessed, kicking at a snow bank as she meandered up the walk behind him.

"Sort of. It's complicated." Justin frowned at her. "Are you okay?"

She shrugged. "So what does the Storm have to do with the Chaos Magic?"

"A few larger Chaos Spirits are living in it, whipping it up when they sense any sort of Power being used," he replied, pulling a set of keys from his pocket and slipping one into the lock on the door. "Which is why all Magic on the East Coast that the Council has the slightest bit of influence over has been suspended, unless performed within a Circle and shielded up the ass. No High Magic at all."

"High Magic?" Nikki wondered if he was going to have to explain to the Council what had happened last night.

"Ritual magic," Justin clarified. "All the older magics, really — ones you don't need to worry about. I think, and this is just speculation on my part, that Shanna found a nest of really icky ritual magic users up there and had to seal everything off to prevent something big from getting out. Who knows what. I know there was a rumor of some Sintetizzi up there — maybe she found them. But whatever she found, she deemed it dangerous enough to lock it in."

"And who or what is a Sintetizzi?" Nikki asked.

Justin removed the key and touched the lock again. It clicked open, and Nikki's eyes widened. He turned and chuckled at her expression. "Edgar gave me permission to key the lock to me, so if

I needed a secure place to cast, I didn't have to go home. Since I'm helping Vashti do some things, it's easier for me to stay up here." He held out a hand. "Are you coming in?"

Behind him, the door opened onto a marble foyer that she remembered all too well, and Nikki swallowed, wondering if she could actually go through this. *They're all gone,* she reminded herself. *Donald, Daphne, Althea...Robin.*

Despite herself, she shivered as she remembered Robin: his hot eyes, and the plans he'd had for her, plans he'd gone to great lengths to bring to fruition, not caring who else he harmed in the process. Robin Rothman, the final scion of a twisted household, whom she'd tricked into hanging himself again, ending his killing spree by recreating his own death.

"Nikki?" Justin stepped back towards her, bringing her back to the present. "Are you okay?"

She nodded, and gestured for him to go first. As she followed him into the mansion, Nikki felt her shoulders tense. *Knock it off, Jeffries,* she told herself. *There's nothing here that can hurt you anymore. You took care of that, remember?* "So what is a Sintetizzi?" she asked, trying to take her mind off the past as she followed Justin into the dusty sitting room. "Some kind of weird magician?"

"Kind of." Justin gave her a brief rundown of the darker characteristics of the Sintetizzi clan, a family of magicians who apparently enjoyed experimenting with the bodily shapes of their neighbors using Blood Magic and demonic spirits. Nikki shuddered.

"Demons incarnated into human bodies? That's so gross," she said.

"Agreed. Which is why the Council hunts them down every chance they get," Justin said, tossing his coat on the chair and pointing his finger at the fireplace. Flames sprang into life, chasing some of the chill from the air. "But they still manage to crop up now and again, usually just after we think we've killed the last of them."

"Unfortunately, the Sintetizzi will be a thorn in the Council's side until the day the universe explodes," came a new voice, and both Nikki and Justin turned to see an older gentleman in hunting attire standing in the doorway to the sitting room, a lovely brunette on his arm. The fact that they were both transparent didn't detract from the happiness in her eyes and the utter contentment in his. Edgar Rothman and Francesca Childers had been born nearly two hundred years apart, but death had brought true love to both of them. It was one of the few good things Nikki felt had come about as the result of that June day when she and Francesca had entered the house.

Robin had pulled both Francesca and Nikki through the World Walls to the Shadow Lands within the house, dooming the caretaker with his lust. The transition to the Shadow Lands had rewired a part of Francesca's brain, reconfiguring her neural cortex to deal with the higher concentration of magical energy in the elemental Lands. But because she wasn't a mage or an Elemental Spirit, the reconfiguration was permanent: had she ever crossed back through the World Walls to Earth, she would have slipped into a coma and died a slow, agonizing death as her brain, shut off from the high influx of magic, withered away in her skull. Instead, Nikki had killed her as she'd asked — taken her life and given her the gift of never-ending death with Edgar.

Now, looking at Francesca's radiant face, Nikki felt warmth flood her, knowing the decision had been the correct one, even if it hadn't felt like it at the time. Francesca's life still sat within her, a small purple orchid that bloomed in Nikki's core and reminded her of the good she could do with her gifts. *I am not just a mindless murderer,* she thought, smiling. *I have to remember that.*

"But you didn't come here to discuss the Sintetizzi, did you?" Edgar asked, giving Justin a sly grin. "Nice black eye, by the way."

Justin flushed. "Rick's got a good right hook," he mumbled.

"I'm surprised he felt the need to use it on you," Edgar said, and gave Nikki a look. She smiled, knowing the make-up she'd put on this morning mostly hid the bruise on her chin. *That, and Rick hadn't hit me as hard,* she thought smugly. His next question punctured her illusions that he hadn't seen her wounds, though. "Or were you two the reason the weather was agitated yesterday?"

"Part of it," Justin allowed. "Nikki needs a teacher — we're discovering rather large holes in her education and frankly, I don't have time to walk her through the basics right now."

"I am no Mage," Edgar said, and Justin nodded.

"I know. But you're a witch, and you ran a coven. You know how the Earth Magics work, especially the basics, and how they intertwine with the other Magics. And it wouldn't hurt her to learn a little witchcraft at the same time." Justin ran a hand through his hair, leaving a trail of spiky locks standing straight up. "And frankly, I can't think of anyone better to teach her about the ways of relationships between Mages, which she also needs to learn."

Nikki raised her eyebrows at that just a little. *Is that a jab at Rick and I? Or did he just mean Mages in general?*

Edgar nodded. "I can do that," he said, and looked at Francesca. "It wouldn't hurt you to sit in on these lessons, love. Then you could help me around here."

"I don't have any magical gifts, though," she said, frowning. "How could I help you?"

"You don't need magical gifts to do witchcraft as a ghost," he told her. "You're in tune enough with the Shadow Lands now, especially since you died here, rather than Earth. And two students are just as easy as one."

"Good," Justin said, breathing a sigh of relief. "I'm glad that's settled." He turned to Nikki. "I'm going to head out to Vashti's for a bit — can I borrow the Jeep?"

"Sure. Just don't forget me here." She pulled the keys from her pocket and tossed them to him.

"You can always take Cerberus home," he reminded her, and chuckled as she flushed. "Bad Horseman, forgetting your noble steed!"

"Get out of here, you brat," Nikki said, still blushing. "Go find someone else to bug."

"You know, you're awfully cute when you blush," Justin said, then ran out of the room as she flipped him off.

"Jerk," she muttered, then turned to Edgar. "Okay, when do we start?"

"Now," Edgar replied, offering her his hand. Nikki took it in her own and felt him pull her through the World Walls, the insubstantial fingers becoming solid as she stepped into the Shadow Lands. "We have a lot to do, and not much time to do it in."

Justin was still chuckling as he opened the door to the Jeep outside. The sky was still grey and stormy, but for the first time in a few weeks, he felt like they might actually come out on top. *And wouldn't that be nice,* he thought, slipping into the driver's seat and starting the Jeep up. *After this is all over, I'm so taking that vacation. Assuming we all survive, of course.*

His good mood lasted until he pulled into the driveway at the farm. The chill in the air as he stepped out of the Jeep had nothing to do with the weather and everything to do with the welcome he knew he was going to receive. Justin squared his shoulders and pushed open the door to the farmhouse, wincing at the silence that loomed within. *Damn, I might not survive today, never mind the rest of this.*

The vast kitchen was spotless, as always, and both Morgan and Vashti were sitting at the large table, drinking tea. "Good morning," Justin said, walking over to the cabinet and pulling out a mug for himself.

"Better than last night," Morgan replied, his deep voice so neutral it was an accusation.

Justin winced as he filled the mug with hot water from the kettle on the stove and dropped in a tea bag.

"Last night was an aberration," he said, turning around. Vashti merely looked at him over the edge of her mug, dark eyes inscrutable.

"Is that what you're calling it?" Morgan asked. "An aberration?"

"Yes," Justin said. "She didn't have a clue what she was doing." He held up his hand as Morgan started to say something else. "I've already got her in with a teacher — apparently Alenya didn't realize how nonmagical Nikki's life was before this. She didn't teach her about Circles — or any of the other real basics we all assumed she knew."

"What?" Vashti frowned. "How could Nikki not know about Circles?"

"She was raised as a mundane, not a Mage," Justin said, sipping his tea. "She's coming into this like a child — a blank slate. She had no idea what she was doing last night."

"But you did," Vashti said, her voice ice. "Would you mind explaining why I felt your touch in that Storm? And why you have a black eye?"

Justin sighed. "She drives me crazy. I don't know how, but she does. I felt her casting and went in to stop her, and we got into a screaming match. Rick had to break it up before we killed each other — and everyone else in the Inn."

"Hence the black eye." Vashti frowned. "I taught you better than that, Justin."

And here comes the guilt. "I know. I'm sorry."

"Not yet," she said. "But you will be." Then Vashti paused. "Do you love her?"

That question hit him harder than Rick's fist. "No! Well, I do, but as a little sister!" Vashti just looked at him, and Justin started to flounder. "Seriously! I am not falling for Nikki!"

"She's a pretty girl, and one of the few that can match you or your sister in terms of Power," Morgan said, and Justin slammed his mug down, almost shattering the heavy ceramic.

"She's in love with Rick, and I do not poach!" he shouted.

"Is that your heart or your head talking?" Vashti asked him, and Justin glared at her.

"Both," he snarled, wondering if it sounded convincing enough. "I do not have any romantic feelings for Nikki. Now, what do we have planned for today?"

Vashti and Morgan exchanged glances but didn't pursue the topic. "More of the same," Morgan said. "Follow me."

And as he did, Justin put all thoughts of Nikki out of his mind. *I don't poach. She and Rick are going to be very happy together, and I'm not ruining that.*

No matter how I feel about her.

CHAPTER TWELVE

"FIREFLIES"

"So, how goes the battle?" Justin asked the next morning.

Rick grunted, staring into the murky depths of his coffee cup as if it held the answers to all the questions in the universe. His brain huddled in the fog of rewrite exhaustion, hiding desperately from the caffeine that beat through the bushes, looking to drag it back out and finish the novel he had contracted.

"I hate sequels," he said, finally looking up. "They suck."

Sarah put a basket of freshly-baked cranberry muffins on the table in front of him; the tart, sweet scent normally would have lifted his spirits, but he was sunk so far into his funk that it barely brushed the surface of his consciousness.

"Can we help?" Nikki asked, reaching for a muffin.

"Not unless you can write the damn thing for me," Rick sighed, shaking his head. "I don't understand. The first book was so damn easy to write. I know the characters. I have a decent plot, I think. I just don't have a decent book."

Nikki and Justin both gave him sympathetic looks, and Rick sighed again. "Maybe if you bounced some ideas off us? Let us read what you have?" Justin suggested, and Rick shrugged.

"Why not? I've tried everything else short of a Ouija board to resurrect this damn plot." He stood up. "Let me go get my stuff."

Rick came back downstairs a few minutes later, carrying a notebook and a mass of printed pages. "Okay, just remember, you agreed to this," he warned them, and both Nikki and Justin grinned at him. "I warn you, it sucks."

"Let us be the judge of that," Justin said, reaching for the stack. "So what's the problem?"

"Besides the fact that I'm a hack trying to make a living at something I suck at?" Rick grumbled. "Nothing."

The kitchen filled with the sounds of papers turning as Nikki and Justin started reading, and Rick refilled his coffee cup. Despite his grumbling, he knew exactly what was wrong with the book — it was flat, boring, without life. He just didn't know what to do about it.

"So who's this Adam guy?" Nikki asked him, dropping the edge of the pages she was holding so she could look at him. "He just kind of wanders in and out. Did I miss something?"

Rick blinked at her. "Adam? He's the hero."

"He is?" Nikki flipped through her pages, frowning. "Then why don't you mention him until...page 120?"

Rick gaped at her. "He's there beforehand..."

"Um, no, he's not." Justin was flipping through his pages too. "Not until Talisman mentions him in passing to Bastian in Ayer. And then it's just a mention. You don't have him in here at all."

Rick stared at both of them, his mouth open. "But, but, how could I forget my hero?"

Nikki tried to smother a giggle, her nostrils flaring as she handed over the pages. "Well, it might explain why the book was so hard to start, right?"

He accepted the pages, his mind whirling. "So where is Adam?" he muttered, dropping the pages and grabbing a pen and his notebook. "And why is Talisman not with him?"

"Well, you have her telling Bastian that he's off on a quest," Justin said, grinning at Nikki over Rick's head.

"He can't be on a quest! Talisman's on the quest!" Rick scowled at the notebook. "Besides, at the end of the last book — oh, shit! That's where he is — he went to go get Dyanna at the Grove!"

"Of course he did," Nikki said, swallowing another giggle. "Did that help?"

Rick didn't answer — he was too busy writing, his brain

suddenly coming out of its fog and spilling forth the story. The world faded from his view as he dropped headfirst into his world, finally able to capture that magic that he'd been missing.

When he finally came up for air, the kitchen was quiet — Sarah was working on some papers at the other end of the table, and the muffin bowl was empty. "Where did everyone go?" he asked, getting up and dumping his cold coffee down the sink.

Sarah looked up and grinned. "Nikki and Justin left about an hour ago — they said something about going back over to Edgar's together to work on something," she said, and Rick felt something green-eyed poke its head up from slumber deep inside his soul. "And unfortunately, this weather has caused a sharp downswing in reservations. No one wants to watch it rain in upstate New Hampshire in November."

"Well, I can't really blame them for that," Rick said, placing the mug into the sink and wandering over to the fridge. "November rain sucks in New Hampshire."

"Yeah, but the song was good," Sarah said, and he chuckled. "I know, I know, I'm old."

"Only as old as you feel." Rick snagged a couple of cans of Dr. Pepper and turned back around to find her holding out a plate of muffins as well. "You rock, cousin. I'm off."

"I figured. There are a few laundry baskets on the stairs as well." She grinned at him. "Please fill them before you get too involved in the story. I don't want your room spontaneously combusting."

"Yes'm." Rick bowed his way out of the kitchen, put his soda, notes and muffins in the baskets and hauled them up to his room. He kicked the door open and sighed.

As usual, his room looked like a library and a laundromat had gotten into a fistfight and killed each other there. Messily. Papers and books were stacked in untidy piles on every available surface and most of the floor, where they fought for dominance over the laundry that crept out of the open drawers and out of the closet. He stepped carefully over the uneven floor, hoping, as always, to not die on his way to his desk.

Which might be the other reason you don't get much action in here, Rick, old son. His conscience/Muse, a personage who looked and sounded like Rutger Hauer, showed up to talk to him far too often for Rick's comfort. He'd always pooh-poohed the idea of a Muse, but Rutger had shown up about four months ago and still refused to leave. *Maybe if you didn't live in a fire hazard, the maiden of your dreams might be a bit more...amiable to certain plans you seem to have.*

"Oh, I think she might be amiable," Rick said, putting the baskets on the bed and grabbing a can of soda before slumping in his desk chair. "She's just busy at the moment."

With Justin, Rutger reminded him, strolling through the mess and leaning over to look at the blank computer screen. *Again.*

"Justin is helping train her magic," Rick pointed out. "That's his area of expertise. And I'm not going to sit here and argue with you over Nikki!" He pointed to the bed. "If you're a Muse, dammit, sit down, shut up and start helping with the damn book!"

Rutger gave him a long-suffering look and started puttering around the room instead, using his cane as an impromptu golf club. *You know, you really need to start acting more like a professional,* Rick thought to himself, ignoring the transparent actor in favor of bringing up a new file. *I mean, honestly. Why is this rewrite giving you such a headache? And how the hell could you forget a character? Especially your hero? What kind of hack forgets a main character like that?*

The kind that's pushing himself far too hard? Rutger interjected, swinging through a mountain of books.

"Tell that to my editor," Rick said, reaching behind him and starting to push the chair back towards the bed to get his notebook. Even though the bed was a good ten feet away, suddenly his fingers closed on a paper cover, and he turned to look at the notebook that had just appeared in his hand. He looked over at Rutger, who was staring back at him, eyebrows raised over the wire rims of his glasses.

Interesting trick, the Muse said, as Rick placed the notebook on the desk in front of him and stared at it. *What's your next one?*

Rick was saved from answering by his cell phone ringing, and the number flashing caused all thoughts of the flying notebook to run screaming from his mind. "Shit."

"Hi Rick. Where's my book?" Lai's pleasant British voice flowed from the receiver and he sighed.

"Well, I have good news and bad news," he said, shifting the phone and tapping a few keys on his keyboard.

"The bad news."

Ah Lai, to the point as always, Rick thought, and said out loud, "I have to rewrite everything I have."

Silence, and he winced.

"But the good news is that I know how to fix everything," he continued hastily. "I should have a brand new outline within about a day."

More silence.

"I know you're not happy, but seriously, it's going to make it a better book." Rick wondered how long she was going to keep him dangling before she said anything. "I forgot a character. That's why it wasn't working."

Then came a sound that he wasn't expecting: barely-muffled laughter. "You what?" Lai asked, and Rick slumped down in his chair, alternating between embarrassment and relief that she wasn't going to skin him alive. "How do you forget a character?"

"I don't know, but I forgot about Adam completely." Grabbing his notebook, Rick opened up to the notes he'd scribbled. "But it was pointed out to me, and I can fix it."

"I need this book by the end of the month," Lai warned him. "I can't hold your slot forever, you know."

"I know, I know." *There's also no way in hell I'll be able to write 100k in a month, even a rough draft.* "Can you give me until the end of February?"

"You're insane. End of December."

"Done," he said, kissing sleep goodbye for the next two months. "I'll have the rough in your hands no later than the 31st."

"You'd better," Lai said. "No matter what."

"So saving the world doesn't get me off the hook?" Rick said, grinning at the monitor.

"No. Finish the book, then save the world," Lai told him. "It'll make great fodder for promotional materials."

Rick chuckled at that and hung up the phone, then he looked over at Rutger, who was still watching him. "Two months," he said to his Muse. "Can we do it?"

Of course we can, dear boy, Rutger said urbanely, setting his cane on the floor in front of him and smiling. *Crack open that soda and let's go.*

Easier said than done, of course. First he had to rewrite his outline, and figure out how long it was going to take Adam to get to the Grove and drag his little sister out by her hair, and then figure out what to do with said hero and little sister afterwards. And what he needed to have his heroine do at the same time. Without the story sucking wind.

Now if only it could be as easy as it is in the movies, Rick thought, narrowing his eyes and leaning back. *I just need a bit of really good plot to start it going...*

You'll find it, Rutger said from the bed where he was stretched out. *That's why you're the writer.*

Rick snorted at him. "Some Muse you are," he said. "I thought you were supposed to be feeding me ideas here!"

My dear boy, you're the one who decided I was your Muse. You never asked me.

"If you aren't a Muse, what the hell are you?" Rick demanded. "Other than a demented figment of my imagination?" A sudden thought occurred to him and he stiffened. "Unless you're a Spirit! Who sent you? Who's spying on me?"

Whoa, calm down, Rutger said, sitting up and looking a little alarmed. *I'm your Muse. I agree. No one's spying on you.*

Rick glared at him, feeling something warm grow within him. "You mean to say..." And then he stopped, smelling smoke. "Did I light a candle?"

No candle, that he remembered, but a small wisp of smoke rose from the pile of laundry moldering near the end of his bed. Rick got up and pulled the pile apart, unearthing a smoking tee-shirt from the bottom.

"I thought I told you to pull your laundry together before it combusted," Sarah said from the doorway, and Rick jumped guiltily. "Can I get the rest of that pile before you burn the Inn down?"

"I...uh, sure, yeah." He looked at the tee-shirt again, thoughts racing through his mind, and then tossed it in the trash can and dumped his soda over it. "Yeah, let's get all of this out of here."

Once he'd helped Sarah carry out four laundry baskets full of clothes, Rick came back into the room and shut his door. Then he locked it.

You didn't tell her that the pile with the burning tee-shirt in it was clean, did you? Rutger asked, and Rick shook his head.

"It's just a coincidence, that's all," he said, starting to clean up the piles of paper that had been unearthed when they'd pulled up all the laundry. "Just a coincidence."

And the notebook flew into your hand by itself, Rutger said, and Rick felt a chill sneak down his spine.

"Yes," he said. "I must have brought it over with me."

If you say so, Rutger said, but his tone was dubious, and when Rick shot him a look, the Muse shrugged and stretched back out on the bed. *Let me know when you're ready to continue writing.*

"I will," Rick muttered, still cleaning. It took him about an hour, but when he was done, the papers were all in neat piles and the floor was clear. No candles burned at all; he'd packed them all away with a shudder. Rick ran his fingers through his hair and sighed, then turned back to his desk. "Now I can start again."

Good, Rutger said, sighting along the length of his cane like it was a rifle. *It's about time. Lai would be proud.*

"Hush," Rick said, pulling his chair up to the desk and setting his hands on the keyboard. The cleaning had given him some new ideas as well, and he started into the outline again.

For a while, the only sound was the clicking of his keys. Rick gradually drifted off into a dreamlike state; the walls of his room faded, replaced by the dusty, warm atmosphere that his heroine Talisman rode through, an alternate America that was stuck in the Wild West, gathering heroes to her cause as she beat back the evil that slunk out from the mountains of the Sierra Nevadas, her hero Adam beside her. *Sort of like Nikki, gathering all sorts of folks to help her against Alex*, he mused idly.

Yes, but who will stand next to Nikki? That green-eyed monster in his soul had a voice that sounded like glass breaking. *Will it be you, or Justin?*

It doesn't matter, as long as she stops Alex, Rick replied, but the monster wasn't fooled.

Will you be able to stand there and watch your best friend ride off with the girl you love? It squirmed around, twining hot fingers around the base of Rick's skull. *Again?*

"Justin wouldn't do that," Rick said out loud, banging down on the keyboard. "Dammit, why am I even worried about this? It's a non-issue!"

Are you sure? Because they go off together every day, looking oh-so-cozy... The voice fed the flames dancing in his head, and Rick ground his teeth together. *Leaving you in the dust...*

Rick! Knock it off!

Rutger's frantic voice cut through the red film spreading over his eyes, and Rick looked around. Smoke poured from one of the piles of paper he'd stacked so neatly: as Rick stared at it in horror, it burst into flames.

"Nonononono!" he shouted, getting up and stomping out the fire. "This is not happening!"

Once the flames were out, he grabbed his cell phone and called Justin. The young Earth Mage didn't answer the first two times he called, but Rick just kept hitting the redial, hoping to get an answer.

"This had better be important," Justin said when he finally picked up, his voice clipped. "I'm in the middle of..."

"I'm lighting things on fire," Rick blurted out, firmly squashing the voice within him that started suggesting exactly what, or rather who, Justin had been in the middle of.

There was a small pause on the other end of the phone, and then Justin said, "Excuse me?"

"I'm lighting things on fire," Rick repeated, panic lacing a high note through his voice.

"Good lord, what is in the water there?" Justin said, and Rick could picture him shaking his head in disbelief. "Hang on." Something covered the phone, and Rick heard a murmuring of voices, none of which he could place. "Okay, where are you?"

"In my room."

"Stay at the Inn — I'll be there in about twenty minutes." Justin paused and chuckled. "Nikki says try not to burn the Inn down — she's got stuff she doesn't want to lose there."

"Very funny," Rick retorted, trying not to read anything into the fact that both Nikki and Justin were together still.

He spent the next fifteen minutes pacing up and down the damp porch on the front of the Inn, wishing he still smoked and concentrating on ice, snow, cold rain — anything but that warm, jealous energy he could still feel lurking deep within him.

I'm not a Mage, he repeated to himself, feeling the notebook in his hands again and trying very hard not to shake. *I'm a Sensitive, and a damn good one. I'm not a Mage! I'm not!*

The muted roar of Nikki's Jeep broke his concentration, and he looked up for a moment. Justin waved, but Nikki was nowhere to be seen.

He drives her car, rides off with her, laughs about you with her, the voice teased. *What more do you need to know?*

No! Not Justin! Rick ground his teeth together, feeling the heat grow around him.

You could take him out now, get rid of your rival. . .

I am not a Mage!

"Unfortunately, repeating something like that to make it true only works in the movies," Justin said, coming up the walk. The snow had turned to grey, musty slush during the afternoon, and Justin picked his way carefully around the half-melted puddles. "So," he continued, coming up onto the porch and leaning against one of the columns. "Tell me everything."

Justin watched as Rick opened his mouth, closed it again, and then, to his private amusement, blushed bright red. *Oh, this ought to be good,* the Earth Mage chuckled to himself. *And I'll bet I know who it involves. Although how she could have done anything to him while practicing in a shielded house, within a Circle, without either Edgar or myself noticing, is something I'll be wanting to know.*

"I was writing," Rick said finally. "And, well..."

"The sequel's not going well," Justin prompted, when his voice trailed off. "Right?"

"The sequel's going fine," Rick said, and sighed. "Okay, it's going, anyways. But not quickly, and I got...frustrated. And then

I smelled smoke."

"I thought you quit?"

"I did, six years ago." Rick shuddered, his amber eyes haunted. "I turned around to see what was burning, thinking maybe I had lit a candle and forgotten about it. But it wasn't that." He quickly summed up the events for Justin, whose eyebrows climbed higher and higher onto his forehead as he listened.

"So then I called you," Rick finished, running his fingers through his hair. "I'm sorry, I didn't know what else to do."

"That makes two of us," Justin said, his mind whirling as he stared at him. *What is going on here? Think, moron. There's got to be a reasonable explanation for this. Come up with some theories.*

Theory number one: somehow, he and Nikki are linked and he's learned how to draw on her Power without her knowledge. Christ, that's a scary thought. Another idea slammed into his head. *Good Christ, what if they're soulbonded?*

Justin shook his head slightly, dismissing the thought as soon as it registered. *No, that's not possible. I would have noticed. Soulbonding kicks up a very definite energy signature, and there's nothing like that on either of them.* A small part of him was very happily smug about that, but he ignored it.

"What are you thinking?" Rick had caught the small movement.

"I'm thinking and discarding possibilities," Justin replied. "Let me get them straight in my head and then I'll share."

This seemed to satisfy Rick, who returned to staring moodily out over the remains of Sarah's rose garden. It had started to rain again, and the cold pattering of the drops tapped an impatient staccato on the porch roof.

He's always been one damned weird Sensitive, Justin thought, chewing on the inside of his cheek. *What if he's not a Sensitive at all, but something else? Christ, you could probably hide an Elemental Lord behind those shields, and we'd never really know.*

When they'd first met Rick, both Shanna and Justin had been impressed with the complexity of his mental shields. Most Sensitives had pretty heavy-duty mental shields as a matter of survival, but his were even more multi-layered and dense, almost as if they were protecting his inner core. Not even Shanna had dared to try and pierce his innermost shields, the ones Rick said his mother had taught him to construct when he was barely three years old.

We always thought she taught him so young because he was a Sensitive. But what if it's because she recognized something else in him, a Talent she didn't want anyone else to see? What if those inner shields are gone?

He controlled a shudder with difficulty. *That can't be it either. It would take something outrageously powerful and skillful to break down those shields without killing him.*

Justin's mind presented him with the energy wave Nikki had unleashed at Gene-Tech and this time he couldn't control the shiver that raced down his spine. *Oh shit, if that was the right frequency...*

"Look at me and don't fight me," he commanded, crossing the distance between them in three quick steps and grabbing Rick's head in his hands, forcing him to look Justin in the eye. After a moment's shock, Rick opened his outermost shields and let Justin slide a mental probe into his mind.

Oh fuck. Justin felt warmth wash over him, magical Power emanating from Rick's core, pulsing and flaring in the space once covered by those innermost shields. Justin let his hands fall from Rick's head and stepped back, withdrawing his mental probe at the same time. "Congratulations," he said, when he could speak. "You aren't a Sensitive after all."

"Don't be ridiculous," Rick said, and Justin heard the panic creeping into his voice. "Of course I'm a Sensitive."

"Sensitives don't light things on fire," Justin pointed out and Rick flushed again. "You're an Earth Mage."

"That's not possible," Rick insisted. "My mother was a Light Mage. My father is as nonmagical as you can get. How the hell could I be an Earth Mage?"

"Same way two Shadow Mages threw off an Earth/Shadow half-breed and the Star-Child," Justin replied. "The aptitude for Magic, the ability to connect with Power, is what's passed along. Not necessarily the sphere you connect with. And who knows?

Maybe you're a half-breed too."

"I can't be a Mage," Rick said. "I can't."

"You can, and you are." Justin watched the emotions play out over his friend's face and got ready for the explosion.

"No!" Rick shouted, and Power poured from him, a sweetly hot flood that slammed into Justin's waiting shield and drained harmlessly away.

"Are you done?" Justin asked; Rick just stared at him openmouthed. "Or did you want to go again? How many more surges like that is it going to take to convince you that you're really a Mage?"

"Why didn't I show before, then? Why didn't Shanna know?" Rick asked, his shoulders slumping.

"Because your mother, bless her, taught you how to shield, remember? If Nikki hadn't blasted those shields to kingdom come on Halloween, we might never have known."

Rick opened his mouth to argue again, and Justin held up his hand to stop him. "Don't bother. I've looked. You're a Mage, and that means learning a different skill set now. Go get your coat."

"Where am I going?"

"To Edgar's." Justin could just picture the look he was going to get from the old witch when he showed up with yet another student for him, and he couldn't stop a wicked laugh from bubbling up. "You need to learn some control."

"But...I've got a deadline!" Rick objected.

"And as soon as you've learned a modicum of control, you can stop the lessons and get back to the book," Justin said, still chuckling. "Until then, you need to make sure you won't cause a fire every time you hit a roadblock. Or daydream about Nikki."

Rick gave him a dirty look and stomped into the Inn.

Chapter Thirteen

"Chasing Shadows"

"Come on, Alex! We're running out of time!"

Behind him, Alex could feel Nikki shift slightly, trying to find a more defensible position in the narrow corridor. White heat emanated from her in preparation to reduce anyone or anything coming after them into ash, and he grinned despite the situation. "Glad you're on my side."

"We're not going to have a side if the military catches up with us," she pointed out. "Open the damn door already!"

"Calm down." His fingers teased open the last little piece of the intricate lock and he smiled in triumph. With a satisfying snick, the entire mechanism whirred for a moment, then vanished into the steel door without a trace. Alex blinked.

"Now what?" Nikki craned her head to look around him at the now-featureless door. "Why didn't it open?"

"I don't know!" Alex ran through the entire sequence again in his head. "It should have worked!"

Tick, tock. Tick, tock. He could hear the clock in his head counting down the seconds until they were discovered, an implacable march of time that he couldn't stop.

"Well, it didn't." Nikki shook her head. "Are you sure it's back there?"

"It's supposed to be."

"We don't have time for supposed to be, Alex," Nikki said,

pushing him aside so she could inspect the door. "I don't suppose you brought any explosives either, did you? Gods, what kind of evil mastermind are you, anyways?"

"I brought you," Alex pointed out. "I thought explosives might be a little superfluous."

"Wrong Horseman," Nikki said. "And besides, as soon as I do anything the least bit loud, the entire complex will be on our asses. I want to be sure it's there before I risk that." She looked back at him. "So are you sure?"

He spread his hands out. "You get us in there, I'll deal with whoever shows up."

"You and what army?" she snorted. "Is it in there?"

"According to the information I received, yes, the chest is in there."

"I hope so." Nikki's eyes started to glow red, and Alex shrank back instinctively. "I'm not a big fan of cells."

Before he could answer, she whirled and delivered a roundhouse kick to the middle of the heavy steel door. It blew inward, bringing most of the frame with it into the room beyond with a deep booming sound that vibrated through him, sending him staggering backwards.

"I thought you said you couldn't open it!" Alex said, choking a bit on the concrete dust that filled the air.

"No, I told you wrong Horseman," Nikki said, looming out of the cloud of the destruction like an avenging angel to give him a hand up. "I never said I couldn't work around it. Next time, bring the right tools. Now come on — they'll be here soon."

Alex followed her through the hole in the wall, thinking that she wasn't so much a Mage as she was a natural disaster on two legs. *And we thought we could control her? Mental note to self: make sure you don't get Horsemen the next time,* he thought, stepping over broken pieces of concrete.

Tick, tock. Time kept running. *Tick, tock.*

Stepping into the room was like stepping into a clock museum. Clocks of every shape and size ticked away on the walls; the floor vibrated slightly beneath him, and Alex looked down to see a giant digital clock counting down to...something. What, he wasn't sure he wanted to know.

"Come on, Alex!" Nikki said, from the other end of the room. "Pay attention. We don't have..."

"Anywhere to run?"

They both turned as another door opened on the opposite wall, and a smiling Tony stepped into the vast clock chamber. "You're quite right," the Blood Mage said, gesturing, and several Spirits and Mages poured in behind him. "You're cornered."

"Not yet," Nikki snapped, bringing her hands up.

"Blow me up, and you'll never find the chest," Tony said. "Did you really think we'd let the two of you just waltz in here and take it?"

"Honestly, your being here wasn't even discussed," Nikki said. "I was betting you guys couldn't get your heads out of your collective asses before we left. I guess I lost that bet."

Alex watched the exchange in shock, too numb by Tony's defection to react.

"What's the matter, Alex?" Tony said, pulling a cigarette pack from his pocket and tapping out a cigarette. "I always end up on the winning side."

"You slimy little bastard!" Rage that the Blood Mage had betrayed him gave Alex's feet wings: he leapt across the intervening space, intent on wringing Tony's neck.

"No, Alex, we need you!" Nikki said, and Alex howled as Power wrapped around him, dragging him backwards. He reached out and grabbed Tony by the collar, pulling against her magic.

"I'll kill you!" he shouted, spraying spittle on Tony's smug face.

"Alex, let him go!" Nikki's voice blurred, shifted. "Dammit, let me go!"

Alex blinked the rage away, realizing that he was in his hotel room, with Tony jacked up against the wall. *Another dream,* he realized, as his fingers unclenched and pain lanced through his midsection. *It was just a dream.*

"Get dressed." Tony smoothed down his shirt, and Alex looked up to see sweat sheening the Blood Mage's bald head. "We have to go."

"Why?" Alex turned, looking for a shirt. "What's going on?"

"Department V's coming for us," Tony replied, grabbing a bag and shoving some other clothes into it. "We've got about 5 minutes, according to my source."

"Damn." *Department V. Damn feds. Damn military.* Alex doubled up as more pain shot through him. *Why can't they all leave me alone?*

"Come on!" Tony shoved him towards the bathroom. "I'll fix you when we get there. Luckily, I've finally found us a place."

I hope I make it... The adrenalin from the dream was fading; Alex stumbled, and nearly brained himself on the doorframe. *It was easier in the dream...*

"Don't die on me yet, Masterson," he heard Tony snarl from somewhere behind him. "I still need you."

"Don't die on me yet, Masterson," Tony snarled, watching Alex fold. "I still need you."

A knock on the other door froze him for a moment. "Mr. Masterson?" an official-sounding voice said, and Tony swore under his breath. "We'd like a moment of your time."

"Not now," Tony muttered, picking Alex up and throwing him over one shoulder, cursing again as he felt the hole in the Shadow Mage's stomach open again and start leaking blood on him. "We're a little busy." He kicked open the bathroom door and slammed his fist into the mirror, shattering it.

Blood welled from the cuts on his knuckles and he cursed again, knowing what he was leaving behind. *Not that I can do anything about it,* he thought bitterly. *At least the moron remembered to let me know they were coming before they showed up. Thank God for small miracles.*

Tony hastily sketched a symbol on the bathroom wall as the front door boomed. *Come on, come on!* he prayed, as the Gate slowly opened. *Dammit, let those wards hold, please!*

Watching the strands of Power open like a flower unfolding while listening to the booms as the cops on the other side assaulted his wards set the acid in Tony's stomach to dancing, and he cursed at himself. *So damn sure you'd lost them,* he growled to himself. *Too damn cocky to set up a Gate ahead of time. Damn fool. At least you were smart enough to ward the entire room, so they had to come through the door.*

The room shook, raining down paint flakes, and Tony risked a glance out of the bathroom. The door was bowing in, and he cursed again as he turned back around.

The Gate was nearly large enough — he breathed a quick prayer that the other end was stabilized and tossed Alex through, just as the front door cracked.

"Stop him!" someone shouted as Tony dove feet-first through the Gate. He grabbed the edge of the spell as he slid by the event horizon, hoping he wasn't about to die, and pulled the spell in after him.

He hit the dirt floor of the cave hard and tripped over Alex's prone body, falling on his face over the unconscious Shadow Mage. More blood oozed from his bald head, adding to his irritation; the cave floor was far from smooth, and he reminded himself that he could have hit a far larger rock than he did.

Keep moving, Tonio. His mother's voice was a whip crack in his mind, reminding him they weren't out of the woods yet. *They'll follow you soon enough.*

Dragging himself to his feet, Tony grabbed a few of the larger rocks, smearing them with his blood, and then set to work.

Each Gate he opened drained him a little more, but he'd been half-prepared for this, at least. In his pocket were four glass vials of blood, specially prepared — the last of his stash. Tony worked methodically, painting the Gate symbol on the walls of the cave, smashing a vial in the center of each symbol and triggering the Gates. Once they were all active, he tossed the blood-covered rocks through three of them, then grabbed Alex's body again and put it over his shoulder. He pulled a small cloth bag from his pocket, squeezed it in his bloody hand, then tossed it into the center of the room. A small red figure rose from it, and fixed Tony with a serious look. "As soon as they show up, collapse the roof," Tony told the imp, and it nodded. "Kill as many as you can."

Then he turned and ran through the Gate.

Wet, hot air hit his face as he came out on the other side: air that tasted of blood and sweat, that wrapped around him like wet cotton bindings and threatened to drown him.

Just the way he liked it.

Tony dropped Alex on the cot in the corner of the room and dismissed the Gate, then took a deep breath. They were safe, for the moment. Long enough for him to get his strength back before they moved again.

He made sure Alex wasn't going to wake up before he got back, binding him with a quick sleep spell so he wouldn't go wandering. Then Tony went out into the kitchen.

The last owner of the shack had stocked the place as if the Apocalypse was imminent; part of the reason Tony had chosen it. It looked like a dump on the outside, but that façade masked a very defensible cottage that, had it been slightly larger, would have been perfect for their plans. Unfortunately, the owner hadn't wanted to share his little fortress with anyone, so it was too small.

The fact that the last owner had also been intensely private and not likely to be missed had also featured in Tony's decision to take it. One never knew when one might need a safe house to flee to.

He rummaged in the large refrigerator, coming up with a thick wedge of Brie wrapped in pastry and a cold beer, and then went into the small living room and flopped into the lounge chair.

I'm getting too old for this shit, he thought, taking a bite from the Brie.

You need to plan better, Tonio, his mother's voice whispered in the darkness. *They almost caught you this time.*

They almost did. Tony took a long pull of the beer. *But it won't happen again.*

Are you sure? She sounded dubious.

I've got the perfect place all picked out, Tony replied, letting another bite of the cheese melt on his tongue, tart and creamy and mixed with some sort of berry. *I just need to get my strength back up, so I can get Alex there.*

Alex. He sighed. The hole in his belly still hadn't healed, and it was getting beyond his mediocre healing ability. And with Andreas' mental state unknown, he couldn't afford to have Alex die on him.

Don't borrow trouble, Tonio, his mother advised. *Just get them all together, and then you can figure out who needs to survive and who doesn't.*

Sitting in the damp twilight, the cool beer chilling his hand, Tony let the bayou noises wash the stress of the day out of his mind. They'd made it so far; barring catastrophic karmic failure, by tomorrow morning, they should be in a place they could finish the experiment.

And then, we can all breathe easier.

Chapter Fourteen

"Cube of Secrets"

"How the hell did he know?"

Derek winced as the bellow shook the windows in his partner's hotel room, which was really too small for the amount of people currently crammed into it. However, Amy's room had at least four additional layers of shields on it, making it next to impossible for anyone to eavesdrop on them.

And since it was becoming apparent that someone was feeding Alex Masterson information on how the hunt for him was going, those shields were necessary.

Derek was currently perched on the bed in the room, shoved up against the headboard, watching Baird McClannahan pace in front of the TV, gesturing in frustration. His dark robes flapped, reminding Derek of a large black bird hopping up and down on a corpse. The flashes of Power that lit up Baird's dark eyes only reinforced the predatory image, and Derek was very happy to not have the Shadow Mage angry at him.

Especially considering what we have for him, Derek thought, shivering a little. *He's already unhappy, and Alex isn't even his problem. Or is he?*

Wouldn't surprise me if this is all connected. What is the StarChild doing?

"Don't be so quick to blame her, Chief," Baird snapped, and Derek jumped. "There's a lot more going on here than you know."

"I wasn't blaming her," Derek replied, stung a bit and only a little afraid of standing up to the legendary Shadow Mage, who had no military rank but could probably disassemble him where he stood. The rumors that Baird was in actuality a Shadow Lord flitted briefly through his mind, but Derek tamped those down. "I was wondering why Ismael has you chasing Alex if it wasn't connected."

"You aren't paid to wonder what the Admiral is doing or why," Baird said, and Derek's jaw tightened. "You're paid to figure out what the hell happened at Gene-Tech. Now, why am I here? What do you have that's so important that you couldn't deal with it?"

Amy, who was standing by the desk, flipped Baird a small object that he caught out of reflex. Derek's faith in the universe was restored when Baird's face went from dark cocoa to ash white in seconds.

"You...you...you found this here?" he choked out, holding the black cube in his hands as if it were a live snake. "Here?"

"Yes," Derek said, as Amy raised an eyebrow at Baird's reaction. "Is it what I think it is?" *I'm thinking yes, judging by the way you look.* That thought was squashed as soon as he thought it, but Baird was apparently too upset to notice it.

"You found a Shadow Cube in the ruins?" Baird demanded, and Derek nodded. "How did he get one?"

"That's one of the questions we'd like to ask Alex when we put our hands on him," Amy said, and Derek silently applauded her dry tone.

"Is it...occupied?" Baird continued to turn the relic over in his hands, the ashy color on his face slowly fading.

"I have no clue," Derek said, as Amy shrugged. "I'm not a Shadow Mage. I can't open it."

Baird opened his mouth, then closed it again, and shuddered. "I'm not opening it here. If I can. Shadow Cubes are legends..."

"That's an awfully solid legend you're holding in your hand," Derek pointed out, and Baird glared at him. "I think this investigation might make us reconsider a lot of things we consider myths."

"There are no Chaos Mages on this side of the Walls, Chief!" Baird said heatedly, and Derek bristled at the man's tone. "I don't care what you think you've sensed, there are no Chaos Mages on Earth!"

"Maybe not anymore, but there sure as hell was something big running through my crime scene!" Derek shot back, tired of being told he was wrong. "Maybe you Mages have missed it, but there is someone practicing Chaos Magic here! Someone who also practices Earth Magic, and that means that at one point in time, they were born here!"

"And I'm telling you that's impossible!"

"And who died and left you God?" Derek snapped, getting up off the bed and standing in front of Baird. The fact that the Shadow Mage towered nearly six inches over him didn't phase him, nor did the Shadows starting to creep up in the corners of the room.

"Watch your mouth, Chief," Baird warned, his deep voice dropping even lower. "I don't have any problems recommending you be removed from this investigation for insubordination."

"It's only insubordination if you're my superior officer," Derek said, and made a show of looking at the shoulders of Baird's robes. "Funny, I don't see any officer's bars there."

"What makes you think I don't have them?" Baird countered in a softly dangerous tone. "Just because I don't choose to wear them?"

"All right, enough, both of you!" Amy stalked around the bed and grabbed Derek by the shoulder, yanking him away from Baird. "Knock it off! These shields are thick, but if you start throwing Power around, that storm is going to come right back around. And I'm not going to be happy if I have to dig my shit out of a crater because you two brought a lightning strike down on us." She glared at Baird, who took in a deep breath and then gave her a curt nod. The Shadows in the corners dissipated, and Derek realized how tense the atmosphere had been.

"Is there anything else the Admiral should know about what's been going on down here?" Baird asked, putting the Shadow Cube in a pocket of his robe.

"We found another office," Derek said. "Untouched by our Chaos Mage. This one had a very familiar signature all over it."

"Oh?" Baird said.

"Yep." Amy pulled out a file folder with a picture clipped to the top and handed it to Baird. "Do you remember the Green

Heights killings?"

"The Blood Magic ritual killings in Louisiana?" Baird's eyes went wide again. "Anthony Keats? Really? I thought he was dead!"

"Everyone did," Derek said. "And there was no Anthony Keats on Alex's payroll. There was, however, an Anthony Ashcroft."

"Ashcroft? Wasn't that the name of the first Green Heights victim?"

Derek nodded. "Violet Ashcroft was bled dry and left artistically arranged in the center of Green Heights Park the night of the full moon. Precisely 48 hours after she was found, her reanimated corpse, powered by a Blood Spirit, killed twenty people in the Green Heights County Morgue before it was stopped. Ballsy little bastard, huh?"

"Indeed." Baird shook his head. "Have you talked to his sister yet?"

"We were just waiting for you to take possession of the...myth," Derek said. "I'm heading out to talk to Chrysanthemum Keats in the morning and see if her brother has contacted her in the last year or so."

Baird squared his shoulders. "Anything else?" Amy and Derek exchanged glances, and he slumped again. "Now what?"

"We found a sealed cell as well," Derek said slowly. "Well, it had been sealed. It was blown open."

"By who?"

"Justin Greystone." Derek watched Baird's face fall. "I know. I didn't want to believe it either. But it was definitely his signature. And our unknown was there as well. He knows who she is."

Several emotions flickered across Baird's face in rapid succession, too fast for Derek to read. "Then go and ask him who and where she is," the Shadow Mage said, a dreadful weight in his deep voice. "And if he won't tell you, bring him to Washington."

Chapter Fifteen

"Ashes, Ashes, We All Fall Down"

"Deck the halls with boughs of holly..."

Nikki lay in bed, listening to the small child in the hall carol her way cheerfully down the stairs and smiled. *At least she can carry a tune reasonably well,* she thought, remembering her own forays into caroling. *My parents put up with so much from me.*

She'd slept late; there was actually weak sunlight streaming in through her windows, but Edgar had given them the day off after nearly two weeks of hard work. Nikki's head was full of magical knowledge, and he'd cheerfully told her yesterday that she'd only scratched the bare surface.

"That's why they call it a lifetime study, my dear," he'd chuckled, when her jaw had dropped. "But don't worry. At least now you won't blow anything up accidentally."

Yep, that's a good thing, Nikki thought, rolling over and feeling for her cell phone. *Bad for property values and all that. Besides, Mom probably wouldn't let me come home if I was lighting stuff on fire when I got pissed off.*

Oh, wait, that was Rick. You're the lightning rod, remember?

She grinned at that thought and punched her mother's number into the phone, then settled back against her pillows.

"You're late, slugabed," Lara Jeffries said when the phone picked up.

"Hi Mom, it's good to talk to you too," Nikki said, chuckling. "How's Dad?"

They chatted for a bit, making plans for Christmas. Lara and Marc were planning on coming up to the Inn for the holidays, so they could meet some of the people Nikki had told them about.

Especially Rick. Lara, Nikki discovered, was extremely interested in meeting the young novelist.

Hopefully he'll be in a better mood by then, she thought, leaning back against her pillows after the end of the call and contemplating the sunbeam shining on the floor. *He's been pissy since Justin outed him.*

Then again, these lessons were cutting into his writing time. And it's got to be hard to switch your entire mindset from being a Sensitive to being a Mage.

The strains of the little girl's singing drifted up the stairs again; she'd switched to "Jingle Bells" and was warbling cheerfully, probably to Sarah.

"Enough laying about," Nikki told herself, sitting up and swinging her legs over the side of the bed. "You've got a day off — time to go Christmas shopping. Who knows when I'll actually get another chance to do so."

Edgar had been so pleased with his students' progress that he'd decreed the day of rest. Both Nikki and Francesca had mastered the basics of ley line magic Edgar was teaching them and could now build Circles on their own, and Rick had mastered his personal shields enough that the old witch had pronounced him safe enough to be let out on his own again.

"Which means he'll be holed up in his room for the next few days," Nikki mused out loud, heading into the bathroom and turning on the shower. "Which gives me a few days to figure out how to break it to him that my mother thinks he's the next Great Thing for her baby girl."

The hot water finished waking her up; after she toweled off, Nikki pulled on clothing, then headed downstairs to grab her keys from the hook on the wall.

"Hey, Sarah, what's the best place to do all my Christmas shopping in one fell swoop?" she asked, strolling into the kitchen.

Sarah's kitchen always smelled heavenly: Nikki took a deep breath, letting the scents of allspice, cinnamon and nutmeg wash over her as the innkeeper mixed yet another batch of pumpkin pies. The little girl that Nikki had heard earlier was parked at the kitchen table, decorating a mound of sugar cookies and still singing to herself.

"North Conway," Sarah said immediately, sliding the next batch of pies into the oven and then turning to her. "There are muffins on the counter — why don't you grab one while I'm writing you directions?"

Nikki helped herself to the large blueberry muffins, sighing in happiness. "Can I kidnap you to cook for me when I finally leave?" she asked around a mouthful of crumbs. "Or maybe I just won't leave. Can I rent my room permanently?"

"Sure," Sarah said, grinning as she handed her a piece of paper with directions on it. "Running a boarding house is a heck of a lot more stable than running an inn. Don't forget your gloves — it's bitter outside."

Nikki grinned back at her and grabbed another muffin before braving the deceptively clear day. Sarah hadn't been kidding; as she stepped outside, the icy air slapped her hard, frosting her cheeks pink within three steps.

Will the Earth ever recover from what happened on Halloween? Nikki wondered, only half-listening to the radio as she guided the Jeep down the road. *Or will the StarChild be forced to finish the Cleansing?*

Edgar had finally explained what a Cleansing was the day before. Nikki and Francesca had listened wide-eyed as the old witch had recounted exactly what was involved in a Cleansing: the release of the Four Horsemen to gather up the random threads of Power that attacked the Walls Between the Worlds, after which they returned to the Council circle and gave the Power they'd collected to the StarChild, who used it to reweave the Walls back together.

"It's a very exhausting process," Edgar had said. "Many times, the StarChild doesn't survive having that much Power inside her for the amount of time it takes to reweave the Walls. It's not a task any StarChild takes lightly, which is another reason the Lords are all in a tizzy now."

"What about the people?" Nikki had asked. "Does the Cleansing destroy the people here as well?"

"Not exactly — it only destroys those who were responsible for the breaks in the Walls in the first place," Edgar had replied. "That's the Horsemen's job — to gather the Power of those who disrupted the Balance in the first place."

"So we're supposed to be able to tell who these people are?" Nikki had asked, her brow furrowing, and Edgar had shrugged.

"I'm not sure how that works. Remember, usually the Horsemen are spirits that the StarChild directs, according to all the legends; perhaps she has a way of marking their targets. I don't know."

And the StarChild is unavailable to ask, Nikki mused, as the sign for North Conway loomed in the distance. *I wonder if Justin would know.*

Not that he's been around much lately either. Jesus, you'd think I was plague, not death, the way he and Rick have been making themselves scarce.

That thought was followed by another, this one a bit more disturbing. *What will happen to me if the StarChild does do a Cleansing? Will I be sucked into the weaving? Is that something I'm willing to do?*

Would I have any choice in the matter?

And what if Alex really has had a change of heart? Can I let the Cleansing kill him if he's trying to make things right?

"Enough," Nikki told herself, pulling the Jeep into a spot in the outlet's parking lot and shutting off the engine. "I have Christmas shopping to do. No more gloomy thoughts today."

She spent several hours cheerfully forgetting about Alex Masterson, odd dreams and the fate of the world as she browsed through North Conway's stores looking for gifts, thankful that her bank account still had some money left over in it — her father must have seen how low it was getting and added more. *Yet another reason for me to look at that consulting job,* she mused, looking at a window display of glittering diamonds. *I should really talk to Justin about what his sister does. After we survive this, of course.*

The back of the Jeep was full by the middle of the afternoon, and Nikki's stomach reminded her that it had been a long time since Sarah's muffins.

"Time for lunch," she said, locking the back of the Jeep. "And if

I remember correctly, Sarah's suggestion for lunch is right around here somewhere."

She'd spotted the little café when she'd driven in, and had walked by it at least twice: a small hole in the wall place with a few tables and the most delicious smell wafting out when the door opened. It was sandwiched between two of the larger outlet stores, and Nikki had caught a whiff of the enticing aroma every time she'd passed.

"Oh yes," she said, stepping inside and inhaling. "I'm definitely in the right place."

A small sign inside the door told her to seat herself, so she chose a small table in one of the corners and opened the menu.

"Can I help you?" A college-aged boy with an intricate braid half-way down his back ambled over with a glass of water and a cheerful smile; Nikki smiled back, unable to resist.

"What's the special?"

"A grilled mozzarella and asparagus panini on a tomato wrap," he said, and Nikki's stomach rumbled in appreciation. "Served with sweet potato fries and broccoli coleslaw."

"Sign me up," Nikki said, closing the menu and handing it to him.

He wrote her order on his pad with a big flourish. "And to drink?"

"Pepsi, with lemon," she requested.

"Coming right up."

As he headed to the kitchen, winding his way through the small café with the grace of a dancer, Nikki caught sight of the TV over the bar. It was tuned to CNN, and in the quiet of the café, she could hear the reporter's voice clearly.

"The federal government is still refusing to comment on the magical shield surrounding the northwestern portion of Vermont and the adjourning Canadian territories, although unsubstantiated reports continue to surface that the StarChild has been seen in the area and may be responsible for the blockade. The Canadian government is also refusing to comment.

"The Pentagon is denying reports that several flyovers of the area have been shot down," the reporter continued. "They also deny that four Mages, including two government agents, are missing in the area, and that a nest of Sintetizzi has been discovered there."

"Of course they're denying it," her waiter said, coming back with a frosty glass of soda, a lemon circle bobbing amid the ice, as the show faded into a commercial break. "What government in their right mind would come out and say, 'Yes, there's a nest of rogue Mages in this area we can't get into, and we have no idea who's put up the barrier that we can't get through.' Not even this administration is that moronic." He placed the glass on her table and grinned at her. "Right?"

"What do you think is in there?" Nikki asked instead, running her finger over the top of the glass.

"Something bad," he said succinctly. "And I think they should just let the StarChild deal with it. Isn't that what she's there for?"

"Sounds good to me," Nikki said, grinning back at him.

"Your food will be up soon," he said, and went back into the kitchen. Nikki picked up her glass and took a drink as the commercials ended and the reporter came back onto the screen.

"In other news, the investigation into the explosion at the former Gene-Tech facility is ongoing. Police Chief Eric Waters stated in his daily press conference that the search for fugitive billionaire Alex Masterson is still in progress, and he denied again any rumors that evidence has been found showing that the research scientists there had created a hybrid magical monster."

Well, they did, kind of, Nikki thought wryly, as the waiter set down her plate in front of her. *You're just twenty-three years too late with your story.* "Thank you," she said out loud.

"Ketchup? Or sour cream?"

"Oh, sour cream," Nikki said, and he put a container on the table.

The reporter glanced down at the papers in her hand and frowned. "Hang on, I've just been handed a new story. Apparently, a woman has come forward claiming that her father was killed at the Gene-Tech explosion. As you know, the site has been off-limits since Halloween, when a massive explosion rocked the complex. We're going to go live now to the front lawn of the town hall in Taylor's Ridge, one of the small towns that supplied workers to the Gene-Tech facility, where Bob Dorr is standing by. Bob, what do you have for us?"

The camera switched, panning to a tall man with a thick black beard and glasses, holding a microphone and standing in front of a small crowd. "Well, Sakelah, we're at the town hall, where Dr. Amy Sturgis has called a press conference, stating she has information the state and federal authorities have been suppressing regarding the explosion at the Gene-Tech facility."

"Any idea what, Bob?"

Bob shook his head. "No idea, and there are no federal or state police here to respond to the allegations, Sakelah." There was a slight commotion behind him and he looked over his shoulder, then turned back to the camera. "Looks like Dr. Sturgis is preparing to make her announcement."

Nikki watched, fascinated, her sandwich forgotten on the plate in front of her, wondering just what the young woman who stepped up to the bank of microphones was going to say. *She looks determined,* she thought.

Dr. Sturgis was dressed in a no-nonsense suit of pale blue, her brown hair pulled back and her eyes steely behind the wire-rimmed glasses she wore. "Thank you all for coming," she said, her voice only trembling a little. "It means a lot to know that people are willing to hear the truth about what happened to my father and everyone else who have disappeared since the explosions."

"Gene-Tech was one of the big employers in this area," she continued, as flash bulbs continued to go off. "My father was one of the senior security guards there. He hasn't been home since Halloween, and he hasn't contacted my mother. I know my father. He would defy an order from God to let my mother know he was okay." She stopped to wipe a tear from her cheek. "So we hired a private detective to find out what really happened Halloween night."

While she had been talking, two men had been assembling a large screen behind her. Dr. Sturgis turned and pointed a remote at it. "He managed to sneak onto the site and take several rolls of pictures. What he documented shocked us."

"To begin with, there was a second explosion, the day after Halloween. This was never reported to the public, no doubt on the request of the military officials that are now running the investigation, no matter what Chief Waters states in his press conferences." The screen bloomed to life, with two obviously military officers walking through the rain. Nikki recognized the background as Gene-Tech.

"The woman is Lt. Amy Elder," Dr. Sturgis continued. "I don't know the man, but Lt. Elder has been investigating special magical crimes for the Pentagon for the past five years. What I really want you to focus on, though, is the black tent in the background."

Nikki had noticed it, and now leaned forward as the camera shifted. "This image was taken the night of the second explosion," Dr. Sturgis said. "My investigator had snuck into the site and managed to get some pictures." She fell silent as the camera moved closer to the tent. A hand came up from the right side of the image and pulled back one of the flaps, and as the image filled the screen, a collective gasp rose from the audience and Nikki's blood went cold.

"I'm sure you can recognize what these are." Dr. Sturgis' voice was flat. "My investigator counted approximately 200 before he had to leave."

Nikki looked at the neat rows of black body bags and swallowed hard, her sandwich turning to dust in her mouth. *Over 200 dead,* she thought numbly. *But how? There weren't that many in the secure building, were there?*

"My father called my mother the day before Halloween and let her know that Mr. Masterson had locked down the entire compound, so he wouldn't be home," Dr. Sturgis said, and Nikki's stomach roiled. "He told her he loved her, and that he would be home as soon as the experiment was over. Something that was going on in the secure wing had kept them all there. And it killed them all."

The picture behind her changed, and Nikki forced herself to continue watching as the footage of the rubble that had once been the secure building at Gene-Tech. "There were nearly 100 people working in this building," Dr. Sturgis said. "I don't think anyone made it out alive. Including my father."

The screen went blank, and Dr. Sturgis turned back to the crowd of reporters. "Don't ask me any questions," she said, more tears running down her face. "Go to Gene-Tech and ask Lt. Elder where our people are. Ask her about the bodies in that makeshift morgue. Ask her about the crater that used to be a building. And ask her about the four hundred people still missing from their families." She turned and left the stage abruptly, even as questions shot up out of the crowd. Nikki tuned them out, slumping in her seat and playing with a fry in the sour cream as voices ran through her mind.

Justin's, assuring her that the three young women left behind had been brought to safety. Rick's, telling her that everything had been okay, that he and Justin had visited Sylvia Richards in the hospital. Edgar's, explaining how the Horsemen gathered energy.

And Morgan's, telling her that her Horseman hadn't wanted to let her die.

So I killed...hundreds instead. The knowledge sat heavy in her stomach, a lead weight dragging her down. *And they lied to me about it. They all lied to me.*

Suddenly, she had to get out, get away. Nikki threw some money on the table and hurried out to her Jeep, rage and horror warring in her system. *Why didn't they just tell me? Why couldn't they trust me to deal with it?*

Probably because they'd just seen you kill over four hundred people, whispered that inner voice that loved to torment her. Problem was, it was right this time.

"I don't know that I killed them," Nikki told herself as she slid behind the wheel, trying to reason the situation out. "I passed out after I stabbed Alex. I don't know that those deaths are on my hands."

You're the Horseman Death, the voice taunted her. *Who else could kill on that scale?*

And it explained so much. Nikki gave up. Laying her forehead against the steering wheel, tears leaking from under her closed eyelids, she couldn't argue with the fact that it explained all those odd little ways everyone had been treating her since Halloween.

Vashti and Morgan, insisting I not exert myself or use my gifts to find Alex. Justin, shadowing my every move. And Rick being distant, pleading his book. I should have known.

Sitting there, she could feel the darkness of her Horseman coiling within her, nestled down deep in her soul, tendrils of smoke and Shadow and Blood snaking through her core. *Maybe Alex was right,* she thought desperately. *Maybe I should have joined him after all.*

I seem to have more in common with him than I do with anyone else I know at this point.

A loud rattle brought her out of her self-absorbed misery; something hard ricocheted off the Jeep, making her jump. Nikki looked up to see the sunlight gone; clouds had rolled in again, and as she stared out the window, freezing rain began to pound down. She swallowed hard, pulling up her shields and forcing her emotions down.

After all, we don't want the Council or the StarChild to come and decide I'm too out of control to live, she thought nastily, narrowing her eyes to keep back the tears. *Of course, maybe I'm too valuable a weapon to kill just yet. Anyone who can kill that effectively must be worth something, right?*

Not that they could tell me that. Not that they could trust me to tell me anything, apparently.

The plaintive strains of "I'll Be Home for Christmas" came over the radio, and Nikki's blood boiled again. She nearly broke the key in the ignition in her haste to shut the Jeep off, and then she shoved the door open, desperate to escape. Standing in the freezing rain, Nikki raised her face to the elements and screamed.

As if summoned, a large black horse thundered up next to her, and Nikki flung herself in to Cerberus' saddle. *Where are we going?* The voice in her head was deep and only faintly curious.

Somewhere that I can't hurt anyone.

Done. Cerberus leapt forward, and Nikki felt him summon a Gate to the Shadow Lands. The rain vanished as they went through the World Walls, but the biting chill remained; the air crackled around them as Cerberus ran.

She didn't recognize this part of the Shadow Lands — it was desolate, almost like a parking lot in the middle of nowhere, but there was no blacktop and trees stood in straggly clumps. Cerberus ran, heedless of her hands on the reins, so Nikki dropped them and pointed at the nearest clump of trees, channeling the anger and hurt at the lies she'd been told into a stream of heat. The trees exploded, flames leaping into the sullen twilight skies with a roar, and Cerberus danced sideways to avoid the sparks.

"Not good enough," she snarled, pointing at another tree and watching it go up in flames. "Too mundane and stupid to be told what was really going on." Boom! Another tree exploded, sap crackling under the intense heat. "Too trusting to realize what was going on around me." Heat pressed in around her as she lit up another tree, trapping herself and Cerberus in a circle of flame.

Should I be worried? The great black horse turned his head back towards her.

"Everyone else seems to be." Nikki bared her teeth at him. "Why should you be different?"

If he replied, she didn't hear it. Nikki held her hands to either side and channeled her frustration and anger through them, urging the flames higher and higher. Trying to burn away the hurt.

If we die here, who would care? The thought made her pour even more Power into the fires. *Would anyone even look for us?*

I would care, came Cerberus' thought, and Nikki ground her teeth together, trying to keep the tears from coming.

She clenched her fists, and the flames died abruptly. "Run," she said, grabbing the reins again and leaning over his neck as Cerberus jumped forward. "Run as far and as hard as you can."

The landscape rolled unseen around them as he ran and Nikki cried, her tears hot as they raced down her chill face.

Eventually, her eyes burning and her throat raw, she looked up. Cerberus stopped, reacting to her unconscious signals, and Nikki sat back, only faintly curious as to where they were.

You said run, he said, almost apologizing. *You didn't say where.*

"Does it matter?" Nikki asked, looking at the tombstones that rose up around her. "Really?"

You need to go home at some point, Cerberus said.

"I don't have a home."

Unbidden came a picture of the Inn into her mind and her jaw clenched again. "I don't belong there."

The image vanished, replaced by an image of Teraisa's house, limned in Shadows.

"As if they won't look for me there."

There is a difference between looking and finding, Cerberus said, unruffled. *And it's not as if you have to let them in. Besides, you need sleep.*

"To sleep, perchance to dream," Nikki said bitterly. "I'm so tired of dreaming."

Dreams are sometimes the only way to see the truth.

"I don't know what the truth is anymore."

Then you obviously need to dream so you can find out.

———

His cell phone rang, startling Derek out of a light doze. The plane ride from Manchester to Arizona had worn him out, especially since his flight had been full of screaming children and harried flight attendants. Not for the first time, Derek wished the higher-ups hadn't decreed no Gates except for emergencies. And since interviewing Chrysanthemum Keats was not an emergency, he had to suffer through the commercial flight. He'd hit his motel room and fallen onto the bed without bothering to undress.

The numbers danced in front of his eyes as he squinted at the phone, and he recognized it after a moment. Amy. Derek opened the phone.

"Are you near a TV?" she said, and his heart sank at the tone in her voice.

"Yes."

"Turn it to CNN," she said. "I'll wait."

Derek got up and grabbed the remote from the top of the TV. CNN was the fourth station he stumbled across, and what he saw made him groan out loud.

"Don't ask me any questions," a young woman was saying to a crowd of reporters, tears running down her face. "Go to Gene-Tech and ask Lt. Elder where our people are. Ask her about the bodies in that makeshift morgue. Ask her about the crater that used to be a building. And ask her about the four hundred people still missing from their families."

"Who the hell is that?" Derek asked, sitting back down on the bed and staring at the screen.

"Dr. Amy Sturgis," Amy replied. "Daughter of Maxwell Sturgis, body number 271 in our morgue."

"What is she doing?"

"Blowing the lid off our investigation." A gusty sigh came over the phone. "Do me a favor and trip over Alex out there, okay? We're going to need some good news soon."

CHAPTER 16

"ICE AND DREAMS"

Justin's cell phone rang just as the skies opened above him, freezing rain that wailed despair and soaked him to the bone in ice. He groaned and booked it to his car, wondering what was wrong now.

Shit. Vashti's number blinked balefully on his phone. He listened to the rain sluice down the sides of the BMW and wondered just how much more of the karmic balance sheet he needed to clear.

The phone rang again, and Justin pushed the button. "Yeah?"

"Where are you?" Morgan's deep voice vibrated through the cell phone. "Can you access a TV or radio?"

"Yeah, I'm in my car." Justin flipped on the ignition and reached for the radio tuner. "What's going on?"

"Turn to NPR," Morgan said, and Justin frowned. "Listen for a moment."

". . scene of utter chaos following the accusations." A breathless voice flowed out of the speakers. "Even if the pictures have been manipulated somehow, this raises a lot of questions that Chief Waters is going to have to answer. Why haven't the workers been allowed to contact their families? Who really is in charge of the explosion site? Is this connected to the ongoing situation in Vermont?"

"Well, Kylie, we're getting word now that the Chief will be holding a press conference this afternoon to address Dr. Sturgis' allegations," a male voice responded, as Justin's blood turned to ice. "What questions he'll take isn't known."

"Will this Lt. Amy Elder be there, Bob?" Kylie asked.

"We don't know, Kylie. No official statements have been issued at this point — only that the investigation is ongoing and that Chief Waters will be addressing the media later this afternoon. Bob Dorr, reporting live from Taylor Township for National Public Radio."

"Thank you, Bob. As we stated at the beginning of this broadcast, Dr. Amy Sturgis, the daughter of one of the security guards who works for Gene-Tech, has just released footage to the media of a scene of destruction inside the research facility. Included in that footage was what appeared to be a morgue with literally hundreds of body bags."

"Oh, hell." Justin leaned back against the seat. "Does Nikki know?"

"We don't know where Nikki is." The absolute neutrality of that statement made Justin's head hurt.

"Shit."

"Why are you people wasting my time?"

Nikki spun her office chair around in a slow circle, watching herself in the multi-part mirror that seemed to be the only other furniture in the room. Every angle magnified details she'd rather have done without seeing: the long, lank, dark hair hanging in dirty hanks around her face, the velvet circles under each eye that made her look as if she'd gone ten rounds with Mohammed Ali, her paper-pale skin stretched taut over sharp facial bones. The black jumpsuit she wore accentuated the paleness, especially since the only thing that broke up the monochromic theme was the dull silver of the iron cuffs on her ankles and wrists.

Nowhere near as elegant as Death was supposed to be.

"What do you mean?"

The voice was emotionless, devoid of sex or humanity, and issued from somewhere above her. Nikki glanced up, but they were hiding from her again. As always. As if they thought she'd actually be allowed do something to them.

"You know what I mean." Nikki let her head loll back against the cool leather of the office chair. "I'm a monster. You don't dare let me out with the normals — so you'll have to keep me here with the crazies. It's safer for everyone that way."

"You've been a model prisoner."

Nikki laughed. "That's because there's no one good to kill here."

"Do you want to kill again?"

"That's what I'm built for." Nikki closed her eyes and remembered the sweet, hot rush of blood and Power from the last time she'd been allowed out. So sweet...

"You're not helping your case, Miss Jeffries."

"That's because I don't have a case, Warden." She smirked. "You aren't going to let me out, and we both know it. I'm far too dangerous for you to let out on the street. The last thing you need is that kind of publicity. And you know how much I love publicity..."

"Your doctors are of the opinion that you can be rehabilitated."

"My doctors are quacks and they're scared shitless of me." She opened her eyes and looked up again at the darkness above the mirrors. "Why are we playing this farce out?"

"The conditions of your sentence..."

"Say I'm never to see the outside of this prison," Nikki said. "Which brings us back to my original question. Why are you wasting my time?"

"We have been approached by a character witness on your behalf, Miss Jeffries."

"Have you now?" Mild interest bloomed. "Who's wasted their time in coming out here to plead for me?"

A crack appeared in the mirror to her right; Nikki swiveled her chair around again and raised her eyebrows at who stepped through the door that opened.

"Hello, Mother."

"You look like hell," Teraisa said, her heels clicking on the polished wooden floor as she stepped into the mirrored chamber. Her sleek black suit was crisp, professional — the exact opposite of her daughter's uniform, and her dark hair was pulled back in a tight braid that snaked down her back. "Have you really slipped this far away from us?"

"Are you here to preach at me or plead my case?" Nikki asked. "Because you're doing a really crappy job of both."

"Neither, actually," Teraisa said, and the mirrored door cracked open again. "I'm just the escort."

"My character witness needs an escort?" Nikki laughed again. "Or do they need protection?"

"Do I need to be protected from you?" Alex asked as he stepped into the room, adjusting the cuffs on one sleeve.

"Everyone needs protection from me," Nikki said, baring her teeth at him. "I'm a monster, remember? The monster you created."

Alex knelt down beside her, heedless of the danger, and cupped her cheek in his hand; she yanked her face away. "You aren't a monster, Nikki."

"No, you're right," she said, looking back at him. "I'm a killer." And she lunged for him, fingers outstretched.

They'd been expecting her to do that. The restraints on her legs grew and tightened, pulling Nikki back into the chair, back away from Alex, but not before her nails left long, angry rents in his cheek and neck. Teraisa pulled him back, blood streaming down to stain his white shirt as he stared at her. "I'll kill you all!" Nikki shrieked, trying to claw her way out of the chair as more restraints appeared out of nowhere and wrapped themselves around her. "If you ever make the mistake of letting me out, I'll kill you all! I swear I will!"

The chair began to roll backwards into the darkness beyond the mirrors, carrying Nikki back to the Shadows as she screamed, "I'll kill you all! I swear, I'll kill you all!"

"I'll kill you all!"

Cleo Smith came awake with a start, the words ringing in her ears. Shadows leered down at her from the walls as she looked around wildly, half-expecting to see a tall, lithe maniac stalking her from the twilight corners with murder in her eyes. There was nothing, of course, and she fell back onto the pillows nearly limp with relief, her heart thumping against her ribs.

"I have got to stop drinking hurricanes with Nora until midnight," she told herself. "The dreams afterwards are hell on my nerves."

As she lay there against the cool sheets, staring at the dark ceiling, the other girl's face swam out of the darkness again, beckoning to her. Pale skin, wide dark blue eyes and long dark hair — she'd been haunting Cleo's dreams for at least a month, but not like this. And yet, even in the midst of the anger and hate that surrounded her, the girl had a strange beauty, a luminous Power that glowed through her like a beacon. Cleo looked at the image floating before her, dissecting her with an artist's eye, wondering what she could do with her.

"Dan wants a Dark Queen for his new club," she said conversationally to the face. "Do you think you can pull that off?"

Phantom claws scratched lightly down the side of Cleo's neck, a faint echo of what she'd seen the girl do to Alex Masterson in her dream and Cleo shivered. *Yeah, you'll do.*

Her right hand snaked out from under the light sheet covering her, reaching for the sketch pad and pencil that lived on the night table on the side of her bed. She didn't need a light; her fingers moved instinctively across the paper, capturing the essence of the face. Then her eyes closed again, and Cleo fell back into a deep, dreamless sleep.

Sunlight dancing across her skin woke her, warm and inviting, a welcome change from the grey, depressing rains that had plagued New Orleans for the past two weeks. Ever since Halloween, the weather had been awful; not nearly as bad as it was back East, with that massive Storm sitting right off the coast, but it had still been worse than normal. Even with the magics her coven and the other three in the New Orleans area had been casting. Cleo rolled over and squinted at her clock.

Ten a. m. "Bleah," she said, rolling back over and stretching, fighting the urge to pull her pillow back over her face. "I really don't want to get up." Something hard jabbed her in the side and after a moment of squirming and gymnast-worthy contortions, she extracted her sketchbook from underneath her. Cleo sat up, a chill snaking up her spine as she saw what she'd sketched in the middle of the night.

Eerie representations of the three figures from her dream the night before stared back at her: the girl she'd seen before, both in her black institutional outfit and smiling, as she'd been when Cleo had first dreamed of the café meeting, and the ageless woman she'd called "Mother."

The kicker, though, was the handsome man with black hair who stared at the girl. A man that Cleo had seen on her television set every time she'd turned it on since Halloween.

Alex Masterson.

"It's just a coincidence," she said out loud, trying to ignore the odd little pressure in the back of her head. "He's in the news, so of course I'm dreaming about him."

The pressure remained steady, but Cleo wasn't ready to face it yet. "No visions before breakfast," she said, and stood up. "I can't face the future on an empty stomach, after all."

No magic before breakfast, and no doom before peanut butter. That had been her mother's favorite saying, back before Caran Smith had lost her mind to religion and turned her back on her gifts. And on the daughter who'd refused to be brainwashed with the rest of the flock.

Enough, she told the sad little girl who stood in the back of her mind, crying over the betrayal. *You made your choice, and they made theirs. Crying over it won't change anything.*

Cleo moved through the little cottage on autopilot, opening curtains and windows as she went from her bedroom to the kitchen, hoping the fresh air would drive away the miasma of sorrow and sleep from her head. *I should have Nora and Donna over to do a purification on this place again*, she mused, filling the teapot and setting it on the little gas stove. *And a cat. I definitely need to get a cat. At least then I'll have someone to talk to besides myself.*

She made scrambled eggs while the kettle heated, and then assembled a breakfast tray and went outside to her little back garden to eat. It was wild, overgrown and luxurious, despite her neglect, and Cleo was never sure what she'd find blooming, but it was a lovely spot to wake up in.

This morning, she noticed a creeping vine that had taken over one shadowy corner of the little garden. Icy white flowers were scattered all over its velvet leaves, and a sweet perfume lay over the yard.

Cleo laid her tray on the little wicker table and poured herself a cup of steaming green and citrus tea from the antique teapot she'd found in a consignment shop in Boston on one of her many travels. Then she laid out a place mat, her plate and silverware, and pulled her sketchpad to her.

A Dark Queen, she sighed, taking a bite and then picking up the pencil. *With a court, of course, because Queens aren't allowed out by themselves. And it has to match the décor, which is...*

"Black and silver," Dan had said, and laughed when she'd rolled her eyes at him. "Hey, it's a gothic martini bar, babe, what do you expect?"

"How cliché can you get?" she'd demanded, and the big bartender had laughed that glorious laugh that had almost kept him in her pants for longer than a month.

"Welcome to Na'Orleans," he'd drawled, making her laugh even harder. "Cliché sells, baby. That's what the tourists want."

Yeah, $20 martinis taste better when poured by an "undead" bartender, Cleo thought cynically, her pencil making random marks in the corner of the sketchpad. *Well, maybe it'll net me some more commissions. I need to pay the rent, after all.*

Hell, he was talking about a gift shop at some point. Prints might sell well, especially if I do some more of the Gothic Princess series. She made herself a note on the corner, under the compass star she'd drawn while her mind was wandering, then drained her tea cup, poured another and flipped to a clean page.

"A Dark Court, deep in the Louisiana bayou," she said, setting pencil to paper. "Gods help us."

And she began to sketch.

Chapter Seventeen

"Slow Burn"

"May I help you?"

Derek shifted his shoulders under his suit and tried not to let the thinly-veiled hostility in the woman's icy voice get to him. Very few nonmagical people were comfortable around Sensitives, but everyone seemed to know what the brown gloves signified. *As if we'd want to go digging through all your paltry secrets*, he thought, letting none of his aggravation show on his face. *Trust me, we don't.*

"I have an appointment with Ms. Keats," he said, giving her a pleasant smile. "Mr. Derek Reynolds. Is she available?"

"Please have a seat, Mr. Reynolds." The woman behind the vast white desk indicated a row of plastic chairs with a brief nod of her head, and Derek held his breath as a wave of Aqua Net-scented air washed over him. "I'll see if Sister Keats is available."

Sister Keats, huh? Talk about separating yourself from your family. Wonder if she took the veil to escape her half-brother. Derek settled himself into one of the uncomfortable chairs and cast a practiced eye over the intricate Nativity scene set up along the opposite wall on a long, low table. The figurines were quite large, and beautifully detailed, but the entire scene was overshadowed by the Crucifix hanging above it. That, like the Nativity set, was highly detailed; Derek could see individual drops of blood processing down the tortured Jesus' leg from the spear hole in his side. *What a place. And this is a family clinic?*

"Mr. Reynolds?" A different voice floated through the still air, drawing Derek's attention to the young woman who had come through the door while he was studying at the décor. She looked more like a doctor than a nun; her crucifix was a simple gold cross on a chain around her neck that glowed warmly against the dark wine-colored shirt she wore. Her hands were shoved into the pockets of a lab coat, and her slacks were pressed so crisply that even his boot camp sergeant would have had trouble finding an issue with them. "Welcome to Colorado Springs. I hope you had a pleasant trip."

Derek got up and held out his gloved hand, noting her minute hesitation before she shook it. "It was tolerable," he said, smiling. "I appreciate you seeing me at the last minute."

"Of course," she replied, while the receptionist glared at him. "I could hardly refuse a referral, especially from the Academy. Please, follow me, and please call me Chrys."

"Derek. I'm sorry, but you don't look much like a nun," Derek said, following her through the door. Chrys gave him a startled look, and he explained, "The receptionist called you Sister Keats."

She laughed. "Lydia calls everyone Sister or Brother here, Derek. It's a term of respect for her, especially since many of us don't have our doctorates, and no one's decided what to call Healers yet." A slight bitterness crept into her voice at the last comment and Derek nodded in sympathy; he'd heard all about the heated debates in the medical community over the role of Healers who hadn't gone to medical school but practiced their craft in hospitals. "But you didn't come here to discuss the medical community's politics," she said, as they walked down the hall. "Did you bring your records with you? The referral said it was urgent, but they didn't send anything."

Derek showed her the large black folder in his hands and then made a show of looking at the other people in the hall. "It's a rather...personal matter, so I didn't feel comfortable in shipping them."

"Oh." She lowered her eyes and sighed. "I understand."

Do you? Derek decided against asking her that, and instead said, "So if you aren't a doctor, Ms... er, Chrys, why did my doctor refer me to you?"

"I'm part of a fellowship, actually," she replied, smiling. "We work mostly with Mages who have suffered traumatic brain injuries and are currently comatose. There is a lot of empirical evidence that prayer and Healing, in conjunction with more traditional treatments, can cure a lot of the burnout that is a result of magical overload. I have a separate specialty in long-term brain injuries as well."

"Really?" Derek gave the slender young woman next to him a new look of respect. "How does your system work? For healing Mages, I mean."

"Well, we don't understand all the mechanics of it," Chrys admitted. "The Lord works in mysterious ways. But," and she explained the process to him as they walked down the bustling halls to a small office.

"That's fascinating," Derek said. "And you say you have a sixty-five percent cure rate?"

"Yes, based on the empirical evidence," Chrys said, blushing a bit with pleasure over his interest.

"I'm surprised that you haven't heard from any of the governmental agencies yet," Derek said, taking the chair she indicated. "That's a better rate than any of the larger military hospitals have right now."

"Only one problem," Chrys said, sitting behind the desk, her smile turning a bit brittle. "The separation of Church and State won't let them admit prayer as a viable treatment option."

"Well, unless you make it prayer specific to the religion of the patient," Derek said, and she shook her head.

"It doesn't work that way," she said. "But again, you didn't come to discuss my work here, Derek. Why don't you tell me what's going on? Why did Dr. Griffin send you to me?"

Derek wasn't surprised that she cut to the heart of the matter and nodded, pulling out a small notebook and a pen out of the black folder. "Actually, Chrys, I'm fine. I needed to talk to you about your brother."

"My. ." She frowned. "Who are you, really?"

"Derek Reynolds," he said, handing her over a card. "I've been asked to look into a few things about your brother, and that led me to you."

Chrys looked at the card and then back up at him, her face oddly mask-like and guarded. "This doesn't say who you work for, or why the Bethesda Military Hospital requested an appointment for you."

"I'm with the Navy," he said. "If you like, you can call that number on the card — they'll vouch for me. And Dr. Griffin really is my doctor."

She continued to stare at him, holding the card between two fingers. "What's your rank?"

"I'm a civilian contractor," he lied easily. "But we have access to the military hospitals."

"Why do you want to know about Anthony?"

He shrugged. "Because my boss told me to find out. I just follow orders."

Chrys looked at him for a few more minutes as if weighing his story, and Derek kept his face bland, wondering why she was so suspicious. *Has Tony already contacted her? Or is she just that afraid of him?* There was more than a touch of fear about her; he could almost taste it on the air.

"What do you want to know?" she said finally, putting his card down on her blotter.

"When was the last time you spoke to Anthony Keats?" Derek asked, flipping his notebook open to a blank page.

"About fifteen years ago," she said. "My father threw him out of the house when he hit puberty and his real personality surfaced."

"Oh?" Derek mentally catalogued the emotions that flickered across her expressive face before that calm mask came back down. *Disgust, fear, shame, fear again, and desperation. What an interesting mix.*

"Yes." Chrys took a deep breath. "Unfortunately, Tony was a product of my father's...indiscretion at a younger age. His mother was a Mage, but when he was younger, he didn't show any signs of following her path, so my father took him in and tried to raise him to be a good Christian man. When he hit puberty, we discovered that his mother had passed on her... predilections for the darker side of Magic. My father tried to get help for Tony, but the sickness was too deep."

"So he threw him out?" Derek's pen flew across the page, taking the entire story down.

"He told him that he either had to change his ways, or get out." Chrys shrugged. "When we got up the next morning, his room had been cleaned out. I haven't seen him since."

"No letters? No nothing?" Derek pressed, and she shook her head.

"He didn't even show up for my father's funeral," she said. "And he had to have known about it."

She gestured to the picture on her desk, and Derek suddenly realized why the name Keats had sounded so familiar.

Well, well, well.

The Right Reverend Henry Keats had been one of the most vocal anti-Mage protesters in the last twenty years, picketing various laboratories and colleges, calling for the outright banning of magic and those who practiced "the black arts," as he called them. He'd created a new church within the Christian Right, raising Healers to near-mythical status while reviling Mages and psychics. *So his legitimate daughter turns out to be a holy Healer, and his bastard son is a Mage. And he threw him out. Shocking.* Keats had been killed when the lab he'd been picketing had blown up in a freak industrial accident, throwing his church into spasms. The funeral had sparked off violence for nearly two months, with Mages all over the country being attacked. The rumors were that the God Squad was somehow affiliated with the now-defunct Church of Divine Healing, but no one had been able to prove that. *And it's not like there aren't plenty of churches out there who want to see Mages dead,* Derek told himself, cutting that line of thought off and bringing himself back to the matter at hand.

"Do you know if he has any other family left?" he asked her. "Anyone on his mother's side?"

Chrys shook her head. "I don't even know her name. My father never mentioned her to either of us. I think he preferred to forget she existed." She gave him a piercing look. "What's he done?"

Derek tried another tact. "What about Alex Masterson? Have you or anyone else here been contacted by him?"

Her eyes widened. "Tony's involved with Gene-Tech?"

"We don't know yet," Derek said. "But there is evidence to suggest your brother may have been at the facility at some point in the last few months. And as this hospital does cater to injured Mages..."

"No one here has heard anything from Alex Masterson," Chrys said firmly. "We're law-abiding citizens here. If he had called us, we would have reported it to the authorities."

Derek stood up and put the notebook away. "If he does happen to contact you, Chrys, we'd appreciate knowing. And I'd like you to keep this visit confidential, of course." Chrys frowned but nodded her agreement.

"I don't suppose there's any chance he died there, is there?" she asked him, and the wistful note in her voice startled him. "My brother, I mean."

"As far as I'm aware, no body has been found, if that's what you're asking." Derek again cursed the ill-timed press conference.

"That's too bad," she said, opening the door for him. "I'd really like to think that's he's burning in Hell right now." Then she sighed. "But that's terribly unchristian of me. I'm sorry, Derek, that just slipped out."

Yes, and it tells me reams about your relationship, Derek thought, but simply said, "Not at all. Thank you very much for seeing me."

"I'll walk you out."

"That's really not necessary."

"I insist," she said, as if she knew he'd try and look around on his own. "This place can be a bit of a maze."

As they walked back down the hall, Derek looked again at the people they passed. Most were clad in what he considered standard doctor/nurse attire — scrubs and lab jackets. Some, like Chrys, wore slacks and a blouse or dress shirt. The patients, and there were very, very few of them, were easy to recognize: many had missing limbs, or horrific burns, and most were unconscious, being moved on stretchers through the halls. *The side to Magic that most people don't see*, he thought, numbed. *The darker side.*

"Chrys!"

They both stopped as a young man and a young woman, both

149 | Valerie Griswold-Ford

dressed in lab coats, came hurrying down after them. The young man's face was flushed with some emotion; Derek couldn't tell what, but he wasn't about to miss whatever was about to happen.

"Chrys, the grant came through! We got the new grant! Now we can..." His voice trailed off as he realized she wasn't alone. "I'm sorry, I didn't realize you were with a patient."

"Actually, I was just walking Mr. Reynolds out," Chrys said. She turned back to Derek. "Mr. Reynolds, these are a few of my associates. Dr. Thomas Smith and Diana Hillerman."

Derek shook hands politely with them, and then said to Chrys, "I can find my way out from here. It sounds as if they have some good news for you. I'll contact you if I need anything else."

"The door is right there," Chrys said, pointing down the hall; he inclined his head at all three of them and then walked quickly to the exit, his mind whirling.

Chrys Keats may not have heard from her half-brother in fifteen years, but one of her associates had some connection to Gene-Tech. The aftereffects of that odd Magical signature danced along his nerves, and Derek narrowed his eyes.

There was definitely more here than meets the eye.

———

Wonder what he wanted? Diana Hillerman watched the tall man walk down the hall, a little bemused by his reaction to her. She'd immediately shaken his hand, not the least bit put off by the brown silk gloves. Thom, on the other hand, had hesitated before shaking and had dropped his hand as soon as possible.

"What did he want?" Thom asked Chrys, who was still staring after the man.

She shook herself and then gave him a smile. "It was a referral."

Thom gave her a raised eyebrow and she shook her head slightly, which piqued Diana's curiosity even more. *Oh, this should be good.*

"You said we got the grant," Chrys said, interrupted Diana's thoughts. "Let's go talk about that."

Once they were safely in Chrys' office, Chrys told them the real reason Derek had come in. "So he's looking for Tony," she finished.

"I was hoping he was coming to tell me the bastard was dead. Although I must admit, when he said he wanted to ask me some questions, I was terrified that they'd finally tracked us down."

"We've been careful," Thom said, leaning back in his chair. "There's nothing to link you or any of us to the deaths recently."

"You know that, and I know that, but it's still a possibility," Chrys said, playing with a plain business card on her desk. "Or maybe I'm just paranoid. I don't like using Magic to cover our tracks."

"That's not our call," Thom reminded her. "The Patriarch decreed the use of the Blessed Amulets to keep the location of the compound safe. And it's the only way we can get back and forth to the labs without anyone following our trails."

Chrys nodded. "I know, I know. I just don't like it."

"Once we finish the experiments successfully, it won't matter anymore," Diana said, leaning forward and propping her elbows up on the edge of the desk. "We'll be able to take our cure to the regular hospitals, and at that point, the Patriarch can destroy the Amulets." She smiled at Chrys. "Don't worry. So why did he want to know about Tony?"

The worry returned to Chrys' eyes. "They found evidence that he was at the Gene-Tech facility before it exploded, and wanted to know if he'd contacted me."

"Really? Did they find his body?" Thom said.

"No. Just his magical signature, apparently." Chrys dropped the card. "I'm supposed to let Derek know if he or Alex Masterson try to contact me."

"Because you're right on Alex Masterson's hot list, huh?" Thom shook his head. "Stupid."

"No, because they found Tony's signature there," Chrys said, putting her fingers on her temples and rubbing. "And honestly, it's a good point. We're a major facility for wounded Mages — if he's hurt, or Masterson's hurt, it's a good bet they might approach someone here. And it's not as if he couldn't just look my name up on the website and find that I work here."

"True," Thom said. "But enough of that. We need to talk about this new grant."

"Agreed," Chrys said. "Who's it from?"

"Markalis Industries," Thom said, and Diana felt a thrill go down her spine. "They're very interested in what we're doing."

I'll bet, Diana thought. Markalis Industries had cornered the market in genetic screening before the government had started favoring the magical research firms, citing more accurate results from the magical labs. It had upset a lot of the traditional science-based firms. *Strange bedfellows. I'll bet they never thought they'd be working with a faith-based organization to eliminate their competition.*

Then again, it's all about business. Some places will deal with the Devil himself.

Diana's mind wandered back to the odd feeling she'd gotten off the Sensitive as he'd shaken her hand; an odd flash, almost like a warning. But a warning of what?

Bah, Chrys' paranoia is spreading like a plague. He's not looking for us. He's looking for her idiot brother. We're fine.

She just wished she could make herself believe that.

Chapter Eighteen

"Lies"

She'd taken Cerberus out again that morning under a sky spitting rain and hail like vicious insults. She pushed the great black horse hard, trying to beat the raging feelings of frustration at her lack of progress into the road beneath her. It didn't work, and she turned back in frustration. By the time she reached her mother's house, Nikki's roiling emotions had settled into an icy, implacable rage. The clouds above her echoed her mood, marching across the sky in sullen, unbroken ranks, but at least the rain had ended.

Nikki unlocked the front door and stalked up to the workroom, Shadows and other Spirits scattering in front of her like startled cats. There was still no sign of the gargoyle when she climbed up the iron staircase, but the fire continued to burn. Nikki threw herself into the armchair in front of the fireplace and brooded.

"You look like your father when you sit like that."

"How would you know?" Nikki snapped, completely unsurprised to hear her mother's voice come out of the gloom. She didn't get up. "We don't know who my father was."

"Of course I know who your father was," Teraisa said, her tone amused and coming from the far corner of the room, which was wreathed in Shadows. "His picture is in my files, if you'd bothered to look that far. He was a very handsome man."

"I'm sure Alex was very concerned about that. Wouldn't want ugly soldiers," Nikki said, biting off the words, then another thought struck her. "Did he use the same donor for all three of us?"

"No," Teraisa said, and Nikki finally looked up. As she'd expected, there was no one else in the room, just a gathering darkness in one corner. "Alex didn't have anything to say about who sired you."

"Who was he, then?" Nikki asked, curious despite her anger. "My father, I mean."

"A researcher, like me," Teraisa said, and a little wistful longing tainted her dark voice. "He was a fabulous cook."

"Too bad he didn't pass that gene on," Nikki muttered. "How well did you know him?"

"Well enough to sleep with him," Teraisa said. "Well enough to want to make a child with him."

"You mean…"

"Yes. I was pregnant before Alex started his little games. Both Caran and I were."

"Was she pregnant by Alex?"

"I assume so," Teraisa said. "Caran Masterson and I were hardly friends. If she was sleeping with someone else, her husband's research assistant would be the last one she told."

"Good lord, the man actually experimented on his own children?" Nikki shook his head. "And he was trying to convince me he'd changed."

"He might have," Teraisa said. "Believe it or not."

"Do you believe him?"

"I haven't spoken to him recently," Teraisa said. "But there's always a chance he's not lying. A small chance, but a chance, nonetheless."

"Wait a minute." Nikki sat up straight and turned towards the darkness. "That Dawn Lord told me that I was her and the Shadow Lord's child."

"You were the product of their Power, not their loins," Teraisa corrected her. "Shadow Lords and Dawn Lords cannot crossbreed. That's why Alex had to start with viable fetuses."

Nikki sank back down, her mind whirling. "What happened to my father?"

"The same thing that happens to everyone Alex doesn't have

an immediate use for." She could hear the shrug that came next. "He died."

"Of course he did." Nikki shook her head. "Why am I surprised?"

"People can change, Nikki."

"Only if given a reason to," Nikki said, glaring into the fire. "And no, before you ask, I don't think Alex is scared enough of dying right now to consider that a reason."

"You're not angry at Alex."

"Of course I am!" Her emotions flared again at the neutral statement and the silence that followed. "They lied to me, dammit!"

"You don't know that," Teraisa said. "The Council..."

"Fuck the Council. They had to know. There's too much that makes sense now." Nikki shook her head. "Justin knew. Rick knew. And they lied to me — telling me that no one died."

"Actually, they didn't," Teraisa said. "They told you the breeders were safe. Technically, if they're dead, they're very safe."

"Sophistry," Nikki snapped. "I killed over two hundred people."

"Over four hundred, actually," Teraisa corrected her. "And it was a very neat job too."

"Do you mind?" Nikki said, shuddering.

"You have to face what you are, Nikki." Teraisa's voice was unsympathetic. "We don't have time to deal with your sensitivities. So grow up."

"And become a monster like you?" Nikki retorted. "Maybe it's genetic."

"Maybe. And maybe we're both just a product of our environments." Teraisa's voice started to fade out. "I'm not staying around while you wallow in self-pity. This house is yours now — do what you will with it. Should you decide to act like an adult and take up your tasks, the tools you need are here."

Nikki felt her presence fade and continued to scowl at the fireplace. Deep within her, she knew the Shadow Mage was right. *What's done is done,* Cerberus' voice whispered within her mind, even though the big horse was outside. *You cannot rewrite the past. You can only move forward.*

What are you, a Zen master? Nikki shook her head. *There has to be some way to fix this.*

There is, the big horse replied. *But you have to let this go before you can see the way. And you'll have to decide how to deal with your compatriots. Soon.*

How soon? Nikki asked suspiciously.

In about five minutes.

"Are you sure about this?" Rick asked, peering through the spotty drizzle coating the outside of the BMW's windshield. "Do you really think she'll let us in? I wouldn't."

"We don't have any choice," Justin retorted, trying not to give voice to the guilt currently churning in his gut, guiding the car down the narrow road. "As soon as her parents got that call from the police about her Jeep, it put Nikki on everyone's radar. We've got to find her before someone higher up starts looking. Not to mention the fact that her parents deserve to know that she's okay."

And if you'd just told her what happened back at Gene-Tech, treated her like an adult instead of a child that needed to be coddled and protected, this situation probably wouldn't have happened at all, his conscience whispered and Justin winced involuntarily.

It wasn't my decision, he told the voice. *I tried...*

Not hard enough, it told him, with a sharp, gleeful edge that cut him apart guilty thought by guilty thought. *You could have told her anyways...*

But the Council...

When have you ever cared what the Council thought? the voice sneered, taking another swipe at his bloody soul. *You're the rebel, remember? The Mage who stands up to the Council, because you think they're wrong, they're hidebound and old, out of touch...*

"Take this turn," Rick said, unknowingly interrupting the voice's ranting, and Justin flipped on his signal, grateful for the distraction. For a moment. Then he saw what was waiting for them. Rick had told him how creepy the house had been the last time, but that hadn't prepared him for this.

"Sweet bloody hell," he said, stunned. He let the car coast to the bottom of the hill, staring in fascinated horror at what towered over them.

"Yeah. I'd say you were right, she's here," Rick said, and when Justin turned to gape at him, he shrugged, trying to hide how the sight had affected him. "What did you expect the house of Death to look like? Especially a Death that's pissed as hell at the moment."

Justin turned back, shaken to his core. *Goddess above and below, what kind of monster have we created?*

He'd been deeper into the Shadow Lands than most mortal Mages, had lived there for a good portion of his childhood, and had always considered the Shadows friendly. Now he saw them as others had: a force to be feared.

The house was barricaded behind a line of tall Shadows that stood shackled in place, held together with chains of brilliant Earth energy that snaked up from the ground and twined around each one, linking it to its fellows. Lightning flashed along the lengths of chain, white-hot and full of rage. The only opening was the driveway, and the Shadows that guarded its edges were particularly tall and solid. The rain fell on them, not through them, and Justin could literally see the demarcation between the Shadow Lands and the Earth. What he couldn't see was any rippling of the Balance — no matter what else she was, Nikki was being very careful to not draw any outside notice to her. And it wasn't as if her mother's house was in a heavily-trafficked area.

Thank the gods for small miracles.

"We could try and contact her from here," Rick said, holding up his cell phone. Justin shook his head.

"She left her phone in the car. Unless you know the number to Hell — somehow I doubt this place has its number registered with the local 411."

He started the car moving again, inching it slowly through the narrow gate. The Shadows turned and watched them go, and Justin realized that the green energy wasn't chains.

It was roots and branches. Every Shadow pulsed with Earth and Light energy, a perfect trinity of Balanced Power.

Holy shit, what has she become?

Once inside the gate, the car coughed twice and died, rolling softly to the curb. Justin didn't even bother to try and restart it, knowing it wouldn't work, but it gave him hope that maybe she wanted them there to talk.

Then Power flared around them; he and Rick both cried out as the car shifted around them, fingers of dark magic lifting up them up, spinning the vehicle around and then slamming it down hard on its wheels, so hard that their heads bounced off the headrests. Once the stars cleared, Justin stared in shock at the open road in front of them: the trees bending slightly in the wind, drizzle weeping down the evergreen needles to the pavement beneath them.

"Where..." Rick said, looking around. "How..."

"Shit." After a few moments, Justin reached out and opened the glove compartment. He pulled his GPS unit out, tapped it to wake it up, then typed in the address they'd been heading to again. After a moment, it pulled up a list of directions, and Rick shook his head. Justin, on the other hand, was fascinated all over again, his guilt pushed aside by his need to know exactly how she'd done what she'd just done.

Somehow, Nikki had managed to teleport their entire car 25 miles north of her house, without so much as a blip in the Balance. A glance at his phone confirmed that: had any of the Lords noticed the transfer, they'd have called him immediately. Especially Morgan, who was particularly worried about Nikki. That told Justin a little, but not enough to satisfy his curiosity.

One, that the house and the small valley it sat in was so deeply shielded that most Mages would never know it existed. Most Lords wouldn't, either, until they came upon the hollow in the Shadow Lands.

Two, that she definitely didn't want to talk to them.

"Now what?" Rick asked.

"Now we go back," Justin said, and Rick gave him a puzzled look when he laughed. "And we try again. She has to get tired at some point."

He spent the drive back trying to figure out how she'd managed to drop them so precisely: the car had been placed on a secondary road that would have taken them back to the Inn, a pointed hint as to where she'd prefer they go.

Not that I've ever been good at taking hints.

This time, he didn't give her time to touch the car; as soon as he crested the ridge, Justin gunned the BMW's motor, shooting forward into the front yard. It didn't matter. As they moved forward, those dark fingers came up again, grabbing the car and throwing it away; the landing was even harder than the first time, and the BMW didn't stop moving forward; trees loomed before them and Justin stomped on the brakes.

The car's tires squealed as the rear swung around on the slick roads, and he scowled, passing a bit of Earth energy down through the frame to stop the skid. The BMW finally stopped inches from a thick trunk.

"Nice driving," Rick said, drawing in a deep breath and releasing his death grip on the door handle. Justin grunted, slumping in his seat as the adrenaline fled. "Are you sure you want to try again?"

"Yes," Justin said, after considering it. "If the others don't find her soon, they'll have no choice but to tell Shanna she's gone rogue. And then..."

"Nikki will die." It wasn't a question. Rick shook his head. "Then let's go. Maybe the third time is a charm."

"Maybe." Justin doubted it, but he put the car in gear and backed it out onto the road again. "Get our directions."

She'd thrown them farther this time, nearly halfway to the Inn. Justin wondered where they'd end up the next time.

The Shadows were even darker as they crested the hill above Nikki's house, and the animosity in the air turned the drizzle into full-fledged rain. Justin set his jaw and drove down, not speeding but not running away either.

You have to let us in sometime, he thought, and felt the barest flicker of an acknowledgement of the statement. *We'll keep coming back until you do.*

He parked the car and turned it off, then turned to Rick. "Ready?"

"Why not?" Rick shrugged. "It's as good a day as any to die."

I hope not.

The door was shut when they came up to it, but not locked; he turned the knob and it opened silently. He exchanged a look with Rick, who shrugged again, and then stepped into the foyer.

"Wow. She's done some redecorating," Rick said when he joined him. Justin was too busy taking in the scene to respond.

Mage lights burned in sconces set into the walls, steady pools of pale green light that spread a cool glow over the room. A large vase stood on the hall table, full of roses; their perfume tickled his nose. What took his breath away was the Spirits that wandered throughout, though: amorphous shapes of amber, sable and jade that prowled the hallway and preened on the staircases, each projecting the same message to the two Mages that stood watching them.

You are not welcome here. You do not belong here. You should leave.

"Why are they here?" Rick whispered.

"Because I'm here," a new voice said, and Justin's eyes widened as Nikki came down the stairs.

He remembered the vibrant creature of Magic and Power that had killed Robin Rothman: Nikki had worn her newfound gifts like a faery's clothe-of-gold cloak, a shiny new toy. At that point, she'd only touched the surface of what she truly was. The creature before him was the next iteration in her transformation: the peacock trading in her brilliant plumage for a predator's claws and teeth.

Two dark curls twined down around her face, black against the pale lavender of her tee-shirt, escaping from the bun on the top of her head. Her slim jeans were tucked into the tops of her faded black boots, and a simple silver bracelet encircled her right wrist. Her face was pale, flawless and calm. Justin tensed, wondering what was going to come next.

"You don't take hints, do you, Justin?" she continued, walking slowly down the stairs, her left hand caressing the dark wood of the banister. "I thought I'd made it very clear that I'd like to be left alone."

"We need to talk, Nikki," he said, and she raised one dark eyebrow, black amusement flaring in her eyes.

"Oh, now we need to talk, do we?" she purred, and he heard the mayhem implicit in her voice. "And just what would you like to talk about?"

Justin opened his mouth to answer, and in that moment, Nikki blurred. Suddenly, his feet left the ground as the creature he'd thought he'd known lifted him up by the throat, the amusement burned away by rage.

"How about we talk about this?" she said, her tone still even, calm and conversational. Rick reached out to stop her; Nikki spared him a single, contemptuous glance and waved one hand, summoning several Spirits to pull him away. Then she turned back to Justin, who had both hands wrapped around her wrist. "Did you know that it takes thirteen pounds of pressure to crush the human trachea? It's the same amount of pressure it takes to crush a soda can. My adopted father taught me a lovely trick for crushing soda cans when I was younger. You just apply a steady grip and they crumple." She slowly tightened her fingers and spots started to dance in front of Justin's eyes. "Early training, you might say."

"Stop it, Nikki! You'll kill him!" Justin could hear Rick struggling, in a far-off way, as if the sounds were coming through a vast sea. Only Nikki's voice was clear, broken glass grinding into his ears, the monster he'd help create coming back to enact her revenge.

"That's what I do," she said silkily, her slender fingers digging into his neck. Blackness edged his vision and Justin knew that if she didn't stop soon, she would kill him.

He just didn't know if she cared.

Then, suddenly, she dropped him; he hit the ground hard and crumpled into a heap, drawing shallow breaths into his burning lungs, feeling the cool marble of the floor beneath him. Nikki knelt down next to him and Justin squeezed his eyes shut, unable to look at her. Her breath was sweet across his face as she whispered into his ear, "I have a message for your precious Council. Tell them to leave me alone. I don't take orders from them anymore. And if you do come back here, I will kill you. And I won't make it an easy death. You don't deserve it."

She stood up and as she walked away, he heard her say, "Now get out of my house."

Rick's hands were suddenly on his arms; Justin forced his eyes open as his friend helped him to his feet. "This...was not...one of my better ideas," Justin said hoarsely, and Nikki paused on the stairs.

"That's the first true thing you've said to me in a long time," she said, and he winced.

"What about your parents, Nikki?" Rick said, and she looked over at him.

"Tell them I'm dead," she said flatly. "It's as close to the truth as they need to be."

"They deserve better than that," Rick said, and Justin closed his eyes again briefly, silently willing his friend to drop the subject. "I can't lie to them."

"Why not?" Nikki said. "You had no problem lying to me." And she went back up the stairs.

"Nikki!"

"Drop it," Justin said, and when Rick turned back to him, he shook his head. "Let's just go." When the other Mage opened his mouth to object, Justin said, "We've found out what we needed to find. She's okay. That's all we needed to know."

"She's not okay!" Rick snapped, his face reddening. "She nearly killed you!"

"We lied to her," Justin reminded him, as the Spirits began to crowd around him. "Now come on. Let's go."

Rick drew in a deep breath, then looked around him and settled for a single nod. The two walked out the front door, which opened for them, and then climbed back into the BMW and drove off.

Justin took a quick look in his rearview mirror as he pulled onto the main road again; the impressions of Nikki's fingers were bruising already, a damning handprint to remind him of exactly what she'd become.

What you helped her become, he corrected himself, and his conscience crowed in victory. *Remember that the next time you decide to withhold information from someone "to spare them."*

"Do you have her parents' phone number?" he asked Rick.

"Yes."

"Good. Call them and let them know she's fine — she's working on a project for the Council and needs to stay incommunicado for a while." Justin hoped he wouldn't regret this lie as much as he regretted the last one. "She'll call them when she can."

"So we're going to lie again." The disapproval in Rick's voice made him grind his teeth in frustration.

"What would you have me do?" he snapped. "Tell them their daughter is now a murderous bitch, bent on destroying everything she can get her hands on, and doesn't give a damn about who she hurts? What good would that do?"

Rick didn't answer. Justin just hoped this time it would work out better.

Hell, it can't get any worse, can it?

Then another thought struck him, turning his blood cold as it occurred to him. "Give me the phone," he said, holding out his hand.

"What?" Rick asked, handing over the phone.

Justin didn't answer immediately, his fingers pressing keys rapidly. He knew she wouldn't answer, but he had to get a message out.

Beep! "Hi, you've reached the cell phone of Shanna Greystone." His sister's voice flowed through the phone. "I'm not available right now, but I am checking messages. Please leave one after the beep."

"Hey sis, I know you're busy, but we're teetering on the edge of a situation, and I need some advice." Justin ignored Rick's strangled gasp and continued, "Don't know how much you've heard, but your Horseman has found out what she did on Halloween and she's none too happy about it. Barricaded herself in her mother's house, and it's becoming a gathering ground for Greater Spirits of all stripes. Call me."

"You...you...you traitor!" Rick said, grabbing the phone back from Justin. "You just signed her death warrant!"

"I know what I'm doing," Justin replied. "Shanna's not going to let the Council bamboozle her into anything. You should know her better than that."

"I hope you're right." Rick settled back into the passenger seat, disapproval apparent in every stiff muscle.

I hope I am too.

Chapter Nineteen

"A Plethora of Choices"

Nikki watched the car drive off from the workroom, her face calm but her insides churning. It had taken every single ounce of her self-control not to crush both Justin and Rick into the ground; the rage that had flared to life when she'd seen the two of them in her front hall. Even after she'd sent them away twice.

"Arrogant bastards," she muttered, stomping back down the stairs and out the door, looking for Cerberus. "I can't believe they actually had the gall to come here and try to talk to me." Spirits scattered in front of her, darting out of the way like diaphanous butterflies. Their emotions passed like silk over her, and Nikki was surprised, as she'd been since they started coming around, how much they reacted to her: their anger was thin but vicious, directed at the car that had just left.

"If only my so-called friends were that worried about me," she muttered. "Sad that I feel more at home with Spirits than with other humans."

They do care about you, the great black horse said, coming over and pushing his soft nose into her chest. *They worry about you.*

"Do they?" she mused, rubbing his forehead. "Or are they worried about covering their own asses?"

I sensed concern, Cerberus said. *I cannot speak for them, but they did seem worried about you, not the Council.*

"If they'd been that worried, they shouldn't have lied to me."

"I agree."

Nikki spun around at the strange male voice, her left hand coming up in a defensive position. He stood by her front door, his hands raised and open in a classic non-threatening position and she frowned. "Do I know you?"

"Not yet," he responded. "But I know all about you, Nikki Jeffries. Or should I call you Nikki Donnelly?"

"You can just call me Nikki," she said warily, not letting down her guard. "And what can I call you?"

"A friend."

"I don't have many friends at the moment," Nikki said, and he smiled, a predator's smile full of promises.

"You have more than you know," he said. "There are those of us who believe as you do, that the Council is running roughshod over innocent Mages..."

"I'm not innocent," Nikki snapped. "And don't presume to think you know what I believe. Who are you?"

"My name is Lucifer."

Her eyebrows rose at that. "The Lucifer?"

"I know of no other."

"Well, well, well. Rarified company." She shifted, leaning back against Cerberus' side but not letting her guard down, and crossed her arms over her chest. "What, I kill enough people and I warrant a personal visit from the Devil himself? I must say, though, that you look disappointingly normal. Where are the horns and tail?"

"I need to work on my PR," Lucifer said, flashing her a smile. "Honestly, mortals believe the most amusing things." He gestured at himself. "What would I do with a tail?"

Several things rose in her mind, but Nikki opted for ignoring the question and asking another one of her own. "So what are you doing here? Recruiting? I'm not interested."

"So soon?" His disappointment was calculated and his eyes twinkled. "And you haven't even heard my offer yet."

"I've had enough of taking orders from immortals," she retorted. "I'm a free agent now, and that's the way I prefer it."

"Do you really think the Council will let you walk away from everything, especially alone?" Lucifer walked over to her, shaking his head; she tensed, but all he did was trail a finger down her cheek. "You're far too valuable an asset, Horseman. If you refuse them, they'll have no choice but to appeal to the StarChild for your termination."

"I've been living under that threat for some time now," she replied, turning her head away from his touch. "And why should I believe that you'd stand up to the StarChild for me? What do you have that the others don't?"

"Conviction," Lucifer said, and Nikki felt something stir within her. "A conviction you share."

"We share nothing."

"Your blood betrays you, Horseman." He laughed, a low sound that rippled Power around her, summoning a response that came from the depths of her soul. "There is a darkness that you haven't even begun to delve into. A darkness I understand. Let me show you what you can truly attain, what Powers await your call."

Nikki looked into his darkly silver eyes, and saw the edges of what he was offering. A family, acceptance... *The same thing I have here,* she realized, as Spirits gathered around her, and the images crumbled.

"Come with me, Nikki," he urged, holding out his hand. "Let us teach you."

Shadows suddenly surrounded and shoved him back, Shadows laced with green and amber. "No, thank you," Nikki said, her voice even, a thin-bladed sword. "I'm done with teachers. Now get the hell off my land, before I throw you out."

For a brief moment, something flared in his eyes, a flash of emotion that sped away too quickly for her to recognize, then he smiled again. "In time, I think, you will reconsider. When you do, I shall be waiting." Then he turned and walked across her lawn. With each step he took, Lucifer's form faded, finally wisping away, a final thread of smoke that drifted away on a nonexistent breeze.

"How very bizarre," Nikki said, watching the spot where the Elemental Lord had vanished. "Do you really think he was the Devil?"

Does it matter? Cerberus turned his head and looked at her. *Really?*

"No, I guess not." She ran her hand down the black's sleek side, turning over the events in her mind. "What kind of Lord was he?"

I don't know.

Cerberus hung his head as she looked at him, startled. "You don't know?"

He felt...odd, the horse said, pawing the damp ground with one hoof. *Normally, I can tell, but not with him.*

"Could he be one of those that Edgar had been talking about? A Chaos Lord?"

No!

Nikki backed up, a bit surprised at his vehemence. "Why not? Wouldn't that make sense why you couldn't tell?"

Chaos Magic cannot exist on this side of the Walls, Cerberus told her, shaking his head. The violence of the gesture had her backing up a bit more. *The presence of Chaos Magic here would mean it was too late for us. That we had failed. He cannot be a Chaos Lord.*

"Okay, okay, he's not a Chaos Lord," Nikki said, holding her hands up. "But he's not anything like I've seen before. Agreed?"

Agreed. Cerberus stamped down hard. *Nothing like you've seen.*

And yet, we resonated, she thought later, back in her workroom, curled up by the fire. *Why? What were you playing with, Alex, that you fucked me up so badly? Why would the Devil himself want me?*

Besides the fact that I'm a mass murderer without even trying, that is.

The Spirits up here were all Shadows, and they draped themselves along the walls, radiating a cool acceptance of her that felt warm against her battered soul. Here, at least, there was no judgment. Only inclusion.

Nikki rode out the next morning, still puzzling over the offer Lucifer had made to her and the strange echo of kinship she'd felt with him. For a moment, they'd vibrated together on an otherworldly frequency that had been touched by the Earth, and then she'd pulled back. Or had he? What did it mean?

Cerberus had taken her into the Shadow Lands, as usual on their rides, but instead of pounding down the endless black top roads that led nowhere, he'd struck off through a dying wood, his steps muffled by the corpses of leaves on the ground. Behind her, four dark knights on sable horses trailed her, an honor guard of Shadow Spirits. She'd been faintly amused when she'd noticed them, then she'd felt their desire to protect her, and been touched. No minor Spirits these, but Greater Spirits, nearly Lords in their own rights, and fully capable of choosing whom they wished to follow.

I've got my own army, Nikki realized, with a thrill that was almost pleasure. *I could take on anyone. Alex. Lucifer. Justin.*

You could, Cerberus said. *But should you?*

Not yet, she replied. *But soon, I think that yes, I will begin moving. Soon, it will be time to remind the other players that I'm not simply a pawn in their game.*

The black horse beneath her didn't respond, but she felt the keen interest and approval of the Spirits at her back.

"Any idea who your first victim might be?"

Nikki turned as another rider joined them, her pale horse moving easily up through the Shadow guards to pace beside Cerberus. Magic shimmered in her wake, and even with exhaustion etching dreams on her pale face, Nikki sensed an underlying strength of steel and determination. The question had been asked in an innocuous way, but there was a glint in the other girl's grey eyes that made Nikki wary.

"I'm still working on that," she said, pulling Cerberus to a stop and turning him to face the newcomer, who also stopped. Her honor guard formed a circle around them; the other girl gave her a weary half-smile and sat back.

Nikki recognized the smile, if not the face it rode on, and a small icy finger touched her heart. *Oh shit...*

"I'd say it's an important decision," the other girl said, and Nikki knew, without a shadow of a doubt, that her companion was aware of the fear starting to bubble in her mind. "The first decision of any good general, in fact."

"I have other things I need to do before I start declaring war on anyone," Nikki said, running her tongue over her lips. The other girl raised one red-gold eyebrow.

"Oh? Like what?" Her horse danced a bit, rustling the dead leaves, and she laid a calming hand on his white mane. He tossed his head and gave a plaintive whinny that shivered in Nikki's ears.

"I have to find the other children," Nikki said, wondering why the girl was asking at all. "And the girl Alex still has." She wet her lips again and then blurted out, "You're Shanna. The StarChild." *And I tried to kill your brother the other day. And still want to kill him, in fact.*

"I am." Two simple words, said without pretense, and Nikki's blood congealed.

"Justin called you." Almost an accusation, but not quite.

"Among others." Shanna gave another half-grin. "You've had a busy few days, Nikki."

"Curse of my life," Nikki replied, raising her chin and deciding to go for broke. "Are you going to kill me?"

"Do you want me to?" Shanna asked, her grey eyes still and cool as icicles, her voice neutral.

Nikki swallowed, well aware that her continued existence rested on her next words, and looked down. "I'd rather you didn't," she said, drawing Cerberus' reins first into one hand, then the other. "I've still got a few things to do."

"Like leading an army?"

"Like fixing this mess I'm in the middle of, through no fault of my own," Nikki said, looking up again, and Shanna's mouth twitched. "Alone, if necessary."

The Shadow Lands breathed around them, a faint whisper of a breeze stirring the skeleton trees, murmuring promises of hope long dead and buried. Nikki felt trapped in a timeless instant, Damocles' sword swinging ever closer, hanging by the thread of the StarChild's will as Shanna looked at her, hoping she wasn't found wanting...

"Ride with me," Shanna said abruptly, breaking the mood by kicking her horse forward. Cerberus danced out of the pale rider's way and then swung around, falling in step with the other horse. They rode in silence, Nikki wondering if this was just a brief reprieve or if she'd signed her own death warrant.

Does it matter? she thought. *We all die at some point, right? And at least I'll see it coming...*

It sounded hollow even to herself, and not even the Shadows

following them offered her any comfort.

Shanna led her along what might have once been a path but had long since deteriorated into the ghost of a game trail, overspread with tree roots and moss. No dead leaves here; the trees had long since given up their raiment, standing mutely bare, emaciated arms raised to an uncaring sky. A solemn, wistful sadness permeated the scene, and Nikki was not surprised to see ornate wrought iron gates rising out of the distance.

It was a small, personal graveyard: only two monuments lay encircled in a jeweled garden, with brilliant flowers a bed of color for the two who slept underneath. A small wooden bench, covered in elaborate carvings, sat looking at the simple stones. Shanna dismounted and opened the gate, then turned and motioned Nikki to follow her.

Well, at least she won't have to go far to dispose of my body, Nikki thought numbly, sliding off Cerberus, then stumbling as he head butted her gently.

Do you really think she'd've gone through all this trouble just to kill you? he asked, and she swore there was a twinkle in his dark eyes. *Trust me. It's not your day to die.*

"Join me, Horseman?" It wasn't a request, and Nikki walked slowly through the gate that Shanna held open, hoping Cerberus was right.

As soon as she stepped onto the gravel that traced a narrow path through the blooms, though, Nikki felt a familiar touch wreath up through her and stiffened. "What is going on?" she asked, turning and looking at Shanna. "Why is he here?"

"He's not, yet," Shanna said, motioning towards the bench. "He's having problems getting away from Rick this morning. Besides, who do you think tends this garden? My talents lie in the same direction yours do: I'm very good at explosions. Not so good at making things grow." She sat down and crossed one jean-clad leg over the other, then patted the seat next to her. "He'll be here soon, don't worry. I need to speak to him too, and my time's a little limited."

"Great." Nikki rolled her eyes. "Just who I wanted to see this morning."

Shanna chuckled. "Not a good parting, huh?"

"You could say that." Nikki shook her head, trying not to let her anger show again, and Shanna laughed.

"Justin always did have a way with women," she said. "And he wonders why he can't keep a girlfriend."

Rather than reply, Nikki looked over at the monuments. The stones were deceptively simple: polished to a high gloss, with a spray of oak leaves and orange blossoms at the top. Incised into the granite were two names: Jared and Natasha Greystone. The birth dates were four years apart, but the date of death was the same.

"What happened?" Nikki asked, reaching out to touch the oak leaves. "And why are they all the way out here?"

There was no answer, and Nikki turned to see Shanna staring at the graves, her eyes bright with unshed tears. "They were killed together," she said finally, her fingers twining around her knee, her knuckles white against the faded denim. "Ambushed and killed."

"Why?" Nikki asked, and Shanna smiled, a sad, self-mocking smile that chilled her.

"Because they'd hidden Justin and I, and we were the real targets." She shrugged. "Well, I was. It's the only way most people know to get rid of the StarChild — kill her when she's still too young to access most of her power." Shanna shook her head. "My parents taught me a lot that day."

"You watched them die."

Shanna shrugged again. "I had to know who I needed to take down."

"How old were you?" Nikki asked.

"Nine," Shanna said. "And by the time I was twelve, my parents' killers were dead."

Nikki looked over at her, but before she could respond, the gate clanked open and Justin stepped through. "Couldn't you find a better place to meet?" he grumbled, pointedly ignoring Nikki and looking at his sister.

"Nice bruises," Shanna said, and Nikki flushed. So did Justin, and then he scowled.

"Did we have to meet here?" he repeated, and rolled his eyes when Shanna nodded.

"I needed a place I knew we wouldn't be overheard," she said, and Nikki raised her eyebrows. "I need to talk to both of you."

Justin muttered something under his breath, then heaved a sigh. "What's going on, Shanna? Why the hell did you seal off Vermont? And why did you start the Cleansing? How the hell are you going to finish it?"

"I'm not," Shanna said, and both Nikki and Justin stared at her. "You are, Nikki."

"Me?" Nikki blinked. "I'm a Horseman, not the StarChild."

"You're a little different than most Horseman, though," Shanna said, and Nikki couldn't dispute that. "You've got enough of both worlds swirling through you that I think you can do it, and the Balance agrees."

"You spoke to the Balance about me?" Nikki didn't know whether to be flattered or scared.

"She speaks to the Balance about everything," Justin said, but the rancor was gone, and he was staring keenly at his sister. "Why me?"

"Who else can I trust?" she said. "If I can't trust you, little brother, we're all doomed." Shanna shook her head. "I can't be here to fix things — I've got my own problems. And no, you can't help me," she added, and he scowled at her again. "I need you here to help Nikki. I can't train her — we don't have time. You have to help her adjust."

"Oh, because I've done such a great job so far," he retorted, pointing to his neck. "How do you know she's not going to try and kill me again?"

"You shouldn't have lied to me," Nikki said, and he scowled at her.

"I didn't have any choice," he snapped, finally turning and looking at her. "I had my orders."

"And you're so good at following them," she snapped back. "Just look at yesterday."

"The difference is that I don't take orders from you," Justin said, clenching his fists at his side. "And if you'd let me explain..."

"I'm tired of hearing you 'explain' things!" Nikki shouted. "I'm tired of everyone 'explaining' things when they don't explain anything! I'm tired of following orders that I don't understand why! And I'm tired of being treated like a child!"

"Maybe if you stopped acting like one, we'd stop treating you like one!" Justin said, and her eyes narrowed.

"Good Christ, is this all you two do?" Shanna said, and the mild tone of her voice cut across the tension, bringing their attention back to her. "No wonder things are so screwed up here. Just jump into bed and get it over with, because I have things for you to do, and you're going to have to work together."

Nikki gaped at Shanna, hearing the words but not believing them. *Justin? He doesn't think of me like that! And I don't...no!*

Then why are you so angry with him now? That little voice was back, smug and sharp. *Why aren't you trying to kill Rick, for example?*

Because Rick was following Justin's lead, Nikki insisted. *I am not interested in Justin like that!*

Justin was sputtering, and he was bright red, but Shanna plowed on, ignoring both their reactions. "Now listen, both of you. This is the most important thing. You can't tell *anyone*. Not Rick. Not Vashti. Not Alenya." When they blinked at her, she shook her head. "I mean it. There's a traitor in our midst, and until I find out who it is, I don't trust anyone not in this graveyard. Got it?"

Nikki nodded, and Justin sighed.

"I'll take that as a yes," Shanna said. "Now pay attention. Here's what I need you to do."

CHAPTER TWENTY

"THANKSGIVING"

"Cleo? You around, babe?"

"In the studio!" she hollered back, and grinned as she heard heavy footsteps come down the hall. Cleo stepped back from the canvas she was still working on and dropped her brush into a can of solvent as one of her best clients and former lovers came into the airy room.

"Hey, beautiful, how's it going?" Dan Sanders leaned down from his six-foot-four height to kiss her cheek and then froze as he caught sight of the canvas in front of her.

"Like it?" Cleo said. Considering it was her fourth attempt at combining both her dream and his wishes, she was pretty pleased with his reaction.

"Oh babe…" His voice trailed off as he slowly straightened up, the kiss forgotten. Dan walked around her and over to the canvas, shaking his head. "You are a fucking genius."

"I try." Cleo picked up a rag and wiped dark orange paint off her hands as she watched him inspect the half-finished painting, his hands clasped behind his back. He'd learned the hard way to not touch a work in progress: it had taken him nearly two days to get the paint out of his hair and ruined a shirt when she'd gone after him in a rage for getting fingerprints on a canvas. "So you like it?"

"It's fucking perfect," Dan said, turning to her and running his hands through his hair, which was currently short and blue. His vocabulary always went to hell when his emotions took over. "She's just...damn, Cleo, she's fucking perfect."

"Yeah." Cleo grinned, unable to hide her pride. "She is, isn't she."

The girl from her dreams glowered out at them, transformed from a chained prisoner to a Dark Queen perched on her throne. Her long, dark hair flowed over her shoulders and down her back, hugging her like a second skin of Shadows and magic. Pale skin accentuated the angularity of her beautiful face; her dark blue eyes pierced the shadowy hollows of her eye sockets, furthering the image of the skull that Cleo had noticed as she was painting. Death stared haughtily out at them, daring her viewers not to notice her as her court clustered around her feet in various positions of adoring, terrified servitude. Behind her stood three men, all looking at her possessively, but the Dark Queen ignored them.

She belonged to no one.

"She's perfect," Dan repeated, turning back to the painting. "I just have one question. Well, two, actually."

Oh shit, what did I fuck up? Cleo raised one blonde eyebrow and watched him walk around the edges of the huge canvas.

"What happened to the background?" he said finally. "And why did you paint Alex Masterson into the picture?"

"What do you mean?" she asked, frowning.

He waved one hand at the painting as he turned back to her. "I mean, I love the sugar maples, don't get me wrong — but what kind of weird creative process led you to put the Queen into a New England evening? Have you even been to New England in the fall?"

"Blame the news," she said, wrinkling her nose. "Anytime I turn on the TV, I see New Hampshire and Vermont, and they're covered with those gorgeous red and gold trees."

"Is that why you painted Masterson in there?" he asked. "Because if that's not him, it's his twin. And I thought you didn't watch the news."

"Aren't you the one who was telling me I needed to stay current?" Cleo said, trying to distract him. "Besides, how can you miss the news these days? It's even infecting my dreams."

"Dreaming again?" Dan said, giving her a sharp look, and she shrugged.

"It makes for good paintings."

Dan chuckled. "Hey, I'm not criticizing! I love it — I'm just wondering what the thought process was."

"Um, honestly, I don't know." *Actually, you wouldn't believe me. And that's just fine.* "It just seemed like New England was a more creepy scene than the bayou setting we'd discussed before."

"I agree." Dan went back to admiring the painting, to her relief, and didn't press her anymore. "Shit, I might have to redecorate the club to match this. She's...God, Cleo, you're a fucking genius, did I mention that?"

"Once or twice."

He went on in that vein for a bit and she tuned him out, looking instead closer at the picture. His questions had stung something out of her memory, teasing out pieces of half-buried dreams and images that flashed in front of her for a moment and then vanished again.

What was I doing? she mused, looking closer at the background of the painting, consciously ignoring the Dark Queen in the center. *I didn't even look anything up for this, did I?*

Brilliant red-gold leaves reached up from skeletal branches to a dark sky, illuminated by a full moon that glowered down on the Court, half-hidden by filmy clouds that partially veiled its scowl. The ground under the Queen's feet was littered with more leaves, desiccated corpses fallen from the trees, gathering in sorrowing piles at the foot of half-crumbling gravestones. The Dark Queen's throne was rough-hewn granite, and the trees formed a desolate gazebo over her head. Cleo noticed writing on some of the stones — words she must have written but couldn't make out now. She made a mental note to look at them more closely once Dan left.

Dan walked around the huge canvas again, distracting her. "You know what would be awesome?" he said.

"A matching picture?" she said, and his eyes widened. "Well, not quite matching. More like a companion piece."

"A King?"

"No. I told you, a companion piece."

"Show me!" Dan was nearly drooling.

She grinned at him, and turned to the other side of the room, where a similarly-sized canvas sat shrouded in a drop cloth. Dan gave a strangled gasp as Cleo yanked the covering off.

"You are a fucking genius. How did you know?"

This time, Cleo had gone pale and pastel in her palette, a sharp contrast to the Dark Queen's jewel tones: greys, blues and purples colored the canvas, pale Spirits that danced against the background of a lush New England autumn. And once again, a Queen dominated the scene.

This Queen was as pale as her compatriot was dark, however. From the top of her ash-blonde head where a crown of diamonds sparkled, to the tips of her fingers as they cupped a clear goblet of blood-red wine, she was icy and haughty, ruling her table with scorn and snow. Her robes bled pastel rainbows onto the leaf-littered ground, the remains of shattered hopes and dreams a misty gazebo surrounding her. Pale eyes, their color a multi-hued mystery, stared off into the distance, ignoring the three men who hovered protectively behind her throne. Frustration etched itself onto her beautiful face and her thin lips were twisted into a mockery of a smile.

Cleo looked over at Dan. "So, what do you think?" she asked, as he continued to gape at the two paintings, switching his gaze from one to the other and back again.

"I want them both." He pulled out his checkbook. "I have to have them both."

Of course you do. That's why I painted them. "Well, she's ready to go now," Cleo said, indicating the Pale Queen. *And I'll be glad to see her go. I'm not sure why, but I will be.* "I have to finish the Dark Queen, though."

"How long?"

"Two more days," Cleo said, and grinned again as he moaned. "Dude, you don't open for another week! You'll be fine — I'll bring her over myself."

"But I need her now..." Dan teased, and she laughed. "How much for the two?"

Cleo named her opening price, knowing he'd counter, which he did; after about fifteen minutes of haggling, he sighed the check and handed it to her.

"Let me pack this one up for you," Cleo said, picking the Pale Queen up from her easel. Normally, it only took her about five minutes to pack a painting up, even a large one, but as her fingers touched the canvas, Cleo felt a frisson of odd Power snake along her skin and the shudder it raised slowed her down. *Yes, I will be very happy to see you gone, my lady,* she thought, fastening the corner of the butcher's paper down with masking tape. *You are far too...I don't know, but I don't like you.*

"I don't suppose you have any plans to do any other paintings with these two?" Dan said wistfully as she brought the wrapped painting back over to him.

Her mind flashed briefly to the small series of drawings she'd started with the Dark Queen, but forced herself to shake her head no. Those were private drawings. "Not right now, but if I do, you'll be the first to know. I've got a few ideas for the Gothic Princess series, though."

"Great!" Dan accepted the painting eagerly and leaned over to kiss her cheek again. "Thanks, babe. Like I said..."

"I know, I'm a fucking genius." Cleo gave him a little shove towards the door. "Now go and let me continue to be a genius so I can finish your other picture."

Once he was gone, Cleo turned back to the Dark Queen, frowning a bit. "Now, my lady, I think you have some secrets to give up."

She went and pulled a small magnifying glass out of the desk in the corner, then knelt down next to the painting to inspect the gravestones more closely.

Twenty minutes later, she sat up again, even more confused. What she was sure she'd intended to be random lines (although she couldn't be sure, as she didn't even remember painting gravestones) had actually formed words: "Edgewood, 1690. Beloved daughter."

"Who's trying to tell me what?" Cleo asked the Dark Queen, who didn't answer. "Who are you, and what did you do in a former life that you're trying to convey through my painting? And what does Alex Masterson have to do with it?"

Again, no answer. The words "Beloved daughter" nagged at her — she reached out, touched the canvas, and again, that strange frisson of Power trembled along her skin, crawling up her arm, causing her to step backwards in shock. "What the hell was that?"

The Dark Queen's smile became a smirk; Cleo backpedaled fast, thinking that she'd been working far too hard lately. *I need a drink. Badly. This is insane.* Then one of the dark Spirits turned, the hood she hadn't known she'd painted falling down...Cleo stared at herself, pale hair glowing with Power and one hand reaching out of the picture towards her, and she did the only thing that she could.

She turned and ran out of the room.

On her way through her living room, Cleo grabbed her wallet and keys, then ran out the front door. There was a corner liquor store only a few blocks down the road that stocked her favorite rum; with luck, she could crawl inside a large bottle of Premium Stock and not come out for a couple of days.

New Orleans was crouched in typical November weather: rainy and warm. Well, the rain had actually gone through earlier in the day. Now it was just misty, with water droplets hanging in midair, a tepid curtain that she pushed through. Her sneakers were soon wet, and she squelched along, trapped in her thoughts, trying to block out what she'd just seen.

She stepped out onto the street, still lost in her mind, not noticing her surroundings. A horn honked, shocking her out of her thoughts. The driver of a large blue SUV shouted something unintelligible at her as she jumped hastily back up onto the curb; the rude gesture he flipped up at her at the same time, combined with the shock she'd just had, snapped the last thread of her control.

Black-edged dark gold Power rose from her, a hunger building. She momentarily lost sight of the world around her as the void opened insistently within her. A roaring filled her ears, cut only by a frantic scream of panic. Then the headache surged, and she came back to herself in a storm of pain.

Goddess above, what is happening to me?

Chaos surrounded her; rain poured from what had been an

overcast sky, mixing the sound of rushing water with the shrieks from the driver. The smell of greenery filled the air, fresh, full of life and yet tinged with decay at the same time. Vines erupted from all around her, covered with large leaves and slithering across the road. Cleo stood in the midst of the downpour looking at the car in front of her, the roof of which was now ripped in half by the vines that snaked around and about it. It was hard to tell through the rain, but the vines looked like they had large purple blossoms on it. The driver was tangled in the greenery, screaming for help.

I should help him, she thought numbly. *I should get up and help him.* Behind the pain of the headache, she could still faintly feel the hunger, an alien sensation of longing and desire. *You can't just leave him there, Cleo. Get moving.*

It was so much easier to say than to actually do. She looked down, and realized that the vines hadn't just sprouted from the ground at her feet; they were tangled around her, spreading out from her body, connecting her with the car and the driver. Cleo reached out with one hand, and the vines responded, wrapping around her and feeding the hunger within her. She closed her eyes and shuddered as warm, wet Power rushed into her, filling the hole within her that she didn't know existed. The screaming of the driver faded behind the pleasure washing over her as the rain poured down around her.

Gradually, she came back to herself. The rain had stopped some moments before, and the sun was streaming down, burning away the clouds. The vines wrapped around her were already dying, falling away from her as she stepped off the curb again. The driver had stopped screaming; Cleo walked dazedly over to his SUV, breathing in the fragrance of rain-cleaned air and morning glories.

The reason he had stopped screaming became immediately clear when she peeked into the driver's side window. Morning glory vines were wrapped around him, pinning him in place and choking the life out of him. Green tendrils clung to every bit of exposed skin, tunneling into the flesh as if it were soil. His mouth was still open, gaping in a final death scream: the vine that had burrowed into the back of his neck had snaked up his throat like a second tongue, and a beautiful bloom, easily the size of Cleo's fist, blossomed off the tip. That wasn't the worst part, though. His entire corpse was skeletal, as if he'd died of starvation, and she realized where the Power filling her had come from.

Sweet hell, I ate him.

Cleo stood looking at the scene for a moment, then fell to her knees and vomited.

Once she'd emptied her stomach, she looked up again. The vines had already started to die, the petals falling from the brilliant blooms like purple tears to puddle in the driver's lap as the greenery shriveled. More disturbing, to Cleo, was the decay of the victim; as she watched, bits of his skin began to fall from his bones, drifting like forgotten snowflakes onto the remains of the flowers, his clothing falling into a pile on the car seat. She pushed herself away from the car and began to run, not caring where she ended up.

It was still early in the day, but this was New Orleans and Cleo had no problems finding a bar. Ducking inside, she welcomed the cool darkness; quiet jazz floated on the air, wrapping around her and soothing the hunger that she still felt curled inside her somehow. She claimed a table and even managed a watery smile at her waitress.

"You look ragged, honey," the waitress said. "Can I get you something?"

Is sanity on the menu? Cleo ordered a kamikaze shot instead, and requested a menu. The waitress simply nodded; after all, it was New Orleans. Kamikazes for lunch was hardly shocking.

There was no TV in the bar, for which Cleo was grateful. She had no doubts that the accident scene would be discovered soon; New Orleans was a major magical city, after all, and the Power surge hadn't been exactly subtle. *At least it was odd enough that no one should be able to connect it with me. I hope...*

Bloody hell, does my aura look like that now?

She spent a frantic few moments with her eyes closed, minutely inspecting herself for any hint of the black-tinged gold, but her aura was back to normal: sunny gold, with shots of white and silver. A normal Light Mage. Then something stirred, deep within her, and she recognized the hunger she'd felt before. *What is happening to me? I haven't used that Power yet!*

Power, the hunger whispered. *We need more Power. It belongs to us. . .*

No! Cleo shivered. *No!*

"You ready to order, honey?"

Cleo jumped again as the waitress' voice intruded on her private battle, distracting her. The hunger reached out, but she squashed it back down. "Oh, yeah. Sorry. Um, can I have the mushroom Swiss burger with fries? And the buffalo wings."

"Any thing else?" The waitress hadn't batted an eyelash.

"Another kamikaze." The image of the driver, entangled in vines, rose in her mind and Cleo shuddered. "A large one."

"Bad night, honey?" Cleo nodded and the woman gave her a sad smile. "I understand. I'll make it a triple."

"Thanks."

It took two of the triples to blunt the edge of the headache. The hunger took longer; Cleo downed not only the burger and fries and wings, but an order of potato skins and a slice of dark chocolate cheesecake. By then, it was nearly four in the afternoon, and people were starting to come in. Cleo was savoring the third kamikaze, enjoying the haze of alcohol that surrounded her, when her phone rang.

Now what? She peered at the display, trying to place the numbers. After a moment, she recognized them, and a chill snaked down through the pleasant numbness of the alcohol. *Shit.*

"You gonna answer that, honey?" The waitress had come up again. "Or do you want me to call you a cab?"

"No cab, but I'll take another drink," Cleo said, shooting down the remainder of the kamikaze and then flipping open the phone, "Hi, Nina."

"Where are you?" The worry hiding behind her high priestess' crisp voice added another layer of guilt to Cleo's soul. "What happened earlier?"

"I'm..." Cleo looked up as her waitress came back. "Where the hell am I?"

The waitress gave her a smile. "Angel Bar and Grill, "she said, and Cleo repeated that.

"Don't move," Nina ordered. "I'll come and get you."

"Not a problem," Cleo said, hung up the phone and picking up her new drink. "Not a problem at all."

Chapter Twenty-One

"Acceleration"

And this is where a decision needs to be made.

Tony stood in the kitchen, sharpening a paring knife with a whetstone, his thoughts whirling. It had been one week since he had consolidated Alex, Andreas and the breeder in one place, the last place anyone would think to look for them. The former owners were now comfortably ensconced in deep graves in the back yard, and deep shields shrouded the house. Part of the reason he'd chosen it — only part, but lucky now for him. Especially with what he knew was coming.

Andreas had been sunk in a deep depression when he'd gone back to collect him; sitting in the garden, drinking heavily. Someone or something had gotten to him, although he denied it when Tony had asked him, but it was obvious that Andreas had lost his nerve. The Shadow Lord had continued his binge in the new house, snapping at Tony when he'd tried to get the location of the spells from him.

"What does it matter where they are?" Andreas had shouted, throwing a bottle against the wall in rage the last time he'd brought it up. "We don't have a Dawn Lord anymore! Or a Light Mage! So it doesn't matter!"

"We'll find one," Tony had said, and Andreas had laughed.

"Oh, sure we will. What are you going to do, Tony, take out a want ad? 'Wanted: one Dawn Lord or Light Mage, willing to commit acts of treason against the Balance and the Council of Nine. Must be able to follow directions and be willing to live on the run for the rest of your short life. 'Oh, stupendous idea."

"Shut up," Tony had snapped, balling his fists in an effort to keep from beating the supercilious smirk off Andreas' face. "Dammit, we can still do this! What is wrong with you? A week ago, you were still ready to go! What about that child? We have to finish this!"

Andreas had leaned back in his chair, the lamp above his head throwing odd shadows across the ruins of his face. "You're so young," he'd sighed, and Tony had grit his teeth at the patronizing tone in his voice." You honestly still think you can pull this off." The Shadow Lord had leaned forward, the alcoholic haze sliding from him like water off a window pane. "Forget it, Tony. Even if you had the spells you needed, the Council will have made sure by now that no one will assist us. Who were you planning on asking to find you a Light Mage, the Sintetizzi?"

Tony shuddered at the thought, just as he had when Andreas had said it. Not even he, a Blood Mage, would deal willingly with the Sintetizzi.

But we have to do something, he thought, pulling the blade steadily across the stone. *We can't just stop. I've invested too much in this now to stop.*

I just need to find a copy of those spells.

An idea had formed in his head, a suggestion, cooed in his mother's voice, that perhaps the Shadow Lord wasn't as necessary as he'd thought. *I can cast the Shadow side, and so all we need is a Light Mage. And once I get my hands on one, I'll make sure she's willing to help us.*

Very willing.

He set the knife and whetstone aside and went to Alex's room, refining the idea as he went. The room stank of infection and sweat; Tony checked the bandage on Alex's abdomen and shook his head. "I don't know why you're even still here, you stubborn bastard," he said, and Alex tossed his head as if he could hear him, even though Alex had been unconscious for the past week." But I can't let you die. Especially not now." He put a new bandage on the weeping belly wound and then went into the adjourning bathroom to wash his hands.

Once his hands were clean, Tony went back to Alex's bedside and put his fingers to either side of the comatose Mage's head. "Tell me it's here," he muttered, pushing his way into Alex's head." Tell me I wasn't wrong."

Andreas had to have had a back-up plan. The Shadow Lord always had a back-up plan. There was no way he would have kept the only copies of the spells in his house, would he? No, there had to be a set hidden elsewhere, and he would have told Alex where they were.

Of course, with Alex still unconscious, Tony had to hope the knowledge was in the part of his mind not hidden behind his inner shields. He wasn't desperate enough yet to try knocking those aside. *Please, don't let me have to do that. Alex had to know where Andreas hid the other spells.*

His mother's voice whispered in his mind again. *You could look in Andreas' mind. Bind him, bleed him and he will be yours...*

Not yet, Tony said, a shiver running down his spine. *I'm not ready yet.* Even in his inebriated state, the Shadow Lord could take him apart if he felt like it. Not until he was completely ready was Tony going to challenge him.

But it has to be here. Alex had to know where the other spells were.

After fifteen minutes of looking, though, Tony was starting to despair. Andreas apparently hadn't trusted his son enough to tell him the secondary location that Tony knew existed somewhere. Which meant only the Shadow Lord knew where they were, and to find them. *Now what?*

You need to make a choice, Tonio. His mother's voice was cool. *You need at least two Shadow Mages to cast some of those spells. You need a Light Mage, at the very least.*

I know, he replied, blowing out a huge breath. *I know.*

Then what are you going to do?

That I don't know. Tony ran his fingers through his hair, trying to look at all the options. Andreas had made his position clear earlier — he wouldn't help them finish the experiment, and Tony wouldn't put it past him to try and sabotage everything by killing the breeder, which is why there was a Blood Lock on her door currently. *But if I kill him, we're down to just the two of us. And it still doesn't help me Heal Alex. Or find a Light Mage. Or find where Andreas hid the spells.*

Unless you bleed him... The malice in his mother's voice matched the evil in his smile. *How many Blood Spirits could you summon with Lord blood, my Tonio? And they could look for the spells and Heal Alex, while you got a Light Mage.*

Oh yes. I could get Greater Spirits with Lord blood. I'm sorry, Andreas, but I don't have time to baby you. Once you're dead, I can find those spells.

Tony decided to wait until nightfall — by then, Andreas would have once again sunk into an alcohol-soaked sleep and that would make everything easier. It also gave him time to run out to the small grocery store around the corner and get a few more necessities.

He stopped in his room and pulled a small, flat box out from under his bed. Opening it, he smiled as he pulled the limp piece of flesh from its bed of fabric, the edges sticky against his fingertips. Tony pulled out a small pocket knife and cut a slit in the flesh of his arm, squeezing the cut to pull some blood out. He smeared the blood on the edges of the mask, then carefully fit the face over his own. It had taken him nearly two hours to pull the face off the skull of the owner of the house, but it was worth it to give him a new identity. A few whispered words, and the face meshed with his own. Tony blinked, then smiled and went out to get his car.

By the time twilight fell, Tony was in the kitchen, wearing his own face again, sharpening a long boning knife and humming a lilting Cajun tune under his breath. A deep red wine glittered slightly in the goblet he'd set out on the counter, and a large, thick steak was marinating in more red wine, garlic, onion and olive oil next to it.

It was so much easier to do Blood Magic on a full stomach, after all.

The oiled grill pan next to him hissed as it came to temperature; he set the whetstone aside and picked the steak up from the marinade. The sound it made as it hit the scorching hot cast iron grill made him smile.

Andreas was upstairs in his bedroom, passed out in a pool of vomit and Scotch. Tony had found him that way when he'd come home from the store, and had taken the opportunity to cast bindings on him. Now, the only thing left to do was bleed him out and then start the experiment again.

And then, I can send out a Spirit, get a Light Mage and we're good to go.

The steak, rare and flavorful, was perfectly accompanied by the wine and creamy mashed potatoes that he'd picked up earlier. Tony took his time with the meal, allowing the components to mingle in his system, giving him even more Power to draw on. Then he took the boning knife and two large gallon buckets and went up to Andreas' bedroom, humming again.

The Shadow Lord lay on his back, his arms folded over his chest in a parody of the death about to come. Tony wrinkled his nose and whispered several words under his breath, and the vomit disappeared. *Now we can begin.*

In a way, it was too bad that Alex had lost the Shadow Cube, he decided, as he used the boning knife to trace a delicate pattern in the air just above Andreas' body, setting the sacrificial spell in place. *One Shadow Lord will give me access to just about any Spirit I want in the World Between the Walls,* he thought smugly. *Two? I could have summoned Madness herself with the blood of two Shadow Lords.*

Yes, Tonio, you probably could, but what would you have done with her when she showed up?

He laughed at that. *Rule the world, Mother. I'd've ruled the world.*

The Shadow Cube could have also been used to keep Andreas handy, which would have given him an inexhaustible supply of Lord blood, but Alex had dropped it in the fight with that bitch from the first experiment, and Tony hadn't dared try to go back and find it. *Stupid chit. You should have joined us when he offered you the chance.*

At least that blonde bitch Richards didn't get a chance to fuck it up even more.

The knife blade continued its precise work, weaving a complex netting of Power around the prone body on the bed, and Tony clamped his thoughts down, bringing himself back to the task at hand.

Plot later, Tonio, came his mother's voice again. *For now, concentrate on the magic.*

He finished tracing the final symbols on Andreas' forehead and then laid the knife on the nightstand. Four candles stood waiting in the four corners of the room: tall white pillars of clean beeswax. They had once been sanctified to his father's ministry, and Tony had been saving them for just such an occasion.

I hope you can see this as you rot in hell, you sanctimonious old bastard, he thought, smirking. The fact that the house he'd chosen had once belonged to the Right Reverend Henry Keats made the ritual feel that much better to the Blood Mage, since he knew how furious his father would be to see it. He pointed to the first candle. "*Nord.*" The candle flared to life, a black flame dancing on the tip of the wick.

He lit the others in order, creating a dark Circle that nestled against the inside of the shields already laid on the house, keeping the Council from realizing what he was doing. Once the Circle was up, Tony began another set of shield spells, around himself this time. That would allow him to move into both the breeder's room and Alex's room to finish the second set of spells once he had the blood to do it. The web was nearly complete; all he needed to do was start.

He picked up the knife from the nightstand and pricked one of his fingers. Blood welled out, jewel-bright in the flickering candlelight and the duskiness of the room. Tony murmured under his breath, Cajun-accented French rolling off his tongue, Power darkening the room even further as he retraced the final rune directly onto Andreas' forehead in blood. The entire web blazed as he connected the last line, and the Shadow Lord convulsed as Power snapped into place around him.

"*Flux, de sang et de mettre votre Power avec vous,*" he said, inserting the tip of the knife into Andreas' right arm. Red blood, sheened with silver, welled up from the cut; Tony placed the arm in the first gallon bucket at his feet and let the spell do its work while he collected the rest of what he'd need.

Nine large silver vials, nearly the size of his forearm, stood on the dresser, waiting his touch. These special vessels would hold the remains of Andreas' blood, once Tony filled the gallon buckets. Tony smiled, a predatory grin that spoke volumes about what his plans were for those vials. *Once Alex is awake again, we'll talk about a Light Mage. And then we'll start.*

Blood Spirits make things so much easier.

"And for once, I have all the blood I'll need," he said after about twenty minutes, swapping out one bucket for the other. Andreas' skin had started to sink in on itself as Power and blood flowed from him; his heart still beat, and would until Tony ended the draining spell.

While he waited for the second bucket to fill, Tony made sure the liquidity spells on both buckets and the vials were effective, and checked to make sure all his other instruments were available. Including the black leather case that now sat on the nightstand.

Tony let one hand linger on the top of the case as he looked down into the bucket, trying to judge how much longer it would take to bleed Andreas dry, and he shuddered in pleasure as Power stroked along his fingertips. These tools had been passed down through his mother's family for generations, and the inherent magic in them proved it.

"Soon," he promised the case, and he smiled as it wiggled in anticipation. "I will let you out very soon."

The second bucket was as full as he needed it to be: Tony whispered, *"Arretez,"* and the silvery-crimson bloodstream slowed. He laid Andreas' arm beside him, and then pointed at the vials in order. *"Débit jusqu'à sec, remplissez jusqu'au complet."* Then he turned back to the prone Shadow Lord. "Sorry to leave you like this, old man," he said, picking up the first bucket and retrieving the case. "But I need to finish up some other things while I bottle the rest of you up. Don't go anywhere — I'll be back in a bit."

His first stop was Alex's room. He wanted to make sure he had enough blood to bind the Shadow Mage securely enough that Tony could control him without Alex realizing he was being controlled. And that meant a Greater Blood Spirit.

Four candles burned in Alex's room as well, and the heady scent of dragon's blood and sandalwood concealed the tang of infection in the air. Tony set down the bucket near the doorway, with the case on top of it, and then walked over to the bed. The bandage he had placed on Alex's wound a few short hours ago was already soaked and green; he peeled it off and dropped it in the trash. *If all goes well, this will be the last bandage you'll need, Alex,* he thought, winding fresh linen across the hole in Alex's belly. Once the bandage was secure, Tony carefully turned Alex over and drew the blanket down, exposing the Shadow Mage's bare back like a canvas, ready to be painted.

Then he retrieved the bucket and the case and brought them back to Alex's bedside. The bucket went on a chair next to the bed, with the case once again perched on top of it. Tony pulled out four lengths of cotton rope that he'd found in the garage and tied Alex to the bedposts, just in case he woke before Tony was done.

Once Alex was secure, Tony climbed up on the bed and straddled him, giving him access to Alex's entire back. He leaned over and opened up the case, exposing the black lacquered brushes to the air.

Seven brushes lay ensconced in threadbare velvet, their handles well-worn by the many fingers that had gripped them over the centuries. The luxurious bristles were the only parts that didn't look aged; Tony smiled as he remembered the little girl who had given her hair to rebuild the brushes the last time. She'd screamed so very long...

Reminisce later, Tonio, his mother's voice said. *Concentrate on your magic.*

He nodded, picking up one of the fine-tipped brushes and dipping it into the blood. Normally, spells to summon a Greater Blood Spirit took several mortal sacrifices on successive nights, but the Shadow Lord's blood should make that unnecessary.

He hoped.

Tony drew the spell on Alex's broad back, each line glistening with Power as the brush skimmed over his pale skin. The web was huge and intricate: within it lay not only Tony's True Name, but the name of the Blood Spirit he wished to summon and the length of the contract. That part he paused over, considering, before he painted the generous terms in.

"You'll just have to die before me, Alex," Tony said, sitting back on his heels and admiring his work. "I'd hate to think I'd allowed a major Blood Spirit to remain incarnate without a Master to control it."

Alex, of course, said nothing. Tony smiled and laid the brush back into the case before sliding off the bed, carefully avoiding touching the newly-drawn spell. "Now for the final part."

He'd left the long blade in Andreas' room, but there were scissors on the nightstand for cutting more bandages and they were plenty sharp enough. Tony reopened the slice on his thumb and allowed three drops of blood to fall on the sigil in the center of Alex's back.

One.

Two.

Three, and Alex's entire back burst into flames.

Tony picked up the black case, closed it and stepped back, pleased, as the Blood Spirit he'd summoned rose from the depths of the magefire raging on Alex's back. "You have nerve, Mage," the Spirit hissed. "I am not used to being summoned."

No, I'll bet you're not. "I humbly beg your forgiveness," he said, giving the Spirit a short, respectful bow. "But I have an offer I think you will be interested in."

Something sparked in the Spirit's empty eye sockets: for some reason, this one had chosen to appear as a giant snake skeleton, bones covered with a transparent skin of scales that danced in the flames. "Tell me."

"I offer incarnation in a Shadow Mage," Tony replied.

"In return for?"

"In return for keeping him alive, no matter what, until I release the spell," Tony replied. "In addition, he must have no idea you're there."

"That requires a lot of Power and skill," the Spirit said, coiling above Alex thoughtfully. "What do else do you offer? I see no sacrifice."

"The sacrifice is the blood of a Shadow Lord," Tony said,

indicating the bucket on the chair. "Drink your fill."

A tendril of flame and smoke snaked down into the bucket, and the Spirit purred in appreciation. "The sacrifice is acceptable. But the vessel is flawed."

"He's wounded," Tony corrected. "Part of your... housekeeping... will have to be to Heal him."

"That will require more blood," the Spirit countered.

"The bucket is not yet empty."

"The blood in the bucket is cooling," the Spirit said. "I must have hot blood to seal this contract."

Tony sighed. *Par for the course.* "Will this do, or would you like me to open a vein?"

He squeezed the cut on his thumb again, and the Spirit reach for him. "This will be acceptable," it said, and bright pain lanced through Tony as fire and smoke dipped into his skin. "For now."

The sheer pull of the Blood Spirit forced Tony to his knees; his vision blurred as Power and blood flowed from him, until his sense of self-preservation kicked in and he broke the connection. The first thing that swam into his line of sight was the cross on the wall — a relic that he vaguely remembered from the last time he was in the house, and he swore.

Will you never leave me, you bastard?

"You have spirit, Mage," the Spirit said, breaking into Tony's thoughts. He watched it sink into Alex's back, pulling the spell web in with it. "This will be a profitable relationship for both of us."

I hope so, Tony thought, struggling back to his feet and pushing thoughts of his late, unlamented father from his mind. *One down, and one to go.*

The bucket still contained a bit of Andreas' blood; Tony dropped it back in the Shadow Lord's room and checked the vials, which were steadily filling, before picking up the second bucket and going down the hall to what had once been his half-sister's room.

How many times did I walk down this hall, under the shadow of his religion, and know I was in the wrong place? The thoughts slowed his steps; Tony paused, the bucket bumping his leg, silvery blood splashing on the dark carpet. *How many times did I dream of doing this to him?*

You had your revenge, my Tonio, his mother's voice whispered, and he smiled. *Don't dwell on the past here. Remember the hole in his chest from the shrapnel, and the look on his face as he saw you in the smoke. Killed by his own pride.*

Yes. Tony smiled, and entered the third bedroom on the hall with renewed purpose.

He had stuck the breeder in his half-sister's old bedroom simply because he hadn't had anywhere else to put her. The people he'd killed had apparently used it for their granddaughter: it was still done up as if a little girl lived there, with princesses and lace and other fripperies that he had no name for. Tony had pulled the bed out from the wall when he'd set the candles up: now, with the black flames dancing in the twilight, the room looked like a gateway into a cotton candy hell.

The girl was curled on her side, one hand cradling her cheek and the other resting protectively against her belly with its precious contents. In the pink and white bedroom, huddled under the pale checked bedspread, she looked about fourteen years old.

Tony yanked the coverlet off and froze as her eyes opened just for a moment, brilliant green in the darkness. *What the hell? She's under a sleep spell! What is she doing awake?* He held his breath as her eyes slowly closed again; her breathing hadn't changed at all, so it must have been an automatic response to the temperature change, nothing more. *She's fine, the spell's fine, everything's fine,* he thought, relief making him a bit giddy. *Let's get this done before anything else weird happens.*

She didn't respond as he pulled her shirt over her head and placed her on her stomach, now just barely starting to round with her pregnancy. Tony used the skin to skin contact to check on the child: it had a steady heartbeat and a strange, half-aware quiescence around it that he attributed to the spells they'd already cast upon it.

Who would have thought we'd really succeed? Tony mused privately, tying her up as he'd tied Alex. *Especially since the Sintetizzi have been trying to do essentially the same thing for god knows how long. Maybe if they hadn't killed the first Elemental Lords to come across them...ah well, their loss.*

The breeder and the bed were both small enough that Tony could draw the web on her back without having to straddle her. His strokes were firm and steady, the artistry of the spell not lost on him. Then the requisite three drops of blood, and the flames erupted again.

This Blood Spirit didn't bargain as much as its brother had; no doubt it had been watching from the World Between the Walls and knew what to expect. It drank its fill of Andreas' blood, took from Tony as well, then started to sink into the breeder's back, winding its tendrils into her mind...

And Tony blinked suddenly, wondering what had just happened. The girl still lay on her stomach, the web slowly fading into her skin, just like it should. The candles guttered, throwing odd shadows on the bedroom walls; he glanced at one and blinked again. It was nearly burnt out.

"What happened?" he asked, disturbed. "Where did the time go?"

No one answered.

Cassandra's Prelude

"Council Thoughts"

She walks through the break in the trees and is hit by it: the hard-edged sensation of anger and discontent, laced with fear. They are eight now, where once they were nine, and the knowledge that they are not immortal is as unsettling now as it was twenty-three years ago. They are Lords, Elemental Spirits — and they are afraid.

Cassandra takes her chair, trying not to look at Andreas' empty seat across the pool from her, and looks instead at her fellow councilors. Her robes are white, pale as the moonlight that floods her beloved Shadow Lands: her companions dress in sunlight gold and holly crimson, Dawn and Earth Lords representing their Spheres. She catches Vashti's eye in passing; the Earth Lord gives her a single nod, but nothing more.

There had been no reason given for this meeting, only a terse summons, but Cassandra can guess. Everyone felt Andreas die. *Stupid man,* she thinks, but not bitterly. Theirs had been a typical Lord relationship: long enough to result in a child, not long enough to form an attachment. Leave love to mortals. If only her daughter had learned that lesson.

"There had better be a point to this."

She turns, as they all do, as a new voice cuts across the conversations. Her granddaughter, for all that the girl that has appeared in the chair at the head of the circle is barely twenty-seven and mortal-born. Shannara Greystone, called Shanna: the StarChild.

Her grey eyes are heavily shadowed, rimmed black with exhaustion, and her cheekbones stick out, making her lovely face almost skeletal. Her long, red-gold hair flows over her shoulders, its richness only accentuating the fatigue in her face. Cassandra wonders idly what is sapping her strength, but now is not the time to ask.

A Dawn Lord stands, his dark eyes hooded with old grief. "So kind of you to join us," he says, and the sarcasm in his voice is at odds with the respectful bow he gives her.

"Get to the point, Xavier," Shanna says to him shortly. "I'm busy."

"Too busy to listen to the advice of your Council?" he replies, and she frowns at him. The rest of the Council holds their breath; Shanna has a short temper, something they've learned all too well, and Cassandra hopes that Xavier has something more on his mind than simply chastising the StarChild for her absence.

"If my Council has advice I need, I will listen," Shanna says evenly after a long moment, narrowing her eyes. "What advice are you offering?"

"You need to come home, StarChild," he says, and gestures to the pool in the middle of the Circle. The still water goes colorless, then black, and then fills with images. One of Andreas, his body lying limply on the ground, flesh sunken in. One of Kymara, Xavier's youngest sister, her throat torn out and her life's blood turning her gold hair dark as it pooled around her. And one of the Gene-Tech Magical Facility, one wing demolished, sinking into the ground. "Your Councilors are being killed, one by one. The Horsemen ride, and..."

"One Horseman rides," Shanna interrupts him, frowning. "By my orders. Do you think she killed Andreas? I can tell you she didn't."

"She should not even be here!" he snaps, and rumbles of agreement rise from some of the councilors. *Interesting*, Cassandra thinks, and makes notes of those who agree with him. This bears watching. The Council has been divided before, but never on an issue of this magnitude.

"And how do you know that?" Shanna snaps back. Xavier starts to reply, but she cuts him off." Listen to me, Xavier, and listen very closely. I'm very busy in Vermont. Nikki Jeffries has my full confidence. And if I catch anyone interfering with the task I've set to her... you'll wish Andreas had succeeded." She looks around at the full Council, and most of them shrink from the steel in her eyes. "Anyone else have any questions?"

No answer, and she looks back at Xavier. "Did you have anything else to tell us? Or can I go back to cleaning up the mess I'm dealing with?"

"That depends," he says, anger tightening his voice. "Would you like to know what Kymara and Andreas were actually doing?"

The Council clearing goes quiet, and Cassandra can see her fellow Councilors drawing in a shocked breath. She wonders what Xavier is going to pull out now. "Enlighten me," Shanna says, and he gives her another bow, this one slightly mocking.

More images appear in the pool: documents and scrolls, scattered on a dark wood table that Cassandra recognizes from Andreas' house. Chanting fills the air, and she hears more gasps as the other members of the Council recognize the spell.

"Did you never wonder how they ended up with a Horseman?" Xavier asks, and she knows that his question is meant for his fellow Councilors, not just for Shanna. "Because my sister and Andreas were playing with these." And he points at the pool, which now shows a single image: an open chest, lined with blue velvet, with seven ancient scrolls resting inside.

Every Councilor knows what these scrolls are. The spells inscribed on the vellum sheets in dark walnut ink carry the last remnants of the Old Knowledge that survived the Elemental Wars: the Summoning Spells.

"And your point?" Shanna's voice is almost bored. Not surprising, as Justin knew about the Summoning Spells, and Cassandra cannot imagine that he hasn't told his older sister yet. "They fucked around with the Spells. They got a Horseman."

"One Horseman, as you pointed out." Xavier's smile is nasty." One quarter of the whole. How can she be Balanced?"

"Congratulations, Xavier, you can count." Shanna's voice drips with sarcasm. "When you learn long division, let me know. The

Horseman is Balanced. I'm not going to kill her. I'm not even going to rein her in. I'm going to let her continue to do her job." She turns to Cassandra. "Is everything else under control?"

"For the moment," Cassandra replies, and Shanna nods, then turns a withering look on her Council.

"I'm going back to deal with a nasty little place called Edgewood," she says, and they all shrink back as that cursed name drops like a stone into the sudden silence. "Unless you all want to help, don't call me back again unless it's something important." And she vanishes.

Cassandra watches Xavier pace angrily in front of his chair, his face thunderous, and wonders where he got his information. Is he the Dawn Lord Andreas was working with this time? Or would that be too easy? She sits back and ponders, watching the other Councilors talk.

"Why will she not address these issues?" Xavier demands finally, flinging himself into his chair.

"Perhaps because she's dealing with Edgewood," Vashti tells him sharply. "Honestly, Xavier, how can you expect her to do anything else? You know what evil lurks there!"

"I know what evil *lurked* there," Xavier corrects her. "The Council dealt with the Edgewoods two hundred years ago!"

"That's bullshit, and you know it," Vashti says. "We sealed it. It has obviously come unsealed. Why are you pushing this so hard?"

Xavier's eyes narrow as he stares at the Earth Lord. "Because I have lost a sister to this insanity," he says softly, malice dripping from his voice. "I have watched the Walls crumble, and I have seen Madness' mists invading my lands." The rest of the Council is silent, watching the interchange. "I will not lose anything more to the Chaos witch. The StarChild must understand that the Walls must not be allowed to fall!"

"She knows that, Xavier!" Cassandra says. "Are you as blind as Kymara was? Can you not see that everything is interconnected? The Web grows, and we are all bound within it. Madness' plans are ripening, and if you do not believe that the StarChild is taking steps to counter her, then you are a larger idiot than I thought." She looks at the faces of the Council and tries to suppress the anger she feels. "We are the Council of 9. We exist to support the StarChild. I suggest the rest of you remember that."

As she stalks from the Council Circle, Vashti falls in beside her. "Stirring speech," the Earth Lord says neutrally.

"We're surrounded by idiots," Cassandra says, and feels the rumbling of Vashti's laughter. "No wonder Shanna doesn't want to let us know what she's doing in Vermont."

"I have news," Vashti says, lowering her voice.

"Has she gone for him?" Cassandra asks, and the Earth Lord nods. "Good. Where is he now?"

Chapter Twenty-two

"Complications"

"So, tell me about Nikki Jeffries."

Nikki laughed." There's not really much to tell," she said, running her finger on the top of her wine glass. She and Justin were sitting in the living room after Thanksgiving dinner; he was on the couch, and she was curled up in one of the large recliners near the fireplace, which was full of scented wood and burning merrily. The lights were dimmed, so the fire provided most of the illumination, throwing her into shadow.

"I don't know anything, though," Justin said, hoping to draw her out a little. "I mean, I know you're a photographer. And a damn good rider. But not much else...well, except for the fact that you know how to crush a soda can with one hand."

The dim light hid her flush, but he could feel her embarrassment. "I did apologize for that."

"I know." The bruises were fading. "And honestly, I didn't blame you."

"You should have."

"Why?" Justin leaned back on the couch and took a long drink from the beer in his hand. "We lied to you. You had every right to try and kill me."

"Can we talk about something else?" Nikki asked. "I'd rather not think about that. Tell me about Shanna."

"What do you want to know?"

"What did she do to the people who killed your parents?"

The unexpected question hit him hard; he blinked several times, wondering where that had come from. Images rose in his mind: Shanna at age nine, covered in blood, holding their mother's corpse and sobbing; then Shanna at age eleven, again covered in blood, holding what she said was the heart of the man who'd ordered the hit. *"Don't worry, Jus. I took care of it."* The alien sound in her voice, the first time he'd truly understood what the StarChild was...

"Jus?"

Nikki's voice broke through the memory and Justin blinked again. "Sorry. That caught me a little off-guard."

"It was that bad?" Nikki asked, and he shrugged.

"Honestly, I don't know. She went out by herself; Alenya was furious when she found out. She was gone for nearly three months, and when she came back..." Justin shook his head. "She never talks about it."

"Huh." Nikki looked over into the dancing flames, her fingers toying with the edge of the wine glass again.

"Why?"

She shrugged." I just wanted to know. She seems to be the closest thing to what I am...and she's so together. I'm a mess."

"You're also barely seven months old as a Mage," Justin said. "Shanna's been training since she was a baby." *And she's got access to more Power than any of us will ever have...*

Can you really say that now? Nikki looked over at him, and in the dim light, her dark blue eyes shimmering, like a great cat's. *With all that she's done to me?* "True, but I still feel like I should have more control."

Well, maybe. We don't know how much she gave you. "It will come, Nikki. Trust me."

How do we find out? "The last time you said that, I killed four hundred people and you didn't tell me."

I don't know. "Are you going to bring that up every time I ask you to trust me from now on?"

Nikki grinned. "Only as long as it works," she said, and he rolled his eyes at her. "Seriously, though, tell me about Shanna."

"What do you want to know? She's as addicted to Dr. Pepper as Rick is, she's grumpy in the morning and she drives far too fast. Her temper isn't the best, and she's got a mouth like a sailor." He took another swig of beer. "And those are her good qualities."

"Who, Shanna?" Rick said, coming into the room. When Justin nodded, he grinned. "How'd I guess?"

"Considering how many times you've been on the receiving end of her tongue, I'm not surprised," Justin said, blinking as Rick turned the lights up. "How's the book coming?"

Rick grimaced. "It's coming, finally. But I'm taking today off. It's Thanksgiving, after all."

"Yes, it is." Justin wondered where Shanna was spending her Thanksgiving. He'd tried to call her, but as usual, she hadn't answered. "What's your favorite Shanna memory, Rick?"

"Hmm." Rick leaned back, thinking. "That's hard to say. The one summer that she and Lucian went toe-to-toe in the middle of campus is kind of memorable."

"In the middle of the campus?" Nikki's eyes went wide. "What happened?"

"Good lord, I'd nearly forgotten that!" Justin laughed. "Poor Lucian. He was so in the wrong place at the wrong time."

"Tell me!" Nikki insisted.

Justin let Rick tell the story, finishing his beer instead and watching the two of them. For a little while, it was almost as if they weren't in the midst of a war; it was just another evening with good friends. *More than good friends,* he thought, the warm glow suffusing him not just the beer and the fireplace. *Some of the best friends I'll ever find.*

One Shanna story led to another, and another; Nikki was an eager listener, and between the two of them, Rick and Justin could go on all night. Especially since it was snowing again, and there really wasn't anything else to do. One beer became two, then three...

"Shit, it's nearly midnight!" Rick squinted at the clock. "I should head to bed."

"Why?" Nikki asked.

"Because I have to write tomorrow," he reminded her.

"Deadlines, tick-tock and all that shit." He stood and stretched. "Night, guys." He gave Nikki a quick look and then left.

"Night," Nikki and Justin said, and watched him leave. They sat together for a short while, and then Justin looked over at her.

"And why haven't you followed him up?" he asked quietly, ignoring the pang in his chest. "What are you waiting for, an engraved invitation?"

"I'm not sure of my reception," she said, curling her feet back up underneath her and looking into the flames. "I think he thinks I'm still mad at him."

"Were you ever mad at him?" Justin said, and she shrugged.

"It was more at you," Nikki admitted. "I don't know why, but I was definitely more mad at you."

His heart leapt at that, but he told it sternly that it was a vain hope. "Then why don't you go explain to him that I'm the one you wanted to beat into a pulp, and see where it leads?"

She continued to look into the fire, her beer bottle dangling from her fingers, and he waited, knowing there was more. When the words finally came, he almost missed them, her voice was so low. "I'm scared."

"Scared of what?"

Nikki looked at him, and unshed tears glimmered in her eyes. "Because I don't have the control, and I don't want to kill anyone else," she said, and Justin's heart wrenched again.

"Oh, Nikki." Justin held his arms out. "Come here." She gave him a confused look, and he nodded. "Seriously. Come over and let me tell you a story."

After another moment, Nikki placed the beer bottle on the table next to her and then came to sit on the couch next to him. He put one arm around her; she stiffened, but then relaxed against him, her dark head against his chest. "A story?"

"A story." Justin rested his chin on the top of her head. "About a very powerful young Mage and the first time he actually did lose control."

"Oh? And what happened?"

"Oh no." He chuckled. "You have to let me set the scene first." The memory rolled obediently out of mental storage, and he said,

"It was summer, and our young hero was all of sixteen. And very full of himself."

"And was she pretty?" Nikki asked.

"Oh yes. Very pretty." She had been, too: all long legs and big blue eyes and blond hair down over her shoulders, flowing down her tanned back...He smiled to himself, remembering. "We'd been flirting for a week or so, and then one of the other kids threw a beach party, so I invited her to go with me. I pestered Alenya until she helped me pack a picnic basket, and then I spent the night before working myself into a tizzy."

"Was it perfect?" Nikki said, and he could feel her smile against his chest.

"It was. I had a blanket for the two of us, a bottle of nice wine, and a picnic basket full of goodies. We drank the wine, and then got...involved." Justin felt his face starting to get hot. "I didn't notice anything wrong, and neither did she... until my sister showed up."

"Oh no!" Nikki's laugh reverberated through him. "What happened?"

"Remember, I'm an Earth/Shadow Mage. When my shields slipped, apparently I set off several brush fires." Justin shook his head at his younger self." Shanna had spent nearly an hour putting them out. She was less than impressed. My young companion, on the other hand, was very impressed. Until her parents found out and banned me from seeing her."

"Just brush fires?" Nikki said.

"Just brush fires." Justin drew in a deep breath. "Over three states."

"Wow." Nikki drew circles on his chest idly, and Justin closed his eyes against the sensations her touch invoked. "Three states, huh?"

"Yep." He patted her shoulder. "But the moral of the story is that it only happened once. I learned, after that. And you've had your loss of control. You've learned."

Her hand stilled. "Are you sure?" she whispered, and the plea in her voice tugged at him.

Justin pulled back and looked down at her, his hand moving

under her chin, forcing her gently to look up at him. "I'm sure," he said firmly. "And if something does happen, I'll make sure no one finds out." He gave her a chaste kiss on her forehead. "Go up to him, Nikki. He's waiting for you."

Nikki wet her lips uncertainly, and he gave her a little shove. "Go on. Follow your heart."

Once she'd left the room, Justin picked up his beer and saluted the ceiling." Have fun, kids. "Then he drained the bottle and went into the kitchen for another, then came back into the living room, pausing to turn the lights back down before taking her place in the armchair.

No wonder you never get the girl, Greystone, he thought to himself, taking a long drink. *Too damned noble to step up for yourself.*

Even if it is for the best.

Chapter Twenty-three

"Visions and Regrets"

"Who's trying to tell me what?" Cleo asked the Dark Queen, who didn't answer. "Who are you, and what did you do in a former life that you're trying to convey through my painting?"

Again, no answer. The painting stood quietly on her largest easel, bathed in candlelight, the studio empty for once. Cleo had decided that the only way to get answers was to go looking for them, so she'd set up a full Circle: tall white pillar candles burned steadily at the four compass points, their golden glow the only illumination in the small room. A small brazier sent a plume of scented smoke curling towards the ceiling, and the air was filled with the smell of myrrh. Clad in her ritual green silk robe, bare feet shushing against the worn linoleum, Cleo moved towards the canvas, determined this time to find out some answers.

Dark gold Power filled her, a solid warmth that made her smile as she reached out to the painting. "Talk to me," the Light Mage whispered. "Let me help you." There was an answering frisson of Power from the canvas, very similar to the one she'd felt while wrapping up the Pale Queen. Even as she registered it, Cleo found herself standing in a clearing, dry leaves crackling under her feet, the full moon above her and an unfamiliar cool, dusty scent in the air. Her robes were still there, but stout boots encased her feet, protecting them from the debris that littered the ground. Cleo turned slowly, a slight breeze dragging chill fingers across her cheeks, wondering what she'd see this time.

Could it be Her? The idea crossed her mind quickly. Her Goddess often chose to manifest this way, giving the Mages who followed her visions of what she wanted them to do, and that would definitely explain the odd feelings from the painting. After all, she'd asked for an answer; maybe her Goddess would be the one to deliver it.

And yet, something felt different this time. Cleo frowned. The Power that had brought her here hadn't had the familiar feel of the Goddess: this was a darker, richer flavor of magic, if possible. As she stood in the deserted clearing, her breath steaming in the chill air, Cleo wondered who else might want to speak with her. And to what purpose?

"If it's someone fishing for unsuspecting Mages, they're in for a surprise," she said out loud, her voice a challenge. "I'm no pushover."

The lonely hoot of an owl was her only reply.

Cleo looked around the clearing again and noticed a small path leading out into the dark woods. There was some sort of light flickering in the distance: a torch or bonfire or lantern, perhaps. She couldn't tell, but investigating the light source beat hanging around the empty clearing waiting for someone or something to show up.

As she started down the path, her robes shimmered and shifted, becoming jeans and a tee-shirt, with a leather jacket settling over her shoulders. *Thank goodness for small favors. I'd hate to spend a few hours freezing my ass off here before whomever I'm looking for finds me.* She squashed the small spurt of fear at that thought. *That's your mother talking, Cleopatra. There's no one after you. You're the one who came here, remember?*

She wandered down the path slowly, remembering the frantic moves from place to place as a child. *Hell, my whole childhood was spent in a fucking van, moving from one city to another "so they wouldn't find us." Except my poor psychotic mother never bothered to explain who "they" were. Until we reached Solitaire, and that damn preacher saved her soul.* Cleo shook her head. *What a crock. And she and Thom sucked it up like Kool-Aid. Luckily I was old enough to head out on my own at that point.*

I wonder if she still thinks "they" are after her. Or if that damn Church has "cleansed" her of the evil magic in her soul, so "they" wouldn't be interested in her anymore.

"Your mother had good reason to fear," said a voice out of the darkness, and Cleo stopped, trying to see who was speaking to her. She'd arrived at the light: it was a torch, thrust into the ground, burning brightly.

"Maybe when she wasn't crazy," Cleo replied. The voice had come from a darker portion of the path, and she squinted, trying to pierce the night. "If there was ever a time like that."

"Don't judge her too harshly," the voice said, coming closer. It was a female voice, sort of, and Cleo frowned. "She had a very hard life."

"What do you know about my mother?" Cleo demanded. "Who are you?"

The speaker stepped into the torchlight and Cleo blinked, unsurprised. The Dark Queen, also clad in jeans and a tee-shirt, stared back at her, vaguely amused. "I'm your future. And your past." She looked over at Cleo, staring at her forehead intently, and Cleo rubbed her hand there. "So, at least one of us was blond. Do you have a twin brother or sister?"

"Brother," Cleo said, completely bemused. "Who are you?"

The Dark Queen reached out for her. "I'm your sister."

Cleo gaped at her. "What?"

"I said, I'm your sister." Before she could move or duck away, the Queen touched her forehead: cool, dark Shadows whispered against her skin, sinking into her flesh, and Cleo felt something dark and hungry within her respond to the touch.

"You're mine," the Queen said softly, and Cleo shook at the Power of that statement. "Flesh of my flesh, blood of my blood."

And then she was gone. The entire clearing was gone; although the scent of torch smoke stayed in her nostrils, when Cleo opened her eyes again, she was back in her studio.

"Wow." That was all she got out, before she looked at what she was clutching in her hand.

A leaf. A brilliant red-orange maple leaf.

"Nikki! Rick! Wake up!"

Justin looked out the hall window and swore again, then banged his fist on the door again. "Dammit, come on, come on!" he muttered under his breath.

Rick appeared at the door just as he was about to hit it again, dressed only in boxers and sleep still in his eyes. Justin pushed past him into the room, where Nikki was sitting up in the bed, wearing only a tee-shirt." Get dressed, "he said sharply, and she looked confused." We have to get you out of here."

"What?" she said. "What's going on?"

"I just got a call from a very close friend," Justin said, running his hand through his hair. "Department V is on the move, and they're on their way here."

"Department V?" Nikki asked, as he grabbed her jeans from the floor and tossed them at her. "Who...?"

"The military's magical arm," he said, grabbing her arm and pulling her up, ignoring her gasp of alarm. "The people we've been trying to keep you from. Get dressed — we have to get you out through the Gate. Come on!"

"What about you?" she said, pulling her jeans on, face flaming.

"Don't worry about me," he said, dragging her from the room. Rick had pulled on jeans as well and followed them out as Justin hustled her down the stairs. "Get to Edgar's and lay low for a day or so. And Nikki..." He grabbed her arm and pulled her back towards him, giving her a hard kiss. "Do not come after me."

Nikki blinked at him, and he murmured against her lips, "Remember, trust no one. That means Rick. I know what I'm doing." Then he shoved her into the pantry, where the Gate was already swirling. Edgar stood on the other side, motioning her through urgently. With one final, terrified look, Nikki turned and sprinted through, and Justin yanked the Gate shut.

And then turned to see Rick staring coolly at him.

Shit. "Rick, I..."

The kitchen door slammed open, interrupting them. They both turned to see two strangers standing there, dark blue suits as stiff as the expressions on their faces. Justin didn't recognize either of them, but it was a safe bet that they recognized him. He let the pantry door go and turned to face them.

"Mr. Greystone." The woman smiled bleakly. "It's a pleasure to finally meet you." She jerked her head at her companion. "Find out what he was doing in there."

The man shouldered him out of the way; Justin stepped aside, knowing he wouldn't find more than a faint signature. Rick was still looking frostily at him, but he didn't say anything.

"I don't suppose you want to tell me where she is, do you?" the woman continued, and Justin schooled his expression to blankness, even when she pulled out a fairly well-drawn picture of Nikki. "This would go much easier if you cooperated."

"I'd cooperate if you told me what you were looking for," Justin said, keeping his voice neutral. Behind him, he heard the other agent curse, and he breathed a sigh of relief. *She got away. They can't pick up a trace.*

He hadn't asked Shanna where she'd gotten her information when she'd called this morning; he knew better than to doubt his older sister, especially on something this important. Now that he knew Nikki had gotten safely away, he could breathe a little easier. The only weak link was Rick — surely he wouldn't jeopardize Nikki's life by blurting something out now...

But the other Earth Mage had turned away, going to the fridge. "You," the woman said, and he turned back around, raising one dark blonde eyebrow at her. "Do you know this girl?"

Rick stared at the picture, then shook his head and turned back to the open fridge.

"He doesn't wake up well," Justin said, watching his friend pull out a Dr. Pepper and one of Sarah's oversized muffins. "A writer, you know. Keeps odd hours. I'm surprised he's even awake." Rick moved to the door, but the woman blocked it, and he gave her an unfriendly look.

"Not yet," she said. "We'll want to speak to both of you."

"About what?" Justin said, as Rick's other eyebrow went up. "We've told you, we don't know who that girl is or where she is. What more do you want to know?"

"How's your sister doing?" the man asked, coming up behind

him, and Justin scowled.

"How the hell should I know?" he said, some of his real irritation at his sibling sliding into his voice. "Christ, if this is about her, you're barking up the wrong tree. I haven't seen her since..."

"Last week?" the woman said, and Justin blinked, startled. "Yes, we know she left Vermont last week, and her signature was felt briefly in this area. You truly expect me to believe didn't get in touch with her only surviving relative at all?"

"We spoke, briefly," Justin said, his mind whirling. "She asked me to check on her house."

"And that's it?" She was clearly unimpressed.

"What do you want me to say?" Justin said, shrugging. "I don't know what she's up to in Vermont. When I asked her, she told me not to worry about it, so I'm not." Almost truth, but he didn't have to feign the frustration that reply had engendered.

"And you didn't press her?"

Justin gave a bitter laugh. "Lady, you've never met Shanna in person, have you? 'Don't worry about it' translates into 'Don't bug me and I won't pound you into the ground.'" The man behind him chuckled, which told Justin that at least one of the agents had indeed run into his headstrong sister once before. "I don't know what she's doing. I don't know what's hiding in the hills in northern Vermont. Did you have any other questions for me that I can't answer, or can I go about my business?"

The woman looked at him levelly. "Oh, I have lots of questions for you, Mr. Greystone. Starting with your whereabouts on Halloween."

Justin straightened up slowly. "I was with friends." Not a lie.

"Where?"

He didn't answer, and her lips tightened. "Are you trying to make this as difficult as possible, Mr. Greystone?"

"What is this about? Who are you?" he countered, and she pulled a set of glossy photos out of her jacket and tossed them on the table. The devastation spoke for itself: Justin looked down once and then looked back at her.

"Lt. Amy Elder, US Navy, currently T. A. D. to the Waterville Valley Police Department," she said, and Justin felt a flutter in his stomach.

They're not even trying to hide who they are from us, he thought, keeping a straight face by sheer willpower. *Shit, Shanna wasn't kidding. They really are pulling out all the stops here.*

"So I will ask you one more time, Mr. Greystone," Lt. Elder said, leaning forward and tapping her finger on the topmost picture. "Where were you on Halloween? And where is the girl?"

Justin didn't look down. "Am I under arrest?"

Her jaw tightened.

"Because if not, I'm leaving," he said, shifting his weight and knowing they weren't going to let him walk out. A hand came down on his shoulder, and Justin smiled grimly.

"Justin Greystone, you are under arrest for mass murder, domestic terrorism and aggravated destruction of property in the explosions at the Gene-Tech Research Facility on Halloween," Lt. Elder said, as her partner pulled Justin's arms behind his back and locked magical-dampening cuffs on his wrists. "You have the right to remain silent. Anything you say..."

Justin ignored her and looked over at Rick. "Call my sister and tell her I need a lawyer, please," he said. Rick was staring at him, jaw open in shock, and Justin gave him full points for acting. "Tell her I've been taken to... where am I going?" he asked, looking over at Lt. Elder.

She smiled, and his heart sank. "Washington." She gathered up the photos from the table and left a business card in their place. "Better yet, tell his sister to come down herself. We have some questions for her too." She looked over at Rick and pulled out a cell phone. "In fact, why don't you call her right now?"

Rick looked at Justin helplessly.

Chapter Twenty-four

"Cleansings"

"She's not coming."

Vashti didn't look up from the rose bush she was inspecting. "You don't have a lot of faith in your sister, do you, Trimaris?"

"It's been a week, Vashti," Trimaris said, running her fingers along the edge of the stone table. Despite the golden sunlight pouring down on the garden, she shivered. "You can't tell me Madness didn't try to reclaim him as soon as that filthy Blood Mage drained him dry. Not even Kymara could stand up to Madness."

"She's an agent of the Balance, though," Cassandra said, and Trimaris shrugged.

"We're all agents of the Balance." She ignored the twinge of guilt, thankful that neither of her companions refuted her statement. "Could you defeat a Chaos Lord?"

"Alone? Probably not." Cassandra looked over at her, and the odd light in her green eyes made Trimaris shiver again. "But she is not alone, and Andreas loves her far more than he ever loved me."

"Not only that, but Kymara gave up her soul to the Spirit of the Balance," Vashti added. "And really, once free of her mortal remains, there is so much more the Balance can do through her."

"Perhaps." Trimaris looked over at the Circle that stood waiting for them to begin the Cleansing. Once they could trust Andreas, they could finally begin to right the situation.

Who would have thought this would end here, she mused, looking down at the table again. *When Vashti and Cassandra showed up here, I thought for certain they were going to kill me. Or toss me through the Walls to the World Between. Not Cleanse me, and offer me a chance to make it right. I had thought that was only a dream Kymara had held out, not a reality.*

The memory of her own Cleansing a few short days ago crawled over her skin and she closed her eyes. Agony, to feel the seeds of Chaos that had been planted in her soul ripped from her, torn out at the roots in a slash-and-burn cleaning that had left her curled in a sobbing pile in the center of her beloved garden. *And I was only involved for months,* she mused, opening her eyes again and looking out to the garden's gate. *How many years worth of Chaos will need to be stripped from you, Andreas? Will you be able to survive?*

He will survive, Kymara's voice said suddenly in her head, and Trimaris sat upright. *We'll be there soon.* The Dawn Lord sounded exhausted, but there was a triumphant note in her thoughts that Trimaris clung to.

"They're on their way," she said out loud, and both Vashti and Cassandra nodded. The Earth Lord abandoned the rose bushes and went to the Circle, lighting the brazier in the center of the stones and conjuring a sparkling stream of water that fell, a musical, healing rain, into the silver bowl beside it.

Cassandra picked up a chair and pulled it over to the Circle, placing it in between the western and northern candles. She sat, arranging her white robes around her, and then spread her hands. Her harp appeared and she began to tune it.

Trimaris supposed she should get ready too, but there was no tools she needed, so she sat, watching the gate and trying to calm the fluttering in her stomach. It didn't work, so she closed her eyes, trying to find her center and reassuring herself that they would fix this.

We have to. Otherwise, I'll never be able to live with myself.

The garden gate creaked and Trimaris felt the wan heat of her sister's presence lap against her shields. Normally Kymara shone like a miniature sun; Trimaris opened her eyes and bit back a gasp at the pitiful shades that dragged themselves into the garden.

"Don't," Kymara warned her, dropping heavily into the other chair. "Just don't say a word, Tri."

Her long blonde hair hung in hanks around her ashy face. The dark circles around her eyes looked as if they had been burned there, and long scratches marred not only her cheeks but tore her robes as well. Andreas didn't look much better; the wounds that he'd carried for the last twenty-three years were gone, but new injuries took their place: bites and gouges along his ribs and stomach, staining his black robes with crusted blood.

Trimaris didn't say a word, but Vashti was under no such compulsion. "Where the hell have you two been?" she said, bustling out of the Circle, concern sharpening her voice. "What did she send after you?"

"What didn't she?" Kymara said, running her fingers through her hair. "Goddess Light, I never knew there were so many different Chaos beasts out there. And they've ALL got claws." She inspected the remains of her robes. "But we did it."

"Indeed." Vashti reached out for her, but Kymara shook her head.

"Save it. I'll be fine. You'll need everything you have to Cleanse him." She reached out and pulled Andreas' face down to her own, kissing him gently. "Be strong, my love. I'll be here waiting for you."

A lump rose in Trimaris' throat as she watched the normally taciturn Shadow Lord touch her sister's cheek softly, one finger tracing the red line of a claw across her cheekbone as he kissed her back. He whispered something to her, and Kymara chuckled, a low, hoarse, tired laugh, then whispered something back to him.

"Come, Trimaris, we must start preparing," Vashti said, and the Dawn Lord rose obediently to follow her to the stone Circle. She took her place between the northern and eastern candles, nodding at Cassandra across from her. Vashti stood at the southern candle, her brazier belching forth scented smoke, and waited.

Andreas finally straightened up from Kymara and strode into the center of the Circle, his dark eyes (how odd to see him with eyes again, Trimaris thought, and then quickly stifled it) at once apprehensive and excited. "You may want to sit down," Trimaris said, and shrugged when he shook his head. "That ground is going to hurt when you fall."

"I will not fall," he said, and her smile turned slightly malicious.

"If you say so."

"Are we ready?" Vashti asked, looking over at her fellow Lords. Trimaris nodded and raised her arms above her head; Cassandra just touched her fingers to the strings of her harp, letting the first low, rumbling notes ripple from the instrument. "Good. Then let's begin."

Cassandra's fingers began to dance on the strings; the rumbling notes calling up a small thundercloud that hovered above Andreas' head. Trimaris reached deeply within herself, calling up her own Power and adding it to Cassandra's clouds, miniature lightning that flashed and arced across the surface of the storm they were brewing. Vashti waved her incense smoke into the growing storm, adding her magic to the other two.

"Light, Shadow, Earth," she said, moving her fingers in an intricate pattern. "Forces of the Balance, gifts of the Spirit that guides and nurtures all of us, wash this soul clean of all the Chaotic, Bloody influence that has taken root in him. Bring him back to us whole and pure, as he was before."

Rain fell upon Andreas from the clouds swirling above him, and he raised his face to the healing shower. Trimaris watched steam begin to rise from his skin, the first remains of Chaos and Blood magic melting away. The downpour increased, drops of water falling harder and harder, as the three Lords continued to combine their Power, washing him clean.

As the fall of water continued, Andreas was forced, first to his knees, then into a crumpled figure on the ground, steam pouring off of him, the corruption of years being wrenched from him. Beyond the Circle, Trimaris was distantly aware of Kymara watching, not anxiously, but patiently, secure in the knowledge that her lover would survive.

I wonder what love like that is like.

The sun had fallen below the horizon and the hazy twilight

that passed for night in the Dawn Lands enveloped them before the storm in the Circle abated. Andreas remained curled up, but Kymara was waiting to kneel beside him, whispering words of encouragement as he shook in the aftermath of the Cleansing.

Lucifer's steps slowed as he approached the last staircase up to the rooms he shared with Madness. The moons outside were hidden from view by grey, sullen clouds that spit a cold, spiteful rain and grumbled low in their throats, a sure sign that his Lady was highly displeased with the events of the last week.

His foot on the final step, Lucifer paused, squaring his shoulders for the storm he knew waited inside for him. Madness did not forgive failures, and he had failed her. *Best to get the lashing done with,* he told himself, and pushed open the door to find...

Nothing. Empty rooms. The suite stood lovely and lifeless, not even the faint scent of her perfume riding the cool wind that walked through the open windows. Lucifer stood in the midst of the stillness and despite himself, he shivered.

This does not bode well. Not at all.

Chill fingers of breeze curled around his neck and he flinched from them. Soft words breathed vague threats and promises, too indistinct to calm his fears. Shaking himself free of the mirage, Lucifer stalked through the rooms silently, looking for the Lady he already knew wasn't there.

He stood at the window in their bedroom and looked out over the maze, wondering where she was. Her mists still clung to the grounds, multicolored pale forms moving around in between the rows of tall, dark green bushes. Today, the maze was a Celtic knot, spiraling in to the gazebo in the center, where mists swirled.

She will be weaving, he thought, relief and trepidation warring with one another. The storm still waited, but his Lady still inhabited this place. He had not lost her. *She has not forsaken me.*

Still, she would not be pleased, and his back would bear the scars of that displeasure before the day was done. A small price to pay to keep her.

He went down to the ground floor, his back already tingling in anticipation of her wrath, and entered the labyrinth. As he passed, Spirits of Chaos and Blood turned to watch him, eyes awhirl with... what? Hunger? Fear?

Or glee?

Lucifer suppressed his shiver and let none of his inner turmoil mar the haughty, confident sneer he normally wore. Despite everything, he was still Madness' favorite.

For the moment, he amended silently, as he stopped at the edge of the clearing in the center of the maze. *For the moment.*

Even more Spirits roamed the lawns surrounding the gazebo: Chaos beasts whose shapes were at the mercy of the Lady weaving at her loom, shifting and blurring in between steps as they prowled.

Lucifer waited for her invitation, knowing if he stepped out of the maze before that, the beasts would rend him limb from limb. The gazebo was hers, inviolate, and he would never trespass.

"You failed me."

Her silky voice lashed across his skin and Lucifer bowed his head. "Yes." No excuses. There were none she would accept, and none he would offer.

"Now what should I do, Lucifer?" Madness' voice never rose, and the cool, calm tone, as if she were discussing what to have for dinner, chilled him more than the violent storm he'd been expecting. "The price for failure here is non-negotiable."

Lucifer closed his eyes, hoping he was correct in thinking she still needed him. "You must do as you think correct, of course."

"Do not patronize me, Lucifer," Madness hissed, and he heard the first pieces of her rage. "You are not irreplaceable, especially not now. The fact that I can still make use of you is the only reason you aren't currently in pieces."

When he opened his eyes, she had paused in her weaving and was looking out over the lawn at him. All the Chaos Spirits had paused and were staring at him as well, and Lucifer's skin crawled. *One word, and they'll be at my throat.*

"How," and she drew the word out mockingly, "did two dead Elemental Lords manage to give the mighty Lucifer the slip?"

"The Balance," he said, and thunder cracked above him as her eyes narrowed. "They called for the Balance."

"Andreas was mine! Tainted! Broken!" Thunder punctuated each word. "The Balance had no claim on him! He was mine!"

She rose from the loom, shaking in fury, and despite the distance between them, Lucifer shrank back. Madness in a full rage was a sight to terrify as her true nature asserted itself.

The paleness that she normally cultivated, the multicolored hues of her native mists, darkened and swirled with her anger just underneath her transparent skin. Blood-red eyes glared out of her bone-white face, and her long hair, normally corn-spun silk, twisted into brilliant white snakes that hissed and spit at him. Her robes wept acid dreams, nightmares that slithered along the ground, leaving a trail of melted hopes in their wake.

She spun around and pointed a long, sharp finger at him. "You will go, now, and you will attempt to redeem yourself, Lucifer. Find me the Dead and bring him back. Do not fail me, or you will be the next prey we hunt."

Chapter Twenty-five

"Threads of Madness"

"So where are we?"

Derek shook his head. "I don't know," he said, frustration etching edges into his voice as he struggled to not lash out at his superior. "All I have is pieces. A strange signature that I can't explain, let alone identify. A Shadow Cube that we can't open and don't know if it's occupied. A single survivor who can't tell us anything, because she's in a coma that none of the Healers can fix. And now, the younger brother of the StarChild in our prison, because he refuses to give us any information to tie it all together."

"That's not good enough, Chief," Ismael said, and Derek's fists clenched. "I know that's not what you want to hear, but I need answers to give the President."

"And I don't have any yet," Derek repeated, as the door opened and Amy came in. "I'm trying to get you some."

"Try harder," Ismael said, and then hung up.

"Here," Amy said, shoving a sheaf of papers at him. "Before you start swearing, look at these."

The retort hovering on his lips died as he scanned the top page. "At the hospital? Really?"

Amy nodded. "Four deaths of comatose Mages in the last two days. All in the immediate vicinity of our survivor. And all..."

"Tainted with Chaos magic." He looked up. "Shit. I've got to get over there."

She smiled. "Car's outside. Let's go."

For once, Derek didn't mind her breakneck speed. The trip to St. Mary's Medical Center passed in a blur of light snow and apprehension — his stomach clenched every time he thought about whom he might be facing when he got there. The guards at the entrance to the room searched them thoroughly, and then opened the door.

There was another guard sitting in there; like the two outside, he held an AK-47 in his hands, pointed directly at them, and gave both of them a magical sweep before stepping away from the bed and lowering his weapon. Derek walked up to the bed, feeling the tingle of Chaos dancing on his skin, and looked down on the deceptively still face of the woman lying on the white hospital sheets.

The doctors had shaved the remains of Sylvia's blonde hair as part of the surgery to save her life; her head was swathed in bandages, gauze imbued with spells to regrow the bones in her skull that had been crushed by the destruction of the spell chamber. Monitors surrounded her bed, magical and medical, delineating her life in a series of beeps and jagged lines, but Derek ignored those. They couldn't tell him anything.

Stripping off one brown silk glove, the Sensitive swallowed once, dismissing fear from his mind by concentrating on his orders. Then he reached down and laid his palm on her flaccid cheek.

The room danced before him, wreathed in pastels that had no name on this side of the World Walls. As his inner sight cleared, Derek looked down and saw Sylvia's body wreathed in a glowing web of Chaos, with the silver strand he knew connected her soul to her mortal clay tangled within it. He watched another piece of Chaos magic drop down, another strand in the web, following the silver soul-strand, and looked up to see where it was coming from.

Crouched in the corner of the room, still within the Walls Between the Worlds, was the giant spider he'd seen before. Sylvia's limp soul lay in the spider's front legs, being wrapped quickly in the sticky strands of Chaos-infused webbing, and poison dripped from her fangs. Derek watched, fascinated, as the great beast moved her head to the side and reached out with another long leg, dragging another portion of the web she sat in closer. Something equally cocooned lay struggling on it; she ripped the webbing with a precise claw, exposing the soul within. Another comatose Mage, Derek had no doubt, and as the spider drove her fangs into his neck, sucking him dry of magical Power, the Sensitive knew why the deaths in this hospital were accelerating.

But how do we stop them?

As if she heard him, the spider paused in her movements and Derek froze. Multi-faceted eyes pinned him in place, her distended abdomen quivering slightly, and a malicious chuckle echoed in his head.

Stop me, precious mortal? Stop me? What a quaint idea.

She dropped the drained soul of the unnamed mage and stalked down the side of the wall towards him, Sylvia's body still dangling from her spinnerets. *And just how do you intend to stop me, Sensitive?*

That was the question that Ismael asked when Derek and Amy reported to him later that evening. The weak early winter sun was just dropping below the horizon, touching pale fingers to the wooden desk Ismael sat behind, caressing the papers scattered across its surface.

"I don't know," Derek said. "I'm on my way back to talk to Justin Greystone again. I'm convinced he knows more about this, and I'm hoping I can appeal to his better nature."

"Better nature?" Ismael leaned forward, his salt-and-pepper eyebrows rising.

"Justin's got more of a conscience than Shanna does," Derek said, and Amy snorted behind him.

"You mean she has one?"

Derek chuckled at that sally from Ismael. "She does. It just doesn't show very often. But Justin's a soft touch — I've seen it. I just need to appeal to that side." He held up the artist's rendition of the girl from his vision." He knows who she is, and where she is. And she's the key to all this. Find her, and we'll find Alex Masterson."

"You think they're together?" Ismael said, and then frowned

when Derek shook his head.

"No, I think she's looking for him, and she's got a better chance of finding him than we do."

Justin was lying on his back on the bed in his cell, ostensibly ignoring the camera in the corner as he tossed a soft cloth ball in the air and caught it. "You really think he'll help us?" Amy asked, as she and Derek watched the monitor.

"I think he'll tell us to go to hell," Derek said, stripping off his gloves and tossing them on the table. "In fact, I'm counting on it. And I'm going to do everything I can to get him to tell me that."

"Why?"

"Because if I rile him up enough, he'll let something slip. Let's hope it's something I can use."

He paused at the doorway, looking up at the monitor above the door. Justin hadn't moved. Derek smiled just for a moment, then schooled his face into an impassive expression and nodded to the guard, who unlocked the door.

Then Derek kicked it open.

Justin sat up, his face wary. "Bad day, Chief?"

Derek slammed the pages down on the table in the room. "You could say that, Mr. Greystone. I've got five dead mages, on top of the bodies you left me in the rubble of Gene-Tech. And so help me God, if I can pin you to them, I will."

"I didn't kill anyone," Justin said, the mantra he'd been repeating for the last two days.

"I know you didn't." Derek tapped the picture he'd slapped down. "She did. And I need to find her."

"I don't..."

"Don't lie to me!" Derek thundered, and Justin blinked. "I'm tired of playing games with you! Dammit, I have people dying out there because of whatever the hell you're involved in, and that blood is on your hands! Is that what you want?"

Justin narrowed his eyes. "What are you doing?" he said, getting up from the bed and tossing his ball on the covers. "You're trying to provoke me."

"I'm trying to get you to see that this silence isn't helping anyone!" Derek didn't have to feign the frustration in his voice.

"You aren't protecting her — you're letting whoever she's trying to stop win! Dammit, Justin, talk to me!"

Justin swallowed, his eyes focused on the picture, but he didn't say anything.

"Let's try something else." Derek pulled the cloth doll without a face from his pocket and tossed it down on the table. "Look familiar?"

When there was no answer, Derek pushed it forward. "Touch it. Go on." He all but forced Justin's hand on it, and when the Earth Mage flinched, held his hand down on top of the doll. "Do you feel that, Justin? Do you feel all that Chaos magic? Do you know what that tells me?"

Still no answer.

"It tells me the Walls are crumbling." Derek watched Justin, but the Earth Mage just shook his head and turned away, so the Sensitive continued pushing. "It tells me that whatever your sister is doing up in Vermont is connected to this, because everyone knows only the StarChild can cross into the Walls Between the Worlds."

"Just because everyone knows something doesn't mean it's true," Justin snapped, and then cursed under his breath.

A brief flash of a vision passed before Derek's eyes: the mystery girl, and Shanna Greystone, but nothing more. Justin glared at him and yanked his hand back.

"Don't ever try that again," he said, anger deepening his voice.

"Then help me!" Derek said, slamming his hand down in frustration. "I'm tired of chasing corpses!"

"Then you're in the wrong line of work," Justin said. "Don't blame me for that!"

"You are going to be found guilty of murder, do you realize that?" Derek said, feeling the tension in the room ripple along his skin. *Come on,* he thought privately. *Give me what I'm looking for.* "You'll hang for deaths that you didn't commit."

Justin looked at him contemptuously. "Do you really think my sister will let that happen?"

"She won't have a choice," Derek said. "Like it or not, Shanna Greystone lives in this world and has to obey the dictates of the law."

"The only law she has to obey is the Law of the Balance," Justin said. "And you know that as well as I do."

"And when her beloved baby brother is convicted of consorting with Chaos Lords, what will the Law of the Balance say then?" Derek gestured to the doll. "It's covered in Chaos and your signature, Justin. How do you explain that?"

"I don't have to," Justin said. "This will never go to trial."

"Want to make a bet?" Derek leaned in close. "Listen to me very closely, Justin Greystone. This case has become one of national security, because it's linked to what's going on in Vermont, and don't even try to deny it. They've pulled some of our most senior agents out of retirement for this case. The American people are now screaming for someone's blood, thanks to Dr. Amy Sturgis, and you just became that someone. So you either start cooperating, or..."

"Or what?" Justin said, standing nose to nose with him. "You'll kill me? Go ahead and try."

"I won't have to." Derek smiled nastily and pulled his last card out. "We'll just dump you in that Shadow Cube we found and then forget where we put you."

The blood drained from Justin's face, leaving it ghostly white. "You found the Cube?"

"We did."

"Let me have it."

Derek threw back his head and laughed. "You have to be kidding me."

"Did you open it?" Justin asked, and the note of pain in his voice surprised Derek, although he tried to hide it. "Did you let him out?"

"Who? Who's in that Cube?"

Justin sat down hard, swallowing. "There's a Shadow Lord named Kith in there," he said finally. "He was trying to stop Alex and got caught." He looked up at Derek, his eyes haunted. "You have to let me let him out. Please. Bring me the Cube."

"Sure." Derek tapped the picture. "As soon as you tell me who she is."

Justin ground his teeth together.

"Then your Shadow Lord can remain in the Cube." Derek shook

his head and turned to leave. "Let me know when you change your mind."

"I want a phone call," Justin said, and Derek chuckled.

"Isn't it nice to want?" he said, and walked out the door.

"Did you get anything?" Amy asked, when he came back into the outer room. She'd been watching the entire exchange over the monitor, of course.

Derek sighed. "Only confirmation that Shanna's involved. And that she knows who that girl is. Which makes this an even bigger clusterfuck than we knew."

"The Shadow Cube hit a nerve."

He nodded. "I only hope we can use it to get some useful information out of him." Derek glanced up at the monitor, where Justin was banging his fists against the wall and swearing. "Sooner, rather than later. I wasn't kidding when I said I was sick of chasing corpses."

Chapter Twenty-six

"A Slippery Slope"

"You have got to be kidding me."

Tony stood in the middle of Andreas' study, scowling. "Come on, old man, where the hell did you hide them?" He turned, trying to see someplace he may have missed. The furniture lay in ruins, even the great mahogany desk, shredded by Shadows in Tony's frantic search for the copies of the spells. Not even the wood paneling on the walls had escaped: he'd ripped them down in large pieces, hoping to find a hidden pocket or something. Nothing.

"Dammit! They have to be here!" He picked up a chair and smashed it against the fireplace. Shards of wood flew, but no paper. No parchment. Tossing aside the remains, Tony stalked through the debris to the next room.

They were here. No one else had been here. Alex had told him Andreas hadn't even told the Dawn Lord where the spells were hidden. Which means either Andreas had been lying...

Or Alex was.

Tony took a deep breath, and sternly told himself to calm down. *There are a lot of rooms here. Alex said he'd always worked on them in the study, but he could have been mistaken. Or Andreas could have moved them again.*

The only thing to do is go through each room. And then, if they aren't here, then I'll worry.

He ransacked the entire house, using the energy of the Shadow

Lands to fuel his fury as it became increasingly evident that Andreas' versions of the Summoning Spells were no where to be found. Then he stomped back up to the study and stood in the center of the room, pondering his next move.

Alex was positive they were here, Tony thought. *Which means someone beat me here.* His blood ran cold at that. *But who?*

Something fell, downstairs, and Tony jumped. A door opened; he stiffened, reaching out to touch the Shadows below, searching to find out who was here. Warmth flowed along the link; not a Shadow Lord, then.

Is this our Dawn Lord? What a lucky catch.

Tony stepped into the corner and deepened the Shadows around him, knowing the Lord below would hear the footsteps and come investigate. *And then... well, there are other ways to keep a Lord than just a Shadow Cube.* He put his hand in his pants pocket and felt the small syringe resting there. *I knew there was a reason I brought this.*

Light spilled through the hallway, and he pulled the syringe out as a tall male Lord came into the room, golden sunlight cupped in one hand. Tony raised one eyebrow — he hadn't realized Andreas had confided in another male. *Then again, I guess it really doesn't matter. I just thought he'd get another female again — he was so into that symbolic crap.*

Then again, maybe he was more in touch with his feminine side than I thought.

The Lord took no notice of him, but frowned as he looked at the destruction, then went to the fireplace. The tall metal screen had been knocked askew — the Lord let his magelight drift above him as he knelt down and started to unscrew the top finial of one of the long rods.

You sneaky son-of-a-bitch.

Tony watched as the Lord tossed the finial aside and dipped his finger into the hollow tube. "Nothing," the Lord said, sitting back on his heels and letting the grating slide to the floor. "And I doubt you have them, little Shadow Mage, else you wouldn't still be hiding there in the shadows." He turned around, and the flames in his eyes danced with barely-contained glee. Tony stiffened as honeyed fingers of light twined around him, pushing the Shadows away from him and teasing him with their warmth. "Why don't you come out into the light?"

He didn't have any choice; the Lord's spells forced him into the center of the room, as the Lord himself rose from the floor to tower over him. "Tell me, little Shadow Mage, what exactly are you hoping to find here?"

"Go to hell," Tony said, and the Lord chuckled.

"Ah, Andreas did like your spirit, Mr. Ashcroft. Oh yes, I know who you are." Light suddenly invaded his body, pushing in through every pore, as the Lord continued, "And now I want to know everything you know."

Agony ripped through him as the Light dug into his mind, and all Tony could do for the next several hours was scream. Once the Lord had what he wanted, he dragged Tony downstairs and out the front door, depositing him on the lawn. The Shadow Mage lay there, drained, unable to do more than watch the Lord go back inside. After a few moments, the upstairs windows smashed out; glass rained down around him, and the Lord popped his head out briefly. "Sorry about that," he called down, and the fake cheeriness in his voice made Tony seethe. "I'll be down soon."

When he came out the door, a trail of smoke followed him, and Tony watched Andreas' house burn, unable to stop the destruction.

"I love a good fire," the Lord said, rubbing his hands together briskly as the flames licked out around the edges of the doorway and another window blew out. "This place is always so damn cold. Don't you agree, Tony? I can call you Tony, can't I?"

All Tony could do was moan. The heat of the fire reached out greedily for him, and the Lord frowned, snapping his fingers. "Come on, now, Tony, up and at 'em." Tony felt heat shoot through his limbs, dragging him to feet numbed by magic. "We have a lot to do."

"Are you certain you want to do this?"

Nikki nodded, concentrating on smoothing the large map of

the United States and Canada out in front of her. "I have to start over," she said. "Right now, we're all tied to Shanna, because she started the Cleansing. According to the book you gave me, I need to recast the first spells to tie them to me instead."

"Did you read the entire book?" Edgar pressed, and she finally looked up at the old witch. His lips were pursed, and the worry on his face touched her.

"I did." She'd had nothing better to do in the last three days as she sat at the Rothman House, hiding beneath its shields, trying very hard not to think about her reaction to Justin's kiss. Or what Rick might be doing now.

The cold look in his eyes chilled her again, and she resolutely shoved the memory away. *He was startled, that's all. He knows there's nothing between Justin and I.*

I hope.

"And you realize that if you start this now, Nikki, you have to follow it through to the end, no matter what?" The intensity of his voice underscored the knot in her stomach, but she simply nodded again. "That this could end..."

"Badly?" she said. "I could die. I understand that. I don't have a choice."

Edgar looked down at her as she knelt there, and to her utter shock, there were tears in his eyes. "I hope not," he said.

"I do too, but I have to accept that it may not be possible to survive a Cleansing," Nikki said, and he nodded. "I accept that. I have no choice, Edgar."

He nodded again. "Is there anything else you need?"

"Just keep those shields up so Department V doesn't find me," she said, and Edgar grinned.

"I've got a distortion spell ready," he promised her. "They'll never be able to figure out where you are, provided you keep your Circle up."

Nikki drew in a deep breath. "Then let's get started."

Edgar stepped back to the edge of the hall — Nikki had claimed the marble foyer as the only place she could spread out easily — and she rose to her feet, turning and pointing at the first candle.

231 | Valerie Griswold-Ford

"In the name of the Balance, I summon the Spirit of Spring," she said, and a brilliant green flame danced on the top of the tall white candle to her east.

In short order, Nikki called the remaining spirits of Summer, Fall and Winter, bid the four to aid her, and then bowed her head, preparing for the next step in the spell. The low chant that accompanied Edgar's distortion spell nibbled at the edges of her mind, but she ignored it.

Raising her head again, she brought her hands out to either side, palms up. She'd read the spells so many times that she didn't even need to look at the book to her right. "We stand here at the edge of Time, staring into the chasm of our own self-righteousness. Our folly has brought us to the brink of madness, and now only the agents of change can right our course and steer us through the maelstroms that loom before us." Each of the flames leaned in towards her: green, yellow, blue and black energies twining into a roiling ball of fire that hovered above her head. Nikki stared up into the whirling mass, wondering just what she would see when she released it.

You can't stop now, she thought to herself. *Not now.*

"I stand on the edge of the chasm and shout into the wind. I call upon those powers who exist only to Cleanse our souls." The fireball began to descend upon her, a deadly New Year's orb, and she tensed, waiting for the flames. "In this instant, I summon the Four Horsemen!"

The multihued flames engulfed her and Nikki bit back a scream as Power invaded every cell of her body, binding her into the spell. Her vision swam; she fell to her knees, reeling from the sheer immensity of the magic she was casting. When it cleared, Nikki's jaw dropped.

She stood in a timeless place, in thin air; beneath her lay the chasm the spell had referred to, energies boiling and churning in a never-ending river of Power. All around her, silvery-grey cords stretched as far as her eyes could see, a living web of magic with flames at nearly every juncture. Most were small, but there were four pillars of multicolored fire, much like the orb that had consumed her. Nikki reached for the nearest one, wreathed in black-edged gold, and stiffened as the image of the girl from her dreams rose in her mind. *My sister.*

Something vibrated the web, and Nikki pulled her hand back from the flames. Sitting in the midst of the strands of mist sat a familiar young woman, with pastel rainbows floating in her eyes. "So you've taken your first steps at last," the woman said, and the edge in her voice underscored the venom in her smile. "Welcome to our world."

"You're not the Balance," Nikki said. "Are you?"

"I never said I was."

"Didn't you?" Nikki said, planting her fists on her hips. "Didn't you tell me I had a glorious destiny to fulfill, should I choose to take it?"

"I did," the woman said, her robes shimmering with dying shards of light. "And you do. But I never claimed to be the Balance. Nor am I claiming that I'm not."

"Why does everyone who thinks they're clever speak in stupid riddles?" Nikki asked herself. "I'm not impressed. If you're the one behind all this, I'll shove you between the Walls so hard you'll never get out."

"You think so, do you, young Horseman?" The teeth behind the smile grew longer, more pronounced. "Now I understand why you're here."

"Do you?"

"Oh yes," the woman purred, and the web shivered. "But I don't want to ruin it for you, Horseman." She rose from the mists and stretched. "I will be seeing you soon, Horseman. Very soon."

Is that a promise or a threat? Nikki watched the mists flow around the woman and between one step and the next, she vanished, the web enfolding her into itself. *And just who are you, anyways?*

The mists didn't answer.

Chapter Twenty-seven

"Searching"

Derek waited patiently as the guard patted him down, watching as the man went through his bag, mindful of the gun trained upon him by the second guard. But when the first one pulled the evidence bag out, Derek laid his hand down on top of his. "No, that stays," he said firmly, pushing the bag back in.

"Sir..." the guard started, and then looked at the set expression on Derek's face.

"Don't make me pull rank," he said evenly, and the guard withdrew his hand.

"If something happens in there, we'll hold you responsible, "the other guard warned, and Derek nodded.

"That is an acceptable risk," he said, and picked the bag up. "Are we done?"

Amy was waiting inside when he stepped through the door, tapping one foot against the side of the small table. "What happened?" she asked, and Derek shrugged.

"They wanted to confiscate the knife. I told them no." He set the bag down on the table and began to unpack it. "It took a little longer than I wanted it to."

Amy peered in at him, and then decided not to pursue it. "Are you sure this is a good idea?" she said instead, and he shrugged again.

"Probably not," he said, setting the bloodstained knife and

the faceless rag doll down, and then pulling out four small white candles. ":But I'm out of ideas at the moment, and the only viable connection to this mystery girl that isn't in a position to argue with me is lying in that bed. I just hope that spider doesn't notice me poking around."

"I'll keep you as safe as I can," Amy promised, and he smiled at her.

They set the candles up at the cardinal points, and then Amy raised a small Circle, enclosing the bed with Dr. Sylvia Richard's still body in the soft, sunlit glow of her magic. Derek stood next to the bed, one ungloved hand on the knife, and let the magic's warmth pulse on his skin for a few moments, composing himself for whatever he might find. The last time he'd touched Sylvia, he'd barely escaped from whatever lurked in her subconscious.

Above them, through the various floors of the hospitals, Mages lay in comas, their lives slipping away, drained by whatever Chaos spirit held Sylvia hostage. Derek knew that if he discovered whom the Chaos spirit was, he could find the mystery girl. If they weren't one and the same.

"Derek?" Amy's voice snapped him out of his reverie. "Are you ready?"

"As ready as I'll ever be." He straightened his shoulders, and then laid his other bare hand on Sylvia's cheek.

Power flowed around and through him; rough-edged, a harsh slap in the face as he stumbled into Sylvia's mind. Images flashed, too quickly for him to process, like a film on fast forward. Somewhere in the background, he heard Amy say something, and then the floor dropped out from underneath him.

When Derek could see again, he blinked, shivering. Once again, the web he'd seen spread out before him: the hospital had disappeared, along with Sylvia and the bloodstained knife. In this timeless space, Power washed over him, a tidal wave of magic that chilled him to the bones.

Why is Shanna casting the first Summoning Spell again?

Derek spun, looking for the source of the magic, and then stopped. Behind him stood the dark-haired girl from his visions, the Spell pouring from her. His eyes widened, and he actually took a few steps back.

"But you don't look like a Greystone!" he blurted out, and then cursed as she turned towards him.

"That's because I'm not, I'm a Jeffries," she said, and then frowned. "Who the hell are you?"

"Does it matter?" Derek asked, his mind whirling. "Maybe I'm a fragment of your imagination."

"I don't like fragments of imagination," she said, and pointed a finger at him. "Get out of my spell."

Derek ducked, knowing that he couldn't avoid whatever she was doing, and her magic slammed into his back, icy fingers that clutched at his heart as it picked him up and threw him out of the Summoning. Power crushed him, a giant hand contracting around his body as it propelled him back to the hospital room, where Amy crouched beside his prone figure. Derek had a split-second glimpse of the scene: thunder crashed above them, and the windows rattled as massive snowflakes and icy rain battered against them, the results of the Summoning Spell. Then pain erupted around him, and he fought to keep his eyes open.

"What happened?" Amy demanded, and her frantic voice pounded against his eardrums, a high counterpoint to the rumbling headache that was the least of his worries. "Why is Shanna casting the Summoning Spell again?"

"Not Shanna." Derek's chest creaked as he struggled to breathe. He had to tell her, before he died. Had to, or this had all been a waste. "Our mystery... her name... is... Jeffries."

"Jeffries? Her last name is Jeffries?"

Derek nodded. "And she's... casting... Summoning Spells." Amy made some sort of response, but it was lost in the roaring that sucked him down into darkness.

"Are you ready to talk about it yet?"

"I don't know," Nikki said, not looking up from the fireplace. She was curled into one of the armchairs in Edgar's sitting room, a steaming cup of tea cradled in her hands and one of Marietta's elegant blankets tucked around her. She was tired, bone-numbing tired, but her thoughts were still running rampant through her head, and she knew she had to make sense of them.

Edgar took the seat next to her, and pulled out his pipe. Soon, fragrant smoke, redolent with vanilla and apple and cinnamon, twined gentle fingers around her face, a polite inquiry that she couldn't ignore. With effort, she turned her head and focused on him.

"The spell took you a bit longer to cast than I expected," Edgar said. "Now, that could be because you've never done anything like that before."

Giving me an out, huh? Nikki smiled. *Nice.* "Edgar, when the Summoning is cast, can others get into the Spell?"

He frowned. "What do you mean?"

She described the woman to him, and his frown turned worried. "I've never heard of anything like that happening. Then again, most of the StarChildren don't often write down what they see in the Spells. There hasn't been a Summoning cast in over a thousand years, so we may have lost things."

"That book you gave me isn't a thousand years old," Nikki said, and he nodded.

"It's been recopied. It will need to be done again soon."

"So who do you think she was?" Nikki asked, bringing herself back on topic with effort. "Could she be the Spirit of the Balance?"

"I doubt it, not if she threatened you," Edgar said. "You're an agent of the Balance, remember? No, I'm more inclined to think she might be one of the Chaos Lords involved in this."

"You mean there's more than one?" Nikki leaned back against the chair and closed her eyes. "Goddess, don't they have anything better to do?"

"Chaos Lords have nothing but time on their hands, and they follow the law of their Spirit," Edgar reminded her. "Chaos always seeks to expand, and some of them look beyond their World to this one. I'm not surprised that there is a female to complement Lucifer."

"So the Spell pulled in my enemy?" Nikki asked, opening her eyes in time to see Edgar nod. "To what? Warn me? Show me what she looked like?"

"Quite possibly." Edgar tapped his pipe bowl thoughtfully. "Or to remind you of the stakes in this game. Did you see anything else?"

"There was a guy who showed up too," Nikki said. "Another Chaos Lord?" Then she corrected herself. "No, he couldn't have been. The Power signature he had was different. Could I have pulled in a mortal?"

Worry painted lines on Edgar's face. "I doubt it," he said, and Nikki's heart sank." He could have been disguising his signature, though. If you saw him in the Summoning Spell, then he must be a Lord. Mortals wouldn't be able to survive the Power levels of the Spell, as far as I know."

"Could there be three Chaos Lords involved?"

"There could be," Edgar allowed. "But I'm wondering if he might be the traitor Shanna was talking about. Did he look familiar?"

Nikki shook her head. "But I don't know any of the Council Lords besides Vashti and Cassandra," she said." Damn."

"Did you say anything to him?"

"Just my last name," she admitted, and he shook his head. "By accident. I think I surprised him as much as he surprised me — he said I didn't look like a Greystone."

"This changes things." Edgar leaned over and tapped his pipe out into the fireplace. "We'll need to move fast — if he saw the locations of the other Horsemen, he may be moving to kill them before we can collect them."

"Kill them?" Nikki blinked. "Why?"

"Because the Cleansing kills Elemental Lords, Nikki," Edgar said. "You're a threat. Why do you think Alex stabbed you? If the four of you get together and mesh your talents the way you're supposed to, you'll be able to finish the Cleansing, and that will destroy those Lords." The look on her face gave her away; Edgar leaned forward and placed one hand on her knee. "This is a war, Nikki. People are going to die. That's what you were created for. The fact that it bothers you is good, because it means that you haven't forsaken your human side, but you have to move on. People die. It's a fact of life."

"I know." The exhaustion in her voice echoed the finality of his words. "I just hope I can live with it afterwards. Maybe I'll be one of the lucky ones and the Cleansing will consume me."

"Is that really what you hope for?" Edgar asked sadly, and she shrugged.

"Let's just say that I'm understanding more and more how Frodo felt when he went back to the Shire after Mt. Doom," Nikki said, and he patted her knee again.

"You're tired," he said. "It's the exhaustion talking. Let's get you upstairs to bed. It won't look that bad in the morning."

"If you say so." Nikki stood up and swayed slightly. "I need to go to New Orleans tomorrow."

"Who is there?" Edgar asked, taking her arm and helping her out the door.

"My sister." The words felt odd on her lips.

Chapter Twenty-eight

"Sisters and Brothers"

You have got to be kidding me.

Cleo stood in front of what had once been an old brick building in the meat packing district, shaking her head in bemused horror. Dan had neglected to tell her the name of the club until today, when he'd stopped by to pick up the Dark Queen. He'd handed her an engraved envelope and grinned when she'd groaned.

"The Stake-Out?" she'd demanded. "Are you joking?"

"Nope," he'd said, unrepentant. "Show up at five. Wear something slinky."

Wear something slinky. She looked down at the outfit she'd chosen after staring at her closet for nearly an hour: a thigh-length black lace dress with a plunging neckline that looked almost opaque — until she stepped into the light. A nude under-dress the exact shade of her skin made it look as if she was wearing nothing underneath the lace, and the black stiletto heels added four inches to her height. Her blonde hair was twisted into a classic chignon, and she wore a set of jet-black onyx beads around her neck, to match the simple black beads that dropped on silver chains from her earlobes. *I hope this looks slinky enough.*

The front of the old building was mostly unchanged, except for the long, low ramp that clung to the brick, and the doorman standing outside the steel door. Somewhere behind that door were both her Queens. With a shake of her head, Cleo walked up the ramp and handed her invitation to the doorman, who opened the door with a flourish.

Music hit her as she stepped inside, a throbbing bass line that nearly knocked her off her feet. Cleo shook her head, and then stopped as she saw what Dan had done with the interior of the building.

It was like stepping back in time. The foyer of the old building had been completely redone, with a shiny black marble floor and icy white accents. And looking haughtily down upon her from the wall was the Pale Queen.

"Cleo!"

Dan rushed out of a side door and nearly ran her down. "Sweet Jesus, Dan, turn the music down!" she shouted, grabbing his arm to keep her balance. "How do you expect anyone to hear anything?"

"They don't have to hear," Dan shouted back, grinning. "All they have to do is pay their cover charge, order drinks and dance. Follow me!"

He led her through a labyrinthine maze of black marble, flashing lights and flickering torches set high in the walls, past doors that opened onto a main room already full of people dancing to the insanely loud music, and up a spiral staircase to a smaller, more intimate bar. As she stepped into it, the bass died away, replaced by a smooth jazz band playing at a more moderate level, and Cleo relaxed.

"Shielding spells on the bar?" she asked, and Dan nodded. "Good plan."

"Thank you." He offered his arm and with a laugh, she threaded her hand through the crook of his elbow. "Let me show you the real attraction."

Cleo had already spotted the Dark Queen above the bar, glowering down on the black glass tables and sparkling martini glasses, but she let Dan lead her to the chrome-inlaid marble counter and lift her onto one of the stools. "This is amazing," she said, as the bartender wandered over. "A Cosmo, please."

"It's on the house," Dan said, and the bartender nodded. "Top shelf. Anything she wants tonight."

"Trying to get me drunk enough to take me home?" Cleo

teased, and he grinned cheekily.

"Will it work?"

"I'll let you know," she said, as the bartender set a blood-red Cosmopolitan in front of her and a small tumbler of scotch (Dan's favorite drink, she remembered) in front of his boss. "Check back with me in a few hours."

The bar was a loft above the dance floor; with the shielding spells muting the music, Cleo could enjoy the view of the dancers writhing beneath her. She and Dan chatted for nearly an hour and another Cosmo, and then the bartender leaned over and handed Dan a phone.

"What?" he said, frowning. "Well, send her away." He listened for a few moments longer and then sighed. "All right, I'll be right down." Dan handed the phone back to the bartender and then leaned over to kiss Cleo's cheek. "Sorry, babe, got a gatecrasher — club doesn't open officially to the public until tomorrow, and the doorman's having issues getting this chick to leave. I'll be right back."

"Have fun," Cleo said, grinning. He grinned back and threaded his way to the door.

She watched the dancers gyrate and sipped her third drink, enjoying the show through a faint alcoholic haze. After nearly five minutes and no Dan, Cleo wondered what was up.

Then the door to the bar opened, and Cleo stiffened, her buzz vanishing as a strong Power signature hit her. She turned on the stool, and looked over at the entrance to the bar.

The Dark Queen stood there, surveying the room with a faintly amused smile on her pale face. Instead of flowing robes, she was dressed in knee-high black boots, skin-tight black leather pants and a red silk sleeveless tank top, but that paled beside the Power shining through her skin. The music faltered and then stopped as she stepped into the room, and from behind her, Cleo heard glass shatter as the bartender dropped something.

"Well, I'll say one thing," Cleo observed in the silence. "You sure know how to make an entrance."

"It's a skill," the Queen said, coming over to the bar. She looked back at the bartender and said, "One rum and coke with ice, please." When he gaped at her, she raised one delicate black eyebrow. "Well?"

The drink appeared as if by magic, and she picked it up and tasted it. "Your buddy has a nice place here."

"What did you do with Dan, anyways?" Cleo asked.

"Nothing. He decided he had better things to do than argue with me about whether or not I could come in."

"He's not dead, is he?"

The Queen smiled grimly. "No."

Cleo heard barely-disguised pain in that word, but the hunger rose within her then, resonating with the Power of the girl sitting next to her and drowned out her thoughts. The Queen laid a hand on hers, and Cleo felt the hunger abate, fed by the touch of her sister's hand. Her sister. "How...?"

"Not yet," the Queen said. "But soon."

Cleo's head swam for a moment, and then she Saw Dan, sitting in his office, another glass of scotch in front of him. The vision lasted only a moment, and then the Queen removed her hand and picked up her drink.

The two of them sat and sipped in companionable silence, each lost in their own thoughts as they watched the dancers below. From behind them, the jazz band started again, a slow, sexy number that oozed darkness and magic the way only good jazz could.

"So what do I call you?" The Queen asked finally. "And where's your sibling?"

"Most folks call me Cleo," Cleo said, her lips twisting in something faintly resembling a smile. "And let's not talk about my asshole brother. What about you? I can't keep calling you the Dark Queen."

"The what?" Cleo gestured with her glass above her, and was gratified to see the Queen's eyes widen. "You painted that?"

"That one, and the one in the lobby."

"Damn." The Queen shook her head in admiration. "You're braver than I thought." She switched her glass to her other hand and held out her right hand to Cleo. "I'm Nikki."

"What do you mean, brave?" Cleo asked suspiciously.

Nikki tossed back the rest of her drink and set the glass on the counter behind her. "Painting Chaos Lords is a great way to draw unwanted attention to yourself."

Ice water sluiced down Cleo's back. "Chaos Lords?"

Nikki nodded. "What did you think your Pale Queen was?"

"A figment of my imagination," Cleo said, and drained the rest of her drink, hoping to find oblivion at the bottom. "Like most of my paintings."

"Sorry." Nikki didn't sound that apologetic. "At least you know the face of the enemy."

"What enemy?" Cleo said, turning to look at... her sister. *How odd to be thinking that.* "What is going on?"

"We're part of the Cleansing," Nikki said, leaning back on the stool with her elbows up on the bar and her booted feet stretched out in front of her. "Horsemen, in fact."

"The Horsemen are a myth," Cleo said, and Nikki laughed.

"Not anymore."

Cleo leaned back, her head spinning again, realizing how much it explained. "But that means..."

"Yep, asshole brother is a Horseman too." Nikki looked over at her. "Any idea which one?"

"Plague," Cleo said instantly. "He's a Healer."

"That should be interesting," Nikki said. "Then we only need to figure out what you are, and find number four."

"Who are you?" Cleo asked, and Nikki gave her a vicious smile.

"Who do you think I am?"

"Thom's worst nightmare," Cleo said, and Nikki laughed again.

"Why?"

"Because you're a Mage," Cleo said. "And Mages are eeeevvvviiillll. Just ask him — he'll quote you chapter and verse as to why God hates us. And why he hates us." She shook her head. "If we need his help, we're all doomed."

"He'll help us." Nikki sounded serenely confident.

"He's a raving religious lunatic," Cleo told her, and Nikki chuckled. "No, seriously. He's given his soul to God and his brain with it."

A raving religious lunatic?

Lucifer's ears perked up at that comment, and he moved closer within in the Walls to the two Horsemen. *Tell me more, child, tell me more.*

"We'll just have to convince him otherwise," Nikki was saying, and Lucifer grinned.

"Good luck." Her companion didn't look that hopeful. "If you can convince Thom to have anything to do with magic, I'll... hell, I don't know what I'll do, but it'll be pretty damn big."

"Where is he?" Nikki said. "I work better face-to-face."

"Last I knew, he and my mother were in the Midwest somewhere," Cleo said. "I'm not sure either of the numbers I have are good anymore — Mom's is disconnected, again, and no one picks up on Thom's."

You look for them, Lucifer thought, heading back to Madness' bower. *I have a faster way.*

"Have you found them?" Madness demanded, as he paused again on the edge of the lawn that surrounded her gazebo. Today, the maze was an infinite spiral, winding in upon itself, and the beasts that roamed the grass had a distinctly reddish tinge to them. Madness herself sat at her loom, weaving jet-black clouds into the ash-grey sky trapped in her frame.

"No," he admitted, and thunder rumbled above. "But I have found something else."

"I do not care what else you have found," Madness said, and the thunder rumbled again, louder. "I want the Dead."

"What if I gave you a sympathetic Horseman instead? One who could track the Dead as only a Horseman could."

There was silence, broken only by the storm grumbling above.

"What do you mean?" she said finally.

"How divine are you feeling, my love?" This time, he couldn't keep the excitement out of his voice.

Madness lowered her hands and stared steadily at him, her pale rainbow eyes unreadable. "What are you talking about?"

"May I show you?" Lucifer asked, and all the beasts froze, looking at him. Madness continued to stare at him, and he wondered for a moment if she would help him after all.

"Come," she said finally, and the beasts parted grudgingly. Lucifer ran lightly across the green lawn, eager to share his idea with her.

Finding the boy was easy enough, once he told her what the girl had said. He could tell she was intrigued; her icy demeanor melting as she wove magic into her web, reading the lines of Power that pulsed from the newest Horseman to her brother.

"A twin," she said finally, raising her face from the web. "A fanatical twin, you say?"

"Highly religious," he said, leaning over her shoulder. "And he hates his sister for being a Mage."

Madness sat back, running a finger over her lips as she thought. "We can use that," she said, and Lucifer smiled triumphantly. She pulled a thread from the web in front of her, a shimmering, sickly ochre strand that snaked out over her hands and disappeared out of the gazebo. "Find him, my Lucifer. Find out as much as you can. I do not like losing Tony like we did for several hours. We need to move the child to a safe place, and this boy may provide us with it. And then, as you say, he can track the Dead for us."

"I hear and obey," Lucifer said, daring to drop a kiss on her pale cheek. She didn't turn away; his heart sang and he favored her with a deep bow before running from the gazebo, following the strand of mist through the World Walls.

The thread led him to a small shrine, deep within a sheltered valley community that nestled behind walls of rock and religion, shutting out the outside world. The statue of a female saint huddled within a small rock garden, evergreens hiding her from prying eyes, and Lucifer paused within the World Walls, listening to the prayers of the tortured soul he sought.

His target knelt on the dead grass in front of the statue, fingers laced together, white knuckles glowing in the soft winter twilight. Lucifer could read the stress in the arch of his spine, and his words only verified the emotions pouring from his skin.

"Send me a sign," the boy prayed, raising his eyes to the statue. "Tell me what I'm supposed to do. I can't stand by and let my mother die, and yet, I can't let this curse lead her into damnation.

Why can't we fix the Cure?"

Lucifer stretched out the lightest of mental touches through the Walls, reaching into the young man's mind, looking for anything they could use to woo him into helping them. What he found inspired a course of action.

He pulled his mental probes back, thinking furiously. Thom Smith the Healer hadn't recognized the dark shape menacing his mother's dreams, but Lucifer had seen that particular Shadow more than once over the years. But why would Teraisa Donnelly, long absorbed into the Shadows that had birthed her, be haunting the other breeder from the first experiment?

Revenge, perhaps? Caran seems to have survived the experiment more or less human. That didn't ring right with the Chaos Lord, although he didn't know why. *Could she still have a role to play in this dance?*

The thread that had led Lucifer here had split when it came to Thom: one strand meandered off into the growing darkness of the winter's evening, out through the hospital's gates. Lucifer ignored that line in favor of the one that snaked into the hospital itself; up through halls of Mages in various stages of mental decay, to a quiet office that looked out over the inner courtyard. He peeked through the door at the blonde working at the desk; another Healer. The thread from Thom wrapped lovingly around her, and Lucifer extended a cautious mental probe, wondering how deep he could go before she'd notice him. But her attention was elsewhere; he sank into her memories without alerting her to his presence, and what he found there made him want to crow in triumph.

You didn't tell us you had a sister, Tony. Lucifer bared his teeth as he withdrew from the Healer's mind. *What else didn't you tell us? I think it's time we found out.*

Chapter Twenty-nine

"Planting Seeds"

"Our Father, who art in Heaven, hallowed be thy name…"

The ancient words echoed in the chapel, bouncing off the wood-paneled walls back to the small group who knelt in the pews, raising their eyes and prayers to the Christ permanently dying on his cross above them. Lucifer stood behind the priest, still within the World Wall, Madness beside him, and wondered why humans were so willing to put their trust in someone they had never seen.

"Everyone needs something to believe," Madness said, when he mentioned it to her. "Even you, my love."

"All I need to believe in stands before me," he said, and she smiled at him. "Are you ready?"

"Always."

Lucifer kissed her gently and then concentrated, shifting his form until it matched the forlorn statue of St. Catherine of Assisi that Thom Smith had been praying to a scant twenty-four hours earlier. Madness called up her mists, twining them around her lover's form and binding herself to him, lending him her voice. Once her spell was complete, Lucifer stepped through the World Walls, masking his presence from all but the one person he wanted to speak to.

Chrysanthemum Keats paled as she saw him, nearly falling off her knees as he stepped around the oblivious priest and pointed at her. The girl next to her glanced questioningly at her, but Chrys shook her head and murmured something, so she shrugged and turned her attention back to her folded hands, and Lucifer spread his arms, pulling Chrys into his spell.

"She cannot see me, my child. God sends me to you and you alone," Madness said through Lucifer, her voice light and sweet, coated in dishonesty. "In this instant, it is only you and I."

"Why do you come to me?" Chrys asked, fear in her eyes.

"Do not fear, child," Madness cooed. "I bear a message from above."

"A message?" Chrys trembled. "What message?"

"The Holy Father has a mission for you, child. There are forces at work that He must combat, and he has chosen you to be one of the ones He works through."

"I am no warrior," Chrys said, but the pallor was fading from her face. "What can I do?"

Lucifer smiled. "You are a Healer, child. You walk the path of the Holy Son. He does not expect you to be a warrior. That is His role. But He will need protectors in the beginning."

Chrys' blue eyes widened as she realized what the figure before her was saying. "He is returning?"

"He is," Madness said. "And His mother is in danger, even as we speak. Her protectors have been corrupted, placing Our Lord in harm's way. His enemies move to take her into their custody, and if they do, He will be unable to return, and the End of Days will begin. He has chosen you to safeguard His mother until the date of His birth."

"But how will I find her?" Chrys whispered, bringing her cross to her lips reverently.

"I will show you the way," Madness promised, and Lucifer reached out to Chrys. Mists flowed from his hand to her head, carrying images of the house and the breeder. "But this will be difficult for you, a test, my child. Can you be strong enough to stand against your own family?"

As they had hoped, Chrys straightened at that. "I have no family left," she said, and Lucifer smiled again. "Where do I go?"

"The Hand of God will guide your heart, child," Madness told her. "Just follow it. Trust only those you hold closest to you, and beware of those who seek to stop Him from returning." A picture of Nikki shimmered into view. "This is the major one who will seek to stop you. Do not listen to her — the Evil One coats her lies in the shroud of truth, and her words are honeyed poison."

"I shall not fail you," Chrys promised.

"We, the Lord and I, have faith in you, child," Madness whispered, and Lucifer let himself slide back through the Walls slowly. "Go and find the mother. Her main protector has been wounded — you will find him with her. Save them both, and you will save the world. He is a Healer too — He will help you with the work you seek to complete."

As he came back to the World between the Walls, Lucifer resumed his own shape and grabbed Madness. "You were perfect!" he chortled. "Perfect! Divine, even!"

"We shall see," she said, but her radiant smile belied her calm words. "Follow her. Make sure they bring the girl and Alex back to this location before Death finds them."

"I hear and obey," Lucifer said, setting her back on her feet and bowing deeply.

―――•+•―――

"We have to obey," Chrys said, tangling her fingers in the chain of her cross. Above her head, the heater kicked on, warming the small office. "We cannot thwart the will of God." She looked at the other two sitting across from her, on the other side of her desk, and asked simply, "Can I trust you to help me?"

Diana didn't answer, but Chrys saw the uneasy look in her eyes. Thom, on the other hand, had lit up when she'd told them what she'd seen during Mass. "So what do we do now?" he asked.

"We have to find out where this house is," Chrys said. "It's odd — I think I know it, but it looks... I don't know. St. Catherine said my heart would guide me."

"And when we get to this place?" Diana said. "Are we really ready to kill someone on purpose?"

"Trust you to be our conscience," Chrys said, smiling to take the sting out of her words. "And we may be able to persuade them to join us. But if not, then yes, I am ready to kill for my Lord."

Thom nodded. "If they are lost souls, it will be a mercy to end their suffering," he said. "And if this is the End of Days, we will all be called upon to kill for our faith. Think of it as treating a disease, Diana. Those who we kill now will weaken the cancer that is the Evil One spreading through the world."

Her face twisted in indecision, and Chrys laid her hand on top of Diana's, noting how cold they were. "I don't like the idea of killing either," she said gently. "But we have to trust St. Catherine. I know, deep within my heart, that God has called us to help him, and I will answer that call. Please help me. I need your help."

Silence echoed as she and Thom watched Diana wrestle with her conscience. Finally, the telepath looked up and nodded. "I can't let you go alone."

"I knew you would find your faith," Chrys said. "Now, we need to get the van..."

Chapter Thirty

"A Lock of Hair to Track Them By..."

"Are you ready?"

Cleo nodded at her from across the circle. Once again, Nikki stood on the marble floor in Edgar's mansion, the chandelier above her sparkling in the dim twilight of the Shadow Lands and a map of the United States spread out before her. Her Light Mage sister had shivered as she'd stepped into the Rothman House, but Nikki barely felt the chill anymore — more proof she was becoming a true creature of the Shadows, she supposed. *But what can I do? It's not as if I can stop it now...*

"Pay attention," Edgar said, and Nikki pulled her wandering thoughts back guiltily. "This isn't as simple as the last one you cast."

"That was simple?" Nikki said, and he nodded. "Good lord."

"Thom will fight us," Cleo warned her. "He's been conditioned to hate Mages, remember. Nothing you say will convince him we're anything other than spawn of the Devil."

"I'm not planning on talking very much," Nikki said. "He may not want to deal with me, but his Horseman won't be able to resist my call."

Cleo shook her head. "Wait until you meet him before you say that."

Nikki looked over at Edgar. "Can you shield my spell again?"

"You shouldn't need it." He nodded at the lock of thick blond hair lying on the floor in the middle of the circle. "This spell is going to be very focused. As long as you don't break your Circle, Department V won't be able to find you."

"Good." Nikki took a deep breath and looked at her sister. "Ready?"

"Sure, why not? I love arguing with my twin." Cleo's mouth twisted. "It makes my day. Who knows, he might even spill something about my mother."

"Then let's begin." Nikki raised her arms and lit the candles with a single word. "We don't have much time."

Cleo raised her arms as well, and Nikki felt her warm Power mesh with her Shadows seamlessly, bolstering her own strength. *And when we are four? How strong will we be then?*

Invincible, came a whisper from deep within her. *When the Four stand together, none can stop us.*

Nikki raised her eyes to the chandelier, focusing on the candle flames dancing there. "I call the quarters to witness my spell. I call the elements to sanctify this space. I call the seasons to guard my call." As she cast the Circle, the tall white pillar candles at the compass points in the room changed color as Spirits glided in, one for each quarter called.

Once the Circle was cast, Nikki paused for a moment, gathering her strength. Then she called out, "Thomas Chamuel Smith, the Horseman Plague, by the Power of the Balance, I summon thee here!" and brought her hands together sharply.

It was midnight — they'd chosen their time carefully, hoping he would be asleep so they could pull him into the Circle without him fighting them. As Cleo and Nikki waited, a nebulous mist wisped up from lock of hair on the floor, slowly growing more solid.

Thom was taller than either of them, but lankier, with blond curls Nikki would have killed to have when she was younger. His blue eyes, so very like his twin's, were confused as he looked at her.

"Who are you?" he demanded. "Why am I here?"

"I'm your sister," Nikki said. "You're here because I need you to help us."

Thom's eyes narrowed. "You're a Mage. I don't help Mages. And you aren't Cleo."

"No, I'm here too," Cleo said, and he spun around. "She's our sister as well, Thom."

"What are you talking about?" he snapped. "We're the only two children Mom had."

"Your mother was part of the same experiment my mother was," Nikki said. "Twenty-three years ago. We're all the result. All Horsemen. And now we have a job to do."

Thom glared at both of them. "I am no Mage! My soul is my own, and I will never help you bring about the End of Days! St. Catherine was right!"

"What are you talking about, you freak?" Cleo said. "End of Days? The world's not ending."

"Not yet," Thom said, and Nikki shuddered inwardly at the fervent light in his eyes. "But soon, Our Lord will be reborn, and He will cleanse the plague of Magic from this world once again."

As he continued to rant, Nikki caught the briefest hint of something emanating from him; a whiff of Chaos, and her eyes narrowed. *Madness. She's already gotten to him. Damn.*

She reached out and touched him on the forehead; he knocked her hand away, but not before she marked him. "Don't touch me!" he spat. "Don't defile me like that. I already have enough of your magical taint on my soul."

"You're going to have a lot more before this is done," Nikki told him. "Like it or not, Thom, you're a Horseman. You *will* stand beside me when the final Cleansing is cast, and you *will* assist us in closing the holes in the World Walls. And now that I've marked you, you cannot hide from me."

"Go back to hell," Thom snarled, and then vanished.

"Good to know that some things never change," Cleo said, and when Nikki looked at her, she shrugged. "Hey, I warned you. He's been spewing that poison since he was sixteen. Did you really think you would just show up and change him?"

"No," Nikki said. "I just didn't think his mind would be that closed."

"Welcome to the world of fanatical religion. Now what?"

Nikki looked out of the Circle at Edgar and nodded. He nodded back and raised his own arms as she turned back to Cleo. "Now we figure out where he went to ground."

She felt him cast the distortion spell even through her shields, and cast her own seeking spell, looking for the mark she'd placed on Thom's spirit as he'd stood in the Circle. Once again, she stood in that timeless instant, looking at the web spread out before her, with the pillars of flame rising. Thom's flame pulsed with a strange, crackling light, and when she touched it, ice coated her fingers. *Not a promising start. I hope you aren't as lost as you seem, Thom. I'd hate to have to kill my own brother after just meeting him.*

Her vision fogged for a moment, and then the image of a hospital filled her mind: a tall, white building that shouldered itself up from the surrounding buildings, holding itself aloof from the rest of the neighborhood. A great cross stood on the very top of the hospital, with an emaciated Christ hanging limply from its arms. *Why am I not surprised?*

When she ended the spell and opened her eyes, she was kneeling down, pointing at a small town in the Southwest. Cleo came over and looked. "Andersonville, huh? That sounds about right. If I recall, Mom rented an apartment there once. Thom's probably got a condo near the hospital."

"Rented?"

Cleo nodded. "Mom never bought anything — she rented furnished apartments, so we could leave at a moment's notice and not have to bring anything. Just in case they found us."

"Wow." Nikki remained kneeling, her fingers on the map, pondering their options. "Sounds like a lovely childhood."

"It wasn't as bad as it sounds — Mom made it fun, until we ran into that damn preacher that turned them into raging lunatics," Cleo said. "So now what?"

"Good question." Nikki frowned. "Do we go to Andersonville and take Thom, or do we go after Alex? I need to get my hands on that slimy bastard."

"Alex? Alex Masterson? Why do you need him?"

"Who do you think your mother was running from?" Nikki said, looking up at her sister. "Didn't she ever tell you?" When

Cleo gave her a confused look, Nikki said, "Alex Masterson is your father."

Cleo blinked. "You're kidding."

"I wish." Nikki stood up and ran her hands through her hair, still trying to make a decision. "I'm not as worried about Thom: that mark won't let him hide from me for very long. So I think we can leave him for the moment. Alex is another matter — I need him."

"We also need to find the fourth Horseman," Cleo said, and it was Nikki's turn to blink. "We're supposed to be four, remember? There had to be someone else."

"But there were only three infants!" Nikki said.

"Doesn't matter," Cleo said, as Edgar joined them. "The spell summoned Four Horsemen. Just because... my father... only had three infants doesn't mean that other spirit just left. Didn't the Summoning Spell show you four pillars?"

"Yes," Nikki admitted. "I figured it was just because that's what the spell called for."

Cleo shook her head. "It's a specific spell, Nikki. You summon four Horsemen — you get four Horsemen."

"Well, shit." Nikki chewed on her lower lip. "Okay, so we need to find the last Horseman as well." She looked at the other two. "So what should we do first?"

There was a light snow falling the next morning when Nikki went outside to see Cerberus. He stood leaning his head over the paddock, blowing snowflakes at another black horse, a mare, that was ignoring him to stare up at the house. They were staying at Edgar's, rather than Teraisa's or the Inn, because they had no idea if Department V was still watching Sarah's house.

Never mind the fact that Rick's being a total ass at the moment, Nikki thought, rubbing the side of his face. *Sleeping together was supposed to clear things up, not make it worse.*

Of course, Justin kissing me like that probably didn't help. But sweet Jesus, I slept with Rick, not Justin!

"Boys are stupid," she announced to Cleo, who had just walked out the front door.

"Well, duh," Cleo said, holding her hand out to the black mare, who sniffed her palm delicately. "What brought that bit of wisdom out this morning?"

"I called Rick."

"Rick who?"

"Rick Jackson. He's been helping Justin and I since we started this." Nikki continued to rub Cerberus' face. "I think I might be in love with him."

"Love or lust?" Cleo asked, and Nikki sighed. "Yeah, it's probably love if you answer like that. I'm sorry."

"Sorry?"

"Love makes people do stupid things," Cleo said. "I'm hoping I never fall in love. Look what it did to my mother."

"Do you really think she loved Alex Masterson?" Nikki asked.

"At one point, yes, I think she did." Cleo put her foot up on the railing and leaned. "She used to look at us and tell us that no matter what happened, she'd always love the streak of our father in us. I always wondered what happened to him — I guess I'd decided he'd died when she escaped from whoever "they" were. She never talked much about her life before us."

"At least you knew her," Nikki said. "My mother dropped me off at a doorstep and hoped they'd take me in."

"At least you got to have a more normal childhood," Cleo retorted, and Nikki conceded the point with a shake of her head. "Nothing's going to be perfect. So why's he being a dork now?"

Nikki gave her a short rundown of the morning Justin had been arrested, and Cleo's eyes widened. Then, to Nikki's surprise, she began to laugh.

"So you slept with one guy, and let another kiss you just before he got arrested?" Cleo burbled. "No, wait, you let *Justin Greystone* kiss you before he got arrested? Damn, girl, you really do pick them, don't you?"

"I guess so." Nikki rested her chin on her arms. "So now what do I do?"

"Well, you've got two choices." Cleo's eyes sparkled. "You can either go with this Rick, who sounds like he's madly in love with you just from the way he's acting, or you can wait for Justin. The big question is, who floats your boat more?"

"I don't know," Nikki admitted. "Honestly, I don't know."

Then another thought slammed into her, and Nikki straightened. "Idiot! Why didn't you think of that sooner?" She whirled and ran into the house, Cleo hot on her tail.

"Think of what?" Cleo called, but Nikki didn't answer until they'd burst into the second-floor library. By then, Edgar and Marietta had joined them, curious as to what the furor was about.

"The hair!" she said, grabbing the Shadow Box that she'd sneaked back to the Inn to get the day after Justin had been arrested off the low table in front of the window. "She collected hair from everyone involved in the project! You, me, Thom..." and Nikki pulled a thick, wavy black lock out and slammed it down triumphantly on the wooden table. "And Alex." She grinned at Cleo. "Now we go hunting your father."

"I get first dibs on kicking his ass," Cleo said.

"Just don't kill him. We might need him later."

CHAPTER THIRTY-ONE

"DREAMS"

"Just a minute!"

Diana stirred the pasta sauce simmering on the stove one last time and then hurried to the door. She peeked through the peephole and gasped, then hurriedly unlocked her door and opened it.

"Sweet Heaven, Thom, what happened to you?"

Thom leaned against the doorframe, his blonde hair hanging in limp hanks around his white face, his eyes sunken deep into his skull. She reinforced her mental shields as she reached for him, guiding him into the living room; exhaustion rolled off him in waves, battering at her. "When was the last time you slept?" Diana asked him, helping him sit down on the couch.

"Last night," he grunted, leaning back. "And it wasn't restful at all."

"What happened?" she asked again as she poured him a glass of water. "Tell me."

Thom accepted the glass and stared down into it, as if the crystal-clear liquid held the answers to all Diana's questions. She took a seat in the chair across from him and waited.

"I think I'm going insane," he said finally, with a haunted, desperate look in his blue eyes. "There's no other explanation for the dreams I've been having, the things I've been seeing. Oh, Di, I'm really losing it!"

"No, you're not," she soothed, extending a calming influence over him, although inwardly Diana shivered. *Dreams? Did someone tell you about your mother's episodes after all? Chrys will be furious if they did.* "You're under a lot of stress right now. Talk to me, tell me about these dreams."

He shivered. "I can't explain them. In some, I'm riding an ash-grey horse through a cold, misty place. There are others, at least three, sometimes four, and we're searching for something. I don't know what, but it's very important that we find it. And there are other riders in the mists, but they're not human — I don't know what they are. And other times, I'm...God, Di, I killed people! With magic!" Thom's voice broke, and he squeezed the glass. It shattered with a sharp crack, making them both jump.

"Don't move!" Diana ordered, getting up and rushing into her small kitchen. She saw the sauce on the stove and turned it off, not wanting anything else to explode, and then grabbed her first aid kit and a kitchen towel. Thom hadn't stirred; he was watching the blood ooze from between his fingers in numbed fascination. He didn't resist as she pried open his clenched fist and removed the shards of glass, didn't wince as she wiped the cuts down with antiseptic, but he did stop her from getting the gauze.

"Don't bother," Thom said, and Diana watched as the cuts closed up. "That, at least, I can still do. I haven't lost everything."

"You haven't lost anything," Diana said, picking up the remains of the glass and carrying it into the kitchen, where she dumped it in the trash. Then she pulled a pair of plastic goblets out of her cupboard and a bottle of chilled white wine from the refrigerator. Thom blinked when she came back out. "Here. Drink this. Then you can tell me why these dreams are bothering you so much."

Thom accepted the glass and she filled it, then poured one for herself and sat back down on the armchair. "They're so real," he said finally, taking a sip. "As if they aren't dreams, but...."

"Memories?" Diana finished for him, and he nodded. "You know they can't be anything other than dreams, though, right?"

"I don't, though, Di, not anymore." Thom shook his head. "Not after last night."

"What happened?"

He described the scene to her: the arching marble foyer and the two young women who had summoned him there to recruit him to their mission. "It wasn't a dream — I woke up still feeling that bone-chilling cold," Thom said, looking up. "And when I went to see my mother today... what's wrong?"

Diana was staring at him open-mouthed — when he said that, she shook herself and took a deep swallow from her glass and then waved him to continue. When she could speak, she said, "I'll tell you in a moment. What happened today?"

He blinked, but when she didn't say anything else, he continued. "I went to see Mother — the nurses said she'd been restless all night, and I wanted to see why. When I went in, she was cowering in the corner, and this dark shadow hovered over her. I could hear it speaking, although I couldn't understand all of it — the voice was deep, throaty, almost female, but not quite. It turned as I came in and hissed at me, and those words I did understand."

"What did it say?" Diana asked, fascinated despite herself.

" 'Grow a backbone, boy, and step up. Can't you see where your cowardice will lead you all?' " Thom said, and for the first time that night, he laughed, a harsh, bitter laugh that scraped against Diana's ears. "Then it vanished."

"Only a dark shadow?" Diana asked, and then realized how it would sound. Thom's head came up sharply and his accusing stare pinned her in place.

"You knew about the shadow?"

Diana chose her next words carefully. "I knew your mother had said she was being haunted by a dark shadow," she said. "It was in the medical reports." Which it had been. Not a lie, not yet. "She also mentioned a being of light, but no one had ever seen them, so everyone thought it was more of her hallucinations. Chrys said she'd discussed the medical reports with you." Also not a lie. Diana knew, though, that Chrys had been pulling out parts of the reports before letting Thom near them, something she'd been against. The way Chrys had dismissed her concerns still rankled a bit.

"I can't have him distracted by his mother's failing mental health, especially when there's nothing he can do for her," Chrys had said, even as Diana fumed. "I understand your concerns, and

I'll speak to him when we have something we can do. Until then, it's best to keep this between us." The look she'd shot Diana had been a warning, coated with false sympathy. "*I can trust you to do that, right?*"

"She didn't." Thom's flat voice pulled her from the memory. "I wonder why."

"Probably because she thought there was nothing you could do, Thom." Diana set her glass aside and went to kneel in front of him, putting her hands around his as they held the wineglass. "That, and we thought it was a hallucination. But if you saw it too, then that proves that she's not crazy — and neither are you."

"You don't know that," Thom said, trying to pull away, but Diana tightened her hands around his and wouldn't let him.

"I do know that," she said. "I saw your dream last night."

He stopped struggling and stared down at her. "You're humoring me."

"I'm not," Diana said. "Your twin sister's let her hair grow again — it's nearly down to the middle of her back, with long curls. The other girl told you that like it or not, you were a Horseman, and you were going to stand beside her, that you couldn't hide from her. She had long black hair and dark blue eyes. Shall I go on?"

"No." Thom shook his head. "You've convinced me. But the other dreams..."

"The one in the café was the oddest," Diana said. "Watching Alex Masterson, the dark haired girl and the other..." She paused, not sure what else to say, and luckily Thom saved her.

"That odd creature...I don't know what to call it," he said, and she nodded, grateful for his interpretation of her silence. *You don't need to know that it was pretending to be my father.* "But do you know what the worst part is?" he asked her, and she shook her head. "Feeling, at least in a part of my soul, like they're right."

"It's not that odd," Diana said. "After all, she is your sister. Even if she is a Mage, and misguided — she's still your family, Thom. Those bonds run deeper than we realize."

"Maybe." Thom looked down at their clasped hands, then up at her, questions hovering in his gaze. "But you haven't told me why you're having these dreams too."

"Maybe we're more connected than we thought." It wasn't really a complete answer, but it was one her conscience could live with, and here, away from the Clinic, Diana felt she could finally say what she'd been waiting a long time to say to him. Especially with no Chrys there to interrupt.

He freed one of his hands and cupped her cheek as she knelt in front of him. "Why didn't you ever tell me?"

"Because you've always been so focused on your work that you've never noticed," Diana said, chuckling. "Besides, I know the rules. No fraternizing on the job." She turned her head, so her lips kissed his hand, then turned back. "But we're not on the job now."

"No, no, we're not." He pulled her up to her feet, the wineglass dropping between them to lie forgotten on the tiled floor as Diana got the kiss she'd been waiting nearly five years for.

Thom's lips met hers and she tasted the sweet residue of the wine. That combined with the mental touch he extended to send her senses spinning, an intoxicating mixture that drowned out the room around her.

He withdrew a bit, and Diana opened her eyes to protest.

"Your phone is ringing," Thom said, his lips moving softly against hers.

"That's what answering machines are for," she breathed, twining her hand up around the back of his head and drawing his unresisting mouth back to hers.

Beep! "Diana, it's Chrys. Pick up, please."

Go away, Chrys, Diana thought fiercely, but Thom had raised his head from hers. *Damn you. Can't you let us enjoy one night? Just one?*

"Diana, I know you're there. Pick up the phone."

They looked at each other, and then Diana sighed and swiveled around. "Yes?"

"What took you so long?"

"I had... something on the stove," Diana said, as Thom slipped his arms around her waist and pulled her back against him. "I'm sorry."

"So am I," Chrys said, and Diana blinked at the odd tone in her voice. "Do you know where Thom is? He's not answering his pager."

"I... I think he said he needed some time to de-stress," she said, trying not to give too much away. "Why?"

"We need to leave."

"Now?" Diana said, trying to ignore Thom's closeness as he leaned over her shoulder, listening intently. "To go where?"

"St. Catherine spoke to me again." Chrys' words rang with an eeriness that tingled on Diana's skin. "She gave me the directions to the child."

"What?" Diana and Thom exchanged astonished glances. "Where is he?"

"My father's watching over him," Chrys said.

"Your..." Diana shook her head, trying to understand. "Chrys, your father's been dead for over ten years."

"Trust in our angel," Chrys said. "And get to the Clinic. We leave in an hour. Tell Thom to come with you when you get off the phone. I know you know where he is."

Diana and Thom exchanged glances again. "Okay," Diana said, but the only the dial tone answered her.

Chapter Thirty-two

"The Beginning of the End"

"Where the hell have you been this time?"

Tony paused long enough to peel the former owner's face from his own before answering. "Sorry, the store was more crowded than I thought it would be." He looked up at Alex, who stood on the stairwell glaring down at him. "What's wrong? Is it the breeder?"

"The breeder is fine," Alex snapped. "I, on the other hand, am about ready to castrate you myself and leave here, taking the child with me. Why are we still cowering here and where is my Light Mage? We need to get this experiment moving again."

"That's rather difficult without the spells," Tony snapped back, dropping the face and the shopping bag on the floor at his feet. "Which you are supposed to be recreating. How is that little project coming along, Alex?"

"Don't change the subject," Alex said, stomping down the stairs. "The next two spells are done — the important ones. I've got them written down upstairs. All I need is a Light Mage to help me cast them. Which you are supposed to be getting. If we don't stabilize the child soon, we're not going to be able to control it when it comes bursting out of her womb like a slavering zombie bent on killing us."

"I know that!" Tony slammed his hand against the wall. "But we can't cast anything here now!"

"Why not?" Alex shouted. "Dammit, Tony, there is no reason

for us not to cast! We have a house with a damned Circle built into it! We are both well-rested! The only thing holding us back is the fact that we don't have a damned Light Mage to cast the other half of the spells!"

"I'm working on it!" Tony shouted back, frustration boiling over. He stalked over to Alex, standing nose to nose with the tall Shadow Mage. "Unfortunately, it's not as if I can just go to Wal-Mart and buy one! People around here would notice if someone went missing!"

"Funny, you've never worried about that before." Alex shoved Tony back against the wall hard. "Get me a Light Mage. I don't care what you have to do to get one, but I'm casting those spells tomorrow. It's the mid-winter solstice in two weeks, and I want that child stabilized before then. Understand?"

"Alex, I really..."

"Get. Me. A. Light. Mage." Alex punctuated each word with another shove, slamming Tony into the wall. "Or I will slit your throat myself."

Then the Shadow Mage turned around and stomped back up the stairs.

Tony slumped back against the wall. Once he was sure Alex had gone, he let loose the shivers huddling inside of him. *We can't start the spells yet. Not yet.*

He might still find us. I don't know if I'm clean yet.

It had been nearly a week since the Dawn Lord had set him free again, after stripping every last bit of information about the experiments from his mind. The last thing the Lord had said, before dumping him back into the Shadow Lands, was a promise: "The child will be mine. I will come and claim it when you least expect it." Then he had patted Tony on the head, like a dog. "And you'll show me the way, won't you, Tony? Take care of my baby for me in the meantime."

Once he brought himself back under control, Tony picked up the discarded face and shopping bag and went into the kitchen. Putting away groceries helped smooth the last of the anxiety from his mind, and he began to think of what he could do to stall Alex without tipping him off to the other Lord's possible presence.

I'll have to find a Light Mage — maybe he'll accept that I'll need to go find one farther away then our current backyard. A young one. Too bad June died of a overdose — she would have been perfect, and I could have bribed her with her drug of choice. Whatever that happened to be at that point.

Maybe Grant knows someone like that. I could call him from a payphone; he owes me...

Gravel crunched outside and Tony froze. *Who the hell?* He went into the parlor and peeked out through the curtains. A large black van stood silently in the driveway.

Shit.

"Alex! We've got company!" He went running into the hall, intent on barricading the door before Department V got through. Upstairs, he heard Alex open the door to the breeder's room and hoped he wouldn't forget the spells. "Don't forget the spells!"

"Don't worry — I'm not my father," came Alex's cool response. "Barricade the door and..."

There was a loud thump from upstairs, and then... silence. Tony swore again as he reached out for the door. *Damnit, John, you were supposed to let me know when they were getting close to us!* As he touched the knob, it twitched under his hand and he flinched back. Then the door slammed open and he looked up in shock.

She really hadn't changed much: same blonde hair, same blue eyes, same cold haughtiness wrapped in almost childlike innocence. Funny how some people would look the same at sixty as they did at sixteen.

"Hello, big brother. Remember me?" Chrys Keats smiled at her older half brother; a mocking smile that chilled his blood. "Good. Now it's time for you to go."

She reached out and touched him lightly on the chest. From anyone else, it would be a tender gesture, but Tony knew better. Especially as the blood in his body stopped moving through his veins.

The last thing he saw was her smile. The last thing he heard was her laughter.

Chapter Thirty-three

"Showdown"

Lord, help us.

Diana watched numbly as Chrys stepped over her dying brother as if he were nothing but a newspaper on the stoop and motioned them inside. It took Thom grabbing her elbow to move her forward; she had to step over the motionless Mage as well, and the look of absolute shock on his face shook her to the very core. *What have I agreed to?*

"We don't have much time," Chrys said, her voice steady, as if she hadn't just killed someone. Diana tore her eyes away from Tony's limp body and tried to focus on what Chrys was saying. "We need to get the girl and Alex Masterson into the van, and get out of here before we call the cops."

"Call the cops?" Thom frowned. "Why?"

"Because we need them to find Tony's body," Chrys said. "That will keep them off our tails long enough to get to the new Clinic."

"It's finished?" Diana asked, the news piercing her stupor.

Chrys nodded. "And that's where we'll be going when we leave here." She turned to Thom. "They should both be upstairs, unconscious. St. Catherine promised God would help us that far. Go and check."

As he went up the stairs, Chrys closed the door, kicking Tony's feet out of the way. "If they find him here, they'll know it wasn't an accident that he died," she said, tapping one finger against her cheek as she thought. "We'll have to move him."

"To where?" Diana asked, her mind whirling.

"The kitchen," Chrys said, then shook her head. "No, the living room. Help me drag him."

It took them a few minutes to drag the limp body into the living room and heave him into the armchair. Then Chrys stepped back to look at her handwork. "Died of a heart attack. Nothing more, nothing less. Rot in hell, you bastard. I'm finally free of you."

"Now what?" Diana asked, shaken by what she'd seen.

Chrys looked out in the hall, where Thom was coming back down the hall from the front door. "Can you carry Alex as well?" she asked him, and he frowned." Yes, we're really taking him with us."

"Like hell you are," came a new voice from behind Thom, and all three of them turned around. For the second time in ten minutes, Diana's world came to a stupefied halt as she stared at the girl who had haunted her dreams for most of the past two months.

She stood in the doorway, framed by a setting sun that washed her in what Diana feared might be a prophetic blood-red haze, her long black hair pulled back into a simple ponytail that showed off how young she really was. That youth was offset by the determination in her blue eyes. As she walked into the house, she was followed by Thom's twin sister: the blonde hair and glittering blue eyes couldn't be mistaken. *How did they know we were here?*

"I don't think we've met yet," the young woman continued, stalking forward, a sleek predator in her jeans and tee-shirt, her boot heels exclamation points to her smooth words. "My name is Nikki. I'm Death. And you're the silly twit Madness and Lucifer have conned into helping them wreck the world, right?" She looked over at Thom. "I told you that you couldn't hide from me."

"I wasn't trying to," he retorted. "We're just picking up a few things and then we'll leave."

"Alex and the breeder?" Nikki said silkily. "I don't think so. I don't trust you with them, funnily enough."

"You don't have a choice," Chrys said, cutting across the confrontation. "They're coming with us. Don't make me move you out of the way."

Nikki actually laughed at her, and Cleo snickered. "You and what army?" Nikki looked up over Chrys' head. "Planning on summoning your Chaos Lord masters to help you, *Healer*?"

Chaos Lords? What is she talking about? There are no such thing. . . Diana followed Nikki's gaze and her eyes widened. On the wall over Chrys' head was a blur, a shimmer — two images trying to hold the same spot and failing. One was the image of St. Catherine that Chrys had said was speaking to her, leaning over her with a hand resting on Chrys' shoulder. But the other... Diana blinked, hoping the image would go away, but it didn't.

A giant, bloated spider crouched on the wall, back legs busily weaving a thick web that dropped down onto Chrys. The web snaked out from the Healer in various directions, and Diana swallowed. *What is going on here?*

"Watch and learn, child," a voice murmured in her ear, and Diana jumped. Suddenly, the whole world seemed to stop, frozen in an instant that only she could see. She looked around, but the voice seemed to come out of thin air. "You need to see how the connections work."

"What connections?" Diana said, frowning.

"There are always connections," the voice said. "You, of all people, should know that. You're trained as a medical professional. Don't you look for connections when someone is ill?"

"Yes, but..."

"The world is ill, Diana," the voice interrupted. "There is a sickness invading from all corners. Connections are still hidden, but they are starting to come to light. Look for the connections, Diana, and see what you need to do to heal the sickness. That is what you do, yes?"

"Yes," Diana said, looking around again.

"Then heal thyself, healer, and heal the world."

There was a flash and Diana blinked. When her vision cleared, time had started again; she looked up at the spider/St. Catherine and shuddered, then looked closer. What she had thought was a single strand of webbing wrapping around Chrys was actually thousands of strands, each one winging off in a separate direction: some towards Thom, some towards Nikki and some...

Diana looked down at her own wrist and shuddered again at the delicate webbing that wrapped itself around her arm like a moving snake. *What is going on here?* Then she realized where the webbing was coming from: not just from Chrys, but from Thom, Nikki and Cleo as well. There was even a strand slithering down the steps from upstairs, and several coming in from the front door. *How closely are we tied? And why?*

Nikki addressed her next comment to the spirit hovering over the Healer. "Come on out and play, Madness," she said. "Oh, wait, you can't, can you? You're still trapped in the World Between the Walls, so you have to work through lackeys here instead. I've got a suggestion, though — next time, choose Mages instead of Healers. They'll at least give me a bit of a challenge before I mow them down."

She watched the spider gnash its mandibles in frustration and smiled. "Of course, you haven't had much luck with Mages or Lords either, have you?" She pointed to Tony's corpse. "Maybe you should just give up and go back to your little hole in the wall realm and chew on your failures a bit more. It's not like you're going to succeed this time either. Just like you failed twenty-three years ago."

Lucifer stepped through the wall and cocked his head at her. "You're mouthy today, Horseman," he said, his dark eyes flashing. "One would think you're feeling confident about your chances of stopping this change."

"One would be right," she said. "You're going to lose, again, Lucifer."

"I don't think so." He put his hand on Chrys' shoulder and, as Nikki watched through narrowed eyes, he stepped into her body. The Healer shuddered and then straightened, and Lucifer's smile twisted her lips. "After all, there are so many ways I can stop you."

"You really think you can? A Lord, against two Horsemen?" She gestured to herself and Cleo. "Especially since you have a Horseman who's too ashamed to admit what he is."

"I don't need him," Chrys/Lucifer said. "He can go get Alex."

"Don't move, Thom," Cleo warned, her voice a low growl coated with Power. "I don't want to have to hurt you, no matter how much you deserve it."

He spat at her and started towards the stairs; she pointed at him, and thick rose vines erupted out of the stairwell, forcing him back with vicious thorns.

"Keep it low," Nikki told her, and Cleo nodded. "Let's not invite the cops to this dance."

"Why not, Horseman?" Chrys/Lucifer said, raising her/his hands. "Are you afraid of a little body count?"

"Don't you dare..." Nikki said, but it was too late. Power arched up from the palms of the Healer's hands, brilliant streams of green shot through with the grey mistiness she'd come to associate with Chaos Magic, and blew through the roof of the house. "Dammit!"

"Now let's see who else we can invite to this little game." Chrys/Lucifer threw back her/his head and laughed. "You cannot stop the Lord's work, Horseman! You still don't understand, do you?"

"Then make me understand," Nikki said, moving farther into the hall and raising her own hands.

"What are you doing?" Cleo hissed, and Nikki shook her head.

"He's right," she said. "That first spark alerted every Mage in the area, not to mention the police." She jerked her head up the stairway. "Get Alex and go. I'll follow you."

Cleo bit her lip, and Nikki spared one glare at her. "Go!"

That one word hit Cleo like a whip crack, and she waved her hand at the vines she'd created.

"Stop her!" Chrys/Lucifer shouted, and Thom moved forward, tackling his sister as she went towards the stairs. Cleo shouted and struggled as her brother took her down.

"I cannot allow you to take the champion of the child," Chrys/Lucifer said, pointing at Cleo. Bright light flashed out, and then ran into a beam of Shadows from Nikki's hand. Chrys/Lucifer snarled at her, and Nikki's lips firmed.

"Do you really want to play this game?" she asked, and Chrys/Lucifer snarled again. "Then so be it. Let's dance."

Chapter Thirty-four

"Wavelengths"

"You cannot hope to stop me, Horseman," Chrys sneered, as green and silver light flared about her. "You cannot stop the will of God!"

"You aren't a god, Lucifer," Nikki retorted, darkness welling up around her, and Diana shivered as the temperature in the room dropped. "Neither is your mistress."

"Neither are you, Horseman," Chrys retorted. "And my Lady has far more power than you shall ever hope to have." Brilliant green light shot from her, aiming for the young woman, and was consumed by her Shadows.

"I don't hope for power," Nikki said, as the darkness reached out for Chrys and was cut away by silver light. "I hope for peace."

"There can be no peace with the Mages here," Chrys said.

"So you would let Chaos ensue?" Shadows and Light leapt out at the same time and grappled together in midair, a crackling echo of the fierce struggle on the stairs as Cleo and Thom rolled and punched each other. "Is that your idea of peace?"

How can we have peace when it begins like this? Diana thought. *Why is God leading us down this path? And why does the Horseman keep referring to Lucifer?*

Have we been duped?

That thought chilled her more than the Shadows in the room, and she shook her head. *No, I can't believe that. Not yet. Not until*

I know more.

Another sound whined beneath the crackling and Diana's eyes widened as she realized what it was: sirens, wailing as they got closer.

"Chrys, we need to go!" she shouted, throwing herself into the middle of the fight. Dark and green Power surround her, shooting sparks into her body. Diana screamed as the two different magical energies fought for dominance inside her, tearing her in two as Chrys and Nikki each struggled to overwhelm the other. "We... have... to... go!"

"Chrys, stop! You're killing her!"

Diana heard Thom's voice as if from a distance as the pain built to a stunning crescendo, surrounding her in a haze of flaring colors and crushing energy that squeezed the life out of her. Grey mist floated around her, drawing her spirit from her body even as she fought to stay conscious.

Maybe...if I die.... she'll stop...

"She'll never stop," said the voice from before, and sadness wafted through Diana, a pale rose red emotion. "She's lost to me now. Don't give up your soul, Diana. I need you now, more than ever."

Abruptly, everything stopped, and Diana crashed to the ground, every nerve screaming in key with the sirens now howling down the road. She blinked and pulled herself to her knees, wondering what had happened.

<hr />

Nikki heard the sirens and cursed, knowing she had to end the fight and get them out of there before the police showed up. *No time for finesse,* she thought grimly, reaching deep inside herself. "Cleo, let go!"

She felt her sister's Horseman roar up from the depths of Cleo's soul in response to her call as her own Horseman uncoiled, reaching hungry fingers for the Chaos Lord ensconced in the Healer opposite her. *This ends now...*

And then the other girl in the room darted in between them, begging Chrys to stop, and was caught in the crossfire. Nikki watched, horrified, as the girl was trapped between her Horseman's energy and Lucifer's Chaos, slowly being torn apart by the dueling Powers.

No! I will not kill an innocent!

She is not innocent! The snarl of her Horseman ripped through Nikki's head. *She is tainted by the same Chaos we fight!*

She is not! She is not a Mage!

Chaos doesn't only use Mages! The Horseman tightened its grip on her, unwilling to give up. *We can kill her, and then kill the Healer, then continue onto the others. This is our purpose!*

No!

Nikki yanked her Horseman back and let the girl go tumbling to the ground. Beside her, Cleo threw Thom across the room and rose to her feet, radiating dark gold Power and a hard-edged desperation that echoed Nikki's. "Get Alex and go!" Nikki shouted, just as someone screeched to a halt outside, followed by several others. "Now!" Cleo nodded and ran up the stairs. Thom got to his feet to go after her, but Chrys/Lucifer grabbed his arm instead and Power flared again.

"God needs you as a Horseman," Chrys/Lucifer told him, pouring Chaos energy into him, and Nikki felt something stir within him. Her own Horseman raged and Nikki clamped down hard on her. *If she releases his Horseman, we have a chance...*

There was a loud banging of car doors, and a voice outside said, "Attention inside the house!"

"Shit," Nikki swore, looking behind her. The door had never closed, and she counted at least four police cars. "This is not going well."

Lt. Benjamin Doom lowered the bullhorn and looked over at his commander. "Are you sure we want to do this now? Shouldn't we wait for Department V or the National Guard to show up?" he asked, and Captain Swift scowled.

"And what do you suggest we do in the meantime?" Swift barked. "I'm not letting these people kill anyone else. You heard what they did in New Hampshire!"

"Sir, we don't know that these are the same people," Doom said.

Swift gestured to the bits of the roof lying on the lawn. "Who else do you know could do that, Lieutenant? Besides, can't you feel them? This is not your normal domestic call."

Doom couldn't argue with that statement.

"Now make sure everyone's ready," Swift said. "Shoot to kill if necessary. Are the houses nearby evacuated?"

"In process, sir," another officer said, and he grunted.

"Good. Let me know when it's complete." He looked around. "Damn, I'm too old for this shit."

The house had gone eerily quiet since they'd pulled up: the front door was open, and a single young woman had been framed briefly in the doorway, but she'd moved when he'd first spoken into the bullhorn. A black van sat in the driveway, the side door open and the interior dark, next to a silver Lincoln Continental.

"Tell them to come out peacefully, Doom," Swift said, and Doom raised the bullhorn. "Hell, maybe we'll get lucky."

"Come out with your hands up and there will be no shots fired!" Doom's voice echoed back from the windows, but nothing stirred in the house.

The air rippled near them; Doom felt wind rush by him, and a pop as a Gate opened somewhere behind the cars. Several police officers whirled with him, guns pointed at the woman who stepped out of the vortex, holding a badge out in front of her.

"Lt. Amy Elder, Department V," she said crisply as the Gate closed behind her. "I'll be taking charge here. What's going on?"

"How did you know to come here?" Swift demanded, and she gave him a scornful look.

"Did you think you were the only one who felt that tremor, Captain Swift? Please." She looked at Doom and the others. "You're facing the wrong way. You might want to remedy that soon."

They turned back to the house, and Doom wondered what she was expecting to come out. Tension rolled off of her, and the circles under her eyes hinted at long hours. *What haven't they told us about these people?*

A rhythmic pounding echoed in the air, and everyone looked around, stunned. *Hoof beats? What the hell is a horse doing here?* Doom looked over to the west, where the sun would be, and shuddered. A sickly-glowing white horse thundered up the road, pushing people out of the way and leaping over the cars with ease. In its wake, officers began to cough: violent, tearing paroxysms, ripped from their throats with such force that the ground was soon speckled with blood. As Doom watched in horror, bloody tears welled up in their eyes, and dark streams poured from their ears as they collapsed on the ground, twitching.

"Stay back from them!" Elder ordered, grabbing his arm as he started to move towards the nearest downed officer. "We don't know if they're contagious!"

"What?" Doom stared at her.

"You heard me." She dropped his arm and grabbed the bullhorn. "Nikki Jeffries! I know you're in there! This is Lt. Amy Elder, and I have a message for you!"

Nothing answered. The horse pawed the ground as it waited in front of the door, then turned as two other horses, both black, trotted around the side of the house, whinnying. The white horse shrilled an answer back, and the larger black horse shook its head.

"Horses?" Doom said, and Elder nodded.

"How religious are you, Lt?" she asked, and when he shrugged, she smiled wryly. "Good. Then the fact that we're probably dealing with the Four Horsemen of the Apocalypse shouldn't bother you very much."

He choked on that.

"What else do you know causes death like that?" she asked him, pointing at the corpses on the ground.

Doom couldn't answer. As he stared at her, the front of the house exploded.

Power poured over them, spreading out like a deadly flood from the young man who stood in the shattered remains of the foyer, his eyes burning, and Doom did the only thing he could: he began to shoot, even as the officers around him began to scream in agony. The Horseman turned to look at him, and Doom faltered for a moment, then fired again. He clearly saw the bullet rip through the young man's chest. . . and then the hole closed, and the Horseman pointed at him.

Doom felt his skin crawl, as if a hundred thousand ants had been dumped upon his hands, and looked down. Then he screamed.

The flesh on his hands was turning black and peeling away, revealing the disintegrating flesh beneath. He staggered backwards, the bloodstained gun falling from his nerveless fingers to discharge into the vehicle in front of him. The sounds of his own screaming faded from his ears, replaced with the pounding of a heart that was slowly being starved of oxygen as the blood that was supposed to flow in his veins poured from the remains of his hands. More blood began to pour from his nose as the Horseman continued to point at him, and Doom stumbled, falling to his knees in a pool of crimson.

His last coherent thought was that at least he'd tried to stop them.

Epilogue

"Aftermath"

It was quiet when Nikki came back to consciousness — too quiet, and her skin crawled with more than the just the aftermath of the Power that had knocked her out. She rose slowly from the shattered remains of the wall Thom had blown her into and looked around.

No one moved as she walked through the rubble to the front yard, and her magical senses told her that at this moment, she was one of the only living things in the area. *I couldn't have been out that long,* she thought, stepping into the yard and cringing at the sight of the silent police cars. The growing twilight hid the bodies she knew would be there, and for that, she was thankful.

Cleo? Cerberus? She threw her thought out, hoping for an answer, and in a moment, the great black horse trotted up the street, shaking his head. *Thank god for small favors.*

We must leave, Cerberus told her, pivoting in front of her. *Others are on their way.*

"I need to know where they went," Nikki said, and flinched as her voice echoed. "And I have to see if anyone survived."

Cerberus snorted, but didn't stop her as she went out to the cars. Nikki swallowed as she moved among the corpses, trying not to step in blood and failing miserably. *I should have known better than to hope,* she thought, as the scent of death filled her nostrils. *Thom did his work well.*

A moan caught her attention, and Nikki followed it to the dark-haired agent she'd seen on TV. "Lieutenant Amy Elder," she whispered, kneeling down next to the woman, who opened her eyes at the voice. "I shouldn't be surprised, but I am."

Amy moaned again, and Nikki placed a finger on her lips." Shhh. Don't try to talk. Just listen, and remember what I'm going to say." The woman's eyes widened and Nikki nodded. "I'm not going to kill you. I don't do that lightly. But this is your only warning — stay out of my way. You can't stop what's going to happen, and I can't minimize the damage if I'm worrying about when you're going to show up. Tell Washington that if they want to keep their country, they'd best leave me alone." She closed her eyes for a moment, and when she opened them again, Amy flinched at the Power glowing down at her. "Do you understand me, Lt. Elder?" Amy nodded. "Good."

Nikki stood up and pulled herself onto Cerberus' back, knowing the agent would continue to haunt her despite the warning. *Did Cleo make it out?*

Yes. She's back at Edgar's, Cerberus said, picking his way through the pools of cooling blood. *With... Alex.*

Good. Nikki pointed at a random open space and opened a Gate to the Shadow Lands as the first of the second wave of sirens cut the silence. *Then let's go.*

Cleo was standing on the steps to the Rothman House, waiting for her. Nikki pulled Cerberus to a halt and the two stared at each other for a long minute.

"He killed them all, didn't he?" Cleo said finally.

"No, he didn't," Nikki said. "And I don't know why." She swung down, feeling her legs wobble. "How's Alex?"

"Unconscious."

"Good." Nikki clung to Cerberus' saddle, exhausted. "Ask Edgar if he minds hosting a meeting. I need to talk to some people." *And then, Madness, I will come after you.*

And you, I will kill.

www.ingramcontent.com/pod-product-compliance
Lightning Source LLC
Chambersburg PA
CBHW022003010726
47494CB00003B/864